Eva Hope

Life of General Gordon

Eva Hope

Life of General Gordon

ISBN/EAN: 9783337095710

Printed in Europe, USA, Canada, Australia, Japan

Cover: Foto ©Raphael Reischuk / pixelio.de

More available books at **www.hansebooks.com**

BY THE AUTHORS OF

"OUR QUEEN," "NEW WORLD HEROES," ETC.

" By the help of God, I will hold the balance level."

—GORDON.

LONDON:

WALTER SCOTT, 24 WARWICK LANE,

PATERNOSTER ROW.

1886.

CONTENTS.

CHAPTER I.

PAGE

Gordon's Birth, Parentage, and Early Work .   1—8

CHAPTER II.

Assistant Commissioner, and First Visit to China .   .   . 9—16

CHAPTER III.

Hung-Tsue-Schuen .   .   .   . 17—23

CHAPTER IV.

The Ever-Victorious Army .   .   .   . 24—35

CHAPTER V.

Successes and Trials   36 43

CONTENTS.

OHAPTER VI.

PAGE

The Rebel Burgevine . . . . 44—51

OHAPTER VII.

In the Thick of the Fight . . , ... 52—60

OHAPTER VIII.

After the Surrender of Soochow . . . . . 61—72

OHAPTER IX.

Gordon again takes the Field . . . . 73—80

CHAPTER X.

The Disbanding of the Ever-Victorious Army . . 81—94

CHAPTER XI.

The Collapse of the Rebellion . . . . . 95—109

OHAPTER XII.

At Gravesend . . . . 110—125

OHAPTER XIII.

Gordon's First Visit to the Soudan , 126—135

CHAPTER XIV.

PAGE

What is the Soudan !   .   .   .   .   136—146

CHAPTER XV.

Gordon's Predecessor in the Soudan .   .   .   .   .   147—156

CHAPTER XVI.

The Slave Trade in the Soudan.   .   .   .   .   .   157—173

CHAPTER XVII.

Hurriyat (Liberty) .   .   .   .   174—183

CHAPTER XVIII.

Near King Mtesa's Land .   .   .   .   184—193

CHAPTER XIX.

In Abyssinia   .   .   .   .   194—201

CHAPTER XX.

The Level Balance   .   .   .   .   202—211

CHAPTER XXI.

Romulus Geasi .   .   .   .   212—221

 CONTENTS.

CHAPTER XXII.

King Johannis of Abyssinia . . . . . . 222—228

CHAPTER XXIII.

Rest or Work ! . . . . 229—239

CHAPTER XXIV.

Troubles in the Soudan . . . . 240—256

CHAPTER XXV.

Gordon's Response . . . . 257—278

CHAPTER XXVI.

Subsequent Events in the Soudan . . . . . 279—290

CHAPTER XXVII.

Slavery and Gordon's Proclamation . . . . . 291—310

CHAPTER XXVIII.

The Year in Khartoum . . . . 311—327

CHAPTER XXIX.

The Relief Expedition . . . . 328—341

CHAPTER XXX.

The End of the Story . . . . 342—360

CHAPTER XXXI.

A Christian Hero . . . . 361—369

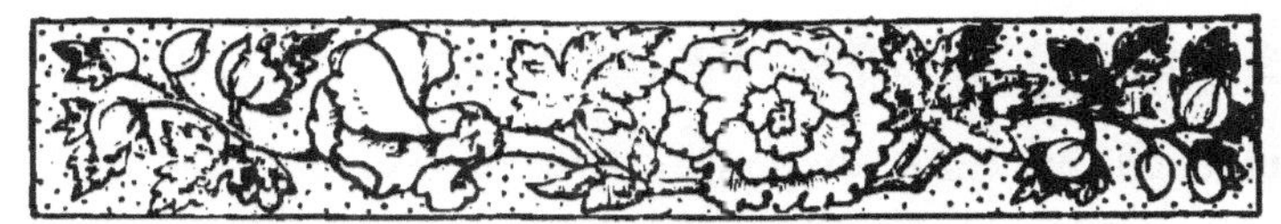

GENERAL GORDON.

CHAPTER I.

GORDON'S BIRTH, PARENTAGE, AND EARLY WORK.

"For myself, son,
I purpose not to wait on fortune, till
These wars determine."
—*Coriolanus.*

WOOLWICH and War, if not synonymous names, are very closely connected; and it was, therefore, in harmony with their lives and characters that in Woolwich Lieutenant-General Henry William Gordon, of the Royal Regiment of Artillery, lived, and in Woolwich his youngest son, Charles George Gordon, was born. The military town on the Thames is not much talked of in times of peace: but no sooner do clouds appear on the political horizon, telling of disquietude which it behoves England to notice, than all eyes and thoughts are turned toward the scene, which, always busy, becomes alive with animation and importance then.

Yet Woolwich is an interesting place to visit at any time. It is only nine miles from St. Paul's, and may be reached by three or four different railways, by trams, or omnibuses, or steamboats; and, when reached, presents features of attractiveness that can be found nowhere else. The Royal Arsenal, which includes the gun factories, carriage department, royal laboratory, and military stores department, is the largest depôt for army stores in the world. Within the arsenal is the ordnance yard, where an immense number of pieces of ordnance, and of shot and shells, with fittings and harness for a multitude of artillery horses, are kept in constant readiness for use. The public are admitted with little difficulty; and no one can look on the Rotunda, with its models of all Her Majesty's dockyards, the principal fortifications in the world, and various kinds of arms, ancient and modern, without intense interest. The Pontoon Ground is also interesting; for there, on large sheets of water, experiments are made with boats and ordnance. On the east side, facing the Military Train barracks, is the Royal Artillery Institution. It includes a museum, theatre, laboratory, and reading-room, for the use of the Royal Artillery officers. There is a small observatory adjoining. South-east of the Repository Grounds is the Royal Military Academy, founded in 1719, for the education of cadets intended for the artillery and engineers; and between the arsenal and the dockyard are the Royal and Marine Barracks, with the Naval and Marine Hospital, which last was erected in 1859. The Royal Dockyard, the most ancient in the kingdom, occupies a narrow strip of land along the south bank of the Thames, and is very extensive. The outer and inner basins are both of enormous dimensions. Graving docks have also been added, which can contain the largest ships in the Royal Navy. This dockyard is under the charge of a Commodore-Superintendent, and is surrounded by lines of circumvallations, under the Fortifications Act. A practice range of several miles in extent lies between Woolwich and Hythe, and the artillery also practice on the Plumstead Marshes. Here, too, the Government ordnance are proved. There is a large place called the Camp, for the servants of the Military Train, and an extensive hospital.

At Woolwich the man who has since become known as "Chinese Gordon," the leader of the "Ever Victorious Army," and the "Good Pasha," was born on the 28th of January 1833. His mother was Elizabeth Enderby of Blackheath, whose father, a London merchant, achieved some notoriety by his success in the whale fishery; by which means he did much to open up the Southern Hemisphere, and to demonstrate the possibility of rounding Cape Horn. The Enderby whalers did good service to Australia and New Zealand, which were at that time little known; and the Enderbys were among the first discoverers of the Auckland Islands. They were, indeed, the means of promoting commerce between our own country and some of our most important colonies; and there is a strip of country in the Antarctic Ocean known by the name of "Enderby's Lands."

Miss Enderby, afterwards Mrs. Gordon, the mother of our hero, was in many respects a remarkable woman, well fitted to guide her children into paths of true nobility and honour. She was exceedingly tender and amiable, bright and hopeful. She lived for others rather than for herself, and proved her ability to rule her children by her perfect mastery of self. She had five sons and six daughters. Sir Henry W. Gordon, K.C.B., and Major-General Gordon, C.B., Royal Artillery, are still living.

Their father, the late Lieutenant-General Gordon, had an ancestry of soldiers. His grandfather—the great-grandfather of our hero—had a very eventful life. He was taken prisoner at Prestonpans, but the Duke of Cumberland used his influence to secure his release. He died at

Halifax in North America, in 1752. His son, the grand father of Charles, fought in several battles, and won some distinction. Henry William, the father of General Gordon, was a soldier of the highest type, honourable, kindly, just, and devoted to his profession.

Charles was a boy of quick but generous temper, with plenty of energy, but not very great physical strength. He was sent to school at Taunton, in Somerset ; and afterwards attended the Royal Military Academy at Woolwich.

A story is told of an occurrence during his cadetship which illustrates the fire and energy of his youthful spirit. "You are incompetent: you will never make an officer," said his superior, in rebuke to him one day ; and, with flashing eyes and flushed cheeks, the lad tore from his shoulders the epaulettes that he wore and cast them down before his reprover's feet.

He was only nineteen years old when he became an officer of Engineers, and received his commission of second Lieutenant. He was ordered to Pembroke, where plans were required for the forts at Milford Haven ; and there he worked for a few months, until, in the winter of 1854, news came that he was to go to Corfu.

This was not at all according to his wish. At this time all thoughts were centred on the Crimea, and thither the ambitious hopes of Charles Gordon turned. He had spent part of his boyhood at Corfu, where his father had commanded the artillery, and would very much prefer to serve in the Crimea than in the Ionian Islands. By some means his route became changed. The young soldier, eager for active service, volunteered to go where men were greatly needed ; and in December 1854 he started for the East, reaching Balaklava on New Year's Day, 1855.

For a few weeks he was comparatively idle, and he spent the time in making observations, and learning lessons for future use. Every one knows long ago the story of the privations and heroisms of the English army before Sebastopol. It has been told again and again by the correspondents of newspapers, and by trusty and eloquent historians; but no pictures were more vivid than those of the young subaltern, who was laying to heart all that he saw. His letters home told the same story which the war correspondents told, of lack of supplies, of food wasting where it was not needed, while men were dying for want of it; of officers and men engaged in foraging expeditions; of the intense cold, which killed Englishmen more surely than Russian guns; of the ravages of cholera; of delays on the part of the officers, and despondency on the part of the men. It is true that at the time when Gordon had joined, things were better than they had been, but they were bad still.

In February some definite work was given to Gordon to do.

The first order he received was to contrive to make rifle-pits between the French and English sentries, who were in front of the trenches, and so unite them. It was hazardous work; and the men and sentries under his command grew frightened, and deserted him. He was shot at by both English and Russian sentries.

But he continued at the work of making batteries in the advance trenches for two months; and although the throwing up of these batteries was a very monotonous occupation, it happened now and then that some excitement was caused by an attack upon the workers, who returned the fire.

On one of these occasions a bullet was fired at Gordon, from one of the Russian rifle-pits, which only missed his head by an inch. He told his friends at home about the narrow escape he had experienced, and added that the Russians were good marksmen, and used a bullet that was large and pointed.

At last, however, there was some fighting. Charles Gordon still took part in the work in the trenches, and was thus brought into all the active life of the time; but although on one occasion he was struck by a stone he escaped uninjured. The war, meanwhile, dragged on somewhat wearily. Justin McCarthy said, "Sometimes it was not easy to say which ought to be called the besieged—the Russians in Sebastopol, or the Allies encamped in sight of it." There were grumblers at home, whose bitter criticisms reached the seat of war, where there were then difficulties which only those who were present could understand. Gordon was noting everything, and laying up stores of knowledge for future use. In the midst of it all Lord Raglan died. His death was, no doubt, the result of anxiety and trouble. On the 18th of June the Allies were repulsed with heavy loss. General Pelissier urged Lord Raglan to consent to the making of a simultaneous attack on the Malakoff and the Redan, and his lordship yielded against his better judgment. The failure of the attempt filled him with grief and dismay. Our Prince Consort wrote in reference to this—"The eighteenth was the nail in his coffin, for he knew that his troops could do nothing under the circumstances which Pelissier had created, and to give them the order to attack was to send them to certain death; and yet had he not done so, the French army would have believed he was deserting them in the hour of need. The choice must have been infinitely hard for him; and yet the French insinuate, and what is worse, the *Times* does so, too, that Lord Raglan is alone to blame." The disappointment and regret, the anxiety and the trouble, were too much for the English commander, who, in circumstances of great difficulty, had sought to prove himself a worthy successor of Nelson, and "do his duty;" and he died on the 29th of June.

The unsuccessful attack of the Allies, which plunged

England into sorrow, and killed Lord Raglan, brought great rejoicing to the Russians. Prince Gortschakoff declared that "the hour was approaching when the pride of the enemy would be lowered, and their armies swept from Russian soil like chaff blown away by the wind."

But, as all the world knows, that was far from being the case. Both the English and the French were brave and courageous. Our men, Gordon among them, worked for long hours in the trenches or the field. Miss Florence Nightingale gave, in a letter she wrote at the time, the following account of their hardships, upon which she dwelt with much more commiseration than the men felt for themselves :—" Fancy working five nights out of seven in the trenches. Fancy being thirty-six hours in them at a stretch, as they sometimes were, lying down, or half-lying down; often forty-eight hours with no food but *raw* salt pork, sprinkled with sugar, rum, and biscuit; nothing hot, because the exhausted soldier could not collect his own fuel, as he was expected to do, to cook his own rations; and fancy, through all this, the army preserving their courage and patience as they have done, and being now eager (the old ones as well as the young ones) to be led into the trenches. There was something sublime in the spectacle."

Such was the training of a hero among heroes; a training that must have been good for all who had sufficient strength of endurance for the trial, and which certainly had an excellent effect on the young subaltern, who was quietly obeying orders, and at the same time realising the whole situation.

He was not present at the taking of the Malakoff tower; but he is said to have been at work in the trenches at the very time when Sebastopol was evacuated. During the night of the 8th of September the Russians withdrew from the south side of the city. A bridge of boats had been made to cross the bay from the north to the south, and over this bridge Prince Gortschakoff, seeing his case to be hopeless—his defences having been almost destroyed by the persistent attacks of the Allies—quietly took his troops. He felt that to try to hold the city longer was only to cause a more terrible death-roll among his men ; and so he decided, before things grew worse, to leave Sebastopol.

But the Allies saw an awful sight on the morning of the 9th of September. The whole city was in flames, and completely ruined. Gortschakoff said in his despatch, " It is not Sebastopol which we have left to them, but the burning ruins of the town, which we ourselves set fire to, having maintained the honour of the defence in such a manner that our great-grandchildren may recall with pride the remembrance of it, and send it on to all posterity." Sebastopol will never again be what it was before. French and English engineers were ordered to destroy such of the forts as were standing, and Gordon was told off to assist in the work of destruction. The war in the Crimea soon afterwards ceased, and the young subaltern of the Royal Engineers received the Order of the Legion of Honour from the French Government. And so Charles Gordon got his first discipline and his first honours.

CHAPTER II.

" These flags of France, that are advanced here
　　Before the eye and prospect of your town,
　　Have hither marched to your endamagement.
　　Their cannons have their bowels full of wrath ;
　　And ready mounted are they to spit forth
　　Their iron indignation 'gainst your walls."
　　　　　　　　　　　　　　　　—King John.

BLE workers are never allowed to remain idle long, and no sooner had Charles Gordon finished his work in the Crimea than he was despatched on other business. In May 1856 he was ordered to join Major Stanton (now Lieutenant-General Sir E. Stanton) at Bessarabia, a province in the south-west of Russia. New frontiers of Russia, Turkey, and Roumania had to be laid down, and Gordon was appointed Assistant Commissioner. Representatives of France, Russia, and Austria were also on the Commission. Eleven months were occupied by the expedition. Gordon's special duty was, in company with another, to trace a boundary that extended for a hundred miles, and compare the English and Russian maps in order to see

if they agreed. The change from the monotonous and exhausting work in the Russian trenches, to leisurely travelling from place to place through beautiful summer weather, was a very agreeable one. When the days were too hot they took their journeys by night, and Gordon felt great interest in his work and the places that he visited. The Commissioners resided at Kichenev, but besides this town Gordon became acquainted with Akerman, Bolgrad, Kotimore, Reni, Seratzika, and Jassy. He saw the district at its best. It is flat but fertile. Bessarabia has a very mixed population, composed of Russians, Poles, Wallachians, Moldavians, Bulgarians, Greeks, Armenians, Jews, Germans, and Tartars, besides a few gipsies. The Dniester, the Pruth, and the Danube are its rivers. It has some beautiful streams, and some salt lakes. The country is traversed by offshoots from the Transylvanian branch of the Carpathian mountains, and the hills are mostly covered with wood. The chief part of the land is in pasturage.

The work that Charles Gordon did in Bessarabia was not monotonous, but he grew a little tired of it; and when, in April 1857, he found that he was ordered to join the Commission for arranging the boundary in Asia, he sent home to ask if he might exchange with someone else. But he was not allowed to do so, and therefore went as he was commanded to Armenia. He was to become a great traveller, and his mind must have been considerably enlarged and strengthened, even as early as the time of which we are writing, by his knowledge of foreign countries, and his intercourse with the men of all nations. Erivan, situated to the north of Ararat, with its fortress and mosques, its stone bridge, and its aqueducts, was visited by him. So was Erzeroum, the busy, prosperous town near the northern source of the Euphrates; and also Kars, which, three years before, had held out so bravely during the siege of the Russians, which lasted from the 16th of June 1855, to the beginning of December. Gordon's labours were diversified by some mountain climbing, for he ascended both Little and Great Ararat. He took observations, and stored knowledge of places and men wherever he went. Mr. Hake, in his *Story of Chinese Gordon,* says of him at this period, that "he found time to study the strategic points of a country illustrious and interesting as the scene of many battles."

After spending six months in Armenia, he went to Constantinople, in order to attend a conference of the Commission; and then, after being absent from home three years, he had six months holiday, and came to England to spend it with his friends. At the end of his furlough, he was sent back to Armenia, not as assistant now, but as commissioner, where he stayed until the end of the year 1858; after which he again came home. The year 1859 was spent at Chatham, where he was engaged as Field-work Instructor and Adjutant.

In the meantime serious circumstances were occurring which were to call Charles Gordon to quite another part of the world.

The Queen's Speech at the opening of Parliament on the 24th January 1860 mentioned the renewal of disturbances in China, and stated that the English and French plenipotentiaries had proceeded to the mouth of the Peiho river in order to repair to Pekin, and exchange in that city the ratifications of the Treaty of Tien-tsin. The plenipotentiaries were stopped, and compelled to retire, and the Royal Speech declared that an expedition had been forthwith despatched to obtain redress.

The Chinese Government refused to make any apology for attacking the British ships, and there was a great outcry raised in England. The military expedition proceeded immediately to China, Lord Elgin and Baron Gros being at the head of it, while the command of the English land forces was given to Sir Hope Grant, and General Cousin de Montauban, afterwards Count Palikao, commanded the French.

Charles Gordon was ordered to join the army—and he started some time in July. He travelled *via* Paris and Marseilles, and visited the towns of Malta, Alexandria, Aden, Ceylon, Singapore, and Hong-kong. From thence he went to Shanghai, and, only halting there for a day, went on to Tien-tsin. He had been travelling sixty-eight days.

The Allies had already occupied that city—having captured the Taku forts—and had marched on Pekin. But the Chinese had endeavoured to stop their progress to the capital by asking Lord Elgin to enter into negotiations for peace, and it was arranged that the Chinese Commissioners should meet the European plenipotentiaries at Tung-chow, a walled town ten miles from Pekin. Mr. Parks and Mr. Loch, Lord Elgin's secretaries, Mr. Bowlby, the *Times* correspondent, and several French and English officers, among whom was De Norman, a friend and colleague of Charles Gordon, went to Tung-chow to make the necessary arrangements for the interview between the envoys and the Chinese Commissioners. As they were returning, some quarrel took place between a French commissariat officer and some Tartar soldiers, and there was a fight. Mr. Parks, Mr. Loch, and others, twenty-six British subjects and twelve French in all, were at once seized by the Chinese General, Sang-ko-lin-sin, and sent off to various prisons. This was a great outrage, committed on men who bore a flag of truce, and had come at the request of the Chinese themselves to arrange a conference with a view to peace.

The Allies resolved to punish this outrage; and they marched on Pekin in October and invested the city, Lord Elgin refusing to negotiate until the prisoners had been returned. The guns of the Allies were in position to blow in the gate of the city, when the Chinese acceded to their terms, and surrendered the gate. The Allies entered the city, and hoisted the English and French flags on the walls.

But then Lord Elgin learned that the captives had been treated with the greatest cruelty and indignity. So horrible indeed had been their sufferings, that thirteen out of the twenty-six British subjects had died in great agony. Among these was De Norman, who had served with Gordon in Asia. The thirteen who were released bore evidence of the abominable treatment to which they had been subjected.

The hearts of the Allied officers and men were stirred to indignation by the perfidy and cruelty of the Chinese authorities, upon whom Lord Elgin determined to inflict an exemplary and signal punishment. He ordered that the Chinese Summer Palace should be burnt down, that the rulers of the nation might understand the danger of treachery and foul play.

"What remains of the Palace," said Lord Elgin, "which appears to be the place at which several of the British captives were subjected to the grossest indignities, will be immediately levelled to the ground: this condition requires no assent on the part of His Highness Prince Kung" (the brother, and plenipotentiary of the Emperor), "because it will be at once carried into effect by the Commander-in-Chief."

And so it was. In two days the Palace was completely destroyed.

The author of *Our Own Times* thus writes of this Summer Palace :—"It covered an area of many miles. The palace of Adrian, at Tivoli, might have been hidden in one of its courts. Gardens, temples, small lodges and pagodas, groves, grottoes, lakes, bridges, terraces, artificial hills, diversified the vast space. All the artistic treasures, all the curiosities—archæological and other—that Chinese wealth and Chinese taste, such as it was, could bring together, had been accumulated in this magnificent pleasaunce. The surrounding scenery was beautiful. The high mountains of Tartary ramparted one side of the enclosure."

Charles Gordon was ordered, with the rest, to assist in destroying this Palace; and, as usual, he gave in his next home letter an account of the work of devastation :— "We accordingly went out, and after pillaging it, burned the whole place, destroying, in a vandal-like manner, most valuable property, which could not be replaced for four millions. . . . You would scarcely imagine the beauty and magnificence of the places we burnt. It made one's heart sore to burn them ; in fact, these palaces were so large, and we were so pressed for time, that we could not plunder them carefully. Quantities of gold ornaments were burned, considered as brass. It was wretchedly demoralising work for an army. Everybody was wild for plunder."

The affair went to the hearts of a good many more people besides that of Charles, now Captain Gordon; and Lord Elgin was considerably blamed for what seemed an act of unpardonable vandalism. It transpired, however, that the French had remorselessly looted and wrecked the Palace before Lord Elgin had given his order—an order which he maintained was a just one, since war would become ten times more horrible than it is already, if it were not one of its essential conditions that the messengers engaged in the preliminaries of peace are to be held sacred from harm.

The Allied armies remained before Pekin until the 8th November, when they left to take up their winter quarters at Tien-tsin, whither Gordon went with his regiment as commanding Royal Engineer. He had received for his services his brevet promotion to the rank of major.

He stayed at Tien-tsin until the spring of 1862. In December 1861, he and Lieutenant Cardew went together on horseback to explore the outer wall of China, at Kalgan. This world-famous structure, " Wan-li-chang" (myriad-mile-wall), was built as a protection against the Tartar tribes by the first Emperor of the Tsin dynasty, about 220 B.C. It traverses the northern boundary of China, and is carried over the highest hills, through the deepest valleys, across rivers and every other obstacle. M'Culloch believes its length to be 1250 miles. The total height of the wall, including a parapet of five feet, is twenty feet ; it is twenty-five feet thick at the base, and fifteen at the top.

Gordon and Cardew were exceedingly interested in their journey, which was not only eventful to them but important to others, for they went to several places that no European had visited before. They had some difficulties, as might be expected. In one place the axle-trees of their carts would not fit the ruts ; in another their carts were stolen from them. The cold was so great that raw eggs were frozen as hard as if they had been boiled.

In one of his letters Major Gordon describes a dust-storm in which he was caught :—" The sky was as dark as night ; huge columns of dust came sweeping down, and it blew a regular hurricane, the blue sky appearing now and then through the breaks. The quantity of dust was indescribable. A canal, about fifty miles long and eighteen feet wide, and seven feet deep, was completely filled up ; and boats which had been floating merrily down the Tien-tsin found themselves at the end of the storm on a bank of sand, the canal being filled up, and the waters absorbed. They will have to be carried to the Peiho, and have already commenced to move. The canal was everywhere passable, and will have to be re-excavated."

In May 1862 Major Gordon had his attention called to the Tai-ping rebellion, in connection with which he was to

do some of the most remarkable and heroic deeds of his
life, and so win the name by which he will be for ever
known—the name of " CHINESE GORDON."

He was at this time a young man, but he had been
unconsciously preparing for future work. He was getting
his lessons in the highest school, for he was a disciple of
Christ, and was learning of Him. Moreover, from his
boyhood upward he seems to have chosen the motto,
" Whatsoever thy hand findeth to do, do it with thy might."
He was in himself the illustration of the words of the great
" Bard of Avon "—

> " Firm of word ;
> Speaking of deeds, and deedless in his tongue ;
> Not soon provoked, nor, being provoked, soon calmed ;
> His heart and hand both open and both free."

CHAPTER III.

HUNG-TSUE-SCHUEN.

"We cannot all be masters, nor all masters cannot be truly followed."
—*Othello.*

THE Tai-ping rebellion was the work of a school-master, who announced himself as the "Heavenly King," the "Emperor of the Great Peace." He said that he had seen God, who had called him the Second Celestial Brother. He got a large following without much difficulty, especially as his clansmen numbered 20,000. He made the announcement that to him was given the power to execute judgment and to deliver the oppressed; and declared that his great mission was to exterminate the Manchoo race. He soon came into collision with the Mandarins; and thinking that some of his people were ill-used, and becoming angry at his own failure to pass certain examinations which would admit him to the circle of the *literati*, he took his converts with him, and went forth to increase their number. When his followers were some hundreds of thousands, he chose five warrior kings—Wangs—from among his kinsmen; and, having his army augmented by bands of robbers and secret

societies, and four thousand warriors brought by some desperate women, he led this immense mob from city to city, from province to province, making raids upon rice-harvests and leaving devastation and ruin wherever they went. The Chinese were frightened at the sight of the gaudy flags and coloured finery in which Hung and his followers were dressed, and they shrank with terror from the knives and cutlasses which the fierce barbarians used.

Hung marched his host to Nanking, to reach which he had to traverse a distance of seven hundred miles. The city fell before him, and he at once took possession of it, and gave it the name of the Capital of the Heavenly King. They put the entire population to the sword, and laid waste the city, spoiling, among other things, the renowned Porcelain Tower, which the Emperor Yungloh erected in memory of his mother in 1414-26. Dr. MacGowan, in his description of this tower, says that it was built nine storeys high, and the bricks and tiles were to be glazed and of fine colours ; and the whole structure was to be of the most superior kind, in order that the virtues of the Emperor's mother might be widely known. There was to be a brass ball, overlaid with gold, on the top of the spire. It was to have one hundred and forty-four bells, and one hundred and forty lanterns, whose light was to illumine the "thirty-three heavens, shining into the hearts of all men, good and bad, eternally removing human misery." A brazen bowl on the top of the highest roof was to contain "one white shining pearl, one fire-averting pearl, one wind-averting pearl, one water-averting pearl, one dust-averting pearl, a lump of gold weighing sixty ounces, a box of tea leaves, 1000 taels of silver, one lump of orpiment, weighing 4000 pounds, one precious stone-gem, 1000 strings of copper coins, two pieces of yellow satin, and four copies of Buddhist classics." The tower was called "Pan-gan-sy "—*i.e.,* "Recompensing Favour Pagoda."

Under this tower Hung-Tsue-Schuen set up his royal state and marshalled his army. He gave to the Wangs, or under kings whom he had appointed, such titles as "Cock Eye," "the Yellow Tiger," "the One-Eyed Dog." He developed into a very tyrannous master, beheading any of his chiefs who displeased him, and kicking to death his discarded wives and concubines. Like the Mahdi in the Soudan, he declared his mission to be altogether a religious one, and he himself a Messiah. He was, he said, and his followers believed him, "the Emperor of the Great Peace." There was plenty of worship, of a certain kind, carried on side by side with war.

The Rev. J. L. Holmes, a missionary, visited Nanking, and learned many particulars about their religious beliefs and ceremonies, afterwards publishing the following, among other interesting information :—

"At night we witnessed their worship. It occurred at the beginning of their Sabbath, midnight of Friday. The place of worship was Chung Wang's private audience-room. He was himself seated in the midst of his attendants—no females were present. They first sang, or rather chanted, after which a written prayer was read, and burned by an officer, upon which they rose and sang again, and then separated. The Chung Wang sent for me again before he left his seat, and asked me if I understood their mode of worship. I replied that I had just seen it for the first time. He asked what our mode was. I replied that we endeavoured to follow the rules laid down in the Scriptures, and thought all departure therefrom to be erroneous. He then proceeded to explain the ground upon which they departed from this rule. The Tien Wang had been to heaven, he said, and had seen the Heavenly Father. Our revelation had been handed down for one thousand eight hundred years. They had received a new additional revelation ; and upon this they could adopt a different mode of worship. I replied, that if the Tien Wang had obtained a revelation, we could determine its genuineness by comparing it with the Scriptures. If they coincided, they might be parts of the same; if not, the new revelation could not be true, as God did not change. He suggested that there might be a sort of *disparagement* which was yet appropriate, as in the Chinese garment, which is buttoned at one side. To this comparison I objected, as comparing a piece of man's work with God's work. Ours were little and imperfect; His great and glorious. We should compare God's works with each other. The sun did not rise in the east to-day and in the west to-morrow. Winter and summer did not change their respective characters. Neither would the Heavenly Father capriciously make a law at one time and contradict it at another. His Majesty seemed rather disconcerted at thus being carried out of the usual track in which he was in the habit of discoursing; and we parted, proposing to talk further upon the subject at another time.

" At day-light we started for the Tien Wang's palace. The procession was headed by a number of brilliantly-coloured banners, after which followed a troop of armed soldiers. Then came Chung Wang, in a large sedan, covered with yellow satin and embroidery, and borne by eight coolies; next came the foreigner on horseback, in company with Chung Wang's chief officer, followed by a number of other officers on horseback. On our way several of the other kings who were in the city fell-in ahead of us with similar retinues. Music added discord to the scene, and curious gazers lined the streets on either side, who had, no doubt, seen kings before, but probably never witnessed such an apparition as that. . . . Reaching, at length, the palace of Tien Wang, a large building resembling very much the best Confucian temples, though of much greater size that these generally are, we entered the outer gate, and proceeded to a large building to the east of the palace proper, and called the Morning Palace. Here we were presented to the Tien Wang and his son, with several others. After resting a little while, during which two of the attendants testified their familiarity with, and consequently irreverence for, the royal place, by concluding a misunderstanding in fisticuffs, we proceeded to the audience-hall of the Tien Wang. I was here presented to the Tien Wang's two brothers, two nephews, and son-in-law. They were seated at the entrance of a deep recess, over which was written, 'Illustrious Heavenly Door.' At the end of this recess, further in, was pointed out to us His Majesty Tien Wang's seat, which was as yet vacant. The company awaited for some time the arrival of the Western King, whose presence seemed to be necessary before they could proceed with the ceremonies. That dignitary, a boy of twelve or fourteen, directly made his appearance, and entering at the Holy Heavenly Gate, took his place with the royal group. They then proceeded with their ceremonies as follows:—First, they kneeled with their faces to the Tien Wang's seat, and uttered a prayer to the Heavenly Brother; then kneeling, with their faces in the opposite direction, they prayed to the Heavenly Father, after which they again kneeled with their faces to the Tien Wang's seat, and in like manner repeated a prayer to him. They then concluded by singing in a standing position. A roast pig, and the body of a goat were lying, with other articles, on tables in the outer court; and a fire was kept burning on a stone altar in front of the Tien Wang's seat, in a sort of court intervening between it and the termination of the recess leading to it. He had not yet appeared; and though all waited for him for some time after the conclusion of the ceremonies, he did not appear at all. He had probably changed his mind, concluding that it would be a bad precedent to allow a foreigner to see him without first signifying submission to him ; or it may be that he did not mean to see me after learning the stubborn nature of our principles, but anxious to have us carry away some account of the grandeur and magnificence of his court, had taken this mode of making an appropriate impression, leaving the imagination to supply the vacant chair which his own ample dimensions should have filled. We retired to the Morning Palace again, where kings, princes, foreigners, and all were called upon to 'ply the nimble, lads,' upon a breakfast that had been prepared for us, after which we retired in the order in which we came."

Chung Wang saw Mr. Holmes afterwards, privately. He was dressed in a loose white silk garment, with a red handkerchief round his head, and a jewel in front. He sat in an easy-chair, fanned by a pretty slip-shod girl. He asked Mr. Holmes questions about foreign machinery, and especially wished him to explain a map, a musical box, and a spy-glass. He became afterwards quite sociable. Mr. Holmes had liberty to visit him whenever he pleased. But he was not willing to be drawn into a discussion in regard to the doctrines of the New Testament, which conflicted with those of Tien Wang ; he admitted that the two did not agree, but declared that the revelation of Tien Wang was more authoritative.

Mr. Holmes, before leaving, entered into conversation with many people, and so got an idea of Hung-Tsue-Schuen's principles and hold upon his adherents, and he concluded that there was very little real religion or elevation of either character or sentiment in them.

Strange to say, there was among foreign nations some sympathy with Hung and his fanatics. It was thought by a few people that his Christianity was better than none, and that possibly the rebels had some right after all. The relations between England and China were at that time anything but cordial, as might have been expected; and that we should interfere was at first improbable. The Imperial authorities endeavoured to drive the rebels towards the sea; and when Shanghai was in danger of an attack, the wealthy traders grew so alarmed that they subscribed funds to induce some foreign forces to protect their city. Already Sung-kiang, a place about twenty miles from Shanghai, was occupied by the rebels, and a reward was offered to two American filibusters —Ward and Burgevine—who were trying to enlist men, to induce them to re-capture the town. Some fighting took place, and at first Ward and his men were victorious. The Faithful King, one of the Tai-ping leaders, hearing of this, led a new army against the "foreign devils," as the Americans were called. They drove Ward back into Sung-kiang, and then marched direct on Shanghai, devastating the country as they went. But the allied French and British troops that were in Shanghai decided now to assist the Imperialists in driving back the rebels, and they were repulsed with heavy loss. They made another attempt, with a similar result, the following day. On hearing this, the Heavenly King summoned his follower, the Faithful One, to Nanking, for consultation and instructions. From that city two months later four immense armies, under the command of four great Wangs, set forth on an expedition to drive the Imperialists from all the cities between Nanking and Hanchow—a district of nearly four hundred miles.

CHAPTER IV.

THE EVER-VICTORIOUS ARMY.

" Let us go thank him and encourage him."
—*As You Like It.*

HEN the news of the onward march of the rebel forces mentioned in the previous chapter reached the British Naval Commander-in-Chief, Admiral Sir James Hope, he decided to visit those ports on the Yangtze which were menaced, and which had been thrown open by the Convention of Pekin to foreign trade. He sailed, therefore, up the river in February 1861, and succeeded in getting into communication with the Heavenly King. Admiral Hope requested of him that the Yangtze trade should not be interfered with, and the rebel leader promised that the armies of the Great Peace should not molest any of the ports, nor at all interfere with Shanghai for one year.

The Heavenly King kept his men to the letter of his promise, and during the year 1861 they engaged themselves in endeavouring to take Hangkow, and make their way into the Yangtze Valley. But they were very unsuccessful, and at last, when the troops were driven back into the neighbourhood of Shanghai, the Heavenly King informed Admiral Hope that as soon as the year of truce had expired he would attack that city. He was warned that it would be not only unwise, but exceedingly dangerous on his part to at all disturb existing arrangements ; but in January 1862 the Faithful King received orders from head-quarters to march his forces on Shanghai, in disregard of all warnings.

In the meantime Ward had not been idle. He was now at Sung-kiang with a thousand well-drilled Chinese soldiers in his army ; and the allied forces at once resolved to join him in his work of putting down the Tai-ping rebellion. From February to June the Imperialists, the Allies, and the army of the Americans, worked together—Captain Dew, R.N., being appointed to the naval command—and they succeeded at once in driving the Tai-pings out of Ningo-po.

In September Ward was killed; and his companion Burgevine, who succeeded him, soon proved that he was incompetent, and altogether unfit for the post. He struck the mandarin, who was the local treasurer, because he did not at once pay the money which he demanded, and ordered his men to break into the treasury and carry off a large sum. Such conduct could not be tolerated ; and the Chinese authorities at once dismissed him from their service.

But now the adventurers who had served under Ward and Burgevine were without a captain ; and Li-Hung-Chang, the great Chinese soldier and statesman, asked General Staveley to select a competent British officer to take command of the Ever-Victorious Army. He promised, under certain conditions, to do the best that he could; and his mind at once turned to Charles Gordon. He knew him ; he had admired his conduct ; and he believed that he possessed very great ability as well as courage.

"What he was before Sebastopol he has been since

—faithful, trusty, and successful. Before Pekin and at Shanghai he has evinced just the qualities that are needed now. Although he has never been in command, he will rise to this occasion, to which he is more fitted than any other man whom I know."

So reasoned General Staveley; and ended by declaring that Charles Gordon must become the new leader of the Ever-Victorious Army.

Gordon was at that time busy in making a military survey of the land around Shanghai; and he did not wish to relinquish this important work, even for the other which was so much more responsible and great. He judged rightly that the knowledge he was now gaining would be of use to him hereafter; and he asked to be allowed for the present to continue at the work. Sir James Hope, therefore, gave the command to Captain Holland of the Marine Light Infantry, who at once besieged the walled city of Taitsan.

This attempt had exceedingly disastrous results. Holland had received false information respecting the defences of Taitsan, and believed it to be surrounded by a dry ditch, when in reality a deep moat ran around it. The consequence was that he was defeated, with a loss of three hundred men and four officers, besides the 32-pounders, which had to be abandoned.

The Tai-pings were of course greatly rejoiced—and Mr. Hake, in the *Story of Chinese Gordon*, reproduces an amusing account of the affair written by one of the Wangs. "'What general is he,' cried our chief, 'who sends his men to storm a city without first ascertaining that there is a moat?' 'And what general is he,' cried another of our leaders, 'who allows a storming-party to advance without bridges? See, oh chief, these unfortunates!' So we laughed and jested as we saw the slaves of the Tartar usurper advancing to destruction. . . . 'Arise,' cried our leader, 'oh, inheritors of eternal peace, and drive these imps from the face of our land.' And we arose at his word as one man—the cry of blood was in our mouths, and the thirst for blood consumed us—we sallied forth on the ever victorious troops, and, behold, they retired as soon as they saw the brandishing of our spears. Many fled, flinging away their arms in their haste; their ammunition and their belts also they cast upon the ground in their fear. The impish followers of the Mandarins set them the example, and many followed it. Little cared they for bridges in their haste—they scattered themselves over the face of the country, and we pursued them as they fled. There were English officers too. Oh, recorder of events, how they ran!'" The precious record concludes thus:—"'We retired before the face of the foreigners, because we knew their might; we withdrew beyond the line which they chalked out, and we will not transgress beyond it; but the country we possess will we hold, and scatter to the four winds of heaven any impish fiends who come against us. Let not the Mandarin slaves think that in their service alone are foreigners employed, and that they alone reap the benefit of their warlike experience. Numbers of them have acknowledged the supremacy of our Heavenly King, and joined us in our efforts to make great peace prevail. Many were in Taitsan, and a Frenchman pointed the gun which carried death into the ranks of our foes. Oh, recorder of events, we, too, have disciplined troops—and we, too, have European firearms, as the imps found to their cost. They have essayed our might, and have experienced the strength of our arms. Let them rest in Sung-kiang. They thought they could take Nanking, but they failed in Taitsan.'"

It was felt that the Ever-Victorious Army would not keep the name it had chosen for itself if a stronger and greater leader were not at once placed at the head of it; and after the Taitsan defeat, Gordon gave up his survey work and took command. It was no easy task that had been given him; but he believed that he might be sure of divine guidance. He had become a commander; but he would take his command from the Great Captain, who is ever on the side of right; and he was not afraid. Self did not enter into his considerations at all: he wished to be useful, and do his duty successfully, and he cared little for what might lie beyond. His letter, dated 24th March 1863, shows the spirit in which he undertook the work :—

"I am afraid you will be much vexed at my having taken the command of the Sung-kiang force, and that I am now a Mandarin. I have taken the step on consideration. I think that any one who contributes to putting down this rebellion fulfils a humane task, and I also think tends a great deal to open China to civilisation. I will not act rashly, and trust to be able soon to return to England; at the same time I will remember yours and my father's wishes, and endeavour to remain as short a time as possible. I can say that if I had not accepted the command, I believe the force would have been broken up and the rebellion gone on in its misery for years. I trust this will not now be the case, and that I may soon be able to comfort you on this subject. You must not fret on this matter: I think I am doing a good service. . . . I keep your likeness before me, and can assure you and my father that I will not be rash, and that as soon as I can conveniently, and with due regard to the object I have in view, I will return home."

Gordon soon proved himself not only courageous, but exceedingly original in his plans, and prompt in carrying them out. Instead of revenging the defeat at Taitsan, as many persons desired him to do, he determined to go away from the neighbourhood, and make war upon some other place held by the rebels. His policy was a bold one. He would go at once to the very heart of the rebellion, and by some military masterpiece of stratagem and skill prove to the rebels the kind of opposition with which they had now to deal. He therefore took two steamers and a thousand men, and went away towards Fushan, which lies on the southern bank of the Yangtze estuary. He landed there, although the Tai-pings saw him; and he went from Fushan to Chanzu, a city ten miles inland, which was loyal to the Imperialists, although besieged by the rebels.

Mr. Andrew Wilson, in his interesting book, says the following in reference to Chanzu:—"The garrison of Chanzu itself had a curious story to tell. They had all been rebels, but had suddenly transferred the town and their services to the other side. Their chief, Lo-Kuo-Chung, had persuaded them to shave their heads and declare for the Imperialist cause early in the year, and this they did in conjunction with the garrison of Fushan; but no sooner had they done so, than, to their dismay, the Faithful King came down upon them with a large force, took Fushan, and laid siege to them, trying to overcome them by various kinds of assault and surprise. He brought against them the two 32-pounders which had been recovered after having been taken at Taitsan, and partially breached the wall. He offered any terms to the soldiers if they would come over; and in order to show his great success, sent in the heads of three European officers who had been killed at Taitsan. Lo, in these trying circumstances, had been obliged to do a good deal of beheading in order to keep his garrison staunch; but he, and probably most of his followers, felt they had committed too unpardonable a sin ever to trust themselves again into Tai-ping hands."

To their help went Gordon and his men. He would be glad to relieve the garrison; and in going there he was showing a bold front to the enemy. He planted his guns among the ruins at Fushan, and opened his fire at once. There was a strong stockade built by the rebels, and towards this he directed his 32-pounders and 12-pounder howitzers. A second stockade on the opposite bank was treated in a similar manner. But, after three hours' bombardment, the rebels gathered in such force that Gordon gave up fighting for the night.

In the morning he saw, with surprise and satisfaction, that the enemy were retreating towards the great rebel centre, Soochow. When they had gone, Gordon hastened to take his force up to Ohanzu; and his men, with a body of Mandarin troops, went through the gates. The inmates of the besieged town were delighted to welcome their deliverer; the Mandarins received them in state, and the poor people testified to their joy. Gordon writes that he saw the young rebel chiefs who had come over. They were very intelligent, were splendidly dressed in their silks, and had big pearls in their caps. The head-man was about thirty-five years old, and was ill and worn with anxiety. " He was so very glad to see me, and chin-chinned most violently, regretting his inability to give me a present, which I told him was not the custom of our people."

This victory, won so rapidly, brought other results than those which seemed to lie on the surface. That which Gordon had anticipated came to pass: his men were put into good spirit, and had strong faith in their leader, who at once set himself to bring about some much-needed reform in the discipline of his army. One thing that greatly encouraged him was the fact that certain British officers whom he knew, and who held him in high esteem, had asked leave to serve under him in China. He was, therefore, strengthened and comforted by his own people.

Besides this, he was now Brigadier-General, the grade of Tsung-ping being granted him by Imperial decree. Li-Hung-Ohung thought well of him, and was anxious to aid him in every possible way; and with his assistance Gordon soon established something like order in his force. He instituted a system of regular payments. Previously the men had looked upon plunder as their chief and legitimate reward; but this was not at all in accordance with the views of their new General, who agreed to give the private soldiers, who were all Chinese, from £3, 10s. to £4, 10s. Lieutenants were to have £30 a-month, and colonels £75 or £85. The commissioned officers were none of them Chinese—they were English, American, Germans, Frenchmen, and Spaniards. All were paid monthly by a Chinese official named Kah, in the presence of Gordon himself.

At first the General had some difficulty with the uniform. It was unlike anything which the Chinese wore, and the men were called by their countrymen, who rejoice in giving nicknames to everybody, " Imitation Foreign Devils." But later, when the force had been everywhere successful, it was thought that their dress had something to do with it, for the courage of the rebels died away when they had to fight foreigners.

Gordon saw that the men were well-armed, as well as well-dressed, well-paid, and well-fed. He was generous in everything. He prepared a flotilla of steamboats and Chinese gunboats ; saw that there was a proper supply of all things that would be needed for transport and actual fighting ; and he had his men well drilled in every respect.

When things were in perfect readiness, and not till then, Gordon summoned his force to action. He decided to march to Quinsan, an important rebel centre. It was known that he intended to attack either that or one of the other two centres, Taitsan or Soochow. He decided to go first to Quinsan, because of the existence there of an arsenal and a shot manufactory, and if that were taken, the power of the other two cities would become less. But as he was marching toward Quinsan, news reached him of an act of great treachery on the part of the rebels, which arrested his progress, and caused him to take his army toward Taitsan

The circumstances that led to this change of route were these : The commander of Taitsan had sent to Governor Li to say that the town would surrender to the Imperialists. General Li therefore sent some men forward to take possession. But as soon as they arrived the rebels changed their tactics, and beheaded two hundred of the Imperialists, making prisoners of the rest.

When Gordon heard of this, he decided that the punishment of such treachery must be swift, sure, and terrible ; and he resolved to be the agent in carrying out the retribution, which had been justly deserved. Without loss of time or hesitation he marched on Taitsan. He knew that there was no comparison between his army and that which he had to oppose. The garrison was manned by ten thousand soldiers, while he had only three thousand to bring against them ; but he did not falter in the least. Making his preparations step by step, with care, but with romantic courage, he took stockades, bridges, and ports, placed his guns in position, and bringing his artillery forward, opened fire upon the battlements. The rebels, headed by some foreigners who had joined them, met the assault with stubborn and energetic resistance ; but it was no use. They gained one temporary advantage ; but when the battle ceased, Gordon had won a decisive victory. He said in his letter home that Taitsan was very important, and its capture well merited ; adding, " It opens out a large tract of country ; and the Chinese generals were delighted, and have said all sorts of civil things about the force. I am now a Tsung-ping Mandarin (which is the second highest grade), and have acquired a good deal of influence, though I do not care about that over much." He had lost a great many men, and among them the brave leader of the assault, Captain Bannen.

An incident followed which gave rise to considerable commotion in England.

Our country has always set its face unflinchingly and resolutely against all cruelty and oppression. As soon as news reaches us of any outrage, we are up in arms immediately. We do not always wait until we are quite sure that the news is true before we become righteously indignant. These feelings are so natural to Englishmen, and on the whole so noble, that none would wish to see them changed; though sometimes, no doubt, the innocent suffer the blame instead of the guilty.

Certainly, Charles Gordon and his associates had a considerable amount of censure passed upon them.

The Imperialists condemned seven prisoners to suffer a slow and ignominious death. They were to be beheaded; but before this was done they were tied up and exposed to view, with arrows sticking in them, and pieces of skin flayed from their arms. That was very terrible: to our English and Christian ideas it was perfectly horrible; and when the news reached this country it awoke a storm of indignant notices in the press. Letters were written which represented the matter to be worse than it really was. The letters were signed "Eye-witness," "Justice and Mercy," and so on, and declared that all kinds of cruelties were practised. In China stories were invented and circulated, which were reproduced in England, and did great harm.

In the deaths mentioned above, Gordon had no part whatever. The Mandarins of their own accord punished the rebels. Gordon was exceedingly displeased at what had occurred, and said so in the plainest and strongest words possible; and General Brown, who commanded Her Majesty's forces in China, went so far as to declare that if such a thing occurred again he would refuse any longer to assist the Imperialists. But there was a great stir made both in China and at home, and Gordon thought it was wise and necessary to write the following letter to the *Shanghai Shipping News :—*

" 15th June 1863.

" I am of belief that the Chinese of this force are quite as merciful in action as the soldiers of any Christian nation could be ; and in proof of this can point to over seven hundred prisoners taken in the last engagement (Quinsan) who are now in our employ. Some have entered our ranks and done service against the rebels since their capture. But one life has been taken out of this number, and that one was a rebel, who tried to induce his comrades to fall on the guard, and who was shot on the spot. It is a great mistake to imagine that the men of this force are worthless. They will, in the heat of action, put their enemies to death as the troops of any nation would do ; but when the fight is over, they will associate as freely together as if they had never fought. . . . If 'Observer' and ' Eye-Witness,' with their friend 'Justice and Mercy,' would come forward and communicate what they know, it would be far more satisfactory than writing statements of the nature of those alluded to by the Bishop of Victoria. And if any one is under the impression that the inhabitants of the rebel districts like their rebel masters, he has only to come up here to be disabused of his idea. I do not exaggerate when I say that upwards of one thousand five hundred rebels were killed in their retreat from Quinsan, by the villagers, who rose *en masse.*"

Gordon needed patience and forbearance as much as courage. Not only did he receive blame from those " who sit at home at ease," and who are always the worst to please of any, but he had some difficulty with his men, and especially with his officers. He had told his soldiers that there was to be no plunder ; but Taitsan was plundered without mercy. He thanked the men and officers for their bravery at Taitsan, but expressed his dissatisfaction at the lack of discipline. Next he chose other officers for certain posts, especially giving an important position to

Deputy-Assistant Commissary-General Cooksley, to whom he gave the title of Lieutenant-Colonel, and whom he placed over the commissariat and military stores. This offended the majors who were to act under him, and they sent in their resignations, which Gordon accepted.

There came a time when everybody praised him, but it was not yet. At present people did not know him as well as they did afterwards; and censure and suspicion tried the soul of the brave man, who had only one desire, and that was to do the right. As we see, not only his Chinese exploits, but his whole life standing out in its grand simplicity, we cannot but feel that he proved himself then and ever a true soldier of the Lord Jesus Christ; and we say, with one accord, " Let us go thank him and encourage him."

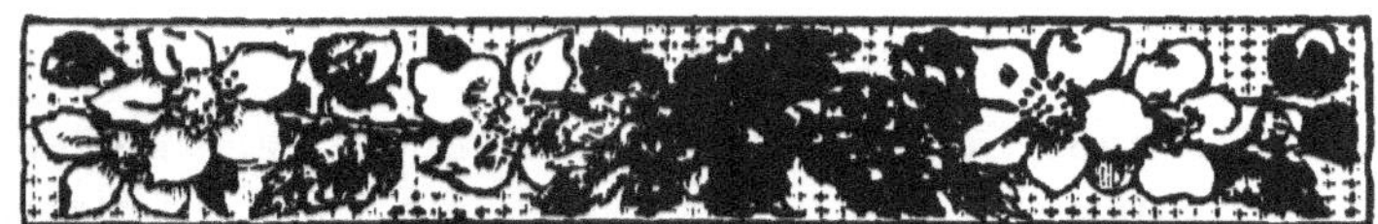

CHAPTER V.

" To the dauntless temper of his mind,
He hath a wisdom that doth guide his valour
To act in safety."

—*Macbeth.*

HE taking of Quinsan was one of the most effective of Gordon's engagements, and it was most cleverly accomplished. He went to the attack with 600 artillery and 2,300 infantry. They were opposed by a force of about 12,000. Quinsan was a large city, four and a-half miles in circumference. There is a high hill in the centre, and the enemy from the top of it could obtain a view of the country all around. It was commanded by a skilful chief, named Moh Wang, who placed men on the hill to telegraph to him all the movements of the Ever-Victorious Army. Gordon made his first attack upon the east gate; but he saw that the best plan would be to bring up his little steamer *Hyson* to work. Quinsan and Soochow were placed between Lake Yansing and some considerable creeks. As the two places, Quinsan and Soochow, depended greatly upon each other, he knew that it

was very important, from his point of view, to cut off all communication between them. So having invested the city by means of his own soldiers and some of the Imperialist forces, in order that the enemy should not retreat to Ohanzu, he brought the *Hyson*, accompanied by a fleet of eighty sail, upon the scene. There was a village only a few miles from Quinsan, which might be called the key to the city; and he therefore came at once to this village, Chanzu, though he had to come through twenty miles of water occupied by the enemy. He was successful in surprising and capturing the rebel garrison at Ohanzu, and there he left three hundred riflemen and a good part of his force in charge. He himself, taking only the well-armed crew of the *Hyson*, commanded by an American of great ability, Captain Davidson, went toward Soochow to reconnoitre. They fell in with a large body of the rebels, and at once fired upon them with such effect that they retreated, leaving Gordon master of the canal. The steamer pursued the fugitives, and went on her victorious course almost unmolested, taking canal, stockades, and ports, with very little trouble.

Gordon's heart was set upon Soochow as the next stronghold to be attacked, and he managed to steam up to its very walls. When he had seen what he wished, he steamed back to Chanzu, arriving just in time, for the rebel garrison were trying to escape. But the *Hyson* was again brought into requisition, and the Tai-pings, who were almost frightened to death, were driven back. They need not have been, if they had only known how to use their vast forces wisely; for they were numerous enough to have won repeated victories where they really had defeat. It was thought that no fewer than 15,000 rebels were beaten at Quinsan.

Gordon and his force at last entered unopposed into Quinsan through the east gate. He gave orders that the prisoners were to be treated as if they had surrendered to British officers. No one was to be beheaded or ill-used. The result of this merciful command was that seven hundred men entered the ranks of the Ever-Victorious. This engagement was of the utmost consequence. Gordon had only two killed and five wounded, but the victory was most decisive and important.

He wrote home, declaring that the steamers would do more than anything to hasten matters. "The horror of the rebels at the steamer is very great. When she whistles they cannot make it out." He told them that he was raised to the rank of Tsung-ping, or Red Button Mandarin. He described the country as wonderful for creeks and lakes, and said that it was very rich. "My occupying this city enables the Imperial Government to protect an enormous district, rich in corn, etc., and the people around are so thankful for their release that it is quite a pleasure. They were in a desperate plight before our arrival, as their way lay between the rebels and Imperialists. . . . You may hear of cruelties being committed; do not believe them. We took nearly 800 prisoners, and some of them have entered my body-guard, and fought since against their old friends the rebels. If I had time I could tell such extraordinary stories of the way men from distant provinces meet each other, and the way villagers recognise in our ranks old rebels who have visited villages for plunder; but I really have no time for it. I took a Mandarin who had been a rebel for three years, and have him now; he has a bullet in his cheek, which he received when fighting against the rebels. The rebels I took into my guard were snake flag-bearers of head chiefs, and they are full of the remarks of their old masters. The snake-flags are the marks of head men in both armies. Whenever they are seen there is a chief present. When they go, you know the rebels will retire. At Taitsan the snake-flags remained till the last, and this accounted for a severe fight. . . . I dare say I shall be loudly attacked in the House of Commons. . . . As you say, the pay is not my motive. I really do think I am doing a good service in putting down this rebellion, and so would anyone if he saw the delight of the villagers at getting out of their oppressors' hands."

After capturing Quinsan, the General had a time of quiet, inasmuch as no big battles were fought, but otherwise he was tried exceedingly. He saw that it would be wise to make Quinsan his future head-quarters, as, from a military point of view, the situation was incomparably better than Sung-kiang. But when the troops heard of it, they became rebellious and mutinous. They preferred Sung-kiang, because there they could easily dispose of the plunder which they hoped and intended to secure, and it was not their wish at all to move. But, of course, Gordon was resolved to have his own way. And there came a time when a severe test must be applied in order to settle once for all the question as to which was the mightier—the Ever-Victorious Army or its dauntless leader.

When the artillery was ordered to fall in, the answer was a blank refusal to do so, accompanied by a threat to attack and kill all the officers, whether English or Chinese. They made a proclamation to General Gordon to this effect, handing it to him in writing. Gordon called them before him, and addressed them: " Now, my men, I want to know who is responsible for this proclamation, and why you did not fall in when ordered to do so ? "

No one spoke. Every one was afraid to confess the truth. Gordon believed that the non-commissioned officers had stirred up the men to mutiny, but he wanted to be sure.

" Now, are you going to tell me ? Very well, then, we will lose no time. *One in every five of you will be shot !* "

This was startling, and the men at once began to groan

and cry. One of the powers which has helped Gordon in his remarkable career is the ability to read character and see into human nature. He noticed one man who was particularly loud in his lamentations. "That is the man who is the ringleader of this affair," said Gordon to himself.

He was always prompt in action, and he now acted upon the impulse of the moment, feeling sure he was right. With his own hand he seized the man and dragged him forth, giving at once the grim order—"*Shoot that man!*"

He was obeyed instantly.

He then called all the non-commissioned officers before him.

"You are ordered into confinement for an hour," he said. "It is an hour given to you for thought. If at the end of that time you do not give up the name of the writer of that proclamation, and if you do not cause the men to fall in, you know your fate; every fifth man will be shot."

This had the desired effect. The name of the person who was responsible for the proclamation was given in, and Gordon had the satisfaction of discovering that he had shot the right man.

After this he had no difficulty from the men; the mutiny was at an end, and they were ready to march to Quinsan and take up their head-quarters there as the General wished.

But Charles Gordon had not disposed of all his troubles, nor could he do so easily. Unfortunately, General Ching was jealous of him, and sought to injure him. Ching thought too much was made of Gordon. Very naturally he believed himself the better man of the two, and did not approve of the rewards and the honours which were given to the foreigner. He wrote letters to Li-Hung-Chang, which he hoped would cause him to view Gordon with disfavour. He did one very dastardly thing—he caused some of his gunboats to open fire on Gordon's army, declaring afterwards that it was a joke. When pressed further he said that he had not recognised the flag on which his troops had fired. Gordon could be exceedingly angry on occasion, and he became so now. He retorted that General Ching knew very well what he was doing ; and he wrote to Li-Hung-Chang insisting upon this. When he got no satisfaction, he resolved that he would go and fight Ching himself ; but Li would not allow this. He sent a messenger to Ching, who obliged him to apologise to Gordon.

But greater troubles still awaited the victorious General. He had to fight with many things besides the rebellion. If he had allowed the men to behave as they pleased with impunity, if he had permitted plunder and self-indulgence on their part, they would have been better pleased. He was too strict and too honourable to give them satisfaction. He was very desirous of making at once an attack on Soochow, and to do this he wished to march on Wokong ; but the artillery officers declared that they would not serve under Major Trapp, whom Gordon had appointed. The intrepid General at once set to work to find other men ; but discovering that he was doing this, the officers yielded, and were forgiven.

Soochow is a most important city on the Grand Canal. To take it was Gordon's intense desire. It is surrounded by water-ways ; and by water Gordon resolved to attack it. If that were wrested from the rebels very much would be gained.

First, Gordon decided to take Kahpoo and Wokong, because, if these places were secured, he would have the keys to the rebel positions. The Imperialists had their ideas and Gordon had his ; and if they were divided as to ways and means, they were united in the wish to win the city of pagodas, the capital of the province. Gordon first attempted to take the two forts of Kahpoo, because then he would have possession of the water-ways and roads leading to Soochow.

He therefore brought his steamers, *Firefly* and *Cricket*, and stormed Kahpoo. He went from thence to Wokong, which place he beleagured on every side. Four thousand prisoners were taken, several important chiefs among them. The leader, Yang Wang, hearing who was coming, had fled; but the two places, Kahpoo and Wokong, were soon in the hands of the Ever-Victorious Army.

And just at that time, with his successes fresh upon him, Charles Gordon became so disheartened that he resolved to throw up the command, and abandon the whole expedition.

He was discouraged by the opposition and want of confidence that he continually met with, when he had a right to look for other treatment. The Chinese Government failed to send him the money that was due to his troops; and the men and officers were both angry with him for his strictness of discipline and determination not to permit plunder. Nearly half the Ever-Victorious Army deserted their commander immediately after he had led them to victory. He could not have kept up the numbers at all, but that he recruited from the rebel prisoners.

His colleague Ching also added greatly to his perplexities and annoyances. He wished to turn more of the prisoners into soldiers, and Gordon, having extracted a promise that they should be well treated, allowed this—to discover that five of the men were beheaded.

What troubled him still more was the fact that Governor Li-Hung-Chang misunderstood him as completely as the rest. He could not believe in the disinterestedness of the brave Englishman with whom he had to deal. Afterwards he knew the man, and loved and honoured him for his worth and true nobility of mind and character; but at present he seemed to suspect that it was for his own ends that he wished to secure the payment of the men. And he kept back supplies, and even broke his promise.

Altogether, though he was sorry on many accounts, Charles Gordon came to the conclusion that it would be well for him to heed the advice of his friends at home, and resign his commission and position in China. So he went to Shanghai for the purpose.

But he did not throw up his commission after all; for when he reached Shanghai he heard tidings that roused all his feelings of courage and chivalry, and sent him back to his post of danger and responsibility with greater resolution than ever.

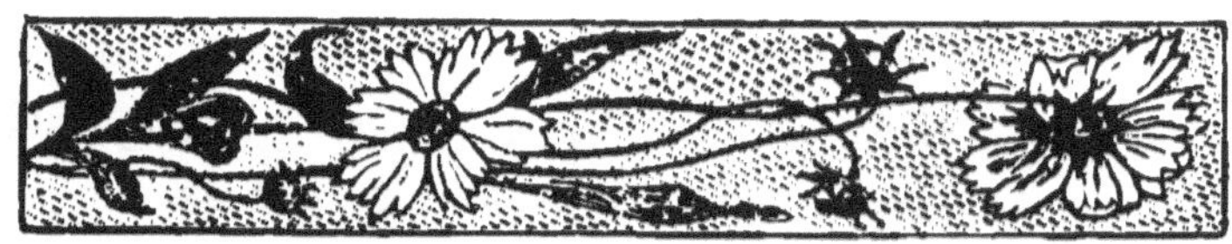

CHAPTER VI.

THE REBEL BURGEVINE.

" Men were deceivers ever ;
    One foot on sea, and one on shore,
  To one thing constant never."
                    —*Much Ado About Nothing.*

HE news which caused Charles Gordon to alter his course and remain at his post concerned the man who, with Ward, had first originated, and then been dismissed from, the Ever-Victorious Army. Burgevine had been hoping again to become the commander ; but finding that this was by no means the wish of the authorities, he became jealous and reckless, and eventually tried to get together an army of his own. He then entered into communication with the Tai-pings, and sought to propitiate those against whom he had formerly fought. At the time when Gordon reached Shanghai, he had contrived, by the help of a man named Jones, the renegade master of the war-ship *Kiao-Chiao*, to seize and appropriate the vessel. The steamer belonged to the Chinese ; but Burgevine manned it with desperate fellows from different parts of the world, and actually steamed up to Soochow.

Gordon hearing of this returned to Quinsan. He felt that so far from giving up now, duty called him to be more energetic and devoted than ever. It was feared on all hands that Burgevine might seduce some of Gordon's men to his side. He had, by his unscrupulous way of rewarding them when he was with them before, made himself popular with the men. He offered the rebels who enlisted with him plenty of pay, and "license to sack every town they took, including Shanghai;" and it would have been little wonder if Gordon's men, angry at being thwarted and kept out of their money, had mutinied. It was a very anxious time; but Gordon was watchful and prompt. He had to personally superintend the defence of both Quinsan and Kahpoo. He had to repulse several attacks, which were made with firm resistance and determination. He was also in a very isolated and dangerous position; but his courage and his trust in God did not fail. People were urging him to make an attack on Soochow; but he thought it would be rash to do so, and he felt that so many lives were entrusted to his care that he would have to exercise the utmost caution. He wrote—

"We have, by the capture of Wokong, very seriously affected the rebels; and if I can carry out my plan of taking Woosieh, and thus surrounding Soochow, I do not think it will be necessary to attack that place, but think they will leave. Burgevine is a very foolish man, and little thinks the immense misery he will cause this unhappy country; for of the ultimate suppression of the rebellion I have little doubt, as it is a government receiving revenues contending with a faction almost blockaded, and drawing on exhaustible funds. The Imperialists are not likely to feel any great liking for foreigners, after the way they have been treated by them. I am thinking of attacking a fortified post of the rebels at Ping Wang, which threatens the city of Wokong, in a few days; and from which they have lately been making raids into the Imperialists' territory."

It was felt by all who knew the true state of affairs that General Gordon and his force were in the greatest possible peril. General Brown sent to the Secretary of War to tell him that Gordon's men had formerly been in the pay of Ward, and that Burgevine had already been joined by some of Gordon's officers. It was quite possible that the guns belonging to the British Government might get into the hands of the rebels through the treachery of some disaffected men, and then General Brown himself and his station at Shanghai would be endangered. He decided to visit Gordon ; and when he saw the efficient state of his garrison, he was more assured. The Imperialists soon joined the Ever-Victorious Army ; and Gordon was at least better protected than he had been before.

At that time he had a remarkable escape. There were some stockades at Patachow which Gordon decided to attack. The Patachow Bridge was three hundred yards long, and had fifty-three arches. Twenty-six of the arches fell "like a pack of cards," and two men were killed. Ten others would have been, but that, hearing the noise, they ran. Gordon had removed one archway to let a steamer pass through ; and this probably weakened the whole structure. He said he regretted it immensely, as it was unique and very old ; in fact, a thing to come many miles to see. General Gordon was one evening sitting on the parapet of the bridge, smoking a cigar, when the stone on which he sat was struck by two shots. He went to see what had been the meaning of the shots, and had not proceeded far before the part of the bridge on which he had been sitting gave way, and went splashing into the water. Was not this another proof that God took care of our hero ?

He was preserved on another occasion, when his life might have been taken by treachery. Some of the

Europeans who had joined the rebels sent to him to say that they were dissatisfied with their position at Soochow, and wished him to meet Burgevine and hold a consultation with him. Gordon recognised the danger, but he did not hesitate. He talked matters over with Burgevine, who told him that he and his men had resolved to leave the Tai-pings; but they would require some guarantee from the Imperialists that they would not be punished. Gordon gave the promise, and offered to take some of the men into his service.

But at the next interview Burgevine had a proposal to make to Gordon. He confessed to him that his great desire was to found an empire of his own in China; and he invited Gordon to join him in the enterprise. He said that together they could take Soochow, and turning out Imperialists and rebels alike, appropriate the treasure in Soochow, and proceed to raise an army and march on Pekin. But he found that he had greatly mistaken his man, for Gordon, by no means allured, treated the proposal as it deserved.

Burgevine, however, had not ceased to treat with Gordon. He sent secretly to tell him that he and his gang intended to desert and throw themselves upon his protection. They asked Gordon to send up from his signal lines a rocket, on which they would board the *Hyson*, as if to capture the steamer. It was carried out as they wished; and so much in earnest did they appear, that a host of rebels rushed to their assistance. The *Hyson*, however, steamed away, and carried the deserters to a place of safety. There were thirty-six of them, but Burgevine was not among them; he and other Europeans, having been suspected by the rebel chief, were retained. The deserters were very glad to find themselves with Gordon, who wrote the following letter to the principal Wangs of Soochow, in order to get them to release the Europeans :—

" STOCKADES, PATACHOW, 16th October 1863.

" *To their Excellencies Chung Wang and Moh Wang.*

" Your Excellencies—You must be already aware that I have, on all occasions where it lay in my power, been merciful to your soldiers when taken prisoners ; and not only been so myself, but have used every endeavour to prevent the Imperial authorities from practising any inhumanity. Ask for the truth of this statement any of the men who were taken at Wokong, and who, some of them, must have returned to Soochow, as I placed no restriction on them whatever.

" Having stated the above, I now ask your Excellencies to consider the case of the Europeans in your service. In every army each soldier must be actuated with faithful feelings to fight well. A man made to fight against his will is not only a bad soldier, but he is a positive danger, causing anxiety to his leaders, and absorbing a large force to prevent his defection. If there are very many Europeans in Soochow, I would ask your Excellencies if it does not seem to you much better to let these men quietly leave your service if they wish it : you would thereby get rid of a continual source of suspicion, gain the sympathy of the whole foreign nations, and feel that your difficulties are all from without. Your Excellencies may think that decapitation would soon settle the matter, but you would then be guilty of a crime which will bear its fruits sooner or later. In this force officers and men come and go at pleasure, and although it is inconvenient at times, I am never apprehensive of treason from within. Your Excellencies may rely on what I say, that should you behead the Europeans who are with you, or retain them against their free will, you will eventually regret it. The men have committed no crime, and they have done you good service, and what they have tried to do by escape is nothing more than any man, or even animal, will do when placed in a situation he does not like.

"The men could have done you great harm, as you will no doubt allow, and I consider that your Excellencies have reaped great benefit from their assistance. As far as I am personally concerned, it is a matter of indifference whether the men stay or leave; but as a man who wishes to save these unfortunate men, I intercede.

"Your Excellencies may depend you will not suffer by letting these men go. You need not fear their communicating information. I knew your force, men and guns, long ago, and therefore cannot get that information from them. If my entreaties are unavailing for these men, of yourself send down the wounded, and perform an action never to be regretted. I write the above with my own hand, as I do not wish to entrust the matter to a linguist, and trusting you will accede to my request.—I conclude, your Excellencies' obedient servant,

"O. G. GORDON, *Major Commanding.*"

It will be seen from this letter how very fearful Gordon was that Burgevine would be decapitated; so he sent the letter and some presents to Moh Wang at once, and all the Enfields that the deserters had brought in. Moh Wang replied that the Europeans need not have left, for they were free to come or go as they pleased; but they had not only ran away, but had taken gun-boats, horses, and arms with them. Gordon replied that he had returned all they had brought. Moh Wang asked the messenger why the Europeans had run away, and was told that it was because they felt sure Gordon would ultimately win and the rebels be defeated.

"Do you think that Gordon will take the city?" inquired Moh Wang.

The messenger promptly answered, "Yes."

" Would it be possible for us to buy Gordon over on our side ? "

" Indeed, no ; it would be quite impossible."

Gordon said in one of his letters, written at this time :—
"This defection of the Europeans is an almost extinguishing blow to the rebels; and from the tone of Moh Wang's letter, so different from the one he wrote to General Staveley a little time ago, I feel convinced that the rebel chiefs would come to terms if they had fair ones offered them. I mean to do my best to bring these about; and I am sure that if I do so, I shall gain a greater victory than any captures of cities would be."

Owing to Gordon's intervention, the rebel Burgevine was not killed. That he was scarcely worth saving was abundantly proved afterward. He had actually, while offering to surrender, been planning with his lieutenant, Jones, to entrap Gordon. But Jones was not so base as to yield to his wishes, although his refusal filled Burgevine with murderous desires towards Jones. On one occasion he fired upon the lieutenant; and it was this that caused Jones and the rest to desert him. Jones thus described the affair, which occurred when Burgevine had been drinking :—

" At noon I went to Burgevine, who was lying asleep on a 32-pounder gunboat, and asked him whether I should assist him to get ashore, as many of our officers and men were making remarks on the condition he was in. On his demanding the names of those who had made the remarks, I declined giving them, and shortly afterwards again attempted to remonstrate with him in company with another officer. On my again declining to give up names, Burgevine drew out his four-barrelled pistol, which he cocked and discharged at my head from a distance of about nine inches. The bullet entered my cheek, and passed upwards. It has not yet been extracted. I exclaimed,

'You have shot your best friend!' His answer was, 'I know I have, and I wish to God I had killed you.'"

Burgevine wrote to a local paper confirming the truth of this statement :—

"Captain Jones's account of the affair is substantially correct; and I feel great pleasure in bearing testimony to his veracity and candour whenever any affair with which he is personally acquainted is concerned."

Gordon succeeded in saving the life of the man who wanted to rob him of his own. He said afterwards, "I am afraid he is a rascal, but I acted to the best of my judgment."

Moh Wang sent him away in safety, and he was delivered to the care of the American consul. No proceedings were instituted against him, in accordance with Gordon's request that he should be allowed to leave the country.

The foreigners whose escape had been made by means of the *Hyson* drew up a document expressing their gratitude to General Gordon, and they gave before the United States consul a full account of the plot in which Burgevine was implicated, and the counter-plot in which they engaged to thwart him.

CHAPTER VII.

IN THE THICK OF THE FIGHT.

"What do you think of me ?"
"As of a man faithful and honourable."

—Hamlet.

N the meantime General Gordon had plenty of work before him. Mr. Andrew Wilson in his interesting book, *Colonel Gordon's Chinese Campaign,* says :—

"In almost all these engagements Colonel Gordon was very much exposed, for he found it necessary, or at least expedient, to be constantly in the front, and often to lead in person. Though brave men, the officers of his force would sometimes hang back, and their commander had occasionally to take one of them by the arm and lead him into the thick of the fire. He himself seemed to bear a charmed life, and never carried any arms, even when foremost in the breach. His only weapon on these occasions was a small cane, with which he used to direct his troops; and in the Chinese imagination this cane soon became magnified into

'GORDON'S MAGIC WAND OF VICTORY.'

His celestial followers, finding that he was almost invariably victorious, and escaping unhurt, though more exposed than any other man in the force, naturally concluded, in accordance with their usual ideas, that the little wand he carried ensured protection and success to its owner. Every one who knows the Chinese character will be aware that such an idea must have given great encouragement to the Ever-Victorious Army, and was of more service to its commander than could have been any amount of arms which he himself could possibly have carried."

Gordon would no doubt have been glad if to his wand had been given the power with which it was credited ; and if, besides winning him victory, it could have warded off disease, and protected him from trouble.

The weather became very hot, and his men fell sick of fever and other ailments, so that it was necessary to remove the troops from Quinsan, and they were taken to a place six miles from Soochow, called Wai Quaidong.

A constant source of irritation and trouble to Gordon was found in General Ching. Although he was supposed to act in concert with Gordon, he much more frequently acted entirely on his own responsibility, leaving his supposed colleague altogether in the dark as to his intentions and movements. Indeed there can be little doubt but that again and again the Chinese general endeavoured to thwart the Englishman, although they were both understood to be fighting in the same cause. This, of course, added greatly to the burden already laid upon Gordon.

"Shall I ever take Soochow ?" was the question that frequently presented itself to him, and sometimes his hope grew faint within him. His friends thought that the odds were so much against him that he would never succeed. He had very little encouragement from the Imperialist Government, in whose cause he was risking his life ; and, indeed, he had little cheer from any side.

The following letter describes better than any other words could do the engagements that followed those already related :—

"You will remember my having mentioned the fact of the Europeans and Burgevine having come over from the rebels. Since then the following have been our movements : we started for the Fifty-three Arched Bridge—alas ! now only twenty-seven arched—Patachow, and made a great detour of the lakes of Kahpoo, to throw the rebels off the scent. We left at two P.M., and although the place, Wulungchiao, which I wanted to attack, was only a mile and a-half to the west of Patachow, I made a detour of thirty miles to confuse them, on a side they were not prepared for. It turned out wet ; and the night of the 23rd of October was miserable enough, cooped up in boats as we were. However, it cleared a little before dawn. About seven A.M. we came on the stockades. I had asked the Imperialists under General Ching to delay their attack from Patachow till I had become well engaged; but, as usual, General Ching must needs begin at half-past five A.M., and he got a good dressing from the rebels, and was forced to retire. His loss was nineteen killed and sixty-seven wounded, while the *Taho* gun-boat admiral, who had abetted him in his tom-fooling, lost thirty killed and wounded. We lost none ; three were slightly bruised. The chief head of Soochow, Moh Wang, knew we were out, but had no idea of our going to Wulungchiao. He is greatly angered, and in addition to this has had trouble with his brother Wangs, who reproach him for having trusted the Europeans, and for neglecting them. Eleven out of twenty-seven Wangs refused to go out and fight. Yesterday afternoon a European left Soochow and came over. I had met him before, and consider that he had acted in a very brave manner in remaining in Soochow. He says Moh Wang does not understand our movements, and is very much put out at the loss of this place. They tried to take it back again on the twenty-fifth at dusk, but got defeated."

After this there was an expedition sent to drive the rebels from Wokong. They had been driven out once, but succeeded in coming back again, and establishing themselves in almost the same position which they had previously occupied. Gordon won another signal victory by making use of the steamer, which compelled them to retire by a narrow road on the bank of the Grand Canal. They were obliged to remain on this road, as there were many large creeks spanned only by high narrow bridges. The steamer kept a fire on the rebels the whole time, and as only two could go over the bridges abreast, of course it took a long time for them to pass. From 3000 to 4000 got away; but 1300 prisoners were taken, and one Wang was among them. Gordon, in his account of it, said —"The value of the victory is that we now have no fear for our rear, and I believe that the rebels in the silk districts seriously think of giving in. In the meantime, I am preparing an attack on the north of the city, which will take place about the 1st of November."

Leeku was the next place to be attacked.

While Gordon was considering the method which it would be best to adopt, he found a letter written by one of his officers to a friend of the rebels, in which the writer, Captain Perry, informed his correspondent of the intended movements of the Ever-Victorious Army. Gordon was rather angry, as he well might be.

"Captain Perry," he said, when the delinquent was before him, "what is the meaning of this?"

"It seems to be a letter of mine."

"Did you write it?"

"Yes, certainly."

"But do you know the harm that such a communication might do? If this information were carried to the Tai-pings, as it well might, and probably would be, do you not see how they might act upon it ?"

"I certainly did not intend to do harm ; my only idea was to convey a little piece of gossip. I thought the facts were of no importance."

Gordon looked upon the matter more seriously. " Such an act might have had grave consequences," he said ; "but I shall pass over your fault this time, on condition that in order to show your loyalty you undertake to lead the next forlorn hope."

His loyalty was proved by his death shortly after. Gordon had forgotten his own remark, until Perry was fighting by his side, and was struck down by a ball. Gordon caught his comrade in his arms, and he died there.

It was at Leeku that Captain Perry was killed. To help Gordon in his endeavour to capture this town, 15,000 of the Imperialist forces joined him. The place was carried with a rush, and Gordon captured their gun-boats, forty other boats, and sixty prisoners.

Soochow was already doomed. Gordon wrote on the 3rd of November :—

" We, yesterday, after a hard fight, took all the stockades up to the walls along the east face of the city, and last night four Wangs came in to negotiate a surrender. I think that this is likely, and the heaviest part of our fighting is over. The rebels are having great trouble among themselves, and have to pay largely for food."

Wanti still remained to be attacked. When that place had surrendered, Soochow would be almost completely invested. Already nearly all the roads and waterways leading to it were closed, and the outposts occupied by Imperialist forces. Wanti was very strongly fortified ; but they managed to surround the place and take it in less than an hour. The rebels lost all courage as soon as Gordon approached, and they began to leave in large numbers at once. Yet some of them fought bravely, and Gordon took six hundred prisoners.

One man, Lai-Wang, who was in charge of some stockades, volunteered to desert the rebels and join Gordon, bringing with him his 20,000 men; but he was killed, and so prevented from carrying out his intentions. Gordon hoped that dissensions within the city of Soochow, and scarcity of rice, would hasten its surrender. He resolved to make the attack at Monding, on the Grand Canal.

Gordon was now ready to commence the great work of taking Soochow. He was determined that before November passed something more should have been accomplished. He knew that he had to contend with overwhelming forces. In Soochow and its suburbs the Tai-ping forces numbered 40,000 men, while 38,000 more were not far away. Gordon had under his own command only between 3000 and 4000. General Ching had command of 25,000 Imperialists.

Gordon had received some information respecting the enemy which encouraged him. Chung Wang, the Faithful King, was in difficulties. He must be exceedingly wary in his movements, or Nanking and Hangchow would be lost to him. If Nanking were once out of the rebels' hands the rebellion would certainly be doomed. The city was besieged, and the works around the Kaiachiao had been evacuated. That which took the strength from the arm of the Faithful King filled the leader of the Ever-Victorious Army with hope; and he thought the time had now come to make the attack.

His first effort resulted in failure. He tried one night to take an inner line of the outer defences, and was defeated.

It was soon after midnight, when Gordon, accompanied by Majors Howard and Williams, made the attempt. All were dressed in white turbans, so as to be seen by each other in the dark. Gordon ordered his men to wait for a given signal before they came on. Everything appeared quiet, and the men who were with Gordon were working at a stockade, when a tremendous fire of grape and musketry was opened upon them from the Tai-pings. Gordon held on with his usual gallantry, but those who came after him were obliged to retire. Moh Wang, who was in the front stockade, fought with great bravery. He had on neither shoes nor stockings; and he and twenty Europeans, who were with him, fought like lions. The rebels, though they won a victory, had very great losses.

Meanwhile the Wangs in Soochow were divided in opinion. Some of them wished to come over to the Imperialists, and some would not listen to such a proposal. Moh Wang was especially indignant with all who thought of it. So some of the Wangs proposed that Gordon should again attack the east gate; and they promised that when he did so, they would shut Moh Wang out of the city, and take affairs into their own hands. Gordon, therefore, brought his guns to bear upon the stockades, which he soon laid in ruins. He had only a few men with him; but he pressed forward, pushed through the stockades, and seized a fort. He thus gained a victory, but not without severe loss of valuable men and lives.

On the 30th of November 1863 Gordon issued the following general order :—

"The commanding officer congratulates the officers and the men of the force on their gallant conduct of yesterday. The tenacity of the enemy, and the great strength of their position, have unfortunately caused many casualties, and the loss of very valuable officers and men. The enemy, however, has now felt our strength, and, although fully prepared and animated by the presence of their most popular chiefs, have been driven out of their position, which surpasses in strength any yet taken from them. The loss of the whole stockades on the east side of the city, up to the walls, has already had its effect, and dissension is now rife in the garrison, who, hemmed in on all sides, are already, in fact, negotiating defection. The commanding officer feels most deeply for the heavy loss, but is convinced that the same will not be experienced again. The possession of the position of yesterday renders the occupation of the city by the rebels untenable, and thus, victualling the city is lost to them."

The Wangs who wished to surrender arranged to have an interview with Gordon, and he met them accordingly. They told him if he would attack the city they would not assist in its defence, on condition that he on his side would engage to protect them from the anger of the Imperialists. The Nar Wang asked Gordon to carry the city by assault, but was told that in that case no one would be able to protect it from being sacked and burnt. He advised the Wangs to give over one of the gates and thus prove their sincerity ; adding that if they would not do that, they must either leave the city or settle the matter in battle.

They agreed to hand over a gate, and while General Ching was settling the terms of the capitulation, Gordon went to have an interview with Li-Hung-Chang in order to get the safety of the prisoners secured.

The rebel chiefs were very brave men, and perhaps the bravest of all was Moh Wang. He would not consent to surrender. He had an idea that some parleying was going on, and he called six other Wangs together that he might confer with them. The conference was conducted with considerable ceremonial. Moh Wang was seated on a dais in the reception hall, and began to discuss the state of the city, of which he was the commander. Four of the Wangs proposed capitulation.

" No surrender ! " said the brave Moh Wang.

" But we shall be overcome, and then it will be the worse for us," urged the rest.

" No surrender ! " replied Moh Wang.

"I, too, would say the same if we had any chance of success. But there is no hope. We are completely surrounded by the foreign devils, and our only chance is in capitulation."

"No surrender!"

"We shall all be killed, and our cause will come to an ignominious end if we stubbornly hold out now. But it is possible to make terms with Gordon. He is an honourable man. He will ensure our safety."

"No surrender!"

"But if we yield now we shall live to fight again ; if we are killed, of what avail will it be that we have stood out against all odds ?"

"No surrender!" again cried Moh Wang.

Kong Wang, in his great anger, threw off his robes, and drew out a dagger. "Will you yield now ?"

"No surrender!"

The brave Wang was stabbed nine times—stabbed until he died.

Then Kong Wang called on the others to assist him, and they carried the faithful Wang from the reception hall into the outer court, and there cut his head from his body.

Gordon had felt the greatest respect for Moh Wang. He knew that in similar circumstances he would have behaved in precisely the same. manner. In his negotiations with Li-Hung-Chang he had laid great stress upon his good character, and Governor Li had given him a pledge that Moh Wang's life should be spared. Gordon was exceedingly grieved to hear when he came back that the brave Wang needed his services no longer.

Now that he was dead, no one else was determined enough to hold out. Very little time was lost ; for on that night Soochow surrendered, and the Ever-Victorious Army, with its intrepid leader, saw the success which they had for so long been desiring.

CHAPTER VIIL

AFTER THE SURRENDER OF SOOCHOW.

"My honour is my life ; both grow in one ;
Take honour from me, and my life is done."
—*Richard II.*

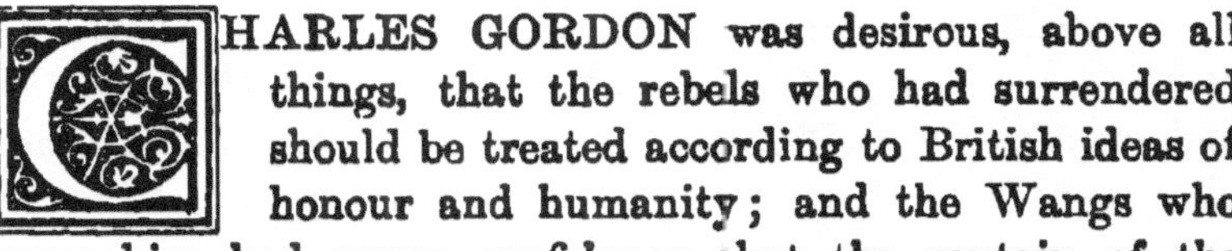

HARLES GORDON was desirous, above all things, that the rebels who had surrendered should be treated according to British ideas of honour and humanity; and the Wangs who knew him had every confidence that the captain of the Ever-Victorious Army would have influence enough to see that his wishes were carried into effect. But Gordon was only one man, and he was crippled and thwarted in many ways. He was especially anxious that two things should be guaranteed: that there should be no looting of the evacuated city, and no punishment of the Wangs.

In regard to the former he did all that he could. So far as his own men were concerned, he was determined to keep them from plunder. So he sent to Li Futai (Li-Hung-Chang) to ask that officers and men should at once receive, as a reward for their gallant services and their obedience in abstaining from plunder, and also as an incentive to future efforts, two months' extra pay. It seemed a reasonable request, and that the men should be satisfied with it proves Gordon to have had considerable power over them.

But to this appeal General Ching brought a denial; proposing instead a gift of one month's pay.

The men were disgusted. They talked of mutiny, and loud threats were issued that they would rush into Soochow, and pay themselves in the way which they liked best—by plunder.

But Gordon was prompt to oppose this; and in order to prevent it he issued his orders and marched the men back to their quarters at Quinsan.

Knowing that they were safe there for the time being, he went to Soochow to see that his Chinese comrades were treating those who were at their mercy with courtesy, or at all events with humanity. He had understood that when Soochow was given into the power of the Imperialists no lives should be taken, and especially that pardon should be given to the Wangs through whose instrumentality the city had capitulated. Ching, who was in Soochow, informed him that Li had given orders for the Wangs to come before him the next day, and formally give up into his hands the keys of the gates of the city; but that the Futai had promised to be merciful to all.

So far from this being the case, the Futai most treacherously had the six Wangs beheaded.

There were many accounts of the event, the Chinese trying to make their own story good, and others telling stories of different kinds; but the following was Charles Gordon's own statement. He wrote a clear account of all that happened, except so far as it related to his own danger and exposure, from the 28th of November to the 9th of December. After describing the conference of the Wangs in the reception hall of Moh Wang's palace, and the assassination of its master, he says :—

"I should have mentioned that Nar Wang had told General Ching, the night of the 3rd of December, that Chung Wang, had assembled the chiefs, after his defeat on the 29th of November, and had proposed to them to vacate Soochow and Nanking, and return to the south. Moh Wang would not accede to it, as he hoped to hold the city, and had all his property there. The other Wangs, knowing of the negotiations, did not also entertain the idea. Another reason for Moh Wang's holding out was that his father and mother were hostages at Nanking with Tien Wang.

"On the morning of the 5th of December there was some musketry to be heard in the city, but it soon ceased, and General Ching advanced some of his men to the east gate, while some of our men went to the north gate; but I soon withdrew them, as I knew their propensities, and I then went to the Futai, and asked him to give the men two months' pay, and let the force push on to Wusieh and Chan-chufu.

" He objected, although the troops had had no remuneration for any of the places that had fallen, and had had very hard and continuous fighting. I told him I could not keep them in hand unless he assented, and gave him until three o'clock P.M., and after that time I could not remain in command. This was a hard fact; but both officers and men were of the same mind, and I had no option. I then went into the city and passed down to Nar Wang's house, and there met all the Wangs. I asked them if everything had gone on properly, and if they were content: they said, Yes, and appeared quite at ease. Their troops were in the streets, and everything appeared orderly. I then went down to Moh Wang's palace, and tried to get his body buried, but the people would not touch it. I then went out to the troops who were under arms, and soon after General Ching came in on the part of the Futai to arrange terms. I referred him to the officers commanding regiments, but they could not agree. Ohing then came to me, and begged me to try and get the force to accept one month's pay. After some demur I determined on making the force accept, as night was coming on, and I was afraid of the troops within making an attack on the Futai, as also on the rebels in the city.

"I therefore assembled them, and addressing them, I let them know that I had succeeded in obtaining one month's pay. The men made a slight disturbance, which was quickly quelled, and, after one attempt to march down on the Futai, dismissed. I kept a guard on the Futai's boat that night, and being apprehensive of further trouble if the troops remained, I marched them back at eight o'clock A.M. on the 6th of December ; and anticipating no further trouble with the men, I ordered the steamers *Tsatlee* and *Hyson* round to Wuhlungchaio, directing my chop to come up to the Pow Mün, or south gate. I then went into the city to Nar Wang's house, reaching it at half-past eleven o'clock A.M. I had heard that the Wangs had to go out to the Futai at twelve o'clock noon, and that then the city would be given over. I should mention that General Ohing had told me, on the afternoon of the 5th December, that the Futai had written to Pekin respecting the capture of Soochow, and stating that he had amnestied the prisoners. At the Nar Wang's house I met all the Wangs with their horses saddled to leave for the Futai. I took Nar Wang aside, and asked him if everything was all right. He said, 'Yes.' I then told him I had the intention of going to the Taho Lake to look for the *Firefly.* He said he was coming down to see me, and would like to stop two or three days. I said unless he thought there was an absolute necessity, the business I was going on was too important for me to stop ; but if he thought he had any reason for wishing me to stay I would do so. He said 'No,' and I bade him and the other Wangs good-bye; and they all passed me a few minutes afterwards, with twenty attendants, going towards the Low Mün, or east gate, on their way to the Futai.

"I went into Moh Wang's palace, and saw General Ching's men come down to bury Moh Wang's body, according to my request. I then went to the east gate, or Low Mün, to while away the time until the steamers got round to Wuhlungchaio, intending to go round the wall to the Pow Mün, or south gate. Just as we arrived at the gate I saw a large crowd on the bank opposite the Futai's boat, and soon afterwards a large force of Imperialists came into the city, and ran off to the right and left along the wall and into the city, yelling as they usually do when they enter a vacated stockade, and firing off their muskets in the air. I remonstrated with the Mandarins and soldiers, as their conduct was liable to frighten the rebels, who might retaliate and cause a row. After a few minutes General Ching came in, and I noticed he looked disturbed. I asked him eagerly if the interview was over, and had been satisfactory. He said the Wangs had never come to the Futai. I said I had seen them going, and asked him what could have become of them. He said he did not know, but thought they might have run away. I asked him what could have induced them to do so. He said they had sent out to the Futai to ask him to keep twenty thousand men, and to have half the city, building a wall inside; that Nar Wang had said before that he wanted only two thousand five hundred; and that at another time he said he wanted no soldiers, but merely to retire home; that the Futai had objected to his demand, and that he had told him to go to the Tch Mün and stockade his men outside that gate; and that he supposed Nar Wang had taken alarm and gone off. He said further that Nar Wang had sent to Chung Wang for assistance. I asked him if he thought Nar Wang and the other Wangs had gone back to the rebels. He said, No; but they would go back to their own homes, and live there. I did not feel very well satisfied, and asked Mr. Macartney, who was by, to go to Nar Wang's house and see if he was there, and to reassure him if he was alarmed at anything. General Ching was anxious I should not go ; and as I had no suspicion, I went round the wall with him to the Pow Mün, which we reached at five o'clock P.M.

"I had frequently returned to the question of Nar Wang, but found that both General Ching and my interpreter seemed to evade the questions. When I got to the Pow Mün, I told General Ching I should go no further, as I felt uncomfortable about Nar Wang, and also heard volleys of musketry in the city, but not of any great amount. I asked General Ching what it was. He said there were some Kwangzi and Canton men who would not shave, and they were driving them out of the city, having left two gates open for their retreat, but they were only frightening them out. General Ching then left, and I asked my interpreter what he thought of the state of affairs. He said that he thought the Imperialists, having got the city, did not care about keeping their agreement. I therefore decided on riding to Nar Wang's house, and seeing him if possible. I rode through the streets with my interpreter, which were full of rebels, standing to their arms, and Imperialist soldiers looting. I went to Nar Wang's palace, and found it ransacked. I met Nar Wang's uncle (a second in command), and he begged me to come to his house and protect it. He then withdrew the female household of Nar Wang, and accompanied them to his house, where there were some thousand rebels, under arms, in a barricaded street. It was now dark, and having seen the state of affairs, I wished much for Nar Wang's uncle to let my interpreter go, taking orders for the steamers to come round and take the Futai prisoner (as he, the interpreter, thought the Futai had not yet beheaded the Wangs), and also an order to bring up my force. They, unfortunately, would not let my interpreter go, and I remained with them until two o'clock A.M. on the seventh, when I persuaded them to let him go and procure assistance. I had kept several bands from looting the house by my presence. About three A.M. one of the men who had gone out with the interpreter returned, and said that a body of the Imperialists had seized the interpreter and wounded him. I was now apprehensive of a general massacre, as the man made me understand that the order I had sent had been torn up, and therefore went out to go to Pow Mün to send by my boat additional orders, and also to look for the interpreter. I found no traces of him ; and proceeding to the Pow Mün, was detained an hour by the Imperialists. It was then five A.M., and I determined on proceeding for my guard to the Low Mün, or east gate, hoping to be able to seize the Futai, and to get back in time to save the house of Nar Wang's uncle.

"I got to the Low Mün at six A.M., and sent on my guard to the house. It was, however, too late. It had been ransacked. I then left the city and met General Ohing at the gate. I told him what I thought, and then proceeded to the stockade to wait the steamers, as I was still ignorant that the Wangs had been beheaded. I thought they were prisoners, and might still be rescued if the Futai could be secured. When awaiting the steamers, General Ohing sent down Major Bailey, one of the officers I had sent him to command his artillery, who told me that General Ohing had gone into the city, and sat down and cried. He then, to alleviate his grief, shot down twenty of his men for looting, and sent Major Bailey to tell me he had nothing to do with the matter, that the Futai ordered him to do what he did, and that the Futai had ordered the city to be looted. I asked Major Bailey if the Wangs had been beheaded. He said that he had heard so. He then told me he had Nar Wang's son in the boat, and had brought him to me. The son came up, and pointing to the other side, said that his father and the Wangs had been beheaded. Then I went over and found six bodies, and recognised Nar Wang's head. The hands and bodies were gashed in a frightful way, and cut down the middle. Nar Wang's body was partially buried. I took Nar Wang's head, and just then the steamers were seen coming up. The Futai, however, received some warning that I had left for Soochow by some other route. I then went to his boat and left him a note in English, informing him of what my intention had been, and also my opinion of his treachery. I regret to say that —— did not think fit to have this translated to him.

"The two steamers then left for Quinsan, and one was sent down with Prince F. de Wittgenstein to inform the General of the state of affairs. This officer had been with the force nearly a month, and had been informed in detail by me of the whole that had passed as above related.

"On the 8th of December the Futai sent —————— to persuade me that he could not have done otherwise; and I blush to think that he could have got an Englishman to undertake a mission of such a nature.

"O. G. GORDON, *Major Commanding.*
" *12th December* 1863.

"*P.S.*—To continue. On the 8th of December I started with an escort and a steamer to General Ching's stockade, to obtain Nar Wang's body and some of his family who had been retained prisoners in General Ching's stockade. These I obtained, and also the body.

"General Brown arrived on the afternoon of the ninth, and took the protection of the force under his command. I had already spoken to the officers, and got them to agree to leave the solution to the British general. The disgust and abhorrence felt by all of them was and is so great as to lead me to fear their going over *en masse* to the rebels; but I have shown them that the sin would then be visited on the Chinese people, and not on the culprits who committed it. The rebels have no government at all, while the Imperialists can lay claim to some.

"C. G. GORDON."

In this description of the events that occurred, Gordon does not lay stress upon his own danger, which was certainly very great; nor does he adequately express the indignation which filled him in regard to the treacherous murders of the rebel kings, and the iniquity of the Imperialists in sacking the city.

He speaks of having gone to the house of Nar Wang's uncle, but does not say that when he did so he was at once surrounded by thousands of armed Tai-pings, who made him their prisoner. It seems wonderful that they did not use their power, and first torture and then kill him. But the Providence that has always been over the man protected him, and he was kept in safety. It seems strange, too, that they did not at least retain him as their prisoner, but they allowed him to leave when he asked to go, that he might seek for his interpreter, who had been wounded. One of the most bitter trials he ever had to endure was that of finding that his word had been broken, though not by himself, and the lives he had hoped to preserve had been sacrificed. It is little wonder that he shed tears of real sorrow. The Wangs were rebels; but whatever they were, he felt that they ought to have been treated with honesty and honour. He wanted— what true Englishman does not?—that the Chinese and all other people should have a high opinion of the motives that guide the men of his nation, and those with whom they have to do—that it should be known that they will keep their promises, and not shirk their responsibilities; and we may be sure that it was with a sore heart, and very hurt feelings, that the heio waited General Brown's investigations.

The result of these were told in the following letter, written by General Brown to Sir Frederick Bruce and Lord de Grey :—

"The circumstances attending and preceding the occupation of Soochow by the Imperialists are so calculated to produce an impression on public opinion unfavourable to the line of policy adopted by Her Majesty's Government in China, that I trust I need not apologise for entreating your most earnest consideration of the whole subject.

"I received the first intimation of events passing in Soochow by a hurried note from Major Gordon, which reached me during the forenoon of the eighth instant ; a second note, which, although written previously, did not reach me until a later period, produced the impression that affairs were proceeding favourably ; consequently I was so far from apprehending the gravity of the crisis, that I decided to carry out my intention of proceeding to Hongkong by the mail steamer, and was on board when Prince Wittgenstein, despatched by Major Gordon in the steamer *Tsatlee*, brought a more complete and detailed narrative of events.

"The additional information then received determined me to accede to the urgent entreaties of Major Gordon, of which the Prince was the bearer, to proceed to Quinsan, the head-quarters of Major Gordon's force, at once. I arrived at Quinsan about three o'clock P.M. the following day, and immediately received from Major Gordon a report which differed but slightly from the more carefully compiled narrative enclosed. Major Gordon has been unable to express in writing the intense indignation and disgust with which the infamous and dastardly conduct of the Futai had inspired him.

"You will perceive by Major Gordon's narrative that he

was able to withdraw his force from before Soochow to Quinsan only under the formal promise from the Futai of one month's pay to the officers and soldiers, and that it required all his influence to prevail on them to accept these terms. The subsequent treachery of the Imperial authorities had, however, destroyed the confidence of all ranks; their cruelties had turned the sympathies of Europeans in favour of the rebels; and I found it necessary, in order to restore discipline, and to avert a perhaps total defection of the men, to take Major Gordon and his force formally under my command.

"This move on my part, I am happy to inform your Excellency, had the best effect; all ranks now express their perfect satisfaction and reliance, and every symptom of hesitation has disappeared from the force under Major Gordon's command.

"I considered it expedient to have an interview with the Futai, with the view of hearing any explanatory statement he might have to offer, and to communicate to him my views on recent events, and explain the future relations between himself and Major Gordon.

"I therefore despatched the interpreter to the consulate (Mr. Mayers), accompanied by two of my officers, to convey to him my desire for an interview.

"Having thus prepared the way, I proceeded the following day to Soochow, but was met at Ching's stockade by the Futai, who had come out from the city to meet me.

"I speedily ascertained that, though the Futai was prepared to take on himself the whole responsibility of murder of the Wangs and sacking of the city, and fully to exonerate Major Gordon from all blame, he was either unable or unwilling to offer any exculpation or explanation of his conduct, and it only remained for me to express my opinion and future intentions.

"This I did in as few words as possible. I expressed the

indignation and grief with which the English people, together with all civilised nations of the world, would regard his cruelty and perfidy. I expressed to him my views on the impolicy of a fruitless severity, which paralysed his friends, and drove the rebels to desperation, at the time when we had good reason to believe they were prepared to capitulate, and return to their homes in peace.

"I then informed him that I should insist on the promised reward of one month's pay; that I deemed it my duty to refer the whole matter to our Minister at Pekin; and that, pending such reference, Major Gordon had received instructions from me to suspend all active aid to the Imperialist cause further than protecting Soochow, knowing its importance to the safety of Shanghai, and warning the rebels to abstain from attacking his positions. I concluded by expressing my unhesitating conviction that, after what had occurred, my Government would withdraw all assistance hitherto afforded to the Imperial cause, recall Major Gordon and all English subjects serving under him, and disband the Anglo-Chinese force."

CHAPTER IX.

GORDON AGAIN TAKES THE FIELD

> "In the reproof of chance
> Lies the true proof of man."
> —*Troilus and Cressida.*

> ' He's truly valiant that can wisely suffer."
> —*Timon of Athens.*

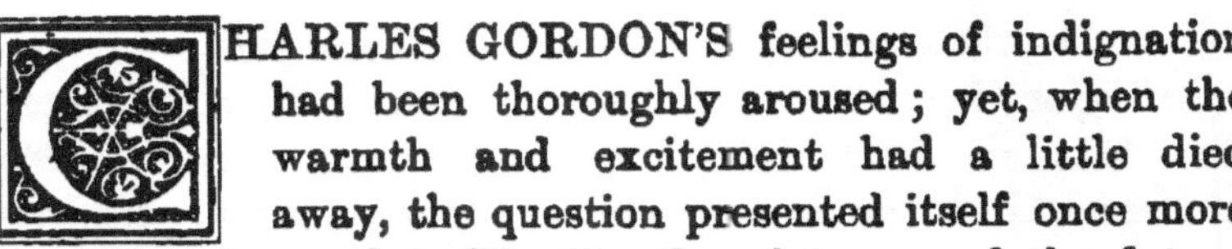

CHARLES GORDON'S feelings of indignation had been thoroughly aroused; yet, when the warmth and excitement had a little died away, the question presented itself once more —" What is my duty?" He thought more of the future than of the past, as he always has done, and does still. It did not occur to him to magnify his deeds or his sufferings; he had tried to do his best, and act with prompt decision, and a measure of success had attended his endeavours. That contented him, and he did not care who had the praise and the rewards, so that he had done the work.

In point of fact, Governor Li had most of the honour. He certainly mentioned Gordon favourably in his despatches, but he did not acknowledge the truth, that it was the Englishman's valour that, more than anything beside, had crushed the rebellion; for crushed it was to all intents and purposes, although a few towns were still in the hands of the rebels. Li very naturally sought to impress his Emperor and the people of his nation with a due sense of his own exploits; and he praised General Ching also for that which he had accomplished. Still the truth remained that neither Li-Hung-Chang nor General Ching could have done very much toward stamping out the rebellion but for the heroism of the gallant Gordon.

The Emperor felt that he must be rewarded; and accordingly he sent through Governor Li a medal of the highest distinction, and a present of 10,000 taels.

And now the illustrious Englishman showed of what stuff he was made.

He gladly accepted the money that had been sent for the assistance of his wounded men, and the reward which had been well earned by, and was forwarded for, his troops; but for himself he would take nothing.

With the true dignity of an English gentleman he returned this letter to the Emperor of China:—

"Major Gordon receives the approbation of His Majesty the Emperor with every gratification, but regrets most sincerely that, owing to the circumstances which occurred since the capture of Soochow, he is unable to receive any mark of His Majesty the Emperor's recognition, and therefore respectfully begs His Majesty to receive his thanks for his intended kindness, and to allow him to decline the same."

This must, more than a little, have astonished both the Emperor and his friends.

Writing home later, Gordon said that he did not want either money or honours. He had the consciousness that he had done good, and that was enough for him. The approbation of his own conscience, and the hope of the Master's "Well done, good and faithful servant," were, indeed, more than sufficient for Charles Gordon.

" But—what next ? "

This was the question that was pressing upon him. Must he really give up the work of repressing the rebellion, although he had ever believed it to be a noble and important one, while yet it had not been completed ? Or should he hope the best of Li-Hung-Chang, and work with him once more ?

It was in accordance with Gordon's whole life and character that he decided to do the latter.

He came to see that even as regarded the slaughter of the Wangs there were some extenuating circumstances, which in the first heat of the occurrence he was unable to admit or to see. He had looked upon it from an Englishman's point of view ; but, of course, there was the Chinese side also—and when he tried the " Put-yourself-in-his-place " plan, he saw that the deed, horrible as it must always appear to him, was not such an unmitigated crime in Chinese estimation. It was open to him to dismiss his army, but if he did, almost certainly many of them would join the ranks of the rebels ; and, perhaps, in time all that he had done would have to be done over again. That so many lives should have been sacrificed for nothing was too dreadful. It would be better that he had never led the Victorious Army to any success than that it should cease its efforts before the end had been accomplished.

But could he lay aside his own personal feelings, and again work with the Futai ?

Yes ; he could do that or anything else when once convinced that it was right. He was a Christian, and, therefore, he must not keep up any feeling of resentment. And he knew who had said, " Vengeance is Mine ; I will repay ! "

His mind was soon made up ; and he communicated the result in a letter to Sir Frederick Bruce, in which he said, that seeing the danger which might arise from inaction since his men were idle, he had arranged with the Futai to issue a proclamation, declaring that he had been in nowise to blame for the execution of the Wangs; and that when this was done he would again take up his former position in the Ever-Victorious Army. He felt this to be the more desirable, because he knew that Burgevine intended to rejoin the rebels; that the Futai was more willing to act with him, notwithstanding all that had occurred, than with any other British officer; and that if he (Gordon) did not act, a less worthy man might be told off to the post. Under these circumstances, although he confessed that it was not an easy task, he decided to go back to his post.

" I am aware," he wrote, " that I am open to very grave censure for the course I am about to pursue; but in the absence of advice, and knowing as I do that the Pekin authorities will support the Futai in what is done, I have made up my mind to run the risk. If I followed my own desire, I should leave now, as I have escaped unscathed and been wonderfully successful. But the rabble called the Quinsan force is a dangerous body, and it will be my duty to see that it is dissolved as quietly as possible, and that while in course of dissolution it should serve to benefit the Imperial Government. I do not apprehend the rebellion will last six months longer if I take the field. It may take six years if I leave, and the Government does not support the Imperialists. I propose to cut through the heart of the rebellion, and to divide it into two parts by the capture of Yesing and Liyang." He adds, " If the course I am about to pursue meets your approbation I shall be glad to hear; but if not, shall expect to be well rebuked. However, I know that I am not actuated by personal considerations, but merely as I think will be most conducive to the interests of our Government."

In the proclamation which is referred to in this letter the

Futai sought to justify himself. He declared that although his intentions were apparently at variance with those of General Gordon, they were in reality identical; that he acted without consulting Gordon because fresh complications had arisen, which hesitation or delay might have made fatal; that not only was no sign of contrition visible among the Wangs, but that they made demands which were in themselves the proof that they wished and intended to return to a state of rebellion when the first opportunity occurred; and that he believed that the death of these few bandits was not only a necessity, but would have most salutary results. He ended by saying that General Gordon had nothing whatever to do with the matter; but that the occurrences which made the execution necessary happened after Gordon had left; that he was not an eye-witness of what took place on the spot, and that he had been misled by rumours. "He was impressed with the conviction that, the terms of surrender having been agreed to, the subsequent execution of the individuals was a breach of the convention entered into; but he was totally unaware of the pressing urgency and extreme danger of the consequences involved, which left not an instant for delay, and which led the Futai to inflict at once the penalty prescribed by military law."

Whatever others may have thought of the wisdom of Gordon's decision, he had the comfort of knowing that Sir Frederick Bruce approved.

"My concurrence," wrote Sir Frederick, "in the step you have taken is founded in no small measure of my knowledge of the high motives which have guided you while in command of the Chinese force, of the disinterested conduct you have observed in pecuniary questions, and of the influence in favour of humanity you exercised in rescuing Burgevine and his misguided associates from Soochow. I am aware of the perseverance with which, in the face of serious obstacles and much discouragement, you have steadily pursued the pacification of the province of Kiang-soo, in relieving it from being the battlefield of the insurrection, and in restoring to its suffering inhabitants the enjoyments of their homes, and the uninterrupted exercise of their industry; and you may console yourself with the assurance that you are rendering a service to true humanity as well as to great material interests. It would be a serious calamity, and addition to our embarrassments in China, were you compelled to leave your work incomplete, and were a sudden dissolution or dispersion of the Chinese force to lead to the recurrence of that state of danger and anxiety from which, during the last two years, Shanghai has suffered. I approve of your not awaiting the result of the inquiry of the Futai's proceedings at Soochow, provided you take care that your efforts in favour of humanity are not in future defeated by Chinese authorities."

In a subsequent letter, Sir Frederick Bruce said that he had obtained a promise from the Emperor that when foreign officers were employed by him, the customs of foreign nations should be observed; and he reminded Gordon that if henceforth it should be impossible for the scenes of Soochow to be re-enacted, he (Gordon) would indeed be the protector of the Chinese. He said, too, that although the action of the Futai was abhorrent to our ideas, it was not a gross or deliberate act of treachery, if the excuses urged by Li were true.

And so Gordon entered the field again; and this time under difficulties even greater than those with which he previously had to contend. He had to win several towns from the lawless men who held them; and he could no longer be supplied from adjacent loyal towns. He set forth on his expedition in the face of great obstacles. The weather was stormy; snow and hail were falling when he started; and these might have been taken as symbolic prophecies of the kind of experience that awaited him. But he was nerved afresh with courage and endurance. He could scarcely meet with greater sorrows and troubles than those through which he had already passed ; and he still trusted in God, and was sure that He would not forsake him.

Almost all his friends would rather that he had not taken the field with Li-Hung-Chang ; but he could not see how it was to be avoided, and he went forward once more to duty, and perhaps to death.

A tedious march was before him and his men, from Quin-san to Woosieh, and it was made all the more irksome because they had to carry their supplies with them. When they reached Woosieh they went on to Yesing, finding every-where marks of the destructive operations of the Tai-pings. A village outside Yesing was just taken ; and Yesing itself, after some little fighting, surrendered. From thence Gordon went to Tajowka, news having reached him that the rebels in the garrison wanted to surrender, but that their captain was resolved not to yield. Tajowka, with its captain, was soon brought to accept Gordon's terms. Liyang came next. The people there were in such a wretched state that they were only too glad to come out into something better. They shut one of their gates on the commandant, who would liked to have fought Gordon, and so rendered him unable to offer resistance.

Kintang was the next place which Gordon attacked ; and there the brave leader of the valorous army was wounded.

The fight was a very desperate one. Wherever the victorious army made a breach, the rebels crowded to the spot, and drove them back with stones and bricks, and anything that could be found.

In the midst of the battle news came that the rebels had beaten the Imperialists at Fushan, and were besieging Chanzu ; but Gordon felt that he must go on with his attack on Kintang.

Suddenly there arose a cry—"THE COMMANDER IS WOUNDED!"

Gordon, who had been looking white and faint, flushed with anger at this, and ordered the man to be silent.

The commander remained at his post, with the blood streaming from a wound. He was urged to retire, but he would not leave until Dr. Moffit compelled him to do so.

Every one was grieved that the brave man was at last laid low. It was ascertained, however, that the wound need not be serious, if only the wounded man would keep quiet. Dr. Moffit said that everything depended upon that, and he urged him to think now more of himself than of anything beside.

Sir Frederick Bruce wrote him a letter to the same effect, telling him that he must be cautious, not on account of the force, but on his own account. "I beg you," said Sir Frederick, "not to look upon your position from a military point of view; you have done quite enough for your reputation as a gallant and skilful leader. We all look to you as the only person fit to act with these perverse Chinese, and to be trusted with the great interests at stake at Shanghai. Your life and ability to keep the field are more important than the capture of any city in China."

These kind words must have been of great comfort to Charles Gordon.

The Emperor of China, who had received a report from Li-Hung-Chang to the effect that General Gordon was wounded, issued a proclamation, in which he said he was deeply moved with grief and admiration. He ordered Li to visit Gordon every day, and keep him well informed of events, that his mind might be at rest; and he also ordered the Governor to "request him to wait until he should be perfectly restored to health and strength before attempting anything more."

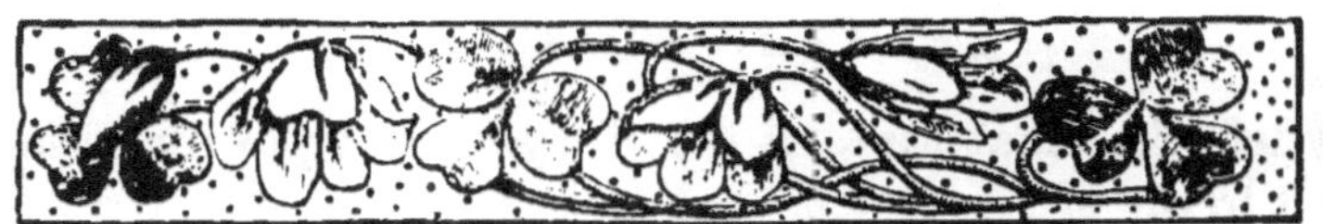

CHAPTER X.

DISBANDING OF THE EVER-VICTORIOUS ARMY.

"Of all said yet, may'st thou prove prosperous.
Of all said yet, I wish thee happiness."
—*Pericles.*

ORTUNATELY Gordon's wound was not a very serious one, but he could not spare himself time to be sufficiently recovered before he was again in action. News came that the Faithful King was back in Fushan, and Gordon felt that he must at once start for Woosieh. He left the principal part of his men at Kintang, and took to assist him a number of the rebels who had but lately joined his forces.

Chung Wang's son was now leading an army of Tai-pings, and Gordon reached a position from which he could cut off his retreat. He found everywhere awful proofs of the devastation and misery caused by the rebels. It is sickening to read of burnt villages, and starving people, so reduced that they actually ate each other. There may have been some good even in the rebels, but they certainly wrought immense havoc among the poor people of the province.

They left the inhabitants of the villages through which they passed to die of starvation.

Gordon's march was, as usual, rapid and decisive. He took very little time to do that which he attempted. But even the Ever-Victorious Army was sometimes defeated. On the 31st of March some of his officers and men, who were travelling by land without their leader—Gordon having taken part of his force by water—were surprised by an immense host of Tai-pings. The Liyangs were panic-stricken and overwhelmed, and compelled to flee before the rebels; losing four hundred men—three captains among them. When Gordon arrived he was compelled to retreat, and great confusion prevailed.

Gordon was obliged to make up his numbers and get his troops into working condition; and when this was done, he was supported by Li-Hung-Chang and a large body of Imperialists. The Governor told him that his colleague, General Ching, was shot. When Gordon heard the news he forgot how frequently Ching had annoyed and thwarted him, and remembered only his good qualities. The two had been comrades in many a terrible undertaking; and generally Ching had seconded Gordon's endeavours with all possible courage. He may have been jealous of the foreigner, who, at the head of the Ever-Victorious Army, had become so illustrious and influential; but under all, there had been so much that was noble in the man that Gordon could only receive the tidings of his death, as Wilson says he did, with tears of real sorrow and regret.

Gordon's next step was to advance on Waissoo. He was well assisted by the Imperial troops, who were placed in such positions as would enable them to prevent the retreat of the rebels, and to make simultaneous attacks. He employed considerable strategy at Waissoo, and his manœuvre was completely successful. The rebels endeavoured to get away by the bridges which had been broken, and hosts of them were slain. The villagers, urged by revenge for the cruelties that had been practised upon them by the Tai-pings, who had stolen their property and burnt their homes, turned out in pursuing crowds to chase their enemies to destruction.

Chanchu-fu was the next city to fall, and it was not taken without considerable difficulty. It had been for some time unsuccessfully besieged by the Imperialists; but the place was full of rebels of the most determined character, and they were bent on holding it, if possible, at any cost. Gordon proposed at once to invest the city; and while this was being done he had another remarkable escape.

Wilson says, that perhaps some of the men wished to discover whether Gordon had really a charmed life. A battery was being constructed by some men of the Imperialist army, a strong picket supporting them, and a covering party being stationed in the rear. Gordon and Major Tapp were superintending, when suddenly the pickets fired into the battery. The Tai-pings at the same time fired into the battery also; and Gordon and his helpers found themselves fired upon on all hands, not only by the rebels but by the Imperialists. It is a wonder that all were not killed. Several men were; and among them Major Tapp, a brave and energetic man, whose life could ill be spared.

There were several ineffectual attempts to conquer the rebels in Chanchu-fu before it was accomplished. First, Li-Hung-Chang tried to take the city with his own soldiers, with very disastrous results. Next, Li asked Gordon to make the attempt, assisted by the Imperialists; but when the time came the Imperialists were not there, and Gordon and his men, fighting alone, had to retreat. Then a united movement was agreed upon; but the rebels were so numerous, and so persistent, that although many were killed, the number did not appear to grow less. In this engagement the officers led the way, but the men refused to follow. Ten officers were killed and nineteen wounded, when the retreat was called.

After that another plan was adopted. Gordon gave the Mandarins some lessons in trench-making; and Li-Hung-Chang had proclamations posted on all the walls to the effect that pardon would be granted to all in the besieged city who came out of it. Hu Wang, or "Cock-Eye," said he would behead any who attempted to escape, and did kill some as an example; but the rebels, encouraged by the promise made to them by the Imperialists, escaped in very large numbers. A letter is said to have been written by some of the chiefs, proposing a plan by which they should treacherously give up the city, without appearing to do so. But Chanchu-fu was wrested from the rebels by assault. Governor Li led the Imperialists; his artillery broke down the city walls, and the generals gained the ramparts. But the Tai-pings were stubborn, and fought in terrible desperation. At one time it seemed that the rebels would again be successful; but just as the Imperialists began to waver, Gordon came forward with one of his regiments and a little band of enthusiastic volunteers, and led his storming party into the city, and all was over with the rebels.

Hu Wang was very loth to acknowledge himself beaten, but fought to the last, and refused altogether to submit to Governor Li. He said that the Futai and all his hosts would not have been able to conquer him but for Gordon. He and four other Wangs were executed.

"I think if I am spared I shall be home by Christmas." So wrote the brave leader of the Ever-Victorious Army on the day before the final taking of Chanchu-fu. And he added, "I do not care one jot about my promotion or what people may say. I know I shall leave China as poor as I entered it, but with the knowledge that through my weak instrumentality upwards of eighty to one hundred thousand lives have been spared."

It was a good thing for himself and his work that the brave leader of the Ever-Victorious Army did not care what people said, for at that time all sorts of false stories were in circulation in England. News came that forty thousand rebels had been massacred by the Allies, and there was naturally great indignation. Mr. Wilson shows that instead of forty thousand there were just nine individuals executed, each one of whom richly deserved his fate; but the feeling in England was so strong that the Government felt compelled to take action. There were very grave and heated discussions in the Houses of Parliament, many people being assured that the reports were true, and many being quite as sure that they were false. The supporters of the Government had faith in Bruce and Gordon, while the opponents of the Government, of course, blamed them for everything, and believed the worst. At last the British Government, early in 1864, revoked the order in Council which permitted Gordon to serve the Chinese Government.

But, fortunately, his work was just finished when the order reached him. The rebellion was, to all intents and purposes, stamped out; and the time had come (at least Gordon thought so, and General Li agreed with him) when the right thing to do was to disband the Ever-Victorious Army. The English merchants at Shanghai did not think so, and were in a state of great alarm. But Gordon considered that there would be less danger in disbanding it than in permitting it to remain in existence. Certainly the army required a strong and wise leader to keep it under control. No one could be sure that the men, left to themselves, would not turn round again and fight with the rebels as many of them had done before. Burgevine might come back, or anything else might happen. The men would assuredly be better at home.

Accordingly Gordon returned to Quinsan, and from the 16th of May to the 1st of June he was occupied sending off the men. He returned all arms to the Government, and then proceeded to pay his soldiers.

He asked no reward for himself; but for his officers and men he asked for very considerable sums. And this time he got what he wanted. He was able to give to the men who had served him and risked their lives at his side, not only generous words of well-won praise, but something much more substantial. The Chinese Government had come to see that Gordon knew best what was right, and they willingly handed over to him the large sums that he requested. They also sent a present to himself which would have made him rich, but this again he declined. It was a real joy to him to present his officers with a sum that more than satisfied them, and to give to his men enough to enable them to make another start in life.

There was, some time afterwards, a letter published in the *Times*, bearing the signature "Mandarin," which, having been written by one who fought in the campaign, and therefore knew all about Gordon, and the spirit and character which he manifested, is very full of interest. It is reproduced in Mr. Edmund Hake's book, and cannot be printed too frequently :—

" It is really surprising how scanty a knowledge English people have of the wonderful feats performed, not many years since, by an officer whose name has lately been rather prominently mentioned—Colonel, or Chinese Gordon: Having served under him during the most eventful period of his command of the Ever-Victorious Army—an epithet, you may be sure, not given by himself—I might fill many of your columns with traits of General Gordon's amazing activity and wonderful foresight, his indomitable energy and quiet, unassuming modesty, his perseverance, kindness, cool courage, and even heroism. My individual opinion may not be worth much, but is it not notorious that any man who has ever served under or with General (as you must allow me to style him) Gordon is an enthusiastic believer in his military genius and capacity? There are not many commanders of whom the subordinates would speak with such unanimous praise. What is, perhaps, most striking in Gordon's career in China, is the entire devotion with which the native soldiery served him, and the implicit faith they had in the result of operations in which he was personally present. In their eyes General Gordon was literally a magician, to whom all things were possible. They believed him to bear a charmed life; and a short stick or rattan cane which he invariably carried about, and with which he always pointed in directing the fire of artillery or other operations, was firmly looked on as a wand or talisman. These things have been repeated to me again and again by my own men, and I know they were accepted all over the contingent. These notions, especially the men's idea that their General had a charmed existence, were substantially aided by Gordon's constant habit, when the troops were under fire, of appearing suddenly, usually unattended, and calmly standing in the very hottest part of the fire.

"Besides his favourite cane, he carried nothing except field-glasses—never a sword or revolver; or rather, if the latter, it was carried unostentatiously and out of sight; and nothing could exceed the contrast between General Gordon's quiet undress uniform, without sword-belts or buckles, and apparently no weapon but a two-foot rod, and the buccaneering, brigand-like costume of the American officers, striped, armed, and booted like theatrical banditti.

"I only know one occasion on which General Gordon drew a revolver. The contingent had been lying idle in Quinsan for three months of the summer without taking the field. This time had been employed in drilling the men, and in laying in large stores of war material, preparatory to the approaching attack on Soochow. The heat all this time was fearfully oppressive; dysentery and cholera had carried off many men and officers, and drill towards the end of the term was somewhat relaxed. This in some measure affected the discipline of the men, and, indeed, of their officers also. But the chief cause of the deteriorated discipline was perhaps to be found in another direction. On the march and in the field the men were unable to obtain opium—the officers but slender stores of liquor; in garrison, on the contrary, they could indulge to the full extent of their monthly pay.

"But whatever the causes, it is certain that when, towards September, orders to prepare for an expedition against strong forts and stockades barring the way by canal from Quinsan to Soochow were issued, the discipline of the troops was greatly inferior to what it had been three months earlier. The artillery, in particular, showed decided insubordination. One company of it refused to embark in the barges which were to take it up the canal, the men declining to take the field before the approaching pay-day. The officers managed to make the men 'fall in,' but from the parade ground they refused to move, although the luggage was already on board the boats, lying fifty yards off. At this juncture General Gordon, who had been apprised by messengers of the state of affairs, arrived on the spot with his interpreter. He was on foot, in undress, apparently unarmed, and, as usual, exceedingly cool, quiet, and undemonstrative.

"Directly he approached the company, he ordered his interpreter to direct every man who refused to embark to step to the front. One man only advanced. General Gordon drew his revolver from an inside breast-pocket, presented it at the soldier's head, and desired the interpreter to direct the man to march straight to the barge and embark. The order was immediately complied with, and then General Gordon giving the necessary words of command, the company followed without hesitation or demur. It may be said that any other determined officer might have done likewise, and with the same results. Not so. It was generally allowed by the officers, when the event became known, that the success in this instance was solely due to the awe and respect in which General Gordon was held by the men ; and that such was the spirit of the troops at the time, that had any other but he attempted what he did, the company would have broken into open mutiny, shot their officers, and committed the wildest excesses.

"In less than a week the spirit of the troops was as excellent as before, and gradually the whole garrison joined in a series of movements which culminated in the fall of Soochow.

"Considering the materials Gordon had to work with, the admirable state of discipline and military efficiency which his contingent eventually attained is really amazing. He certainly had a few first-rate officers—rough and ready ones, no doubt—perhaps half-a-dozen altogether, of which General Kirkham, at present in Abyssinia, was one ; but as for the remainder, or the great majority of the remainder, I scarcely like to use the epithets which would be most applicable to them. This I remember, during the month of July when the corps was in Quinsan, out of a hundred and thirty or a hundred and forty officers, eleven died of *delirium tremens.* There was no picking or choosing ; the General was glad to get any foreigners to fill up vacancies, and the result, especially in garrison, was deplorable. They fought well, and led their men well, however ; and that, after all, was the chief requisite.

" Well, notwithstanding such drawbacks, every regiment could · go through the manual, and platoon, and bayonet exercises to English words of command, with a smartness and precision to which not many volunteer companies can attain; could manœuvre very fairly in companies or as a battalion; and each regiment had been put through a regular course of musketry instruction, every man firing his ninety rounds at the regular distances, up to three hundred yards, the scores and returns being satisfactorily kept, and the good shots rewarded.

"It was a most fortunate thing for General Gordon that, a few years before he accepted the Chinese command, he had been employed in surveying and mapping precisely that portion of the country in which his future operations were carried on. This part of China is a vast network of canals and tow-paths; there are absolutely no roads, wheeled vehicles are never used, and the bridges still remaining were scarce and precarious. It was an immense advantage to know what canals were still navigable, which choked with weeds, and what bridges were left standing; where the ground would be likely to bear artillery, and where it was impassable swamp. Gordon knew every feature of the country better than any other person, native or foreigner— far better even than the rebels, who had overrun it, and been in partial possession for years.

"But even these advantages would go but a short way towards accounting for the complete and thorough success which marked Gordon's career, where his predecessors had gained merely temporary advantages, fruitless toward securing the main object in view—the expulsion of the enemy from the province. The reasons for Gordon's great successes, for his unparalleled feat, must be sought for elsewhere; and they are, without doubt, firstly, his military genius, and secondly, his character and qualities, which were such as to cause all brought in contact or serving under him to have unbounded faith in his capacity, and to feel firmly that the best means at his disposal would be used to the best purpose.

"To persons who know General Gordon—his unassuming ways, and quiet, retiring manners—it speaks volumes that the ignorant men and rowdy officers composing his contingent should have looked on him in the light they did, and in the manner I have attempted to describe.

"That a swaggering, ostentatious, dashing, and successful general should be looked up to by such men would be natural enough. If one were to draw inferences, one might, perhaps, say the ignorant Chinamen were better judges than certain well-educated folk nearer home."

Mr. Hake says that there is one mistake in this appreciative letter, and that Gordon had not the advantage of a previous knowledge of the district in which his exploits were done.

Gordon had disbanded his army, but he had not therefore ceased to feel an interest in China.

He went to Nanking, and visited Tseng Kuo-fau there, and also the Governor of the province of Chekiang, the commander of the troops at Nanking, and conferred with them as to the best means of completing the work. Gordon thoroughly examined the defences and the works, and thought the place would be easy to capture. He advised the introduction of some changes into the Imperial army, such as instructing the natives in the use of other arms than their own, of paying the men regularly, and of augmenting the army.

He soon after wrote a letter, which proved that with his usual insight he had quite understood the Chinese nature. He said it was no use to drive them even into a course of action that would be for their good ; and that the only way to manage them successfully was to lead them, and not offend their prejudices.

In what esteem our hero was held by the Chinese was proved in many ways.

When he went to Li-Hung-Chang to take leave of him,

the Futai showed him every respect and honour. The more he had known of Gordon, the more profoundly had he been impressed by his perfect blamelessness of life and his great ability. He had misjudged him sometimes; but the two men, now altogether reconciled, and each admiring the other, did not scruple to unsay what they had said before, and give every expression to their cordial sympathies toward each other.

Gordon did not care for honours, but plenty were showered upon him. He received several titles. He was made a "Ti-tu," which gave him the highest rank in the Chinese army; and the Emperor himself commanded that he should be rewarded with "a yellow riding jacket, to be worn on his person, and a peacock's feather, to be carried on his cap; also, that there be bestowed on him four suits of the uniform proper to his rank of Ti-tu, in token of our favour and desire to do him honour."

These were very grand presents—indeed, the greatest that China could bestow—and although Gordon refused to take the Emperor's money, he did not refuse these honours. He wrote to his mother in his own affectionate way, "I do not care twopence about these things, but know that you and my father like them." The Emperor wished the British Minister to bring before the notice of Her Majesty the Queen of England his appreciation of the splendid services which Gordon had rendered. He hoped that he would be rewarded in England as well as in China for his heroic achievements.

A subsequent letter in the *Times* said that Prince Kung, who was then the Regent of China, had waited upon Sir Frederick Bruce, and said to him—"You will be astonished to see me again, but I felt I could not allow you to leave without coming to see you about Gordon. We do not know what to do. He will not receive money from us, and we have already given him every honour which it is in the power of the Emperor to bestow; but as these can be of little value in his eyes, I have brought you this letter, and ask you to give it to the Queen of England, that she may bestow on him some reward which would be more valuable in his eyes."

Sir Frederick Bruce sent this to London with a letter of his own :—

"I enclose translation of despatch from Prince Kung, containing the decree published by the Emperor, acknowledging the services of Lieutenant-Colonel Gordon, Royal Engineers, and requesting that Her Majesty's Government be pleased to recognise him. This step has been spontaneously taken.

"Lieutenant-Colonel Gordon well deserves Her Majesty's favour, for, independently of the skill and courage he has shown, his disinterestedness has elevated our national character in the eyes of the Chinese. Not only has he refused any pecuniary reward, but he has spent more than his pay in contributing to the comfort of the officers who served under him, and in assuaging the distress of the starving population whom he relieved from the yoke of their oppressors. Indeed, the feeling that impelled him to resume operations after the fall of Soochow was one of the purest humanity. He sought to save the people of the districts that had been recovered from a repetition of the misery entailed upon them by this cruel civil war."

It does not seem, however, that anyone mentioned the affair to the Queen, or that any particular notice was taken by the Government of the heroic deeds of the Englishman, of whom any land must have been proud; and it was a good thing, therefore, that the heart of the Christian soldier was not set upon either fame or reward.

He did receive what he must have valued very highly, an engrossed and illuminated address from the merchants of Shanghai, who expressed in very generous terms their respect and admiration. To this Gordon wrote in reply :—

"SHANGHAI, 25*th November* 1864.

"Gentlemen—I have the honour to acknowledge the receipt of your handsome letter of this day's date, and to express to you the great satisfaction which I feel at the honourable mention you have made therein of my services in China.

"It will always be a matter of gratification to me to have received your approval; and deeply impressed with the honour you have paid me —I have the honour to be, Gentlemen, yours obediently,

"C. G. GORDON."

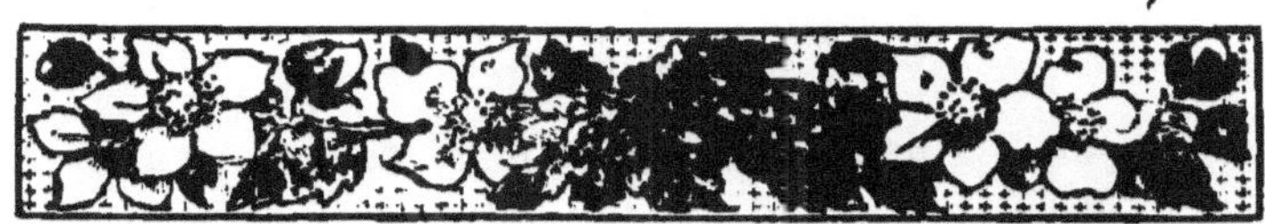

CHAPTER XI.

THE COLLAPSE OF THE REBELLION.

"The guilt of conscience take thee for thy labour,
But neither my good word, nor princely favour;
With Cain go wander through the shade of night,
And never show thy head by day nor light."
—*Richard II.*

"THE back of the rebellion had been broken;" indeed the rebellion itself was all but dead. There still remained Nanking, the royal city of the rebels, now in desolation, but striving to hold its own against starvation and all other foes. The Rev. Joseph Edkins, of the London Missionary Society, visited the city about this time, and thus describes what he saw:—"Where the porcelain tower once stood, there is now a mass of glazed bricks, whole and broken, white and coloured. The Tai-ping people, had they the power, would destroy all the idol temples and pagodas in China. Their religious fanaticism is too essential a part of the movement to allow of any change in this point. Nanking was famed for the grandeur of its monasteries and the number of its priests. They have all disappeared.

"Hung-sien-tsiuen lives within a double wall, with imperial dragons painted on the gates. Every morning a few scribes may be seen copying new edicts, written on yellow satin, and pasted on boards near the palace entrance. They are in red ink, in the chief's own handwriting, and consist in great part of statements on the subject of the Tai-ping religion. In some I read he attempted to deprive the relation of our Saviour to the Father in regard to his divine nature, and in doing so expressed Arian views. The door of the palace is called 'The holy heavenly gate of the true God.'

"A walk in the Manchu city helped us to appreciate the intense hatred of the Tartar rulers felt by the Tai-pings. Only one house was left standing in a city of 25,000 inhabitants. The city walls and gates, too massive to be thrown down, are overgrown with wild flowers and weeds. All ornamental structures of coloured bricks, which once stood upon them, have been carefully destroyed. Broken bricks and porcelain of many colours lie along the wall and near it.

"The great river Yang-tse-kiang sweeps past Nanking to the north-east. A fine range of hills appears on the north side. One of their summits has on it a pagoda, seen from Nanking. We asked the Tai-pings why that edifice was not, like others of the kind, destroyed. 'We have not yet found time for such a thing,' was the reply. On the Nanking shore two hills frown at one another. One of them is the 'Purple Forbidden Hill,' on the southern slopes of which are the tombs of the founder of the Ming dynasty and his father. The other hill is inside the walls, and has been included within the palaces of ancient emperors, when Nanking was the temporary capital. It is now used as a site for a high look-out by the rebels. Beyond it and the north wall are batteries placed on the riverside."

Mr. Edkins came out of his experience in Nanking unharmed by the rebels; but another missionary, an American, the Rev. J. L. Holmes—whose letter, taken from the *North China Herald*, and giving an account of his visit, is inserted in an earlier part of the present volume—was cruelly murdered by the Tai-pings in 1861, the year after his visit to them. He had written other letters which offended the rebels; and especially one which he intended the chief to see, but which fell, instead, into the hands of his subordinates, containing grave and direct charges against the opinions and practices of the Tai-pings. One life more or less was of very little consequence to the rebels; and Mr. Holmes, near Chefoo, fell a sacrifice to the prey of a party of the rebels who were called Nien-fei.

Things became worse and worse with the Tai-pings who were shut up in Nanking. It was estimated that the Faithful King lost no less than 100,000 men from the attacks of a foe, who worked surely but silently among them, and whose name was *Starvation.* They died because their commander had no rations to give them. But the Faithful King was very true to his name, and altogether worthy of it. He would not yield until the city was completely invested, and there was positively no hope. At last the Imperialists entered Nanking—to find that the Faithful King had set fire to it, and that the whole place was in desolation. Grass was growing in the streets, and nearly the whole city was in ruins. Hung-sien-tsiuen, the originator of the trouble, did not remain to suffer the penalty of his misdoings from others. He endeavoured to maintain some dignity to the end, and would not allow it to be thought by any that he was afraid. When the worst had come to the worst, he killed himself to prevent any unholy hands from slaying him.

The Faithful King and other Wangs were arrested, and sentenced to be executed. He spent the time that remained to him in writing an autobiography, which had some merit as a literary production, and was especially designed to show strong and sufficient reasons why he—the Faithful King—should not be put to death. But they were not strong enough to convince the Imperialists, and he shared the fate of the other rebels. It was, perhaps, necessary that he should die; but no one can read the story of the Faithful King, as told by Mr. Wilson in his *Ever-Victorious Army*, without feeling that there was a considerable amount of nobility and even heroism in the man.

Indeed, looking at the Tai-pings and their doctrines as a whole, it is impossible not to see that, especially at first, they were certainly not all bad. They set their faces against a great many of the corrupt practices of the Chinese. They endeavoured to abolish opium-smoking. They would not countenance the slave-trade. They denounced the use of torture and bribing in courts of justice, and the tail-wearing slave-badge of the men. They commanded that the feet of the women should not be crippled by tight shoes, but should be allowed to grow to the natural size. They disregarded the Chinese idea of lucky and unlucky days. They instituted literary examinations, though the parade of Christianity, and the requirements of the adherence of the students to obey the doctrines of Hung in connection with these examinations, prevented them from doing much good. The theme was "Uniting to elevate the Heavenly Father and Heavenly Brother to the Headship over all duty and morality." The publications of Hung-sien-tsiuen were used as reading-books among the rebels and their families; but they all insisted upon one central assertion—that Hung himself was divinely appointed to be the head of the world, which should be regenerated through his instrumentality, and become under his reign "the heavenly kingdom of great peace" (Tai-ping-tien-kno). He demanded from all his followers faith in him as a sort of Messiah, second only to Christ. This will be seen from a communication made in a letter from the chief himself to an American missionary, Mr. Roberts:—"Add to your faith. Do not suppose that I am deceived. I am the one saviour of the chosen people. Why do you feel uncertain of the fact of divine communications to me? When Joshua formerly destroyed the enemies of God the sun and moon stood still. When Abraham sat under the oak three men stood by him. Carefully think of all this. Do you become conscious of it? Do you believe? I am grieved at heart, having written very many edicts on these matters, and all men being with me as one family. When Kan Wang came to the capital, he also had a revelation. To recognise these divine communications is better than being baptised a thousand times. Blessed are they that watch. Your Father, your Lord, comes to you as a thief, and at a time when you know not. He that believeth shall be saved. You will see greater things than these. Respect this."

"Respect this" is always the conclusion to an emperor's edict; and so Hung used it, to give his letter more effect.

It will have been seen throughout that the religion which Hung professed and taught had some Christianity in it, though it was rather a caricature than otherwise. Still, at first many hoped that the rebels might bring about a change for the better; and perhaps if the Heavenly King had found an empire of willing subjects, and had met with no resistance, it might have been so. Certainly he talked of many improvements which he intended to introduce, such as gaslighting, railroads, telegraphs, and a higher system of education. But since he was not at once acknowledged, and had to take his armies into unwilling villages and towns, he had to plunder the people in order to provide for his men; and this, of course, greatly incensed them, and turned them into enemies. The consequence was that every year the rebels became more lawless, until at last it seemed that there was no right feeling among them; and their cruelties became so great that Gordon, humane as he was, felt that they ought to be extirpated.

When he began his work, whole regions, rich in silk and tea, were overrun by hordes of Tai-pings. His force, as we have seen, was altogether disorganised. The men were ready to fight, and, indeed, were eager to be engaged; but they did not care very much with whom, or on which side. In the army there was no discipline; and he found no supplies ready to his hand. There were no regular roads by which he could take his men where they were needed; and difficulties of all kinds surrounded him. He was very much alone in the burden of responsibility that was laid upon him; for he could not be sure of sympathy or help from England, or even from China. But of one thing he could and did feel sure—namely, that the cause in which he was engaged was one of righteousness and mercy, and that God was on his side; and this conviction kept him brave and patient through all. And he never forgot whose servant he was. He was in himself an illustration of the truth that the Christian is the highest type of man. Because he served God he served his fellows also.

"In a position of unequalled difficulty," said the address presented to him by the Shanghai merchants, "and surrounded by complications of every possible nature, you have succeeded in offering to the eyes of the Chinese nation, no less by your loyal and throughout disinterested line of action, than by your conspicuous gallantry and talent for organisation and command, the example of a foreign officer serving the Government of this country with honourable fidelity and undeviating self-respect." His name, which will ever be revered in China, began to be known and honoured in England also. In the *Times* of 5th August 1864 was a leading article showing great and just appreciation of our noble countryman :—

"Never did soldier of fortune deport himself with a

nicer sense of military honour, with more gallantry against the resisting, with more mercy toward the vanquished, with more disinterested neglect of opportunities of personal advantage, or with more entire devotion to the objects and desires of his own Government, than this officer, who, after all his victories, has just laid down his sword. A history of operations among cities of uncouth names, and in provinces, the geography of which is unknown except to special students, would be tedious and uninstructive. The result of Colonel Gordon's operations, however, is this: He found the richest and most fertile districts of China in the hands of the most savage brigands. The silk districts were the scenes of their cruelty and riot, and the great historical cities of Hangchow and Soochow were rapidly following the fate of Nanking, and were becoming desolate ruins in their possession. Gordon has cut the rebellion in half, has recovered the great cities, has isolated and utterly discouraged the fragments of the brigand power, and has left the marauders nothing but a few tracts of devastated country and their stronghold of Nanking. All this he has effected, first by the power of his arms, and afterward, still more rapidly, by the terror of his name."

Gordon had not left China when Nanking was subdued. At that time almost nothing remained of the rebels. Gordon had fought in no less than twenty-three battles, and had met with not quite but almost invariable success. Eventually, on 16th April 1865, eight thousand Govern ment troops caused the rebels to evacuate Hangchow and retreat towards Tungshan. They were pursued and sur rounded on all hands, until the little remnant of the great host fleeing to the mountains, broke up and got lost. Thus ended the rebellion of the Tai-pings.

Some lasting good has no doubt resulted for China. Mr. Andrew Wilson shows the good effect of introducing Euro pean medical arrangements into the Ever-Victorious Army ;

and he has published in his book some very interesting
statistics respecting the grand work which Mr. Moffit was
able to do among the wounded and diseased. Before that
time the Chinese knew very little of surgery. It was found
that fevers were most fatal, and that diarrhœa was very
common, especially in the hot season, and among those who
indulged themselves in opium-smoking. The Chinese
have almost no taste for alcohol; and they can live
quite comfortably on a simple diet of rice, vegetables, and
fish.

Gordon's work in China has been the means of awaken-
ing considerable interest in the country, hitherto so little
known; and the last few years have seen many books
produced upon the subject. What China now wants is
·thus summed up in a little book, entitled, *The Foreigner in
Far Cathay*, by Mr. W. H. Medhurst, H.B.M. Consul at
Shanghai:—" Let the commercial enterprise of the people
be taken advantage of to introduce the thin end of the
wedge of progress whenever the opportunity offers itself;
let knowledge be sown broadcast throughout the land by
means of suitable and instructive publications in the native
language; and let foreign powers combine to treat China
justly, and at the same time see to it that she acts justly by
them, and not only will progress be possible, but no long
time need elapse before a regeneration ensues, which shall
at once satisfy the longings of the diplomatist, the merchant,
and the missionary."

This book bears the date 1872; and a pamphlet re-
printed from *The Phœnix—A Week in Nanking*, by the
Rev. Thomas Bryson, of the London Missionary Society,
Wuchang, China, of the same date, describes Nanking as
it was then :—

" One feature of the prospect, both outside and inside the
walls, was very conspicuous—viz., the absence of trees.
This, and the presence of ruins in all directions, especially

in the less inhabited portions of the city, and when seen after the sun had set, gave a weird, desolate character to the place. In some marshy places one had also to be careful how he walked, lest he should get a fall into a ditch. Usually at these dangerous points we found a septangular stone pillar, with a figure of Buddha carved on each face, and an invocation cut down the side. These are piously set up as a kind of talisman, to ward off the unseen evil spirits who are supposed to infest such roads, and attack the unwary traveller.

" The want of trees is attributable to the possession of the place by hostile armies for so many years during the late rebellion. There were other vestiges of the horrors of that siege to be seen besides these. We came across a plot of ground literally crammed with grave-mounds, and found many officers and men living in tents close by with a number of newly-made coffins at hand. They were engaged in exhuming the bones and dead bodies, to be carried out and re-interred in a cemetery without the walls. It is well known that the rebels were reduced to awful extremity before the city fell. They were falling thick of starvation. Individuals used to be dropped over the walls at night to dig up every root they could find. And such was the slaughter at the taking of the city that the streets literally swam with blood, and heaps upon heaps of dead had to be hurriedly buried within the walls."

Nanking, however, the city beautiful for situation, is becoming more beautiful every year as it recovers from its sorrows of twenty-five years ago. The streets are wider than those of any other city in China, the shops and houses are rebuilt, and business and pleasure fill the place once so desolate. The Imperial Satin Manufactory is carrying on its work, and a stranger arriving for the first time would not, unless he knew its history, dream that Nanking had passed through such an awful experience.

General Gordon has been to China once since all this happened. He went at the request of his old colleague, Li-Hung-Chang. Some time afterward his counsel in regard to China appeared in the form of a letter, or proclamation, said to be addressed to Li-Hung-Chang, and which was published in the *China Mail.* It is an exceedingly characteristic letter, and is important, because it treats of the military strength of China, and how that strength may be developed, and also because, as the *China Mail* remarks, "the writer's simple honesty comes straight from the heart, and he is entirely unencumbered by anything outside of his inborn convictions." The following is the memoranda :—

"China possesses a long-used military organisation, a regular military discipline. *Leave it intact. It is suited to her people.*

"China, in her numbers, has the advantage over other powers. Her people are inured to hardships. Armed with breech-loaders, accustomed to the use and care of breech-loaders, and no more is needed for her infantry.

"Breech-loaders ought to be bought on some system, and the same general system made applicable to the whole nation. It is not advisable to manufacture them, though means of repair should be established at certain centres. Breech-loading ammunition should be manufactured at different centres. Breech-loaders of various patterns should not be bought, though no objection could be offered to a different breech-loader in, say, four provinces, from that used in another group of four provinces. Any breech-loaders which will carry well up to a thousand yards will be sufficient. It is not advisable to spend money on the superior breech-loaders, carrying further. Ten breech-loaders carrying up to one thousand yards could be bought for the same money as five breech-loaders of a superior class, carrying to one thousand five hundred yards. For the Chinese it would cost more time to teach the use of the longer-range rifle than it is worth, and then, probably, if called to use it, in confusion the scholar would forget his lesson. This is known to be the case. Therefore, buy ordinary breech-loading rifles of a thousand yards' range, of simple construction, of solid form. Do not go into purchasing a very light, delicately-made rifle. A Chinese soldier does not mind one or two pounds more weight, for he carries no knapsack or kit.

"China's power is in her numbers, in the quick moving of her troops, in the little baggage they require, in their few wants. It is known that men armed with swords and spears can overcome the best regular troops; if armed with the best breech-loading rifles, and well instructed in every way, if the country is at all difficult, and if the men with the spears and swords outnumber their foe ten to one. If this is the case when men are armed with spears and swords, it will be much truer when the same are armed with ordinary breech-loaders.

"China should never engage in pitched battles. Her strength is in quick movements, in cutting off the trains of baggage, in night attacks, not pushed home; in a continuous worrying of her enemies.

"Rockets should be used instead of cannon; no artillery should be moved with the troops. It delays and impedes them. Infantry fire is the most fatal fire. Guns make a noise far out of proportion to their value in war. If guns are taken into the field, troops cannot march faster than those guns. The degree of speed at which the guns can be carried along dictates the speed at which the troops can march. Therefore, very few guns, if any, ought to be taken; and those few should be smooth bored, large bore breech-loaders, consisting of four parts, to be screwed together when needed for use.

"Chinese accustomed to make forts of earth ought to

continue this, and study the use of trenches for the attack of cities.

"China should never attack forts. She ought to wait, and starve her foes out, and worry them night and day.

"China should have a few small-bored, very long range wall-pieces, rifled and breech-loaders. They are light to carry, and if placed a long way off, will be safe from attack. If the enemy comes out to take them, the Chinese can run away ; and if the enemy takes one or two, it is no loss. Firing them in the enemy's camps a long way off would prevent the enemy sleeping ; and if he does not sleep, then he gets ill, and goes into hospital, and then needs other enemies to take care of him, and thus the enemy's numbers are reduced.

"When an enemy comes up, and breaks the wall of a city, the Chinese soldiers ought not to stay and fight the enemy, but to go out and attack the trains of baggage in the rear, and worry him in the roads he came by. By keeping the Chinese troops lightly loaded with baggage, with no guns, they can move two to every one *li* the enemy marches. To-day the Chinese will be before him ; to-morrow they will be behind him ; the next day they will be on his left hand, and so on, till the enemy gets tired and cross with such long walks, and his soldiers quarrel with their officers, and get sick.

"The Chinese should make telegraphs in the country, as a rule, to keep the country quiet, and free from false rumours ; but with the Chinese soldiers in the field they should use sun signals by means of the heliograph. These are very easy, and can do no harm. For this purpose a small school should be made in each centre.

"The Chinese ought not to try torpedoes, which are very difficult to manage. The most simple torpedoes are the best and the cheapest, and their utility is in having many of them. China can risk sowing them thickly, for if one of them does go astray, and sink a Chinese junk, the people of the junk ought to be glad to die for their country. If torpedoes are only used at certain places, then the enemy knows that he has to look out when near those places, but when every place may have torpedoes, he can never feel safe; he is always anxious; he cannot sleep; he gets ill, and dies. The fact of an enemy living in constant dread of being blown up is much more advantageous to China than if she blew up one of her enemies, for anxiety makes people ill and cross. Therefore China ought to have cheap, simple torpedoes, which cannot go out of order, which are fired by a fuze, *not* by electricity, and plenty of them. She ought not to buy expensive, complicated torpedoes.

"China should buy no more big guns to defend her sea-coast. They cost money. They are a great deal of trouble to keep in order, and the enemy's ships have too thick sides for any gun China can buy to penetrate them.

"China ought to defend her sea-coast by very heavy mortars. They cost very little. They are easy to use. They only want a thick parapet in front, and they are fired from a place the enemy cannot see, whereas the enemy can see the holes from which guns are fired.

"The enemy cannot get safe from a mortar shot. It falls on the deck, and there it breaks everything. China can get five hundred mortars for the same money she gets one 18-ton gun for. If China loses them the loss is little.

"No enemy could get into a fort which is defended by 1500 large mortars and plenty of torpedoes, which must be very simple.

"Steam-launches, with a torpedo on a pole, furnish the best form of movable torpedo.

"For the Chinese fleet, small, quick vessels, with very little draught of water, and not any great weight of armour, are best. If China buys big vessels they cost a great deal, and all her eggs are in one basket—namely, she loses all her money at once. For the money of one large vessel China would get twelve small vessels. China's strength is in the creeks, not in the open sea.

"Nothing recommended in this paper needs any change in Chinese customs. The army is the same, and China needs no Europeans or foreigners to help her to carry out this programme. If China cannot carry out what is here recommended, then no one else can do so. Besides, the programme is a cheap one.

"With respect to the fleet, it is important to consider that in the employment of foreigners China can never be sure of them, in case of a war with the country they belong to; while, on the other hand, if China asks a foreign power to lend her officers, then the foreign power who lends them will interfere with China.

"The question is—

"1. Is it better for China to get officers here and there, and run the risk of these officers not being trustworthy; or,

"2. Is it better for China to think what nation there is who would be likely to be good friends with China in good weather and in bad weather, and then for China to ask that nation to lend China the officers she wants for her fleet?

"I think No. 2 is the safest and best for China.

"Remember, with this programme China wants no big officers from foreign powers. I say big officers, because I am a big officer in China.

"If I stayed in China it would be bad for China, because it would vex the American, French, and German Governments, who would want to send their officers. Besides, I am not wanted. China can do what I recommend herself. If she cannot, I could do no good.

"(Signed)   O. G. GORDON.

"CANTON, *7th July* 1880.

" *P.S.*—As long as Pekin is the centre of the government of China, China can never afford to go to war with any first-class power.   It is too near the sea.   The Emperor (Queen Bee) must be in the centre of the hive.

" No ironclads or iron gun-boats can help China till she has a place to keep them in.   But China can have no place (asylum) to keep them till she has an army.

" China cannot have an army when generals keep twenty thousand men and draw pay for five thousand.   Those generals ought to have their heads cut off.

" (Signed)   O. G. G.

" HONG-KONG, *23rd August* 1880."

CHAPTER XII.

AT GRAVESEND.

"There is no news, my lord; but that he writes
How happily he lives, how well beloved."
—*Two Gentlemen of Verona.*

 NE evening, in the year 1865, a doctor stepped out of a small house in Gravesend, and entering his carriage, ordered the coachman to drive home. The door of the cottage was closed by a young woman with a pale face, and eyes dim with tears, who held a baby in her arms. There happened to be passing at the moment a young man, who, at a glance, took in the whole situation, and whose natural insight into human life and character, and power of imagination, enabled him to comprehend more than was revealed.

He stopped at the cottage door that had just been closed, and gently tapped it. The young woman with the baby responded to the knock, and looked into the kindly face of a gentleman who was a stranger to her and to Gravesend.

"Good evening; may I come in?"

"Certainly." The stranger stepped into the little room, put his hat upon the table, and at once made himself at home.

"Your baby is a fine little fellow. It is not the baby

whom the doctor has been to see? He looks as if nothing had ailed him since he was born. How old is the young man?"

"He is two years and a-half, sir. Yes, he is very hearty, bless him! and never has anything the matter with him except when he is teething. That troubles him a little, and makes him cross. He has not had the measles yet, nor the whooping-cough, and I hope he will not, for my hands are tied so much at present that I don't know what I should do if I had any extra work."

"What is the matter, then?"

"My husband is very ill, sir."

"I am sorry to hear that. From what complaint is he suffering?"

"Oh, he has been very bad. He is a working man, but for some time he has not been able to work. His stomach has been bad; he has had such dreadful feelings—so weak, and sinking, and full of pain; and then he used to get cold all over, his skin was white, and looked all shrivelled up and turned into goose flesh, and then his teeth chattered, and his knees knocked together, and he had dreadful shivering fits; and he shook so that it seemed to shake the whole house; and his face, and lips, and finger-nails all turned blue, and he seemed to be dying of cold, although he was in front of a big fire."

"Yes," said the stranger, smilingly; "and when that had passed away he became just as hot as before he had been cold. His face got red, and he had palpitation, and his breathing was bad, and his head ached, and he felt as if it would burst; wasn't it so?"

"Yes, it was, sir."

"And then, when they had passed away, another change came. The pain in his head and his back got better, and he broke into a great perspiration, and presently felt all right again."

"No, sir, not all right, but better. The fits left him so awfully weak that I didn't know what to do; and the worst of it was, that they were sure to return the next day; so it quite depressed us."

"Yes, your husband has, or has had, the ague."

"Yes, that is what the doctor calls it. I never saw it before. I come from Derbyshire, and among the beautiful hills there we don't have such dreadful diseases."

"Perhaps they will not always have them in Gravesend. When our people get more scientific, and have better sanitary arrangements, ague will die out."

"I hope that will be soon."

"I hope so, too. But your husband is better, isn't he?"

"Yes, sir, he is better," said the woman, the tears again coming to her eyes; "but he is so dreadfully weak. The doctor has been scolding me about it; he says he must have nourishing things. I don't know what to get him; isn't milk nourishing, sir?"

"Very."

The strange gentleman had not looked about him much; he had seemed to keep his eyes upon the woman's face, or the baby's form; but he had taken in every detail of the little room with its plain furniture, and he could not see a superfluous article, except a little vase that had probably cost twopence.

"Yes, milk is, I suppose, one of the most nourishing kinds of food of which we can partake. And it is cheap, too. Have you given your husband plenty of it?"

"Well, that is the worst of it, sir. He cannot take milk. It makes him sick."

"Ah, then it is no use giving it to him. Could he eat a few grapes?"

"I dare say he could, sir. But grapes are dear."

"I will fetch a few; do not tell him until I come back."

The stranger was out of the house almost before he had

concluded the sentence; and before the woman had ceased wondering who he was, and why he had called, he was back again with a beautiful bunch of grapes, and a piece of beef.

"You know how to make beef-tea, don't you ?"

"Oh, yes, sir. Thank you; this is just what we wanted."

"See to it at once, and make it good. May I go and see your husband ?"

The poor man scolded a little when his wife brought a stranger into the bed-room; but there was something in that same stranger that won the sick man's heart at once.

"Can you eat a few grapes ?" The invalid's dry lips scarcely framed an answer in words before the cool, luscious fruit was between them.

"They are good. They are the only nice things I have seen or tasted for a month."

"I am glad you like them."

"What beauties they are! Splendid! Such grapes do not often fall to the lot of poor folks. Thank you for them, sir."

"Eat them up. They won't hurt you, and you shall have some more when these are gone."

"Who are you, sir ? I don't know you."

"Never mind who I am. I am a stranger. I have not been in Gravesend long."

"But what made you call at my house, sir ? Who told you about me ?"

"No one."

"But how is it that you are here."

"Oh, I saw a doctor's carriage leave the door, and supposing that someone was ill, I thought I would come in and see who it was, and if I could do anything."

The man looked faint. "I am not going to stay long

this time, but I shall come again. I have been sent to you."

"Sent?"

"Yes, sent by God. None of these things happen by chance. You in your weakness need just what I can give you, and so I was made to pass your door just as the doctor left it. Don't you see that all this must have been arranged by One who knows all things, and directs events according to His will?"

The sick man shook his head; and the stranger, with a kindly smile, left him to consider the subject at his leisure.

He came again the next day with some more beef for beef-tea, and also some jellies and other delicacies, which the poor man needed more than medicines, but which were quite out of his reach.

"How are you?"

"Oh, I am better to-day, sir, thanks to you."

"No; thanks not to me, but to some One else. Have you thought about what I said?"

"Yes, but I don't know anything about these things. I am only a poor man, and I have had to work hard all my life."

"And so have I; but I could not have worked if I had not had the assurance that all things were under the control of God."

"He is very wonderful and very great, I know."

"And He is very merciful and very good, *I* know."

"But you see, sir, your life and mine have been so different."

"How do you know that when you have not the least knowledge of my life, and cannot guess where it has been passed, or what I have had to do."

"But you are rich."

"Am I? But I assure you that many a time I have not

known where my food was to come from, nor if I should
find a place in which to lie down at night. But that is of
very little consequence. Your heavenly Father knoweth
that ye have need of all these things. He has taken care
of me; He will take care of you."

"But why has He let me be ill?"

"How can I tell? You must wait. Sometime, perhaps,
He will reveal a reason. And if not, there is always left
to us faith."

The man found afterwards the truth of the stranger's
words; for his new friend, with a persistent kindness that
astonished the invalid, continued to bring and send him
nourishing food, and occasionally to have short talks with
him. By degrees the man grew strong; and as strength
came back, so did resignation and cheerfulness. He began
to read for himself the Bible that his visitor gave him; and
he read, not as a duty to be got over as speedily as possible,
but as a delight and a help; and it became to him a light
to his feet and a lamp to his path. When he met with
any difficulty he told it at once to his friend, and the
trouble seemed to melt away, and everything appeared plain
and easy to be understood. The man's illness was the best
thing that had ever happened to him, for when he went
back to his work his whole life and character appeared
changed. His mates met him with congratulations—

"Glad to see you back, old fellow. How are you getting
on?"

"I am getting on well. I have found a friend, who has
been kinder to me than a brother."

"Who is he?"

"He is the gentleman who lives at the Fort House; he
has only lately come to live in Gravesend."

The gentleman at the Fort House was Lieutenant-
Colonel Gordon.

He was sent to Gravesend to serve in the capacity of

Commanding Royal Engineer, and there he remained from 1865 to 1871.

Nothing could prove more clearly than his life there the marvellous ability that he possesses to turn with facility from one kind of work to another, and become well-nigh perfect in all.

At the close of our last chapter we saw in him the master of all the tactics of war, and the valued counsellor of the greatest statesman of a great nation. In the present chapter we see in him the devoted philanthropist, the beneficent peacemaker, the lowly servant of the Lord Jesus Christ.

Gravesend, at the time when Colonel Gordon went to reside in the town, was still a very favourite watering-place. It is only twenty-four miles from London, and every summer thousands of Londoners resort thither to enjoy the salubrious air and picturesque scenery of the great river-port of England. In these days the railways do such wonders for the people, that they can be carried in a few hours not only to Ramsgate and Dover, but any place north, south, east, and west of the country; and a holiday at Gravesend has ceased to be as great a treat to our children as it was to ourselves. It is still, however, "the place to spend a happy day," for the far-famed Rosherville Gardens have not lost all their charms, nor are the views from Windmill Hill less interesting than of old; while the steam-boat ride from London down the Thames is, on a fine summer's day, full of enjoyment. To wander about on the hills, or rest on the piers, or gather water-cress in the beautiful streams, or eat the "shrimps, brown shrimps," for which Gravesend is famous, or to search for wild flowers in the pleasant Kentish lanes, or walk by the side of the broad river, are pleasures that do not pass away with passing years; and Gravesend is not likely to cease to be a well-known and favourite resort to all, and especially to the young dwellers in the metropolis.

It was in the vicinity of the river that Colonel Gordon spent most of his time, for it was his special duty to superintend the construction of the Thames defences. This brought him into connection with a great many men and boys belonging to the working classes, who soon found that a friend had come to live among them.

To the boys—and there are hundreds of them engaged on and about the river—he was especially kind. Not one of those with whom Gordon came into contact could ever utter the bitter complaint, "No man careth for my soul," for Gordon cared for that, and the body too.

"Come up to the Fort House this evening," he would say, when he saw a boy in trouble, and in need of counsel and help.

The house was large, and the colonel's wants were small; there was in it, therefore, abundant room and opportunity for all kinds of charitable work. The writer has quite lately met many people in Gravesend, who, although thirteen years have passed since Gordon resided there, still say he was "the best man who ever lived in Gravesend." In his home he lived in the simplest and most economical manner, and all that he saved he distributed with lavish hand.

"The furniture in his bed-room," said one, "consisted of a bed, a chair, and a box; but he made many of the bed-rooms of the sick poor beautiful with exquisite flowers and fruit."

"It is a comfort to have a garden," said a poor man who was allowed to walk in the Fort garden. "I often think if I were rich I should like to cultivate my own potatoes and green peas. It would be a pleasure to watch them grow, and see the progress they made from week to week."

"But anybody can do that. Have you not a bit of ground attached to your house ?"

"Not a square yard."

" Very well then, I will lend you a yard or two of mine. Put what you like in that corner yonder, and come and gather in the crop when it is ready."

The man looked into the merry face of his friend to see if he were joking; but he knew the colonel meant it, and he took him at his word. It gave the man and his family so much pleasure that Gordon extended the privilege to others, who are now only too glad to talk of the gentleman whose whole life seemed to be one of bounty and generosity.

He had eyes that were very quick to see sorrow. He was once watching a young bricklayer at his work, when he perceived that there was something on his mind which was making him unhappy. In his own pleasant way he soon entered into conversation with the young man, and almost before the latter knew it he was pouring out his tale of sorrow into the sympathetic heart of Colonel Gordon.

"Mother has left us, and gone away from home; and everything there is so miserable that it is not like home at all."

" What do you do with your evenings?"

" I cannot do anything with them, sir. There is no light, no warm place in which to sit, no quiet in which to read; so I stand about the streets when I have finished work."

" Come and spend your evenings at the Fort House. You will find books and papers there, and pen and ink, and other lads too."

"Thank you, colonel, I shall be very glad to do that."

So the young bricklayer became a nightly visitor, and had many a talk with the colonel. Very happy evenings they were, both to him who did good and to him who received it; for no one could be in the company of Gordon without being morally and spiritually elevated.

One evening the young bricklayer was at Fort House as usual, when he was suddenly taken ill, and hæmorrhage of the lungs set in.

The colonel at once sent for a doctor. He found the young man very ill, and likely to continue so for some time. What was to be done ? He could not be sent in his present state to his own miserable home—that was not to be thought of. But the doctor and the colonel consulting together decided that he might be removed in a cab to the house of Mrs. Smith (to whom the writer is indebted for the narrative), where he would receive all necessary attention.

The colonel delivered him into Mrs. Smith's charge, giving the good Samaritan's injunction and assurance, "Take care of him; and whatsoever thou spendest more, when I come again I will repay thee."

He was not long before he came again, for he visited him continually.

"What can you take ? Can I bring you anything ?" he would ask ; and would never forget to say to Mrs. Smith, " Be sure to let him have everything he fancies."

He bore the cost of everything, met the doctor's expenses, and paid for the lodgings, and was constant in his thoughtful helpfulness. He had plenty of work to do, but could always find time to read the Bible to the young man, who liked listening to that, and to the colonel's talks and prayers, better than anything.

At last the doctor advised that he should be removed to the local infirmary, for he was in a rapid consumption.

"Shall I see you there, colonel ? " he asked, with wistful eyes.

"Certainly ; I have a good many friends there, and am often calling to see them."

"I know that I am going to die."

"But you are not afraid, for now you know who says, ' I am the Resurrection and the Life.' He will be as near to you in the infirmary as here, and as near to you in death as in life."

"Oh, yes, I know Him now;" and so he did, for as the narrator said, "The colonel had led him to Christ by his life and teaching."

So the young bricklayer, who would do no more work, was taken to the infirmary, and was able to show to the patients there what Christianity could do for a dying man.

"Read the Bible to me," he would say to the nurse; "there is nothing like it."

"But you are tired."

"Yes, I am very tired. I do long to go to Jesus."

On another occasion he said, "I can see such beautiful sights, like little peeps into heaven. Can you see them? I shall soon be there."

"Is there anyone you would like to see before you die?" asked his good friend, the colonel, when he saw the end was near.

"Yes, I should like to see my mother."

So the mother was telegraphed for, and arrived in time to see what the Saviour of the world is able to do for those who trust in Him.

And then the young bricklayer went away, as he was longing to do, to be with Jesus; and to thank Him for sending him a friend and teacher in Colonel Gordon.

Another incident in the colonel's life at Gravesend was the following :—

A boy in the employ of a tradesman in Harmer Street robbed him. The culprit was discovered, and the master angrily declared that he would send him to prison. The mother of the boy was almost heart-broken, but she had heard of Colonel Gordon, and knew that, like his Master, he never turned away from the sad and troubled ones who sought his help. So, with all the mother's earnestness, she went at once to the colonel, and trying to check her tears, she told him the story.

"I cannot understand it, sir; he has always been an

honest boy, and I do believe that this is the first and the last time. If he could only have another chance! But if he is sent to prison I am afraid it will end in his ruin."

"I am afraid it will. I will do what I can for him. What would you like me to do?"

"Oh, sir, if you would intercede with his master, and persuade him not to send my boy to jail, I will be grateful to you all my life!"

So the colonel went to Harmer Street and saw the tradesman who had been robbed. He was very angry. He thought the boy deserved to be punished, and that it would do him good, and serve him right, and be a warning to him and to others, if he had a few months in prison.

But Gordon pleaded very earnestly for him, and every one respected the colonel, and was glad to do as he wished.

"What will become of the boy? I cannot keep him here now."

"Oh, no, of course you cannot. But if you will promise not to prosecute him I will take charge of him, and perhaps we can make a man out of the rascal yet. At least I should like to try, if you will let me."

"Very well, colonel. I will not punish him, and I hope he may repay your kindness."

"Thank you very much."

The colonel spoke very gravely to the boy, telling him how he had barely escaped going to prison, and pointing out to him how he had broken the laws of God as well as man. "But you shall have a chance," he said; "your master has kindly forgiven you, and if you ask God, He will forgive you also. And I will help you, if you behave well in the future and try to do your best. Will you?"

"Yes, sir, indeed I will," said the boy, through his tears.

" How would you like to go to sea ? " asked the colonel.

" I should like it very much indeed, sir."

" Very well.　Now you must go to school for a year.　I will pay for you ; and you must attend to your lessons, and try to learn as much as you possibly can in the time. Will you ? "

" Yes, sir ; I will try to be a good boy in everything."

" You must come up and see me sometimes at the Fort House ; and you must spend your evenings at the Boys' Home, and I shall see you there.　By these means I shall know whether you are keeping your promise.　If at the end of twelve months I find that you have really been a good boy, then I will get you a berth in a good ship, and you shall go to sea."

The boy thanked the colonel, and so did his mother ; and, in fact, they continue to do so, though perhaps he does not know it, to this day.　My informant says, " The lad is now a man, and goes to sea ; while his mother resides in Gravesend still.　He has a good character, and both the mother and the sailor bless the name of Gordon, who saved the lad from prison and the mother from disgrace."

Another mother residing in Gravesend says that she thinks her son would never have recovered from his illness if it had not been for the large amount of nourishment supplied him by Colonel Gordon.　Her boy was ill of fever, and the colonel bought or sent everything that he needed ; and not only so, but visited him, and read to him and prayed with him constantly until he recovered.　After he was better, the colonel often invited him to Fort House, where he always had happy times.　The colonel was the friend of all the family during the whole of his stay ; and when he went to bid them farewell on leaving Gravesend, so fully had his kind heart sympathised with them, that he wept.　The father of the boy, at that time a policeman, and now a detective, says he thinks that " Gravesend never had, before or since, a better Christian gentleman, nor one so deeply interested in young men and lads."

That is certainly true, although Gravesend has had, and has still, as the writer knows by personal acquaintance, many earnest Christian workers. One of the first established ragged schools in the country was at Gravesend ; and in this school Colonel Gordon was an indefatigable worker. The boys loved him, and honoured him above all others. There used to be testimonies borne to him written in chalk (of which there is always a bit to be found in the neighbourhood of Gravesend), ornamenting, or otherwise, the palings and walls ; such as these, "O. G. is a jolly good feller," "God bless the Kernel," "Long life to our dear teacher, Gordon." In the ragged school he always took the roughest and the raggedest boys into his class, and taught them to be more gentle in their manners, and more honourable and true in their lives and characters.

"We loved him so much," said a young man, "that many of us went to the night school only that we might be near him."

A lady who takes great interest in lads at the present time in Gravesend, says that she visited a good many of the poor and sick in that town with the colonel, who read and prayed with them, and always had some kindness to show them of a substantial sort. She thinks that occasionally his kindness was imposed on. She remembers with pleasure the address which he gave at the opening of her Mission Room in Passenger Court, and speaks of the great comfort which his presence brought, not only to the patients in the hospital, but also to the poor and the aged in the workhouse, to whom he not only spoke, but whom he cheered with the singing of hymns.

Visitors to the ragged schools are shown some Chinese banners which the colonel left behind him. One is his own name, exquisitely worked in Chinese characters. These are proudly borne by the present Gravesend boys when they walk in procession on Sunday-school festivals or other gala occasions.

A missionary now labouring in Gravesend in connection with the British and Foreign Sailors' Society, who has kindly furnished the writer with some information writes :—"Throughout the town it is said of him, like the Master, that he 'went about doing good;' and as he never courted the praise of men, only eternity will disclose the results of his sojourn in Gravesend."

Great sorrow was felt by all classes when he left. A doctor declared that he quite missed him, as whenever he found a case particularly needing attention, he always commended it to Gordon, and never in vain. On one occasion he stepped into the doctor's carriage and asked—

"Have you any work for me?"

"Yes," was the reply; "there is a lad at Perry Street" (a village about a mile from Gravesend) "who requires a little help and instruction."

"I am glad of that," replied Gordon; and he went to see the boy every evening from that time, until he no longer needed help.

When Colonel Gordon left Gravesend, the following appreciative testimony to his worth appeared in one of the local papers :—

"Our readers, without exception, will learn with regret of the departure of Lieutenant-Colonel Gordon, C.B., R.E., from the town, in which he has resided for six years, gaining a name by the most exquisite charity that will long be remembered. Nor will he be less missed than remembered, for in the lowly walks of life, by the bestowal of gifts; by attendance and ministrations on the sick and dying; by the kindly giving of advice; by attendance at the Ragged School, Workhouse, and Infirmary; in fact, by general and continual beneficence to the poor, he has been so unwearied

in well-doing that his departure will be felt by many as a
personal calamity. There are those who even now are
reaping the rewards of his kindness. His charity was
essentially charity, and had its root in deep philanthropic
feeling and goodness of heart; shunning the light of
publicity, but coming even as the rain in the night-time,
that in the morning is noted not, but only the flowers bloom
and give a greater fragrance. Colonel Gordon, although
comparatively a young man, has seen something of service,
having obtained his brevet and order of Companion of the
Bath by distinguished service in China. He is thus
eminently fitted for his new post, and there is no doubt
but that he will prove as beneficent in his station under the
Foreign Office as he was while at Gravesend; for it was
evidently with him a natural heart-gift, and not to be eradi-
cated. Colonel Gordon's duties at Gravesend terminated
on the 30th of September, and by this time he is on his way
to Galatz, in Turkey, where he will take up his residence as
British Commissioner on the Danube. He is succeeded by
Colonel the Hon. G. Wrottesley, as Commandant of Royal
Engineers for the Gravesend district. All will wish him
well in his new sphere; and we have less hesitation in
penning these lines from the fact that laudatory notice will
confer but little pleasure upon him who gave with the
heart, and cared not for commendation."

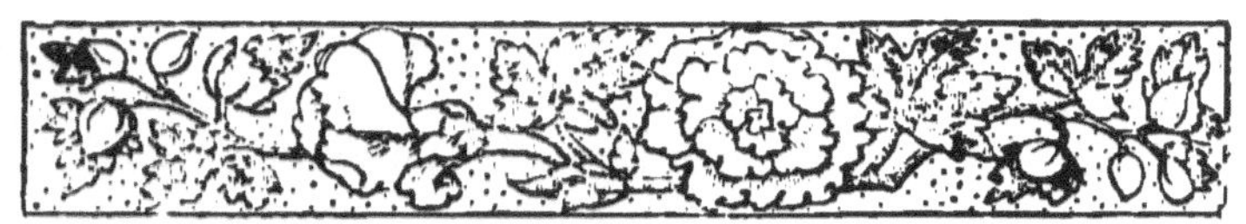

CHAPTER XIII.

GORDON'S FIRST VISIT TO THE SOUDAN.

" The force of his own merit makes his way;
  A gift that heaven gives."
                                    —*Henry VIII.*

HAT is the meaning of the name which for so long has been occupying a prominent position in our newspapers, and has been heard in fragments of conversation among all classes of people? The Soudan is "the country of the Blacks." It is in Central Africa. It is bounded on the north by Egypt, and on the south by the Nyanza Lakes. It extends from the Red Sea on the east to the western boundary of Darfour on the west. Its length is about 1600 miles, and its breadth 1300. It has at present no railways and no canals, although there is some talk of making a railway from Suakim to Berber. If this were done, very happy results might follow, for it would make commerce between Egypt and the Soudan possible, and would bring the country of the Blacks in connection with the whole world by means of the Red Sea. At present the people take their journeys on the backs of camels, excepting when the White Nile is navigable, as it is at certain periods of the year.

Egypt first took possession of the Soudan in the year 1819, when Ismail, the son of Mehemet Ali, was sent by his father to establish an Egyptian Government at Khartoum. From the first the Soudan has been an exceedingly difficult land to maintain. Ismail and his army managed to establish themselves; but they had not been long in possession before the Blacks had their first rising. They did not want the Egyptians either then or afterward. One of the native rulers invited Ismail and his friends to dine with him. He drugged the wine which he gave them to drink; and when they were overcome by its effects, he set fire to the house in which they were feasting, and so burnt them to death. Of course, after that, the Soudanese were compelled, whether they wished or not, to submit to Egyptian rule—Senaar and Kordofan being wrested from them. In the year 1826 there was a Governor appointed in the person of Khurishid Pasha, who ruled over Fashoda for eleven years. A rebellion broke out in Kassala in 1841, at which time the Soudan was divided into seven provinces; and there was so much difficulty connected with them that Said Pasha, when he visited the Soudan, was very much disposed to give it up altogether, but that a strong representation was made to him to the effect that if he did this there would be constant warfare between the tribes. He therefore appointed a Governor; and there have been Governors of the Soudan ever since.

There was for some years a gradual pushing southward of the Egyptians; and the country was further opened by adventurous traders, who, for purposes of their own, sought to traverse the strange wild region of which almost nothing was known; and in the year 1853 the English Consul for the Soudan, Mr. John Petherick, succeeded, in the interests of trade, in making a voyage along the upper waters of the White Nile. He found that ivory was plentiful and cheap; and henceforth considerable trading was carried on. At that time Egypt's possessions on the Nile only extended a hundred miles south of Khartoum; but since then she has been rapidly extending her rule, and the last conquest, that of Darfour, has added many miles to her territory.

Unfortunately the European traders did not long content themselves with dealing in ivory, for they found that to deal in slaves was very much more profitable. In the Bahr Gazelle country bands of armed men kept the posts for the traders, so that their horrible traffic could be carried on in safety. In the year 1860 the world was fully aroused to these matters, and the indignant voice of the people became so loud, that the Europeans could not for very shame carry on their infamous work. So they sold their slave stations to the Arabs, who contrived to keep the peace with the Khedive by paying a yearly rental. The poor people who were caught and sold into slavery were no better than before; and the thing itself was, of course, as unrighteous as ever. Indeed, the Arabs were more ruthless than the Europeans had been. They were provided with arms and ammunition by the Egyptian Government and the Europeans who had before held the posts, and they stopped at nothing. They actually made the slaves catch each other; for they trained some boy-negroes whom they had stolen, and so taught and urged them, that they became adepts in the art of securing their fellows. The result of all this was to devastate the whole district. Captain Speke wrote:—"The atrocities committed by these traders are beyond civilised belief. They are constantly fighting, robbing, and capturing slaves and cattle. No honest man can either trade or travel in the country, for the natives have been bullied to such an extent that they either fight or run away, according to their strength or circumstances."

Dr. Schweinfurth, in his interesting work, *The Heart of Africa*, writes:—"There are traces still existing which demonstrate that large villages and extensive plots of cultivated land formerly occupied the scene where now all is desolation. . . . The population must have diminished by at least two-thirds."

The men who were doing so much harm to these villages were becoming very powerful themselves, on account of their number and influence; and at last the slave-dealers set up a king of their own, and refused to pay taxes to the Imperial Government. The name of the man who ventured to oppose the authority of the Khedive was Sehehr Rahama. When Dr. Schweinfurth saw him he was surrounded with a court that was little less than princely in its details. . . . Special rooms, provided with carpeted divans, were reserved as ante-chambers, and into these all visitors were conducted by richly-dressed slaves. . . . The regal aspect of these halls of state was increased by the introduction of some lions, secured, as may be supposed, by sufficiently strong and massive chains. . . . His wealth matched even his superstition. It was reported, on good authority, that to foil the black art of an enemy, whose charms were a proof against lead, he had 25,000 dollars melted down into bullets, as the amulets did not apply to silver.

This man was the owner of thirty fortified posts, and his power was so great that the Egyptian Government tried to check its growth, and sent out some soldiers, under the command of an officer named Ballal. But Sebehr brought a force to oppose him, and Ballal was slain, with some of his men. The Khedive was angry, but he had to submit to that which he could not prevent, and Sebehr was more than ever like the king of the slave-dealers.

At last the Khedive became afraid that Darfour would come into the hands of Sebehr, in which case he might in time wrest the whole of the Soudan from Egypt. He tried to secure the rebel on his side. He made him a Bey, and invited him to join him in an expedition to Darfour. The Sultan of Darfour fell before the enemy, and his two sons were slain; and though other members of the family succeeded, they were in turn killed, and Darfour became part of the Soudan.

Sebehr was made a pasha, but he wanted to be more than that.

"What will satisfy you?" was asked of him.

"I have done the fighting and won the victory," was the reply; "I ought to be Governor-General."

From that time the Khedive set his face against slavery, although previously he had not only allowed it, but received some of the proceeds arising from it.

He, therefore, in 1869, called in the aid of Sir Samuel Baker to assist him "to strike a direct blow at the slave trade in its distant nest;" and Sir Samuel, in his celebrated book, *Ismailia*, published in 1874, gives a graphic account of his journeys and experiences. We shall refer to these in a subsequent chapter; for later events have made Sir Samuel Baker's mission appear of even greater importance than it did—at all events as far as British interests were concerned — when it was first undertaken.

Sir Samuel Baker undertook the work with all its responsibilities, and for the next four years worked hard, opening up the Nile country as far as the lakes, and doing his best to suppress the slave trade; and in 1873 he resigned his post.

The difficulty now was to find a worthy successor. But the man was ready when the time of need had come.

At the sitting of the Danubian Commission, in Constantinople, Nubar Pasha had met Colonel Gordon, and was much struck by his ability, force of character, and honourable disposition. Nubar Pasha, therefore, resolved to consult Gordon in the emergency which had arisen; and he asked the Englishman if he could recommend some suitable person to take the post vacated by Sir Samuel Baker. Gordon took time to consider; and the next year he wrote to Nubar Pasha to say that if the Khedive would apply to the English Government for him, he would himself accept the position of Governor of the tribes of the Nile Basin.

The Khedive accordingly applied to England, and England gave permission for Gordon to go to the Soudan in order to assist the Egyptians. The Khedive informed him of the result of his application, and then he said that he would pay Gordon £10,000 a-year for his services.

But Gordon would not accept so much money.

"Fix your own terms, then," said the Khedive; and Gordon said that he would take £2000 a-year, as he believed that would cover his expenses.

The Khedive explained his duties. He was to endeavour to put an end to the traffic in slaves. If the brigands were willing to give up their former habits, and become servants of the Government, Gordon was to accept their services, and pay them well. If they were determined to follow their old course of life, Gordon was to punish them severely. Care was to be taken that proper supplies of corn were at hand. The troops were to till the land and raise crops; and if the seat of government proved to be placed in an unproductive locality, they must move to a more fertile region. Gordon was also to endeavour to establish some system of post-communication, and to endeavour to get the assistance of the tribes among whom he was going to live, in order to help him in his efforts to put down the slave trade.

Gordon went home for a short time before commencing his duties; and in February 1874 he reached Cairo, on his way to commence work.

Dr. Birbeck Hill has published in his book, *Colonel Gordon in Central Africa,* the letters which Gordon wrote home. It may be questioned whether any man's letters were better worth publishing. No novel is as interesting —no book of travels more graphic. Added to his other powers, Charles Gordon is one of the best letter-writers of his time : he is chatty and pleasant, breezy and bright, almost all through.

In his first letter he said that he thought he saw through the affair, and that the expedition was a sham got up to interest and please the English people. But though he made this discovery, he was hopeful of being able to achieve some good results.

He spent a few days at Cairo ; but he said that he and Nubar Pasha did not exactly "hit it off." He wanted to travel by a steamer that would be shortly leaving for Suakim, for by doing so he would save something like £400. But Nubar Pasha did not like the new Governor of Upper Egypt to go to his field of office and honour except in becoming state. So a steamer was engaged, and a number of servants provided, and he started off with all the pomp and ceremonial of state.

He, attended by an equerry of the Viceroy's, was sent to Suez by special train. But their journey was not very satisfactory. An engine had run off the line, and this made a block on the railway, which stopped the special train in which the new Governor was travelling. There occurred a delay of two hours ; but though Gordon could be very quick tempered and annoyed by some things, he was only amused at this. In relating the incident he said, " We were shunted into a common train with a great many people—begun in glory and ended in shame."

They went down the Red Sea to Suakim, and there were put in quarantine for the night. Gordon guessed it was because the governor was not ready to receive them. They had on board two hundred and twenty troops, who were to accompany him across the desert. This journey was taken on camels, and occupied a fortnight.

On the 13th of March he arrived at Khartoum. He thus describes his reception :—" The Governor-General met your brother in full uniform, and he landed amid a salute of artillery, and a battalion of troops with a band. It was a fine sight. The day before your brother had his trousers off, and was pulling the boat in the Nile, in spite of crocodiles, who never touch you when moving. He cannot move now without guards turning out. I have got a good house here, and am very comfortable."

He was glad to be told that the rest of his journey would be less difficult and tedious than it might have been ; for the " sudd," the undergrowth of vegetation in the river, had been cleared out by the soldiers, so that the distance which had taken Sir Samuel Baker more than a year could now be accomplished in three weeks.

He spent a few days in Khartoum, and held a review ; besides which he visited the hospital and the schools, to the great delight of the little black children. He wrote, "Your brother's title is 'His Excellency General-Colonel Gordon, the Governor-General of the Equator ;' so no one can or ought to cross it without permission of His Excellency."

He issued a decree which put the district under martial law, declaring that the Government of Egypt had the monopoly of the trade in ivory ; that no one should enter without a passport ; and that arms and powder were not to be imported.

He described the air as being so dry that nothing decayed ; everything was dried up. The Khartoum people saluted him with a shrill noise that was very musical.

They left Khartoum amid a salute of artillery, and steamed up the Nile. He thought the crocodiles were dreadful-looking creatures, as they lay basking in the sun with their mouths open.   Little birds might always be seen flying about these glistening creatures.   There were large flocks of geese and other birds flying south.   They had a pleasant journey, and time and opportunity were given to Gordon to get used to his party, and his party to him. His staff consisted of Colonel Long of the United States, Major Campbell of the Egyptian staff, Mr. Kemp, an engineer, Mr. Linant; and Messrs. Anson, Russell, and Gessi.   Gordon had decided to take with him Abou Saoud, a slave-hunter known as the "Sultan."   No one approved of this, but Gordon felt sure that he was right to take him, and that he would find him very useful.   He said that none but poor people spoke in Abou's favour.   One gentleman said that Gordon ought never to eat with him, lest he should poison him; but he felt sure that the Sultan would be nothing but a help to him.

The steamer went very slowly, and they had time to notice the animals all around them—the storks, the monkeys, and the noses of the hippopotami.   He said they passed some people who wore gourds for head-dresses, and "also some Shillooks, who wear no *head* or *other* dress at all."

One night he was thinking rather pensively of the friends whom he had left at home, and of the dangers and difficulties of the work which he had engaged to do, when suddenly he heard loud peals of laughter.   "I felt put out, but it turned out to be birds who laughed at us from the bushes in a very rude way.   They are a species of stork, and seemed in capital spirits, and highly amused at anybody thinking of going up to Gondokoro with the hope of doing anything."

He saw troops of buffaloes, and camelopards looking like steeples, and eating the tops of the trees.   He said the villages looked like haystacks.   They saw a tribe of Dinkas, and the chief came on board, in full dress—a necklace—who seemed inclined to salute him in the usual way, by spitting in his hand. Gordon gave him some food, which he seemed to enjoy, and after eating which he wished to kiss his feet ; but the general would not allow this, so he sang a hymn of praise to him instead. Gordon gave him a string of beads as a present, with which the chief was highly delighted.

The mosquitoes annoyed him very much, and the heat was great, but they got on tolerably well. They passed some natives who had rubbed their faces with wood until they looked like slate-pencils; and he gave one chief a picture from the *Illustrated London News,* which he was to keep to show that he was protected.

At a place called Bohr he found the people angry because he had come to put down slavery. But at St. Orcix, a missionary establishment, the people danced with joy to see him.

At last there is this entry in his diary :—

" Gondokoro, 16th April.—Got here to-day, much to the surprise of the people, who never expected one's arrival at all, and did not know of my nomination."

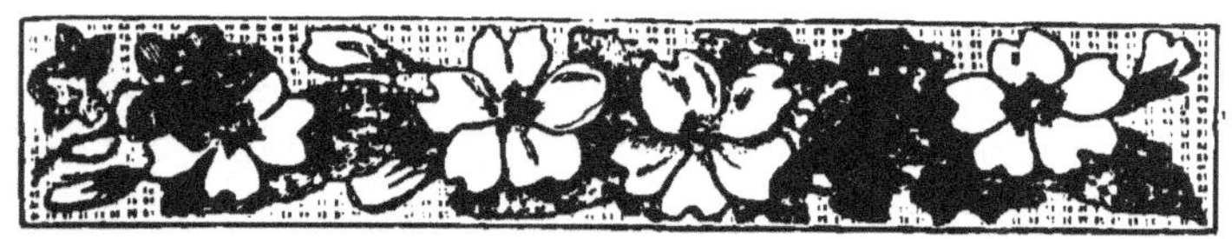

CHAPTER XIV.

WHAT IS THE SOUDAN?

"I think our country sinks beneath the yoke ;
It weeps, it bleeds ; and each new day a gash
Is added to her wounds. I think, withal,
There would be hands uplifted in my right
From gracious England."

—Macbeth.

E think a little more information respecting the country in which Colonel Gordon had now taken up his abode will be interesting, especially to the young readers of this book, many of whom are saying, "Tell us something about the Soudan." We have already given the explanation of the name, and the size of the country, which is at present but sparsely inhabited. It is a district full of romantic interest. It was only a short while ago lonely, unknown, and unexplored. For ages people have being reading of the wonderful river, *The Nile*, and have welcomed all information respecting it. For many years this amounted to very little ; but Speke and Grant, Sir Samuel Baker and Dr. Schweinfurth, have, during the last twenty years, thrown the light of their researches upon the land of mystery, and

given us much knowledge that we never possessed before. One reason why it was so little known was, that there were no roads by which it could be reached. The only method of travel is by means of camels, which can traverse the deserts at great speed. Egypt has endeavoured to occupy the Soudan since the year 1819; but it has cost many wars to keep the possession even of the tribes who were at war among themselves.

One of the first to give the world a written account of the Soudan was Mr. John Petherick, whose name has already been mentioned. He entered the service of Mehemet Ali Pasha, Viceroy of Egypt, in the year 1845. He secured the necessary stock of provisions and camels at Assouan, and started early in January 1847, going first to Korosko and then to Berbera, then to Kordofan, and then to Khartoum.

He gives some interesting descriptions of the country and the people of the Soudan.

He one day wished to have a Turkish bath to refresh him after his journey, and was told that one would be brought to him. To his surprise he found the bath consisted of a small wooden bowl and a teacup. The bowl contained dough, and the cup sweet oil. The dough was to be rubbed into the skin to cleanse it, and the oil, which was perfumed, was afterwards applied for refreshment. The operation was called the "dilka." The better class natives use the dilka every evening, and it is supposed not only to keep them clean, but to be conducive to health.

The dress of the Soudanese women is very simple. They attire themselves in dark blue calico, which they wrap round the waist, and which covers them down to the knees. Besides this they wear a white muslin veil, which covers the head and the face, leaving only the eyes exposed. They are very fond of ornaments, especially of beads, which they wear not only round their necks, but also round their waists, and their wrists. They further decorate themselves with necklaces of "saumeet," or pieces of agate an inch thick, with alternated colours of black, brown, and white. They wear ear-rings and nose-rings of gold. Those in the ear weigh half an ounce each, and that in the nose is so large as to cover the mouth. It is worn on the right side of the nose. When they cannot afford the gold rings they put a piece of coral through the nose. Not only are the neck, ears, and nose ornamented, but the ankles also. Strings of glass beads, or filigree ornaments fastened with a silk tassel, generally red, above thick-soled brown leather sandals, adorn the feet of the Soudanese girls. The girls themselves are thus described in Petherick's interesting book, *Egypt :—*

"Their colour partakes of various shades, from light to brown, almost black ; and although they scarcely ever wash—using the "dilka" instead of water—their skin appears clean and fresh. The hair, which never reaches below the shoulders, and inclines to be woolly, is plaited into a variety of forms, but generally closely to the head, fitting like a skull-cap, and hanging down in thick masses of innumerable small plaits all round the side and back of the head. Another form is to plait the hair so as to adhere close to the top of the head, as in the former case, but the ends, instead of being plaited, are combed out and stiffened with a solution of grease, forming a thick bushy circle around the head. With this head-dress, as the lady only arranges her hair once or twice a-month, she cannot recline upon a pillow, for which she is obliged to substitute a small wooden stool, hollowed out to fit the neck, upon which she reposes."

The houses of the people in the Soudan are as simple as their dress, and more simple than their ornaments. They are built of sun-burnt bricks, plastered with a composition made of manure and grey sand. There is generally only one large room in the house, which is used both for living and sleeping in, and a small one used as a lumber-room. Often there are no windows, but if there are any, they are placed in very high positions.

They call their bedsteads " angareb "—a frame with no posts, having strips of hide drawn across it, and a mat of palm leaves placed on the top. There are no chairs in the house ; but a few stools and the angareb are the entire furniture—the latter being the sofa by day and the bed by night.

Mr. Petherick found some willow-pattern plates and basins in some of the houses, but generally wooden bowls are the utensils used. Water is the chief drink of the Soudanese ; and water in the desert is a great desideratum. The water is stowed in earthen pitchers, and, instead of glasses from which to drink it, the rim of a gourd is used. The principal food is " assida," which is maize flour made into thick porridge. Each woman grinds her own, for which purpose each family possesses a mill, which is generally placed in a separate hut used as a kitchen. The mill consists of two stones, one two feet in length and ten inches wide, with a smooth surface, fixed into the centre of a slightly raised mound of clay, concave in shape, so as to hold the flour, and a smaller stone, which the woman presses over the larger one, using both hands and kneeling, the better to perform her work. She can grind half a peck of corn in an hour. The fire over which the porridge is boiled is made of wood, kept in its place by three large stones or lumps of clay. When the porridge is cooked sufficiently it is put into a wooden dish, and heaped up in the same way that our blanc-mange is. It is eaten with a sauce of a curious vegetable called baymeh, and powdered meat very highly seasoned. No spoons are used ; each person conveys the food to his mouth with his fingers. Sometimes the flour is made into thin cakes, and baked on the hot ashes as a change from porridge; but always the same kind of sauce is eaten, and nearly always the men dine first, and the women after they have finished.

The children are never dressed until they are eight or nine years old, and they are very young when they are married. A mother carries her baby on her left hip: the baby is always naked, and sits astride.

At the time of Petherick's visit the Governor-General of the Soudan was Hhalid Pasha, and the Egyptian dependencies were Dongola, Berbera, Khartoum, Sennaar, Fazogl, Taker, and Kordofan; Khartoum being the capital. The Government stores were there, and an arsenal used for the construction and repair of boats. The only stone building in Khartoum was that of the Roman Oatholic mission. There was a church in connection with it, and a school. At that time, with the exception of the Roman Catholics, there were only five Europeans in the place. Yet Khartoum was of considerable mercantile importance. There was then no communication, as there is now, by means of the Red Sea from Suakim to Suez and Cairo, and the thought of the canal had scarcely entered men's minds. But Manchester goods were brought into the Khartoum market—for all the dresses of the Soudanese were of cotton; and there were some exports, such as ivory from the White Nile, and gum arabic, ostrich feathers, and bees-wax from Abyssinia. Round about Khartoum there were extensive date groves and good gardens; and in the centre of the town were two large bazaars, where all the manu-factured goods that were needed could be bought. When the markets were held booths were erected, and all sorts of wares spread out to tempt the purchaser. " Saddles for all kinds of beasts, cords, bridles, swords, lances, hoes, hatchets, cowry shells, needles, brass thimbles, oil, odori-ferous herbs, spices, antimony (called ' rohl '), for tinging the eyelashes, pepper, salt, onions, garlic, tobacco, grain, coral, amber beads, ivory, iron bracelets, glass bead neck laces, hedjas, sandals, small looking-glasses, gaudily striped handkerchiefs, dyed cotton Manchester goods, red-bordered plain scarfs, and a thousand other things were to be bought in the Soudan market."

Merissa is the favourite drink. It is intoxicating, but drunkenness is infrequent, and is looked upon as a disgrace. Merissa is made from grain, either dourra or duchu (millet). This grain is moistened, and then spread between two layers of the leaves of the nsher, a poisonous plant, which attains its greatest perfection in Kordofan. This gives the merissa a flavour. The dourra is then dried in the sun, and ground in a mill. The flour is then mixed with water, and worked into a thick paste. It is afterwards baked on a large earthenware pan into thick cakes, which are next broken up, put into a pot, and boiled in water. Then, when the process of fermentation is at its height a few days later, it is filtered through bags made of the reeds of the date palm, and is ready for use.

The water melon is of great service to the Soudanese, and is, no doubt, not only more refreshing, but much more beneficial than merissa. At Kordofan it grows wild, but if the seeds are sown, it is reproduced in large quantities. It can be kept for some time; and the inside of the fruit becomes liquid, and is such a good substitute for water, that when the latter is scarce, as it is in the hot season, both man and beast can live upon it. Another useful tree which is abundant in the neighbourhood of Kordofan is the baobab. It grows to the height of thirty or forty feet, and its immense trunk and large branches are hollow. It flowers in August, and is then covered with blossoms that look something like our double-red hollyhock. Its fruit looks a little like a cocoa-nut. But the most wonderful thing about these trees is that they form natural tanks, in which water is kept. In the rainy season they get filled, and in the dry season the natives tap them, and find within them water enough for use, and so are able to live in districts where otherwise they could not exist during the drought.

A great many of the trees of the Soudan are gum-producing. These were the sources of considerable profit to the Egyptian Government until it became a trade, free from taxation, and thrown open to all.

Petherick was the means of opening up the Soudan for purposes of trade, especially that of ivory. In 1853 he turned his attention to the district of the White Nile—very little known in those days, but lately become very famous—and began to see what could be done to establish the gum-arabic and ivory trades, of which the Egyptian Government no longer held the monopoly. He resided at Il Obeid, and made expeditions from that place. Petherick's *Egypt* contains the account of his voyage up the White Nile. He went beyond the confines of the Egyptian Government, and left behind him all traces of civilisation, passing primitive forests never disturbed until he and his Khartoum traders went into them to cut down the timber for boat-building. There were herds of antelopes and gazelles, and now and then a lion might be seen. Blue monkeys played among the branches, and flocks of wild fowl, from the teal to the goose, were plentiful. And so, too, were the crocodiles.

Petherick and his men sailed past beautiful islands, with trees growing upon them such as we have scarcely heard of in England—mimosa, and heglig, and others. They made acquaintance with the strange tribes among whom afterwards Charles Gordon was to live—the Djibba, the Dinkas, and the Shillooks—people who were all naked, except the married women, who wore leather aprons behind and before. They were generally friendly, and willing to exchange what they had for a few glass beads. They astonished Mr. Petherick by their mode of salutation, which was not shaking hands, or kissing hands, but spitting upon the hands.

He tells an amusing story of the way in which he purchased an elephant tusk :—

"My interpreter and myself seated ourselves opposite to the owner of the tusk, who obstinately retained his seat, refusing us an inspection of it. Placing a hide on the ground, a variety of beads, cowry shells, and copper bracelets were displayed thereon. The beauty of these provoked striking signs of approbation, the vendors and bystanders grinning and rubbing their stomachs with both hands. A consultation then took place between the party and his friends as to the relative merits of the beads, which resulted in the following dialogue :—

"*Vendor.*—'Ah, your beads are beautiful, but the bride (tusk) I offer is lovely! Like yourself, she is white and tall, and worthy of great price.'

"*Self.*—'Truly, the beauty of the bride is undeniable; but from what I can see of her, she is cracked, while my beads are perfect.'

"*Vendor.*—'The beads you offer are truly beautiful, but I think they must have been gathered before they were ripe.'

"*Self.*—'Oh, no; they were gathered when mature, and their colour is peculiar to them, and you will find that they will wear as well as the best red; they come from a different country.'

"*Vendor.*—'Well, let me have some more of them.'

"His request being complied with, rising from the tusk and throwing himself upon the beads, he collected them greedily. At the same time the possession of the tusk was disputed by half-a-dozen negroes, stating they had assisted to carry it on their shoulders, and claimed a recompense. On this being complied with, by a donation to each man, another set of men came forward, under the same pretence; and the tusk was seized by my men at one extremity, whilst they had hold of the other, and in perfect good humour struggled for its possession. At last, to cut the matter short, I threw handfuls of beads amongst the crowd, which resulted in the immediate abandonment of the tusk for a scramble after them. In the meantime, the purchase was carried off, and safely lodged on board. After a fortnight's sojourn, leaving an establishment of ten men and a stock of merchandise wherewith to continue barter-trade, I returned direct to Khartoum."

Other expeditions were made into the interior, and in this way the ivory trade was well and firmly established. It was fairly remunerative; but another trade was becoming possible to the Soudanese, which was very much more profitable, and that was the slave-trade.

At Kordofan it had always been easy to procure slaves, for the station is so near to the homes of the negroes that catching them was very possible. Mr. Petherick mentions the fact that a lad of fifteen or twenty years could be bought for from £5 to £8; a girl of the same age costing about a-third more. This was a regular trade then, and has been since. The slave-merchants brought them from their native hills, and sold them in Kordofan. They were often treated kindly, and trained to do field and domestic work. If they ran away they were pursued, and could be easily traced by their footprints in the sand. The Arabs would run after them for the sake of the reward which was offered. They would soon know whether the slaves had fled to some encampment, hoping for protection, or were fleeing from the encampment in fear; and would "follow them until, from various dodges and attempts to elude observation, they became convinced of their being on the track of a fugitive negro. The pursuit is then no longer continued in the heretofore inquisitive manner; but, like a pack of hounds in full cry, if the track is followed by more than one, they exultingly proclaim their convictions, and full swing, keeping up a steady trot, are off in pursuit. If the footprints are not very fresh, or if they show that the fugitive is riding any animal superior to a donkey, horses are immediately resorted to; and a chase after a fugitive negro partakes of as much excitement by participators and lookers-on as a fox-hunt creates in England."

Of course there could be no slaves to run away if there were not slave-traders. Since the time of Mr. Petherick's visit the buying and selling of slaves has gone on, and there have been shameful cruelties practised, and terrible sufferings undergone by the hapless slaves.

In 1856 His Highness, Said Pasha, visited the Soudan, in order to inquire into the abuses that were reported, and to decide as to its future, so far as Egypt was concerned. He saw so much that annoyed and perplexed him, that he was almost inclined to altogether withdraw the Egyptian protection and governorship from it. But a strong representation was made to him from all the principal chiefs, that if he did that there would be constant war among the tribes, and the spirit of anarchy would reign in place of order. He therefore consented to retain the power and responsibility of the Soudan; but he declared that before any good could be accomplished, slavery must be abolished. He commanded that his army should no longer be recruited by slaves; that they should no longer be received, as they had been, in payment of taxes; and he himself liberated large numbers of slaves from their bondage.

But, in spite of all this, slavery is to-day the great difficulty, the crying evil of the Soudan.

Ivory is still sought, and elephants are still hunted and caught for the purpose; but the slaves are hunted and caught yet more fiercely. In the one case the animal is great, and can protect itself, even though eventually it is slain for the sake of its tusks; but in the other, the poor wretches are frightened and starved into submission, and there appears no hope for them. And yet there is hope. Livingstone's last words called down blessings upon those who should cure the moral evil of slavery; and Gordon may yet prove to be the man whom God has appointed to do the work. There is something picturesque in the elephant hunt—the march through the bush, the prairie on fire, the elephants standing stupefied in the midst of the smoke, and alarmed at the roar and the crackling of flames, the hunters rushing on their prey with a whoop and a shout, and then the swift lance that does its work effectually, and slays the animal with as little suffering as possible. But there is no picturesqueness, nothing but horrible misery and cruelty practised toward the slaves. They are stolen, and beaten, and harried, and starved, for no reason but that others may get rich—by no right but that of might. And England, which has done so much for the slaves, must do her part, if possible, to crush the slave trade in the Soudan.

It was to do this that Sir Samuel Baker and Colonel Gordon were sent into the country of the Blacks.

CHAPTER XV.

GORDON'S PREDECESSOR IN THE SOUDAN.

"Home-keeping youth have ever homely wits;
I rather would entreat thy company
To see the wonders of the world abroad."
—*Gentlemen of Verona.*

IT was in June 1869 that His Highness Ismail Pasha, Viceroy of Egypt, paid his second visit to England. He spent eight days in our country; and received every possible respect from the English people. He reached Charing Cross on the 22nd of June, and the Prince of Wales tendered him a royal greeting in the name of the Queen of England. A great multitude of people shouted their welcome as he drove to Buckingham Palace. He visited the Metropolitan Railway and the Thames Embankment, th Zoological Gardens and the Crystal Palace. At the latter place there was a public festival in his honour, more than 30,000 persons being present. The Duke of Sutherland had provided a banquet, and there was a concert of sacred music in which an orchestra and chorus of 3000 persons took part. On the 24th of June he visited the Queen

at Windsor Castle.   Everyone united to shew him respect ;
he was taken in the royal saloon, with a guard of honour,
and as the train drew up to the station the band played the
Egyptian National Anthem.   The Viceroy and a select
party of distinguished guests dined with Her Majesty, and
stayed all night at the castle.   The next day the Viceroy
dined with the Prince of Wales ; the Prince and Princess
afterward giving a concert at which the celebrated artistes,
Madame Patti, Mdlle. Christine Nilsson, Signor Gardoni,
and Mr. Santley, sang.   The Viceroy was entertained with
a review in Windsor Park on the twenty-sixth ; and on the
thirtieth he inspected the Fire Brigade in the garden of
Buckingham Palace.   He appeared greatly delighted with
his visit ; and no doubt desired that England might think
well of him and his country.

He left England on the 1st of July, the Prince of Wales
taking leave of him at Charing Cross.

His Highness the Khedive could not be long in England,
nor mix with English people of any rank, without seeing
that the abhorrence of slavery was one of the strongest
feelings in the English heart.   That the Prince of Wales
would honour him all the more if he used his influence to
abolish slavery in the Soudan, he had abundant proof, not
only during his stay in London, but also during the visit of
the Prince to Egypt.   It will be remembered that not only
the Prince, but the Princess went to Egypt ; and they were
greatly interested, and hospitably entertained by the
Khedive.   Mr. Russell wrote a very interesting account
of the visit, and so did Mrs. Gray, a lady who accompanied
the Princess.

In one place Mrs. Gray writes :—" The money spent on
pipes in this country must be fabulous ; they say that in the
Viceroy's treasury there are pipes, the value of some of which
amounts to no less than £6000 a-piece.   I could not resist
the temptation of following the example of the rest, as I

thought smoking out of these lovely pipes must be quite different from any other smoking ; but I am sorry to say I soon found the taste very like what it is elsewhere, and gave it up at once. In fact, I only tried out of curiosity, though I must confess I constantly had to accept a pipe, when offered afterwards in the course of our tour."

Mrs. Gray also says of the food in Egypt :—" She never felt more inclined to be sick—two dozen of dishes, alternately sweet and savoury, interchanged, apparently, after no order reconcilable with European tastes or notions, many of these washed down by mouthfuls of vinegar, with additions of herbs and cucumber; moreover, each article being generally, and *de rigneur*, taken from the same dish by the fingers. This formed a combination, doubtless, of the highest interest to the Oriental, but of anything but interest to his hungry, yet patient European guests.

" The dresses the princesses wore to-day were splendid, as far as jewels go. One had on a white moire-antique dress, richly embroidered nearly all over with gold. Another had a red one; and blue and grey were worn by the younger ones, all equally embroidered. The shape of their dress was very odd : it seemed to me equally long in front as behind, where it formed a long train. The skirt was cut open about two feet on each side, showing their legs wrapped up in some soft material or other. The train in front was passed behind, and their walk, in consequence of all this, was anything but graceful; for, having this heavy gown between their legs, they waddled along like ducks."

Among the members of the expedition was Sir Samuel Baker, who had been specially invited by the Prince to accompany him, and to whom the Khedive, as we have already mentioned, gave the honour and the responsibility of becoming the Governor of the Soudan, for the express purpose of putting down the slave trade. Sir Samuel Baker received his commission in the following terms :—

"We, Ismail, Khedive of Egypt, considering the savage condition of the tribes which inhabit the Nile Basin :

"Considering that neither government, nor laws, nor security exists in those countries :

"Considering that humanity enforces the suppression of the slave-hunters who occupy those countries in great numbers :

"Considering that the establishment of legitimate commerce throughout those countries will be a great stride towards future civilisation, and will result in the opening to steam navigation of the great equatorial lakes of Central Africa, and in the establishing a permanent government :

"We have decreed, and now decree as follows :—

"An expedition is organised to subdue to our authority the countries situated in the south of Gondokoro ;

"To suppress the slave trade ; to introduce a system of regular commerce ;

"To open to navigation the great lakes of the equator ;

"And to establish a chain of military stations and commercial depôts, distant at intervals of three days' march, throughout Central Africa, accepting Gondokoro as the base of operations :

"The supreme command of this expedition is confided to Sir Samuel White Baker, for four years, commencing from 1st of April 1869 : to whom also we confer the most absolute power, even that of death, over all those who may compose the expedition :

"We confer upon him the same absolute and supreme authority over all those countries belonging to the Nile Basin south of Gondokoro."

This was a very large and important commission, but it could scarcely have been given to a more suitable man ; for Sir Samuel Baker had already visited the Soudan, and made himself acquainted with, not only the country, but the peoples who inhabit it.

In 1861, when those two great pioneers of African travel—Speke and Grant—were pursuing their lonely journeys, and making their remarkable discoveries, they one morning walked into Gondokoro. They were on their way to call upon a Circassian merchant, named Kurshid Agha, and they saw hurrying towards them an Englishman. They had been on the look-out for Mr. Petherick, whom we referred to in our last chapter, and who had been despatched with supplies to the help of the illustrious travellers. They had heard of him a few days before, when a very black man, named Mahamed, had rushed at them, throwing himself into Speke's arms, and begun to hug and kiss him.

" Who is your master ?" asked Speke.

" Petherick," was the reply.

" And where is Petherick now ?"

" Oh, he is coming."

" How is it you have not got English colours, then ?"

" The colours are Debono's."

" Who is Debono ?"

" The same as Petherick."

This man promised to take the travellers to Petherick, but delayed so long that they left him, and went on their journey. When, therefore, in Gondokoro they saw the Englishman, they concluded that he was Petherick. But another had come out in search for them—namely, Mr., now Sir Samuel Baker, and it was with him they were, to their great delight, shaking hands.

Speke said afterwards—" What joy this was I can hardly tell. We could not talk fast enough, so overwhelmed were we both to meet again. Of course we were his guests in a moment, and learned everything that could be told. I now first heard of the death of His Royal Highness Prince Albert, which made me reflect on the inspiring words he made use of, in compliment to myself, when I was in England. Then there was the terrible war in America.

and other less startling events which came on us all by surprise; as years had now passed since we had received news of the civilised world."

Baker showed them the greatest kindness, and he continued the work which they had begun. Sir Samuel Baker was accompanied by his wife. No white woman had ever before been seen in those regions, and it is quite possible that Lady Baker, who possesses great personal attractions, as well as tact, ability, and imperturbable courage, contributed more than a little to the success of the expedition.

Sir Samuel Baker was at Berber, on the Nile, for the first time, in May 1862. Berber is a town of considerable size and importance, lying in the direct caravan route between Cairo and Khartoum. He made his way to the latter place, and reached it a year later, having visited all the Nile tributaries of Abyssinia—the Atbara, Settite, Salaam, Angrab, Rahad, Dinder, and the great Blue Nile.

Next he went to the distant south to accomplish one of the greatest of his life-works—viz., to discover the White Nile source.

Even then, and at the very commencement of his labours, he got an insight into the slave trade which fitted him for the work he was afterwards to undertake in the Soudan.

There was another eminent traveller, who, a little later, achieved the success which he and Sir Samuel Baker alone, of all the explorers, had won, of penetrating Africa from north to south—Dr. George Schweinfurth. We have already referred to his book, *The Heart of Africa.* Schweinfurth was born at Riga in 1836, and took his degree of Doctor of Philosophy at Berlin. During his school life he was under the care of a teacher whose father was a missionary in South Africa. Schweinfurth seemed to have, born with him, a passionate love of botany; and in 1863 he went to Egypt and travelled as far as Khartoum. He made subsequent journeys; and by his discoveries of many kinds, added greatly to the interest felt in the Soudan, and the knowledge which is possessed respecting it.

It will be seen that Sir Samuel Baker was, of all men, the best that could have been sent on the mission. He took with him some troops, and the provisions they were likely to require; also some steamers and sailing vessels. It was a great mass of heavy material, and would have to be transported for a distance of about three thousand miles, four hundred of which would be across the scorching Nubian deserts.

On the 8th February 1870 he wrote in his journal—"My original programme—agreed to by His Highness the Khedive, who ordered the execution of my orders by the authorities—arranged that six steamers, fifteen sloops, and fifteen diahbeeahs should leave Cairo on the 10th of June, to ascend the cataracts to Khartoum, at which place Djiaffer Pasha was to prepare three steamers and twenty-five vessels, to convey 1650 troops, together with transport-animals and supplies.

"The usual Egyptian delays have entirely thwarted my plans. No vessels have arrived from Cairo, as they only started on 29th August. Thus, rather than turn back, I started with a mutilated expedition without a *single transport animal.*" But although he started at such a disadvantage, his expedition was altogether a splendid one. He had all kinds of things to do—to make a canal in one place, to cut down the "sudd" in another, to warn Kutchuk Ali, a great Khartoum ivory and slave dealer, to send no more slaves down, and to punish the desertion of his soldiers. He discovered the Governor of Fashoda in the act of kidnapping slaves, for he found seventy-one slaves concealed in a boat, and eighty-four hidden and guarded on the shore; and he liberated the captives, to their great joy. This was followed by similar actions in other places.

Sir Samuel Baker explored the old White Nile, and at Gondokoro he officially annexed the country to Egypt, having invited all the head men to be present. The troops and artillery formed into a square round a flag-staff which was in the centre, and from the foot of which was read the official proclamation, which described the annexation of the country to Egypt, in the name of the Khedive. The Ottoman flag was then run up; after which the officers saluted it with drawn swords, the troops presented arms, and the artillery fire a royal salute. At dinner they had roast beef and plum pudding—the latter had been brought out in tins for Christmas day, but as it could not be found then, the author of *Ismailia* says it was added to the feast on the "day of annexation," and was "annexed accordingly by English appetites. This was washed down and rendered wholesome by a quantity of pure filtered water from the river Nile, which was included in the annexation, and was represented in the Nile Basin, mixed with Jamaica rum, sugar, nutmeg, and lemon-juice from the trees planted by the Austrian missionaries."

This regulation was posted :—

" No person shall trade in ivory, neither shall any person accept ivory as a present or in exchange; neither shall any person shoot, or cause to be shot, elephants : all ivory being the property and monopoly of the Government of His Highness the Khedive of Egypt.

" No person shall either purchase or receive slaves as presents or in exchange.

" Any person transgressing by disobedience of the above laws will be punished as the will of Baker Pasha may direct."

The new arrangements did not please the Baris, and force had to be used. Besides that, the cause they had at heart was hindered by Abou Saood, who had himself profited by the slave trade. The expedition suffered from scarcity of food, and from the half-heartedness of the troops, the treachery of the slave-hunters, and the opposition of the Baris who were constantly at war with them; but the brave commander kept ever before him his commission—he was to suppress the slave trade and annex the equatorial districts.

He had with him a body-guard of very fine men, which became famous as the " Forty Thieves " corps. These men were brave and valiant; and at the last, in spite of their name, so honest that they would scorn to commit a theft. They overcame innumerable difficulties; travelling south to Loboré, thence to the Shooa Mountain, and on through the " Paradise of Africa " to Fatiko, and thence to Unyoro and Masindi, about twenty miles from the Albert Nyanza. Here Baker set up a seat of government, and endeavoured to make the chief or king, Rabba Rega, understand that he must submit to the Khedive, and use his influence to establish a system of merchandise with the north, the route to which had now been opened. Unyoro was annexed to Egypt officially in the name of the Khedive on the 14th of May 1872. Every effort was made to cultivate the law, to establish commerce, to open a school, and to bring about improvements of many kinds. But the little party was continually in danger; the troops were poisoned, and a battle had to be fought at Masindi. Even that did not compel submission, or make the natives less treacherous. Baker himself had a narrow escape from a poisoned arrow, and the natives set several places on fire. At last Baker was compelled to leave the station and go on to Kionga. As they were preparing to march, and wondering what they were to do for food, Lady Baker awakened the gratitude of the whole expedition by showing a quantity of flour, which when it was plentiful, she had stored for a hungry day that might come. The discovery brought a shout of joy from the officers and men—" God shall give her a long life."

The story of the march of Sir Samuel Baker from

Masindi to Foweera, as told in *Ismailia*, is one of the most exciting that has ever been written. Every one should read it in order to understand the perils and the protection which attended the mission. At last the task was completed : and the brave Englishman had accomplished that which he had been sent to do He was thankful for peace, and rest, and victory. It was not his fault if, after he had suppressed the slave trade, the Government allowed it to be revived. He was able to say with satisfaction that he had "rendered the slave-trade of the White Nile impossible, so long as the Government is determined that it shall be impossible." And he gave up his commission in generous words when he said, "The Khedive of Egypt, having appointed Colonel Gordon, R.E., has proved his determination to continue the work that was commenced under so many difficulties. The Nile has been opened to navigation ; and if the troubles that I encountered and overcame shall have smoothed the path for my able and energetic successor, I shall have been well rewarded."

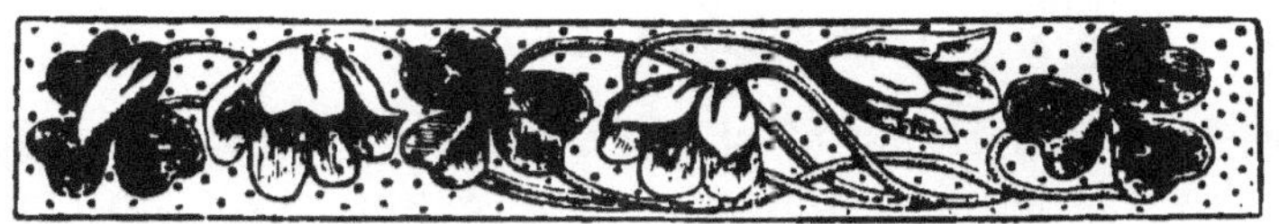

CHAPTER XVI.

THE SLAVE TRADE IN THE SOUDAN.

" We do pray for mercy,
And that same prayer doth teach us all to render
The deeds of mercy."

—Merchant of Venice.

E left Colonel Gordon at Gondokoro, but he only stayed there a few days. His luggage had not come, and he returned to Khartoum.

The latter town, Khartoum, which has a population of 25,000, is the capital of the Soudan. It lies at the junction of the Blue and White Niles. Khartoum, at that time, was said to live on what was called the White Nile Trade. Sir Samuel Baker thus described the town, and the slave trade connected with it, as they were at his first visit in 1863:—"Without the White Nile Trade," said Sir Samuel, "Khartoum would almost cease to exist; that trade is kidnapping and murder. The character of the Khartoumers needs no further comment.

"The amount of ivory brought down from the White Nile is a mere bagatelle as an export, the annual value being £40,000. The people for the most part engaged in the nefarious traffic of the White Nile are Syrians, Copts, Turks, Circassians, and some few *Europeans.* So closely connected with the difficulties of my expedition is that accursed slave-trade, that the so-called ivory trade of the White Nile requires an explanation.

"Throughout the Soudan money is exceedingly scarce, and the rate of interest exorbitant, varying, according to the securities, from thirty-six to eighty per cent.; this fact proves general poverty and dishonesty, and acts as a preventive to all improvement. So high and fatal a rate deters all honest enterprise, and the country must lie in ruin under such a system. The wild speculator borrows upon such terms, to rise suddenly like a rocket, or to fall like its exhausted stick.

"Thus, honest enterprise being impossible, dishonesty takes the lead, and a successful expedition to the White Nile is supposed to overcome all charges. There are two classes of White Nile traders—the one possessing capital, the other being penniless adventurers; the same system of operation is pursued by both, but that of the former will be evident from the description of the latter.

"A man without means forms an expedition, and borrows money for this purpose at one hundred per cent., after this fashion; he agrees to pay the lender in ivory, at one-half its market value. Having obtained the required sum, he hires several vessels, and engages from one hundred to three hundred men, composed of Arabs and runaway villains from distant countries, who have found an asylum from justice in the obscurity of Khartoum. He purchases guns and large quantities of ammunition for his men, together with a few hundred pounds of glass beads. The piratical expedition being complete, he pays his men five months' wages in advance, at the rate of forty-five piastres (nine shillings) per month, and agrees to give them eighty piastres per month for any period exceeding the five months advanced.

His men receive their advance partly in cash and partly in cotton stuffs for clothes, at an exorbitant price. Every man has a strip of paper, upon which is written, by the clerk of the expedition, the amount he has received, both in goods and money; and this paper he must produce at the final settlement.

"The vessels sail about December, and on arrival at the desired locality, the party disembark and proceed into the interior, until they arrive at the village of some negro chief, with whom they establish an intimacy. Charmed with his new friends, the power of whose weapons he acknowledges, the negro chief does not neglect the opportunity of seeking their alliance to attack a hostile neighbour. Marching throughout the night, guided by their negro hosts, they bivouac within an hour's march of the unsuspecting village doomed to an attack, about half-an-hour before the break of day. The time arrives, and quietly surrounding the village while its occupants are still sleeping, they fire the grass huts in all directions, and pour volleys of musketry through the flaming thatch. Panic-stricken, the unfortunate victims rush from their burning dwellings, and the men are shot down like pheasants in a battue, while the women and children, bewildered in the danger and confusion, are kidnapped and secured. The herds of cattle, still within their kraal, or 'zareeba,' are easily disposed of, and are driven off with great rejoicing as the prize of victory. The women and children are then fastened together, the former secured by an instrument called a sheba, made of a forked pole, the neck of the prisoner fitting into the fork, secured by a cross piece lashed behind, while the wrists, brough together in advance of the body, are tied to the pole. The children are then fastened by their necks with a rope attached to the women, and thus form a living chain, in which order they are marched to the head-quarters in company with the captured herds.

"This is the commencement of business; should there be ivory in any of the huts not destroyed by the fire, it is appropriated; a general plunder takes place. The trader's party dig up the floors of the huts to search for iron hoes, which are generally thus concealed, as the greatest treasure of the negroes; the granaries are overturned and wantonly destroyed, and the hands are cut off the bodies of the slain, the more easily to detach the copper or iron bracelets that are usually worn. With this booty, the *traders* return to their negro ally; they have thrashed and discomfited his enemy, which delights him; they present him with thirty or forty head of cattle, which intoxicates him with joy; and a present of a pretty little captive girl, of about fourteen, completes his happiness.

"But business is only commenced. The negro covets cattle, and the trader has now captured, perhaps, two thousand head. They are to be had for ivory, and shortly the tusks appear. Ivory is daily brought into camp in exchange for cattle, a tusk for a cow, according to its size— a profitable business, as the cows have cost nothing. The trade proves brisk, but still there remains some little customs to be observed—some slight formalities, well understood by the White Nile trade. The slaves and two-thirds of the captured cattle belong to the trader, but his men claim, as their perquisite, one-third of the stolen animals. These having been divided, the slaves are put up to public auction among the men, who purchase such as they require; the amount being entered on the papers (serki) of the purchasers, to be reckoned against their wages. To avoid the exposure, should the document fall into the hands of the Government or European consuls, the amount is not entered as for the purchase of a slave, but is divided for fictitious supplies. Thus, should a slave be purchased for one thousand piastres, that amount would appear on the document somewhat as follows :—

Soap ...	...	...	...	50	Piastres.
Tarboash (cap) ...	...	...	100	,,
Araki ...	...	...	...	500	,,
Shoes ...	...	...	...	200	,,
Cotton Cloth	...	...	...	150	,,

1000

" The slaves sold to the men are constantly being changed and resold among themselves; but should the relatives of the kidnapped women and children wish to ransom them, the trader takes them from his men, cancels the amount of purchase, and restores them to their relatives for a certain number of elephants' tusks, as may be agreed upon. Should any slave attempt to escape, she is punished either by brutal flogging, or shot, or hanged, as a warning to others. An attack, or razzia, such as described, generally leads to a quarrel with the negro ally, who, in his turn, is murdered and plundered by the trader—his women and children naturally becoming slaves. A good season for a party of a hundred and fifty men should produce about two hundred cantars (twenty thousand lbs.) of ivory, valued in Khartoum at four thousand pounds.

" The men being paid in slaves, the wages should be *nil*, and there should be a surplus of four or five hundred slaves for the trader's own profit—worth, on an average, five to six pounds each.

" The boats are accordingly packed with a human cargo, and a portion of the trader's men accompany them to the Soudan, while the remainder of the party form a camp or settlement in the country they have adopted, and industriously plunder, massacre, and enslave, until their master's return with boats from Khartoum in the following season, by which time they are supposed to have a cargo of slaves and ivory ready for shipment. The business thus thoroughly established, the slaves are landed at various points within a few days journey of Khartoum, at which places are agents, or purchasers, waiting to receive them with dollars prepared for cash payments.

"The purchasers and dealers are, for the most part, Arabs. The slaves are marched across the country to different places; many to Sennaar, where they are sold to other dealers, who sell them to the Arabs and Turks. Others are taken immense distances to ports on the Red Sea— Suakim, and Massowa—there to be shipped for Arabia and Persia. Many are sent to Cairo; and, in fact, they are disseminated throughout the slave-dealing east, the White Nile being the great nursery for the supply. The amiable trader returns from the White Nile to Khartoum; hands over to his creditor sufficient ivory to liquidate the original loan of £1,000; and already a man of capital, he commences as an independent trader."

The previous chapter has shown how Sir Samuel Baker resolutely set his face to abolish the trade which was so hateful to him.

He felt sure that the Khedive was sincere in his desire that it should be put down: how could he be otherwise? when he knew, not only as a humanitarian, but because he was acquainted with the sentiments of the Great Powers of Europe, that civilisation demanded the extinction of such horrors. But, of course, this could not be accomplished without great difficulty and loss; and it may be that Europe will yet have to speak out in unmistakable tones before the great evil is swept, as it ought to be, from the face of the Soudan.

"This latter thought the thing real, and found it a sham, and felt like a Gordon who had been humbugged," wrote Sir Samuel's successor, almost as soon as he had started on the expedition.

Gordon found that even when he visited Khartoum the difficulties which beset his predecessor were his also. The slave stations remained, and the slave trade was still carried on.

Gondokoro had been at some time a mission station. Baker found, during his first visit, that the ruins of the brick church and house were still remaining, and he could see where the garden had been. A few miserable grass huts were all that formed a town, and the ivory traders had possession of it. The natives of Gondokoro are the Bari. The men are tall, and the women plain-looking. Livingstone once said of some women he was describing:— " Many of the women were very pretty, and, like all ladies, would have been much prettier if they had only let themselves alone." The Bari women who live in Gondokoro are not pretty, but they do not let themselves alone. They shave their heads, and anoint themselves with an ochre made into a paste by an admixture of grease. All that they wear is a lappet made of beads, or small iron rings worked up like a coat of mail in front, and a tail of fine shreds of leather behind. These are fastened by a belt worn round the waist. Gondokoro was neither a healthy nor a pleasant town in which to reside. Sir Samuel Baker found that the Baris, who were warlike people, had been secured as allies by the slave-hunters, and were very valuable. "They were people," said he, in *Ismailia,* " by whom the blessings of a good government were hardly to be understood."

When Gordon was passing between Khartoum and Gondokoro he made acquaintance with the strange tribe called the Shillooks. These people have been already referred to. They were miserable enough as our hero found them ; but they had been a very powerful tribe— indeed the most powerful of the Blacks on the banks of the White Nile. Their dwellings are mud huts, thatched, having a very small entrance, looking at a distance like rows of button mushrooms. They navigate the river on their raft-like canoes, formed of the ambatch wood, which is so light that they can very easily carry their vessels about. The ambatch tree is about the thickness of a man's waist, and tapers to a point; it is, therefore, easily cut down, and several of them being lashed parallel to each other, and the ends tied together, the raft is made. It was supposed to carry two persons.

The Shillooks are shrewd traders, and they are industrious, being clever at agriculture, pasturage, fishing, and the chase. Their country is easily cultivated, because the soil is naturally fertile, and is benefited by rainy seasons, numerous canals, and the rising of the river. It is, indeed, more moist and less hot than most of the surrounding districts. They grow cotton, which, in its raw state, they are glad to exchange for cotton goods. They also cultivate large quantities of dhurra and maize. Their domestic animals are oxen, sheep, and goats; and they also keep poultry and dogs, especially dogs. The dogs are like our greyhounds in shape and our pointers in size. They are of a foxy red colour, with a long, black muzzle. They are so fleet that they outrun the gazelle, and so agile that they can spring over walls ten feet high, or leap over a space four times the length of their own bodies.

The male Shillooks do not wear clothing, but cover their bodies with ashes. They pay great attention to the arrangement of their hair. Dr. Schweinfurth says that "amongst the men the repeated application of clay, gum, or dung, so effectually clots the hair together, that it retains, as it were, voluntarily, the desired form; at one time like a comb, at another like a helmet, or it may be, like a fan. Many of the Shillook men present in this respect a great variety. A good many wear transversely across the skull a comb as broad as a man's hand, which, like a nimbus of tin, stretches from ear to ear, and terminates behind in two drooping circular lappets. Occasionally there are heads for which one comb does not suffice, and on these several combs, parallel to one another at small intervals, are arranged in lines. There is a third form, far from uncommon, than which nothing can be more grotesque. It may be compared to the crest of a guinea-fowl, of which it is an obvious imitation, just as among ourselves many a way of dressing the hair would seem to be designed by taking some animal form of a model."

The Shillooks greatly need some religious instruction. It seems as if they have some dim idea of God, for they speak of the Father of their race, and believe that his hand guided them to their place of abode, and gave them the land which they possess. They pray to him for a good harvest, and call upon him in their time of trouble, and perhaps hope that "the unknown God," whom they ignorantly worship, may pity and love them. They have old traditions and legends among them, and they imagine that their dead are still among them like ministering spirits.

Colonel Gordon was kind to the Shillooks, and soon made friends with them. Those that he saw at the entrance of the Saubat River were poor, and he gave them some grain for their present needs, and also some maize to plant.

He became acquainted about the same time with another curious tribe, that of the Dinkas. Their territory extends north and south of the river Saubat for nearly four hundred miles, and there embraces an area of nearly seventy thousand square miles.

Dr. Schweinfurth has an interesting chapter in his work, *The Heart of Africa*, on The Dinka, and he gives illustrations of "Dinka profiles," a "Dinka Dandy," Dinka instruments for parrying club-blows, a view of a Dinka cattle-park, and some pictures of the Dinka cattle.

The Dinka houses are curious little round huts, situated in a farm or park. They call them the murah, which means a resting-place, and has more reference to the animals

than the men. The Dinkas take great care of their cows.
There is a kitchen in the hut with a fire-place in it; a
screen of clay keeps the wind off. Goats are kept at
hand, in a space fenced off. Some of the huts are forty feet
in diameter ; their foundations are made of clay and straw,
chopped in small portions. The roof is made of acacia
wood and cut straw ; the buildings last for eight or ten
years. The Dinkas cultivate sorghum and penicillaria.

The Dinkas are very dark, chocolate-coloured, or bronze ;
they have long necks and wide jaws ; the men have their
heads shaven. They pierce their ears, and fasten in them
iron rings, or little bars of iron ; and the women bore the
upper lip, and fit in an iron pin running through a bead.
The men tattoo their foreheads and temples. The Dinkas
hold iron in very high estimation. The richer women are
often quite heavily laden with iron. Dr. Schweinfurth
declares that he has seen some of them carrying about on
their persons quite half-a-hundredweight of iron ornaments.
They wear immense iron rings on their ankles and wrists,
which clatter like the fetters of slaves. Men prefer ivory
rings, which they wear on the upper part of their arms.
Those who can afford to do so cover their arms with rings
of various sizes and kinds, which are put so that they touch
each other, and quite encase the arms. On the neck they
wear plaited leather, and bracelets made of the hide of the
hippopotami, and tails of cows and goats. The Dinka,
indeed, likes to ornament with these things not only his
person, but also the weapons which he uses. He has very
little hair on his head, and therefore does not dress it up as
the Shillooks do, so he makes a cap or head-piece of bugle
beads or ostrich feathers. When he loses a relative he goes
into mourning by wearing a cord round the neck.

The Dinkas use clubs and sticks in warfare, and they have
several kinds of shields, or instruments for parrying the
blows of clubs. "They are of two kinds. One consists of a

neatly carved piece of wood, rather more than a yard long, with a hollow in the centre, which protects the hand. They are called 'quayre.' The other, which has been mistaken for a bow, is termed 'dang,' of which the substantial fibres seem peculiarly fitted for breaking the violence of any blow."

The Dinkas are cleaner in their habits, and in the preparation of food, than most tribes. Dr. Schweinfurth thinks they are more intellectual and refined than any other tribe in Africa. Their farinaceous and milk foods are not inferior to those we use in England. They take great pains in the reaping, thrashing, and sifting of their grain. "In seasons of scarcity their talent for cooking has led them to the discovery of various novelties in the way of food." They behave well at the table; not dipping their hands in the dish all at once, but one at a time. A large dish of farinaceous food is placed in the centre. Each guest reclines around it, and has a gourd shell of milk or butter at his side. He pours milk on the portion he intends to take, and then passes it on to his neighbour.

Snakes are common among the Dinkas; indeed, they inhabit their huts, and are looked upon with friendliness, if not reverence. The Dinkas call them their brethren. The Dinkas make soup of turtles, and are very particular as to the kind of flesh they eat. They will not touch the flesh of the dog, but consider that of the cat to be a delicacy. They also greatly esteem the flesh of the hare.

It seems a very great pity that the Dinkas could not be left to themselves, to live their harmless lives as they pleased in their own country; but Sir Samuel Baker found a great change in the aspect of things when he went the second time to the Soudan.

"Although this country was exceedingly rich in soil, it was entirely uninhabited on one side (the east) of the river. This had formerly been the Dinka country; but it had been quite depopulated by razzias made for slaves by the former and present governors of Fashoda. These raids had been made on a large scale, with several thousand troops, in addition to the sharp slave-hunters, the Baggara Arabs, as allies. The result was almost the extermination of the tribe. It seemed incomprehensible to the Shillook natives that a Government that had lately made slave-hunting a profession should suddenly turn against the slave-hunters." *

Perhaps in this connection we may recall some words of Dr. Livingstone on the general results of slave-capturing :—

"I came near the party of Said-bin-habib, close to the point where a huge rent in the mountains of Rua allows the escape of the river Lualaba out of the Lake Moero ; and here I had, for the first time, an opportunity of observing the differences between slaves and freemen made captives. When fairly across Lualaba, Said thought his captives safe, and got rid of the trouble of attending to and watching the chained gang by taking off both chains and yoke. All declared their joy and perfect willingness to follow Said to the end of the world or elsewhere; but next morning twenty-two made clear off to the mountains. Many more, on seeing the broad Lualaba roll between them and the homes of their infancy, lost all heart, and in three days eight of them died. They had no complaint but pain in the heart, and they pointed out its seat correctly. This to me was the most startling death I ever saw. They evidently died of broken-heartedness, and the Arabs wondered, seeing that they had plenty to eat. I saw others perish, particularly a fine boy of ten or twelve years of age. When asked where he felt ill, he put his hand correctly and exactly over the heart. He was kindly carried, and as he breathed out his soul, was laid gently on the side of the path. The captors were not usually cruel ; they were callous—slavery had hardened their hearts.

* *Ismailia,* vol. i., p. 111.

"When Said, who was an old friend of mine, crossed the Lualaba, he heard that I was in a village where a company of slave traders had been previously assaulted for three days by justly-incensed Babemba. I would not fight, nor allow my people to fire, if I saw them, because the Babemba had been especially kind to me. Said sent a party of his own people to invite me to leave the village by night and come to him. He showed himself the opposite of hard-hearted; but *slavery hardens all within, and petrifies the feelings; it is hard for the victims, and hard for the victimisers.*

"I once saw a party of twelve who had been slaves in their own country—Lunda or Londa—of which Cazembe is chief in general. They were loaded with large, heavy, wooden yokes, which are forked trees, about three inches in diameter, and seven or eight feet long. The neck is inserted in the fork, and an iron bar driven in across from one end of the fork to the other, and riveted; the other end is tied at night to a tree, or to the ceiling of a hut, and the neck being firm in the fork, the slave is held off from unloosing it. It is excessively troublesome to the wearer, and when marching, two yokes are tied together by their free ends, and loads put on the slaves' heads besides. Women having, in addition to the yoke and load, a child on their back, have said to me in passing, 'They are killing me. If they would take off the yoke, I could manage the load and child; but I shall die with the loads.' One who spoke this did die, and the poor little girl, her child, perished of starvation. I interceded for some; but, when unyoked, off they bounded into the long grass, and I was greatly blamed for not caring to preserve the owner's property. After a day's march under a boiling vertical sun, with yokes and heavy loads, the strongest are exhausted.

"The party of twelve above-mentioned were sitting singing and laughing. 'Hallo,' said I, 'these fellows take to it kindly ; this must be the class for whom philosophers say slavery is the natural state ; ' and I went and asked the cause of their mirth.   I had to ask the aid of their owner as to the meaning of the word *rukha,* which usually means to fly or leap.   They were using it to express the idea of haunting, as a ghost, and inflicting disease and death and the song was, 'Yes, we are going away to Manga, abroad in the white man's land, with yokes on our necks but we shall have no yokes in death ; and we shall return to haunt and kill you.'   A chorus then struck in with the name of the man who had sold each of them, and then followed the general laugh, in which at first I saw no bitterness.   Peraube, an old man, had been one of the sellers.   In accordance with African belief, they had no doubt of being soon able, by ghost power, to kill even him. Their refrain might be rendered :—

> " ' Oh, oh, oh !
>   Bird of freedom, oh !
>   You sold me, oh, oh, oh !
>   I shall haunt you, oh, oh, oh !' "

Dr. Livingstone's books had been read by Colonel Gordon ; and his kind heart was again and again touched with pity for the slaves.   He related in one of his letters, in his own way, an incident which occurred during his stay at Saubat, which was so beautiful, that to read of it must have brought tears into the eyes that read the letter. It does not refer to a slave, but it reveals the heart of the man who had come to live among them.

Colonel Gordon's character is an illustration of the combination, in a remarkable degree, of both strength and tenderness.   The latter quality, which was so strongly brought into play at Gravesend, must have been filling his heart in his lonely life at Saubat.   "People are dull in England," he said ; "but, oh, dear me ! how dull they would be here."

But he relieved the tediousness of his life by gracious acts of mercy, as the following—which deserves to be written in gold—shows :—

"I took a poor old bag-of-bones into my camp a month ago, and have been feeding her up; but yesterday she was quietly taken off, and now knows all things. She had her tobacco up to the last, and died quietly. What a change from her misery! I suppose she filled her place in life as well as Queen Elizabeth. . . . . A wretched sister of yours is struggling up the road, but she is such a wisp of bones that the wind threatens to overthrow her; so she has halted, preferring the rain to being cast down. I verily believe she could never get up again. I have sent her some dhoora, which will produce a spark of joy in her black and withered carcass. She has not even a cotton gown on, and I do not think her apparel would be worth one-fiftieth part of a penny.

"*August* 4.—I am bound to give you the sequel of the lady whom I helped yesterday in the gale of wind. I had told my man to see her into one of the huts, and thought he had done so. The night was stormy and rainy, and when I awoke I heard often a crying of a child near my hut, within the enclosure. When I got up I went out to see what it was, and, passing through the gateway, I saw your and my sister lying dead in a pool of mud; her black brothers had been passing and passing, and had taken no notice of her. So I went and ordered her to be buried, and went on. In the midst of the high grass was a baby about a year or so old, left by itself. It had been out all night in the rain, and had been left by its mother—children are always a nuisance! I carried it in, and seeing the corpse was not moved, I sent again about it, and went with the men to have it buried. To my surprise and astonishment, she was alive. After some considerable trouble, I persuaded the black brothers to lift her out of the mud, poured some brandy down her throat, and got her into a hut with a fire, having the mud washed out of her sightless eyes. She was not more than sixteen years of age. There she now lies; I cannot help hoping she is floating down with the tide to her haven of rest. The babe is taken care of by another family for a certain consideration of maize per diem. I dare say you will see—in fact, I feel sure you will see—your black sister some day, and she will tell you about it, and how Infinite Wisdom directed the whole affair. I know this is a tough morsel to believe, *but it is true.* I prefer life amidst sorrows, if those sorrows are inevitable, to a life spent in inaction. Turn where you will, there are sorrow and troubles. Many a rich person is as unhappy and miserable as this ray of mortality, and to them you can minister. 'This mustard is very badly made,' was the remark of one of my staff some time ago, when some of our brothers were stalking about showing every bone in their poor bodies."

"*August* 5.—The Rag is still alive. The babe, who is not a year old, seized a gourd of milk and drank it off like a man last night, and is apparently in for the pilgrimage of life. It does not seem the worse for its night out—depraved little wretch."

"*August* 5.—Just a line. Your black sister departed this life at four P.M., deeply lamented by me."

The humour and tenderness of the man are well exhibited in this letter. As for the strength of mind, promptness of action, and uncompromising hatred of slavery, which he also possesses, they were brought into play as soon as he reached the Soudan.

He had gone to put down slavery, and of course he meant to do it as far as it was in his power.

He was not long in making the discovery that slave-trading was carried on; and when Nassar, a slave dealer, whose practices were reported to him, came upon the scene, he promptly arrested him. He said that Nassar was a miserable creature, but he had one good point, for "when he was taken to prison he prayed very fervently, with the knowledge that God could help him."

CHAPTER XVII.

HURRIYAT (LIBERTY).

" There is a kind of character in thy life
That to the observer doth thy history
Fully unfold."
—Measure for Measure.

COLONEL GORDON had not been long in the country of the Blacks before many of his staff fell ill; and he expressed himself very glad to have for his body-guard Baker's Forty Thieves. He declared that he had made it known that the motto of the province was Hurriyat—which means liberty; and that in regard to the expedition and his management, those who did not like it were at liberty to leave it. But his people had no license to do wrong; and he soon discovered that Abou Saood, whom he had been disposed to trust, was altogether untrustworthy.

Sir Samuel Baker had known this all along, and was surprised and pained by his appointment; for Abou Saood had been the greatest slave-hunter of the White Nile, and almost the most troublesome man with whom he had had to deal. He was the representative of the great firm of traders, Agād & Oo.; and he was "the *incarnation of the slave trade.*" It was he who attempted to poison Baker and his men, and he who had urged Kabba Rega to attack them. He set false reports afloat concerning the expedition again and again. He intrigued to thwart all efforts to suppress the slave trade, at the same time that he cringingly professed to be anxious to assist the Government. He swore eternal fidelity to Baker at the same time that his station was crowded with slaves. At last he had the effrontery to appeal to the Egyptian Government for protection against any interference with his trade, which was really that of kidnapping and murdering the slaves, and stealing their goods. The slave trader must have been really backed by the authority of some high personage, notwithstanding the fact that the Khedive had sent out an expedition to abolish the slave trade. The Khedive promised that he would have Abou Saood judged by a special tribunal, for the purpose of which Baker Pasha handed to Nubar Pasha seventeen documents; but he was released without a trial. Three vessels, containing seven hundred slaves, which belonged to him, were captured; and yet he became an assistant of the man who hoped, above all things, to be able to abolish slavery. But Gordon's suspicions were aroused by finding that Abou had stolen some of the Government ivory, and grossly deceived him on several occasions. He had treated him fairly and kindly enough, but his kindness did not avail to keep the man from double-dealing and robbery, nor from conniving at the slave trade. So Colonel Gordon saw that there was nothing to do but to let him go altogether; and he accordingly dismissed him. This was not done too soon, for it became evident that the treacherous man was trying, not only to circumvent Gordon's plans in every possible way, but to have his life taken also.

From Sobat River Colonel Gordon had now removed to

Gondokoro, and from thence to Rageef. Here he had many things to trouble him. Already he had been compelled to make acquaintance with some people of the Niam Niam tribe. These are mentioned both by Petherick and Schweinfurth. Very strange tales were at one time in circulation respecting them. An Italian discoverer—Piaggia—went to live among them for a year, in order to enlighten the world respecting them, which he did by means of an interesting book. The name Niam Niam signifies great eaters, and has especial reference to the fact of their being cannibals. They are exceedingly curious people, and seem to occupy a place in creation that is altogether unique. They have round, broad heads, and thick, frizzy hair, which is long, and which they wear plaited. They have large, full, almond-shaped eyes, with a wide space between them, and their eyebrows are thick and large. Their noses are flat and square, the chin is round, the mouth has thick lips. The body is longer than the legs, and the Niam Niam are rather inclined to stoutness. They are not as black as the Nubian; they are chocolate coloured. They tattoo their faces, and have a kind of cross tattooed on the breast. When they want to be particularly smart on their gala days, they colour their bodies with red and black. If they dress at all, they wear a skin fastened across the loins, and they like to wear a monkey's tail as a sort of finish.

The men are far more particular in regard to their hair than the women ; they dress it up into all sorts of forms, and part it in the middle. Then they gather it up into rolls and curls, and long plaits and tufts. They spend more time every day in dressing their heads than even an English girl who wants to look her best for her first ball. The men wear a fringe over their foreheads—but the fringe is made of dogs' teeth. The Niam Niam fight with lances and trumbashes—a boomerang—made of iron. They have a shield of Spanish reeds woven together, and the trumbash is carried inside of it. These shields are very light, although they are large enough to cover more than half the body. They also use sharp knives with sickle-like blades. The farm-work of the Niam Niam is done by the women; the men occupy themselves with the chase. The land is exceedingly fertile, and the agricultural work is much more easy among them than among most of the tribes. The grain they use most is the *eleusine coracana*, of which they make not only bread but beer. They also grow the manioc, sweet potato, yam, and colocasiæ. They smoke gundy— a kind of tobacco—and use clay pipes, with long bowls and no stems. Poultry and dogs are the only domestic animals, and the latter wear bells round their necks. The dog's flesh is eaten, and considered a great delicacy. Their name, Niam Niam, is not wrongly given. The pure air of their country makes them hungry, and they have always a stock of provisions near. They are like some English people, who cannot take a railway journey but they must feed all the way; the Niam Niam carry a little basket of provisions with them wherever they go; and they have little boxes fixed up outside the houses, and in all convenient places, where food is kept at hand, from which they constantly help themselves. Meat—or as they call it, pushujoh—is liked by them more than any other kind of food; and, alas! most of them enjoy eating human flesh.

The houses of the Niam Niam are made of clay, and all have conical roofs. Separate huts are used for sleeping and cooking purposes. Sometimes they ornament the points of their houses with a wisp of straw, into which they occasionally weave snail-shells; and they now and then make a cross on them of some coloured materials. They are able to do a little work in iron and pottery; indeed they are clever at the latter. Their drinking cups are pretty, and their water flasks are well made. They take great pains in making their pipes look well. They carve wood; some of their dishes and basins, as well as their stools, are beautifully carved. Their mode of greeting is peculiar. They extend their right hands, and so join them as to make the two middle fingers crack, and they nod at each other and wave their hands in very curious fashion. The men greet each other when they meet, but the women are very retiring. A woman's duties consist in "cultivating the homestead, preparing the daily meals, painting her husband's body, and dressing his hair." They are very fond of music; Piaggia thinks that great eaters though they are, they would go without food at any time to listen to sweet sounds. They have several kinds of oracles which they consult, to try to discover whether success will attend them in war or hunting; but though they have the form of the cross on some of their instruments and buildings, and even seem to regard it with some superstition, they have no knowledge of the true God and His Son Jesus Christ.

Colonel Gordon said that the Niam Niam ladies wore a bunch of leaves for full dress.

While he was at Rageef he tried to teach the chiefs how to use money. He made a shop, and sold beads. He bought a tusk of one, who wanted in exchange two bells; but Gordon gave him two dollars for the tusk, and then sold the bells for a dollar each. The people seemed to like it, and to take to it easily. Gordon also amused the soldiers by showing them a magic lantern. He introduced piece-work instead of day work among them, and thus made them more industrious and self-reliant.

While he was at Rageef he ordered the men to make a mosque and keep their Ramadan. The name is that of the ninth month in the Mohammedan year. It was in this month that the prophet received his first revelation. It happened to come at an inconvenient time to Baker, but Gordon was able to spare the men that they might attend

to its requirements. The " Faithful " are supposed to keep
a strict fast from dawn to sunset—when a white thread
can be distinguished from a black one. Eating, drinking,
smoking, bathing, smelling perfumes, and other bodily
enjoyments, are strictly prohibited during that period.
Even when obliged to take medicine, the Moslem must make
some kind of amends for it, such as spending a certain sum of
money among the poor. During the night, however, permission is given them by the Koran to take what is
necessary, and then they are very apt to make up by
indulgence for their fasting during the day. But it is
sometimes a very severe infliction upon those who wish to
observe it religiously, especially when the month—which is
lunar—falls upon the long, hot days of midsummer. In
time of war, or when travelling on long journeys, they may
postpone the fast, but they must not omit it altogether;
and there are exemptions allowed in cases where the fast
would prove really injurious.

There is a tradition to the effect that not only Mohamed,
but also Abraham, Moses, and Jesus, received each their
revelations during the month of Ramadan.

Towards the end of October Colonel Gordon went to
Gondokoro, where he remained until after Christmas. He
made friends with the tribes all around, who soon learned
to trust him. The Khedive wrote to him to stop the slave
trade, and he answered that he would like to do so, by
using summary measures with the Khartoum merchants
themselves.

In January 1875 he went to Lardo. He was anxious
to bring the stations for the government of which he was
responsible in more direct communication. It took six
months, and required a band of one hundred men, to get news
from one station to another. The Khedive wished his flag to
be placed on the Albert Nyanza; and Gordon asked him to
allow him to establish fortified posts, a day's journey apart.

But he had some trouble with the Sheikh Bedden, a Bari chief, to whom Baker had made a present of a blue shirt and a grand dress of gold and silver tissue; but who afterwards treated him with great treachery, refusing to allow his people to carry the travellers' baggage, though he had previously engaged to do so. Gordon on his arrival sent a present to Bedden, whose territory was very near the district in which he had settled; but the messenger brought back the threat that the next man who went to him would be killed. It was necessary to do something with Bedden in order to make him understand that he must not molest the Government station; and so it was decided to take his cattle. Accordingly they went to his zeriba—the cattle enclosure of the sheikh—and took two thousand head of cattle; "so that," wrote Gordon, "without any effusion of blood on either side, or burning of villages, we punished Bedden severely." He added, "I hope Bedden and Lococo will both submit before many days are over. I do most cordially hate this work; but the question is, What are you to do? You must protect your own people, and also the friendly sheikhs, and you cannot make them give in except by the capture of their cattle."

Bedden came to him afterwards; and then he gave him back twenty of his cows, and also a present of some copper, and a pair of scissors. Poor old Bedden was blind, and not now capable of doing so much harm as his son.

Gordon was interested in everything he saw. He shot two hippopotami. He thought it was too bad to do it, but the people wanted food, and there was as much meat in one of these as in twenty cows. The hippopotamus is found all over Africa, and nowhere else. It is almost as large as the elephant, is aquatic in its habits, and can be found in rivers, lakes, and estuaries. Its skin is two inches thick on the back and sides. Its colour is dark brown, and it has no hair. It has a large head and small eyes and ears. It breathes very slowly, and can keep under water for a long time. It eats the weeds that grow at the bottom or on the banks of shallow streams. The fat of the hippopotamus is exceedingly nice. It is salted, and at the Cape of Good Hope can be bought as our bacon is in England, and is liked quite as well. It is called there Zee-roe-speck, which means "Lake-cow-bacon." The tongue is a delicacy, and there is a very good and nourishing jelly made of its feet. The hide is useful, and the teeth are valuable ivory, for which there is always a good sale.

On one occasion Colonel Gordon secured the friendliness of one of the tribes by giving them some of the flesh of the hippopotamus—a delicacy which they could not resist.

Gordon was anxious to make stations between Rageef and Duffli. He began to feel that time was getting on, and he had not accomplished what he wished. He wanted to know how to get his steamers up the Nile above the cataracts; he tried with nuggars—the usual Nile boats already described. He started toward Labore, and then went to Kerri. After various difficulties and dangers, and experiences of many kinds, he got the nuggars up the dangerous currents. "It is the violent eddies which are so terrible. The slightest faltering in the haulers would be fatal. We have about sixty or eighty black satin-skinned natives hauling on each boat. Your brother prays the nuggars up as he used to do the troops when they wavered in the breaches in China; but often and often the ropes break, and it all has to be done over again." A nuggar got lost and floated away. They had many hindrances, but at last reached Labore. He felt sometimes that his work was not a very great one. "What is the work? The placing of a chain of posts along a river, and the hauling-up of some boats over rocky channels." Yet the small work—very difficult and dangerous, though small—might lead to great ends; and, in any case, Charles

Gordon would obey the command of his Master, whom he served in the Soudan as in China or Gravesend: "Whatsoever thy hand findeth to do, do it with thy might."

On 28th August he established a station to which he gave the name Moogie. He was joined by Linant, who had just come from Mtesa's county, where he had met Stanley. Gordon was interested in finding that some magicians were cursing him very earnestly, and he thought this boded no good; so he sent a few shots among them, which stopped the magic quite suddenly. The natives soon after made an attack on the party. Linant, who wanted to go and burn their houses in order to teach them better, was set upon by them and killed. Gordon had given him a red shirt, and this shirt seemed to annoy them. The commander of the expedition had, with a very mournful heart, to write to the bereaved father of Linant, and tell him that his son was dead. This was the second son he had lost; one died at Gondokoro.

The Mudir of Fatiko joined Gordon on the last day of August, bringing 500 men with him; so that the brave commander was able to rest a little and to doctor himself, for by this time he was feeling far from well; he had got his feet wet on several occasions, and his liver was out of order. He had some Niam Niam warriors on his side now; and with those he fought the Baris, who were continually attacking him. As far as the finances of his expedition were concerned, he had been very successful, for he had sent £48,000 to the Khedive, and had by him £60,000 worth of ivory.

In September he set himself to collect the taxes from the natives, or to make raids on them. The result was 200 cows and 1,500 sheep. A daughter of one of the hostile shiekhs was taken; but Gordon sent to say her father could have his daughter back again if he promised submission. There was intense excitement among the people; and in the midst of it the over-worked man at the head of affairs was glad to welcome a good officer—Nuehr Agha, from Fatiko. On the 15th September he was able to say he believed he had only one hostile tribe on the left bank of the Nile, between Moogie and Makadé.

After the usual delays and difficulties, his steamer was got off, and they went from Moogie to Labore. He had resolved not only to make the stations, but to well equip them. The Arabs tried his patience exceedingly. He was so quick, and they were so indescribably lazy. From Labore they went to Duffli, where he stayed a fortnight. He had ague there; so he crossed the river, and took up his station at Fashelie, though he thought his illness was caused more by the carelessness of his servants than the air or the water. The place was healthy and quiet, and he (Gordon) had the pleasure of feeling that he had done good work by opening a road. He wanted to subdue the Moogie tribe completely before he left; and although a complaining letter from the Khedive made him half inclined to throw up his commission, he decided, after hearing again from the Khedive, to remain and complete his work.

With the end of the year he came to the conclusion that it was not his work to explore the Lake Nyanza. He was so pressed with other work that he declared he was not concerned as to whether there were two lakes or a million, or whether the Nile had a source or not.

He would leave the Albert, and try to go to the Victoria Nyanza. He resolved, therefore, as soon as possible, to make for the South. His heart was often very sad. The people among whom and for whom he worked disappointed him greatly. "I am not," he wrote, "after nine months of worry, in a fit state to explore anything but my way out of the province." But he had accomplished a good year's work, little and disappointing as it appeared to himself.

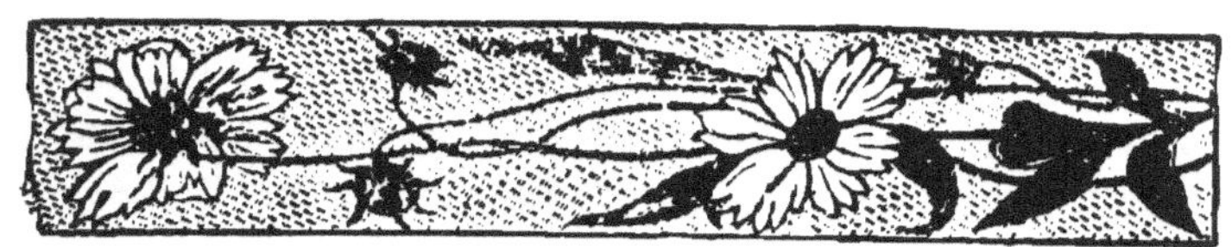

CHAPTER XVIII.

NEAR KING MTESA'S LAND.

" What thou would'st highly,
That would'st thou holily : would'st not play false."
—*Macbeth*.

ON the 2nd of January 1876 Colonel Gordon reached Fatiko. The New Year did not begin with very good promise, for although he reports himself as able to walk fourteen miles a-day, he suffered considerably from pain and fatigue. From Fatiko he went to Foweira, which was reached after a most uncomfortable march. The road by which they travelled was one along which a troop of elephants had lately come ; and the big, unwieldy creatures—so interesting in English menageries, so common in Africa—had made great holes in the road with their heavy feet, and trodden down the trees, leaving them in the paths, so that the clothes of the travellers were torn to pieces by them. The Colonel had more than a little difficulty with Baker's old enemy, Kabba Rega, whom Sir Samuel had deposed, setting in his place Rionga—by far the better man of the two. Rionga was a favourite with the natives, and a man who

had been much persecuted by Kabba Rega. Gordon received Rionga, and assisted him into his rightful place at Mrooli, "a miserable country, full of mosquitoes." Kabba Rega was at Masindi, and when he heard what Gordon had done he fled, taking with him "the magic stool," the throne of the kings of Unyoro, to which was attached so much importance, that the people believed the loss of it would mean the loss of all the authority of the kings. The throne was a very small piece of furniture, made partly of copper and partly of wood.

In March 1876 Colonel Gordon had a letter from Mtesa, the powerful king of Uganda, the country on the shore of the Victoria Nyanza. This man had been much written about during the preceding years ; and the facsimile of his letter is not the least interesting thing in Dr. Birkbeck Hill's book, *Colonel Gordon in Central Africa.* Mtesa, as was only natural, resisted the advance of the Egyptians towards his territory. He said he wanted to be a friend to the English, but he certainly did not want an Englishman to bring Egyptian troops nearer to him than they already were.

The year before this, Henry Stanley, the gallant American, who went to the help of Livingstone, and has subsequently made his name as famous as that of any discoverer, visited Mtesa, and wrote the following account of his visit for the London *Daily Telegraph* :—

"Mtesa is about thirty-four years old, and tall and slender in build, as I have already stated, but with broad shoulders. His face is very agreeable and pleasant, and indicates intelligence and mildness. His eyes are large, his nose and mouth are a great improvement upon those of the common type of negro, and approach to the same features in the Muscat Arab, when slightly tinted with negro blood. His teeth are splendid and gleaming white. As soon as Mtesa began to speak, I became captivated by his manner, for there was much of the polish of a true gentleman about it—it was at once amiable, graceful, and friendly.   It tended to assure me that in this potentate I had found a friend, a generous king, and an intelligent ruler.   He is not personally inferior to Seyd Burghash, the Arab Sultan of Zanzibar, and, indeed, appears to me quite like a coloured gentleman who has visited European courts, and caught a certain ease and refinement of manner, with a large amount of information.   If you will recollect, however, that Mtesa is a native of Central Africa, and that he had seen but three white men until I came, you will perhaps be as much astonished at all this as I was.   And if you will but think of the enormous extent of country he rules, extending from E. long. 34° to E. long. 31°, and from N. lat. 1° to S. lat. 3° 30', you will further perceive the immense influence he could wield towards the civilisation of Africa.   Indeed, I could not regard this king, or look at him in any other light than as the possible Ethelbert, by whose means the light of the gospel may be brought to benighted Middle Africa.

"Undoubtedly, the Mtesa of to-day is vastly superior to the vain youth whom Speke and Grant saw.   There is now no daily butchery of men and women ; seldom one suffers the extreme punishment.   Speke and Grant left him a raw, vain youth, and a heathen.   He is now a gentleman, and, professing Islamism, submits to other laws than his own erratic will, which we are told led to such severe and fatal consequences.   All his captains and chief officers observe the same creed, dress in Arab costume, and in other ways affect Arab customs.   He has a guard of two hundred men— renegadoes from Baker's expedition, Zanzibar defalcators, a few Amini, and the elect of Uganda.   Behind his throne— an arm-chair of native manufacture—the royal shield-bearers, lance-bearers, and gun-bearers, stand erect and staid.   On either side of him are his grand chiefs and courtiers, sons of governors of his provinces, chiefs of districts, etc. Outside the audience house the lengthy lines of warriors begin with the chief drummer and the noisy goma-beaters; next come the screaming fifers, the flag and banner-bearers, the fusiliers, and so on, seemingly *ad infinitum*, with spearmen and attendants.

"Mtesa is a great king. He is a monarch who would delight the soul of any intelligent European, as he would see in his black Majesty the hope of Central Africa. He is King of Karagwe, Uganda, Umagoro, Usoga, and Usui. Each day I found something which increased my esteem and respect for him. He is fond of imitating Europeans and what he has heard of their great personages, which trait, with a little tuition, would prove of immense benefit to his country. He has prepared broad highways in the neighbourhood of his capital for the good time that is coming when some charitable European will send him any kind of a wheeled vehicle. As we approached the capital, the main road from Usavara increased in width from twenty feet to one hundred and fifty feet. When we arrived at this magnificent breadth we viewed the capital crowning an eminence commanding a most extensive view of a picturesque and rich country, all teeming with gardens, of plantations, and bananas, and beautiful pasture land. Of course, huts, however large, lend but little attraction to a scene; but a tall flag-staff, and an immense flag, proved a decided feature in the landscape. Arrived at the capital, I found that the vast collection of buildings crowning the eminence were the royal quarters, round which ran five several palisades and circular courts, between which and the city was a circular road, ranging from one hundred to two hundred feet in width, and from this radiated six or seven imposing avenues lined with gardens and huts. The next day after arrival I was introduced to the royal palace in great state.

"Now, until I arrived at Mtesa's court, the king delighted in the idea that he was a follower of Islam; but, by one conversation, I flatter myself that I have tumbled the newly-raised religious fabric to the ground, and if it were only followed by the arrival of a Christian mission here, the conversion of Mtesa and his court to Christianity would, I think, be complete. I have, indeed, undermined Islamism so much here, that Mtesa has determined henceforth, until he is better informed, to observe the Christian Sabbath as well as the Moslem Sabbath, and the great captains have unanimously consented to this. He has further caused the ten commandments of Moses to be written on a board for his daily perusal—for Mtesa can read Arabic—as well as the Lord's Prayer and the golden commandment of our Saviour, 'Thou shalt love thy neighbour as thyself.' This is great progress for the few days that I have remained with him; and, though I am no missionary, I shall begin to think that I might become one, if such success is feasible. But, oh, that some pious, practical missionary would come here! What a field and a harvest ripe for the sickle of civilisation! Mtesa would give him anything he desired—houses, lands, cattle, ivory, etc.; he might call a province his own in one day.

"It is not the mere preacher, however, that is wanted here. The Bishops of Great Britain collected, with all the classic youth of Oxford and Cambridge, would effect nothing by mere talk with the intelligent people Uganda. It is the practical Christian tutor, who can teach the people how to become Christians, cure their diseases, construct dwellings, understand and exemplify agriculture, and turn his hand to anything, like a sailor—this is the man who is wanted. Such an one, if he can be found, would become the saviour of Africa. He must be tied to no church or sect, but profess God and His Son and the moral law, and live a blameless Christian, inspired by liberal principles, charity to all men, and devout faith in heaven. He must belong to no nation in particular, but the entire white race. Such a man, or men, Mtesa, King of Uganda, Usoga, Umgoro, and Karagwe—a kingdom three hundred and sixty geographical miles in length, by fifty in breadth—invites to repair to him. He has begged me to tell the white men that if they will only come to him he will give them all they want. Now, where is there in all the Pagan world a more promising field for a mission than Uganda? Colonel Linant de Bellefonds is my witness that I speak the truth, and I know he will corroborate all I say. The Colonel, though a Frenchman, is a Calvinist, and has become as ardent a well-wisher for the Waganda as I am."

The Colonel Linant mentioned here was the one already referred to. Colonel Gordon was himself much interested in Mtesa. He once wrote, " The glory of Mtesa's conversion would lead to other things ; but these tribes, and this slow, dull life, would need a self-abnegation which would be difficult to find."

Mtesa did not appeal for missionaries in vain ; for when Stanley's letter reached England a gentleman offered £5000 to the Church Missionary Society as a beginning of the good work.

On 19th March, Gessi Romulus (Gessi Pasha), one of the most illustrious members of Gordon's staff, left him to go to Magungo and the Lakes, while Gordon went to Lardo and Kerri. He had at that time the satisfaction of feeling that he had established stations all along the line from Duffli to Lardo—these two stations being termini, and having between them the important main stations, Laboré and Kerri ; besides Rageef, Bedden, Moogie, and Tyoo.

It had not been easy to accomplish all this. He had made many journeys and met with many adventures. On one occasion, when he was assisting a boatman to pass a rope across the river, the rope slipped and dragged him into the water. A man who sprang in to rescue him got his dress over his head, and looked, Gordon said, "like the veiled prophet of Khorassan." Both were saved, and almost the next day Gordon was again in danger from a whip-snake. But nothing was permitted to harm him; and the dangers which he saw only made him feel the more certain of the Divine protection. Wherever he was, by the African lakes and rivers, as well as in the midst of the Tai-pings of China, there was ever an undertone of solemn music sounding in his heart.

"*He that dwelleth in the secret place of the Most High shall abide under the shadow of the Almighty. Surely He shall deliver thee from the snare of the fowler and from the noisome pestilence; thou shalt not be afraid for the terror by night, nor for the arrow that flieth by day, nor for the pestilence that walketh in darkness, nor for the destructions that wasteth at noonday. A thousand shall fall at thy side, and ten thousand at thy right hand, but it shall not come nigh thee. Because thou hast made the Lord thy habitation there shall no evil befall thee, neither shall any plague come nigh thy dwelling. For He shall give His angels charge over thee, to keep thee in all thy ways.*"

One of Colonel Gordon's pleasures at this time was that of reading Dr. Schweinfurth's *Heart of Africa*. He said that he envied his love of botany. He himself grew restless under the inaction which seemed perfectly agreeable to the Egyptian garrison. He described the country as very beautiful. "Such glorious glades of forest, and away north of the tail of the Neri Hills there is such an expanse of fine land quite unexplored. No one knows what tribes are living here." He was amused by the children; indeed they always interested him. "The children of the natives are quite extraordinary; at a year old they walk, and carry gourds of water. They are fearfully op-heavy—*i.e.*, their heads are enormous, and at a distance hey are like regular tadpoles. Their heads and stomachs are *they;* their legs and arms are merely antennæ to them."

His friend Gessi returned on the 2nd of May, having gone round the Victoria Nyanza in nine days. He had been in a terrible storm, which had swept over the lake and driven him into dangerous quarters with Kabba Rega's men. Such a storm can scarcely be imagined in England. The drops of rain were as big as a dollar, and the waves so tumultuous that almost everyone was ill, and quite everyone was frightened. The Arab sailors declared that nothing should ever induce them to go to that lake again as long as they lived. The natives had been very much afraid of Gessi, for they thought he was a fiend; they would hold no converse with the sailors until he had gone away.

Colonel Gordon was at this time longing for the steamer to come and take him away. He went from Kerri to Lardo to look for it, and try to hasten its preparation. On his return to Kerri he had another narrow escape. A heavy thunderstorm set in, and, while he was adjusting the side of his wet tent, he was struck by a flash of lightning, and received two rather severe shocks. But although these things showed him how near he was to danger, nothing was suffered to hurt him. The letters that he wrote at this time are very beautiful. He was sometimes prevented by circumstances from carrying out the plans that he had laid; but always he yielded to any necessary change, feeling that God overruled everything.

" I feel that I have a mission here (not taken in its usual sense)," he wrote in July. " The men and officers like my justice, candour, and outbursts of temper, and they see that I am not a tyrant. Over two years we have lived intimately together, and they watch me closely. I am glad they do so. My wish and desire is that all should be as happy as it rests with me to make them ; and though I feel sure that I am unjust sometimes, it is not the rule with me to be so. I care for their marches, for their wants and food, and protect their women and boys if they ill-treat them—*and I do nothing of this. I am a chisel which cuts the wood—the carpenter directs it.*"

Colonel Gordon had said that he did not care to enter upon the work of geographical discoveries; but the reading of Dr. Schweinfurth's book had made him greatly desire to assist a little in exploring the wonderful district into which Providence had sent him; and in July we find him *en route* to Magungo, in order to traverse the seventy miles between that place and Foweira. Dr. Schweinfurth said, "It may be that Lake Albert belongs to the Nile Basin, but it is not a settled fact, for there are seventy miles between Foweira and Lake Albert never explored, and one is not authorised in making the Nile leave Lake Albert. The question is very doubtful."

Colonel Gordon set himself to settle the question, and on 5th August he dates his letter from *three miles west of the Murchison Falls.* The task was one of exceeding difficulty, but he accomplished it, and proved that if that had been his mission, he had in him plenty of the stuff of which the greatest discoverers are made. It was an awful task—eighteen miles of jungle, fifteen miles of ravines, and gullies, and rain, eight miles through fearful grass. "To-day and half of yesterday we had no path, but have had to force our way through the jungle. It has been terrible work, for what with wild vines, and convolvuli and other creepers, you sometimes got bound hand and foot. I have had several severe falls."

Toward the end of August he was at Mrooli, and began to turn his thoughts toward home. He had been absent three years—"a very long three years without a Sunday." He had to give up one scheme which he had formed—namely, to explore that portion of the Nile from Urundogani to Nyamyongo. That was the only bit of the Nile from Berber to Victoria that he had not traversed. But he knew it was not wise to attempt it then ; and so he left his personal feelings out of the question, and gave up the idea, the more readily, as he confessed, because if he did not do it he would the sooner reach his home.

He had yet another peril to pass through, for the troops that he had left at Masindi had moved away. They did not meet him as they had been ordered to do; and Kabba Rega's men were uncomfortably near him ; but Kabba went off to the Lake as they approached, and Gordon was able to take all his men and the sick who were with him safely away.

Before he left he organised a force to go and fight Kabba Rega. The soldiers did as the Colonel wished them ; but the man, although he lost a good many cattle, managed to get back to his country when the troops had left.

Colonel Gordon then went to Kerotos, Magungo, and Chibero, and on the 29th October he had reached Khartoum. It seemed like coming home. He was pleased to see English sparrows there. He reached Cairo on the 2nd of December; and hastening homeward, he arrived in London on the 24th of December, in time to spend Christmas Day with the dear friends whom he had not seen for three years.

CHAPTER XIX.

IN ABYSSINIA.

" Men of merit are sought after : the undeserver
May sleep when the man of action is called on."
—*Henry IV.*

HEN away in the Soudan, Colonel Gordon had often relieved the tedium of his weary days by thinking of home, and the leisures and comforts of a quiet life in England. But he was not long allowed to rest. "Men of merit are sought after," said Shakespeare; and as soon as it was known that Gordon had come home, it seemed that he was wanted in several places at once. Britain is often in difficulties of some kind, and there is always plenty of work for hands that are able and willing.

When Gordon came home at the time of Christmas 1876, English eyes were turned to Bulgaria, for terrible news had come from thence of atrocities, and cruelties, and wholesale massacres. A man was needed—a man who was a hero— who would be wise, and clever, and strong for the work in hand. And soon there were whispers in many quarters such as these: "Gordon is at home; he has finished his work in Egypt; he is the man for the hour." The *Times* especially directed attention to the Colonel and his work. "Surely," it was said in that paper, "his genius for government and command might be utilised for his own Government as well as for the Khedive. If the jealousies of the Powers would permit him to be made Governor of Bulgaria, he would soon make that province as beautiful as an English county." And there was a good deal of correspondence on the subject.

But would Gordon be willing? Had he really finished the work that had been given him to do in the Soudan?

To that question he would himself have replied in the negative. However others might praise him, he felt that he had accomplished but little.

And the reason was, that he had been thwarted and hindered by the Khedive's own Government.

He had been told to abolish slavery in the Soudan; but the Governor-General of the Soudan, the Khedive's own representative, Ismail Pasha Yacoub, nad allowed Khartoum, the capital of the Soudan and the seat of government, to remain the head-quarters of the slave system. Gordon frequently felt that he was in an exceedingly ambiguous position, and this had hindered him in accomplishing much of the work on which his heart had been set. "I am almost inclined not to go back," he said; but he wanted to be quite sure as to what was his duty in the matter. He was determined not to return on the same footing as before. He would not go and exert his power to suppress the slave trade with the knowledge that another, also high in power, would encourage it. Rather than submit to a repetition of former troubles and disappointments, he would throw up the expedition entirely. But the Khedive would not hear of his doing this. He was too sensible of the marvellous results of Gordon's endeavours to be at all willing to lose the services of such a man. Eventually Gordon went to

Cairo to consult with the Khedive, who asked him to become himself the Governor-General of the Soudan. Under such circumstances, assured that now he would have no one to hinder him in his work and thwart his designs, he readily agreed to return. He was to have to assist him—for the work was too great for any one man—three deputy-governors.

Now, as before, General Gordon was to direct his attention to the two great duties which had occupied him previously. He was to suppress the slave trade, and improve the means of communication in the Soudan. But besides these, a new responsibility was put upon him. He was, at the Khedive's request, to act as mediator between Egypt and Abyssinia, the two countries being then engaged in dispute.

He left Cairo for Massawa on the 18th of February, and arrived eight days later. "I am so very glad to get away," he wrote from the former place, "for I am very weary. I go up alone, with an infinite Almighty God to direct and guide me, and am glad to so trust Him as to fear nothing, and, indeed, to feel sure of success."

The Soudan lies between Egypt and Abyssinia; and the two Governments could not be otherwise than deeply interested in the country of the Blacks. Considerable jealousy existed between the two countries, and several battles had quite lately been fought.

It will be remembered that ten years before there had been an English expedition to Abyssinia. At that time Theodore was king, and he then held in captivity a number of men and women who were British subjects. Why they were in durance was not precisely known, excepting that Theodore was angry because England would not help him against the Turks. He wrote a letter to Queen Victoria, which was not answered. There was a story afloat at the time to the effect that he had asked the

hand of the Queen in marriage, declaring that he was
a descendant of the Queen of Sheba, and not unworthy of
becoming allied to the Queen of England. Whether this
was so or not, no notice was taken of his letter; and considering himself slighted by England, he seized all the
British subjects—several missionaries among them—who
were in his power, and had them put in chains, and
confined in his rock tower at Magdala. He kept them
there for some time, always with the fear of death before
their eyes. Our Government was almost afraid to act, for
it was feared that at the first intimation of an invasion
Theodore would have all his prisoners slain. So at first
three persons were sent over with a conciliatory message
from the Queen, and a request that King Theodore would
at once liberate Her Majesty's subjects. Theodore kept
the messengers in suspense for a time, and then imprisoned
them also. But England did not choose to be treated in
this way; and in November 1867 an expedition was sent
out under the command of Sir Robert Napier, afterwards
Lord Napier of Magdala. The expedition made short
work of the affair. The army had to march four hundred
miles across a mountainous country that was without
roads—sometimes under a burning sun, and sometimes
through storms of sleet and rain; but they reached
Magdala in April. The Abyssinians at once made an
attack upon them; but, of course, they were repulsed.
The Abyssinians had five hundred killed, and nearly two
thousand wounded, while the English had none killed and
only nineteen wounded. Then Theodore sent the English
prisoners out of Magdala into the English camp, and very
glad they were to get there safely. But as Theodore
himself would not surrender, Sir Robert attacked his
stronghold, and Magdala was captured. The soldiers who
entered found King Theodore self-slain inside the gate;
and Magdala was completely destroyed.

The widow of Theodore died in the English camp a few days later. Their orphan boy, the heir to the Abyssinian throne, Alamayou, aged seven years, was to be, by the Queen's own orders, taken care of. He was first sent to school in India, and then brought to England, where he was treated with every possible kindness. But he faded away, and died before he reached the age of maturity.

The man who succeeded Theodore was one of the chieftains who had revolted against him—Prince Kassai. He managed to get an Abouna, or Archbishop (without the laying-on of whose hands no man of Abyssinia can be made king) to crown him, and he became King John the Second of Abyssinia, better known as Johannis. He was not the heir to the throne, and the rightful heir—Goobasie—opposed him, but without success. Johannis became firmly seated in power. He had not, however, the whole of Abyssinia to reign over, for in 1874 Egypt took possession of Bogos, and endeavoured to secure the neighbouring province of Hamacem. These two places belonged to Walad el Michael, who had been imprisoned for opposing Johannis, but was now set free to fight for his own. The Abyssinians beat the Egyptians in one battle after another; until in 1876 a large army of Egyptians, under the command of Ratib Pasha and Loring Pasha, invaded Abyssinia. They were joined by Walad el Michael. The Egyptians were thoroughly beaten; it is said that 9000 were slain. Later the Abyssinians attacked the Egyptian force, and this time Egypt won. Some time after Johannis offered to give up Hamacem to Egypt, if Egypt would surrender Walad el Michael to him. But the envoy who took the message from Abyssinia to Egypt was not treated well by the Khedive; and he was at last sent back without a definite answer. This, as may be assumed, greatly incensed Johannis; and it was at this critical juncture that Colonel Gordon came on the scene.

Walad el Michael was a great stumbling-block in the way of any terms being made. He had 3000 men with him; and such an Abyssinian chief on the side of Egypt, and at the place where peace was to be made, was very much in the way.

Dr. Hill, in his book, gives a beautiful letter written by Gordon "between Massawa and Keren." He was in the midst of solitudes, riding on a swift-footed camel over the desert, with plenty of time for thought, and good thoughts to fill up the time. He was cheered because the Khedive's despatches were kind (how could they be otherwise when addressed to the man who had done so much for him ?), and very restful and happy in the assured presence of God. "These interminable deserts and arid mountains fill the heart with far different thoughts than civilised lands would do. It was for this that the Israelites were led there. . . Of course, I cannot converse with the Arabs; so on one goes, stalking along."

Before he reached Keren he was met by two hundred cavalry and infantry to act as his body-guard. He found this much more irksome than solitude. "I am most carefully guarded. At six yards' radius round this tree where I am sitting are six or eight sentries, and the other men are in a circle round them. Now, just imagine this, and put yourself in my position. However, I know they will all go to sleep, so I do not fret myself. I can say truly, no man has ever been so forced into a high position as I have. It is irksome beyond measure. Eight or ten men to help me off my camel, as if I were an invalid! If I walk, every one gets off and walks. So, furious, I get on again."

A grand procession met him as he neared the capital; drums were beaten, and musicians played, and dancers danced before him. The troops were drawn up in line to receive him.

It was not long before Walad el Michael came to see him, attended by a body of men. Gordon took him into his house, and gave him a paper which he had prepared, stating that Egypt would not continue the war, and that Walad should have a government either under Johannis or under Gordon himself. The result was that he was made the governor of two or three tribes.

This was scarcely settled with Johannis before Gordon had to be away again to fight with Menelek, king of Shoa, who had attacked Gondar, an important town in the south of Abyssinia. Gordon was afraid that Michael would take the opportunity of Johannis's absence to advance on Hamacem. But he left things in as safe a condition as he could, and then left Keren for Duggam and Kasala, having heard that Darfour was in revolt, and that he was needed there. So, having arranged with Aloula, the chief general of Johannis, to deliver a message to him, to the effect that he *must* agree to the conditions which Gordon had placed before him, he started on his journey, travelling at a great rate, although the weather was intensely hot. Several interesting incidents occurred on the journey. He had to receive and pay a return visit to a great religious man from Mecca. This man traced his descent in an unbroken line from Mahomet, and was everywhere received with the greatest veneration. At another time he arrived at a village where a *fête* was being held. The men were dressed in long shirts of mail, and they had helmets of iron, and fringes and nose-pieces of chain armour. Even the horses were covered with armour. Their swords were the same as those used by the old Crusaders; in fact, the whole affair was a remnant of the Crusades.

General Gordon and his escort travelled very rapidly, doing as much as forty-five miles a-day, resting at mid-day when the sun was very hot, and making the journey in the evening and morning. As his swift camel went over the desert he had plenty of time for thought, and he often faced the difficulties of his position. He had to contend with many vested interests. He had to fight with fanaticism, to attend to Greeks and Turks and Bedouins, and the large province which the great rebel, Sebehr, had appropriated to himself at Bahr Gazelle; and he was quite alone, with no means, no paraphernalia of power to surround him. One man against fearful odds, but with God on his side: that has been the story of General Gordon's whole life.

CHAPTER XX.

THE LEVEL BALANCE.

"You drop manna in the way
Of starved people."

—*Merchant of Venice.*

HE new Governor-General of the Soudan reached his seat of Government early in May. He found that his home was a palace as large as Marlborough House, pleasantly situated on the bank of the river. It had probably been put in repair before his arrival; but nearly one hundred and fifty of the windows had been broken by the sister of the ex-Governor, Ismail Yacoub, who had also cut the divans into pieces, so angry was she that Gordon had been sent in the place of her brother. However, the people had a warm welcome for the new Governor-General. To look at Gordon is to be inspired with confidence and trust.

He found that, however he disliked it, he would have to live in state. There were two hundred servants to wait upon him. There was quite a ceremony of installation—the firman was read, and the Cadi presented an address, after which a royal salute was fired. The people then waited for an address or proclamation from their Governor-General. It was very eloquent, and very much to the point. It was also very short; there were no need of reporters to assist the memory of those who heard, for it was an address that no one would forget. The address was as follows :—

" *With the help of God I will hold the balance level.*"

The people were delighted. That was a royal speech that every one could understand—and it promised them all they wanted. Fairness—justice—who deserves or has a right to ask for more? A level balance is the one need of the whole world.

There was a great holiday at Khartoum. The new Governor at once set himself to begin reforms. The water-supply of the town was bad ; and Gordon at once promised to have water pumped up, so that all might have that great necessary of life. Moreover, he made the hearts of the very poor glad with gifts. A friend says that in three days he gave away a thousand pounds of his own money among them. He resolved also, that, if he could possibly avoid it, he would have no flogging. The whip had been very freely used before, but Gordon did not like it. Then, too, he would hear what the people had to say. It had been as difficult before for a person who had a grievance to lay it before the Governor, as it would be for a private person to get an interview with the Czar of Russia. Indeed, only those who required help least had been able to secure it; for those who were about the person of the Governor had to be heavily bribed before they would arrange the interview that was desired. Gordon soon altered all that. He wanted the people to trust him, and he wished to know all about them. So he had a box placed at the door of the palace, with a slit into which petitions and letters could be dropped ; while the depositors might always be sure that they would receive attention.

On the 19th of May General Gordon left Khartoum for Darfour, the most westerly province of the Soudan, in order to quell the revolt that had broken out. There were ninety-seven days of camel-riding before him, and plenty of stiff work at the end of the journey. But travelling was good for him: the rapid movement through the air always brought back courage and hope, and confidence in himself, which was, however, not so much self-confidence as confidence in his mission and his God.

He reached El Obeid, the capital of Kordofan, by the end of May. El Obeid has a population of 10,000. It has lately been much talked of in connection with the terrible disaster that overtook General Hicks. Gordon did not stay at Obeid, but pushed on to the frontier of Darfour. He knew that the rebels were besieging the garrisons at Fascher, Dara, and Kolkal. Hassan Pasha had gone with a force of 16,000 men from Fogia to Fascher, but the force had not been heard of. Gordon had very few men with him; but he had faith, and he could pray. He had prayed the Ever-Victorious Army into victory. He had prayed his boats up the Nile, and now he prayed the revolted tribes into helpers. "Now, I think God will enable me to make friends with the different tribes between Fascher and Fogia, and I trust He will enable me to go to Fascher with two hundred men, and escorted by the chiefs who are at present rebels." It was that faith which could remove mountains. A little later, at Oomchanga, he could write that he had made peace with the tribes that were around. Many of the rebels came to ask for pardon. They had been treated so abominably by the Bashi-Bazouks that Gordon sympathised with them, and said we ought to ask pardon of them.

He was at this time not far from Shaka, and he decided to go there, and try to get troops, the better to relieve Fascher. Shaka was the head-quarters of the great robber chief and slave dealers' king, to frustrate whose designs the Khedive had first solicited the help of Baker, and then of Gordon. Sebehr himself was at Stamboul, but his son had command of his hordes. Gordon described Shaka as the Cave of Adullam, where all murderers and robbers were assembled, and from whence raids were made upon the negro tribes for slaves. Sulieman had 10,000 soldiers to fight for him; and Gordon had to face not only this formidable foe, but others quite as terrible. He had only five hundred "nondescript troops," not more in number than his little "Ever-Victorious Army," and men of a very different stamp, who were cowardly and disloyal again and again, and at one time certainly were planning how they could take the life of their leader.

At Toashia he found nothing but a half-starved garrison of three hundred and fifty men, fit for nothing. He had hoped that they would swell the number of his army, but they had not been paid for three years, and were so miserable and useless, that instead of taking them with him, he decided to send them back to Kordofan to be disbanded.

Then he hoped to be assisted by a sheikh, whose brother he had released; but here again he was disappointed. He increased his numbers by pardoning other rebel chiefs; but he felt all the time that he could not depend upon his troops, and this was his greatest trouble. In the midst of it all he was surrounded by thousands of determined Blacks, who looked as if they meant murder, and nothing less. Gordon knew that the firearms he and his "troops" had were almost useless; and he felt the shadow of death steal over him. "I prayed heartily for an issue," he said; "but it gave me a pain in the heart like that I had when surrounded at Masindi. I do not fear death, but I fear, from want of faith, the results of my death—for the whole country would have risen. It is, indeed, most painful to be in such a position. It takes a year's work out of one,

However, thank God, it is over, and I hope to reach Dara to-morrow." He found afterwards that he had been absolutely defenceless, for the man who had carried his rifle had dropped it, and it was broken, so that if he had wanted to fire he could not have done so.

Every one at Dara was surprised to see him. Troops had been sent out to meet him, but had taken another direction from that which he had travelled. Both here and at Fascher the Pashas had been doing nothing but wait for reinforcements.

Gordon was obliged to send an expedition against Haroun, who declared himself the King of Darfour; and nothing could be done until he was subdued. While waiting to see what would be the result of this effort, the Governor-General received a visit from the chief of the Razagat tribe, who had come to declare that he was ready to side with the Government against Sebehr's son, who had pillaged and ill-treated them continually. But another trouble now faced the commander of the Soudan. Food was scarce, and how was he to feed the Razagats who were willing to join him ! Food was wanted in other directions too. Two hundred and ten slaves were brought to him, rescued from their captors, who were so miserable, and thin, and starved, that at sight of them the tender-hearted Governor burst into tears. He gave them some dhoura, though he had so little that he did not know what he should do. But he left that to God. "I declare solemnly," he wrote "that I would give my life willingly to save the sufferings of these people; and if I would do this, how much more does He care for them than such imperfection as I am. You would have felt sick if you had seen them. Poor creatures ! thirty-six hours without food." They had positively been living on grass !

From Dara the Governor-General went to Wadar; for news reached him that there was difficulty with another tribe—the Leopards, as they called themselves—who had attacked Toashia. They were overtaken by a fearful thunderstorm, which lasted all night. "I put on my great-coat, put up my umbrella, and wished for dawn!" A battle was fought in the morning, and the Leopards were beaten; but they afterwards made a determined attack, and although there were only seven hundred of them, they were so resolute that they nearly won a victory. Gordon had now the Masharin tribe to help him; and in this engagement their chief was mortally wounded. Gordon was disgusted with his own troops, who were always afraid to fight, and let others do their work. Indeed, the true-hearted man had to endure sorrow of all kinds. In order to subdue the Leopard tribe he had to keep them from water; but he sympathised so much with their sufferings that he suffered with them. "Consider it as we may, war is a brutal, cruel affair," he said. But his determination to conquer them helped him to be victorious even over his own kind feelings. He would not allow the Leopards to drink until they sued for pardon. Thirst overcame them. They swore fidelity and gave up their spears; and then Gordon, with as much pleasure as they felt themselves, signed their pardon and rewarded them with water.

Next, the Governor-General went to Fascher, to relieve the hemmed-in capital of Darfour; which he did, although Hassin Pasha had not done it with more than ten thousand men, and Gordon had only three hundred.

About this time he discovered that a lieutenant-colonel, who had been sent out from Dara with an expedition, had accepted a bribe from the chief he was to attack, and had done nothing. This same man—who was supposed to be supporting Gordon, and helping to carry out his orders—had tried to excite the fanaticism of the people against him, by giving them to understand that Gordon would not allow the usual call to prayer to be issued. This was very far from being the case. Only a short time previously he had a mosque, which the Egyptians had before seized and appropriated as a powder magazine, cleared and re-opened for worship; and especially ordered the crier, or muezzin, to call the people to prayers. "To me it appears that the Mussulman worships God as well as I do, and is as acceptable, if sincere, as any Christian," a sentiment which, whatever way we may judge it, certainly made it exceedingly cruel of this lieutenant-colonel to pretend that Gordon prevented the crier to prayer from doing his duty; and he was so angry that he gave the crier two sovereigns, and sent the lieutenant-colonel into banishment, so that he might have time to reflect.

Troubles and perplexities thickened around General Gordon. He described the chief of them in very few words :—

"Sebehr's son, with his 3000 men, *now* want to help me (*i.e.*, ravage the country) against my will! Haroun is ravaging the country to the north, and I am placed between these two forces. The whole of the tribes around Sebehr's son are hostile to him, and partially hostile to *me*, and in favour of Haroun; but asking me to help them against the armed force of Sebehr's son—a triangular duel."

In the midst of it he received intelligence that the slave traders, with 6000 troops, had reached Dara. He hurried there at once, arriving long before his escort, having ridden eighty-five miles in a day and a-half. There was no dinner for him, but he had some sleep; and then, rising at dawn, he put on the golden armour the Khedive had given him, and rode off to the robber bands. On his way he was met by the son of Sebehr, "a nice-looking lad of twenty-two," and then he went into the rebel camp. "The whole body of chiefs were dumfoundered at my coming among them. After a glass of water I went back, telling the son of Sebehr to come with his family to my divan. They all came, and, sitting there in a circle, I gave them in choice Arabic my ideas—That they meditated revolt; that I knew it, and that they should now have my ultimatum—viz., that I would disarm them and break them up. They listened in silence, and then went off to consider in silence what I had said. They have just now sent in a letter stating their submission, and I thank God for it."

Gordon was able to tell Sulieman that he knew he had only three days before fired three shots close to his tent.

Sulieman was forgiven; but the trouble was not soon over. Gordon feared he would have to make him a prisoner, which he did not wish to do, for he had a good deal of admiration for him. "I cannot help feeling for him," he wrote, "for he is a smart little fellow; the terror in which he has kept the mightiest of these freebooters is something wonderful. They are all afraid of him, and he made men of all sorts prisoners."

Sebehr's son got very angry with Gordon because he would not give him robes. It is a wonder that he did not kill him. He might have done so. Even then Sulieman could feel far more sure of his men than Gordon of his.

At that time General Gordon had the grief to discover that his black secretary had taken £3000 backsheesh. He said it was horrible. He sent the man to Khartoum to be judged; and in his place appointed Berzati Bey, a clever young Mussulman, with whom he was very well pleased. The black secretary was sent to Khartoum to meet the justice that was due to him.

In September he decided to ride to Shaka and complete what had been begun by the submission of Sulieman. He rode through the forest; and when he was six hours from Shaka he had an invitation from Sebehr's son to come and see him. When he was nearer still, Sulieman and his officers came to meet him. They were very subdued, and apparently sincere in their penitence. Sulieman said that Gordon was his father, and he wished him to make his home with him. Gordon decided to go. He wrote a note in the " Cave of Adullam," as he called the home of the robber chief's son. He had made himself quite at home, and rather rejoiced in the astonishment which he knew would be felt at his unceremoniously taking his seat. " I am in the son's house. He never used to let anyone sit in his presence, and must be shocked at the familiarity with which every one was treated by me. He is sitting out in the verandah—I expect to excite my pity. However, a short diet of humble pie will not be bad for him. What an amount of trouble he has given me and everyone !"

He stayed there for two days, and then went to Obeid, taking Sulieman with him. The town of Shaka was full of slaves. The Arabs were quarrelling as to whom they would choose for chiefs. They selected one man, and crowned him with corn-leaves.

As he went to Obeid, Gordon had a suspicion that actually a caravan of slaves was going with him. There were many women and children, but the merchants declared they were their wives and children. He found at last that eighty slaves were really going up with him in chains. He was very disheartened ; slavery met him everywhere, but he did not see that he could release them ; he only insisted on the chains being removed.

General Gordon got very tired just at that time with the thought of the 2300 miles he had ridden over the desert, and the many miles he had yet to go.

On the road to Obeid he picked up slaves constantly. He found a little black boy who had been left behind, and also a lad with a string of slaves ; some were dying, and some were ill. He lost all patience and hope. It seemed no use trying to subdue the trade. It was more than man could do; he felt that none could accomplish it but God.

The people at Obeid were delighted to see him again. But he did not stay there long. He went on to Khartoum. He was wanted to do so much that his camels could not keep up the pace which he required. At Khartoum he had petitions to read and hear, and trials of murderers and others to attend to. "You can have little idea of the amount of work I have to do, and I never have a Sunday or a day of rest. Now that I have given up all drinking of wine or spirits, I am much better, and sleep well; but it is a fever life I lead. Were it not for the very great comfort I have in communion with God, and the knowledge that He is Governor-General, I could not get on at all."

CHAPTER XXI.

ROMULUS GESSI.

ROM Khartoum General Gordon started to visit Walad el Michael's camp at Hellal. This necessitated a sail up the Nile, and gave the rest which he needed, and which was of the utmost use to him. From Berber to Dongola the journey was again made on camels, and he happened not to have very good ones provided. At Berber he found that there was to be an illumination in his honour, which he did not at all admire. At Meroc he was surrounded by people. A real live Governor is not often seen in those parts; and the people were so eager to pour their complaints into his ears, that they actually shouted after him for hours when he left. They threw dust on their heads, and waved their clothes, and shouted, " We are miserable," until Gordon felt inclined to shout back, " So am I." And, indeed, he was; for he was at that time not only tired, but ill.

When he reached Abou Heraz, he found that of the twenty-eight camels which he owned, fourteen had died of small-pox. To compensate for that worry, the next thing he recorded was that the nights were wonderful with the new moon. The air was exceedingly clear, and they saw the crescent and the whole circle. He heard that the Greeks at Kassala and Katarif employed gangs of slaves to cultivate tobacco and other things; so he decided to have the slaves seized. On his way he had a little incident with the "holy man" among the Mussulmans who was before mentioned. Gordon had once, by mistake, sat upon his divan, and so broken through the rules of Mussulman etiquette; but on this occasion he was careful to leave the seat of honour for the priest, and he also presented him with twenty pounds.

The good man could not help wishing that Gordon would become a Mussulman. Others had wished so too; but the Governor-General did not intend to change, and he knew that if he did, he would be less, and not more respected by the people.

On the 16th of December he reached the camp of Walad el Michael. He found it on the top of a high mountain. To reach it two hills had to be scaled, and this was terrible work for the man, already exhausted. He found Walad with 7000 men, all armed and drawn up to receive him. The chief himself was not there, but he sent his son. Gordon went on towards the camp of the chief, who was said to be ill with a bad knee. A procession of priests with sacred pictures walked before Gordon, and in front of him was Walad's general-in-chief. At length the sheikh was reached; and having paid his respects to him, Gordon was taken to a hut which was appropriated to him during his stay. The hut looked suspicious, especially as similar huts for his ten attendants were grouped around, and they found themselves boxed up into a very small space.

"What does this mean?" asked the eyes of his ten soldiers.

Gordon himself felt that the position was more than a little dangerous. But he was able now, as in all the crises of his life, to retain his coolness and courage.

"If Michael wants to make me a prisoner, of course he can do so," he said to the interpreter, "but he'd better not; it would be worse for him in the end."

Both Michael and his son at once commenced to make such profuse apologies that the General knew that at present, at all events, he was not a prisoner.

"It is all right," he said to his host; "only if the news reached Senheit that I was so boxed up, they might think I was a prisoner, and that would cause too much excitement to be pleasant for any of us."

The next day he had a long talk with Michael, in which he advised him to show a little humility toward Johannis, and ask for pardon. "That is impossible," replied Walad el Michael, "and we need talk no more on that point, for it is waste of time."

He asked Gordon to give him more districts—that he might plunder them, of course—and declared that if Gordon would not prevent him he could take another Abyssinian town, Adoua. But the Governor-General would not hear of that.

News came to Gordon at this time that the troops had attacked some of Johannis's tribes, which annoyed him. Gordon was trying to make peace between Egypt and Abyssinia—a peace that should be satisfactory, and therefore lasting; but he was hindered at every turn. He sought to get from Johannis a promise of pardon for the men of Walad el Michael; but Johannis was so long in answering his letter that by the end of the year he went back to Khartoum, travelling *viâ* Suakim and Berber. He was not well—so much travelling on camels had shaken him.   He had ridden during the year nearly four thousand miles.

In the beginning of January 1878 Colonel Gordon was summoned to Cairo by the Khedive, who wanted to consult him on the state of his finances, which, at that time, was anything but satisfactory.   He was obliged to obey the summons, although he would rather not have done so; and he started off at once on the long journey, taking with him a present of some curious old armour and regalia, which the Khedive afterwards presented to the Paris Museum. He was received by the Khedive with the greatest respect, and lodged in the palace which the Prince of Wales had occupied during his visit.   Every honour and attention was lavished on the Governor-General of the Soudan, who certainly deserved it all, and more, but who scarcely appreciated it.   The change from the desert to so much grandeur was so great and sudden, that he and his men were quite dazed.

His visit to Cairo, instead of proving, as it ought to have done, a season of rest and recreation, only served to wear and trouble him more.   The difficulties so thickened around him that he sometimes grew tired, and wished himself away " where the wicked cease from troubling, and the weary are at rest."   The Khedive would not agree to the plans which he proposed; and yet Gordon would not give way, for he had that confidence in himself which every man has who does any good or great work in the world.   He felt afterwards that he had been almost too outspoken; but that was one of his characteristics, and no one would have wished otherwise of him.

Colonel Gordon remained in Cairo until the end of March, when he left for Suez.   He had now to go to Zeila, which formerly belonged to Turkey, but had been annexed to Egypt.   From Zeila he went to Harrar, where Raouf Pasha, whom Gordon had deposed four years before, was again carrying matters with a high hand. The road was very bad, and he had to go on horseback. He found that the road was used for the conveyance of slaves, and at once resolved to stop that. His thoughts were not pleasant. The Khedive was trying to compel him to make bricks without straw—to carry on everything at the Soudan in an expensive way, without allowing any expenses for it. But in the midst of everything Gordon remained faithful to his duty.

On the route he met a caravan conveying £2000 worth of coffee, which was to be sold for the private benefit of Raouf. He at once confiscated it—for Raouf had no right whatever to it—and dismissed the man from office.

When Gordon reached Harrar, he found that three cows had been slaughtered in honour of his arrival. It was worse than the illuminations, for the death of the animals distressed the man, who could not bear the sight of suffering in any shape. He paid five pounds for the cows, and felt so vexed they had been killed, that, for the moment, it prevented him from noticing Raouf, for whom after he felt sorry in turn.

Bad news reached him at Massawa, for he heard that Walad el Michael had attacked Ras Bariou, the general of Johannis, and slain him. On his way back to Khartoum he wrote :—" In one month I have turned out three generals of division, one general of brigade, and four lieutenant-colonels. It is no use mincing matters."

At Khartoum he found all work greatly in arrears. He had to attend to the prisons, which were in a very bad state, and to examine into the case of each prisoner. The Khedive also had wished him to look into the difficulties which beset his scheme of making a railway. The finances, too, were very unsatisfactory. It is impossible to make the Soudan pay its own expenses—it never has done so ; and Gordon found that in one year it had cost £259,000 more

than it had produced. Things seemed to be wrong every
way; and the cares and troubles of state so oppressed the
brave man at the helm, that if he had not been a Christian,
and able to rely on God, and felt assured of divine support,
he must have broken down altogether.

One result comforted him, however: in two months he
had stopped twelve caravans of slaves.

He became very summary in his dealings with the
traders. He hung a man for mutilating a little boy,
and established a "government of terror" over those who,
for their own greed, seemed determined still to traffic in
human bodies. It greatly troubled the Governor-General,
who would have given his life to prevent it.

But in the meantime a crisis was approaching.

On the 8th August he wrote:—"I have a nasty revolt
Bahr Gazelle, and do not know how it will end."

Sulieman, the son of Sebehr, had revolted, and again
had taken possession of that province.

This meant that all kinds of cruelties would be practised
by the slave dealers, and that Sebehr's gang, if unsuppressed,
would undo all the work of reformation which had been
going on for several years. Clearly, a force must be sent to
fight and overcome Sulieman.

The Governor-General took prompt steps at once. He
seized and imprisoned all the relatives of Sebehr whom he
could find, and confiscated their goods.

Then he sent an expedition to Bahr Gazelle, under the
command of Romulus Gessi, the Italian before mentioned.
He was thus described:—"Aged forty-nine. Short, compact figure; cool, most determined man. Born genius for
practical ingenuity in mechanics. Ought to have been born
in 1560, not 1832. Same disposition as Francis Drake.
Had been engaged in many political affairs. Was interpreter to Her Majesty's forces in the Crimea, and attached
to the head-quarters of the Royal Artillery."

Gessi was a very suitable man for the expedition.

He went into the equatorial province for troops, and then started on his mission. He was at first greatly hindered. It was flood time: all the tributaries of the Bahr Gazelle were overflowing. This was a sore trouble to Gessi, for news came which made him wish more than ever to meet the rebel Sulieman. These tidings were to the effect that he had proclaimed himself the Lord of the Bahr Gazelle. He had surprised a garrison, massacred the troops, and appropriated to himself the stores of ammunition. Of course he had been opposed by the chieftains near; but he had slain the men, and, worst of all, had made slaves of the women and children whom he did not butcher. The people were starving; for Sulieman had stolen their grain, and they had nothing to eat but leaves and grass.

Gessi could not at once begin, and the Arabs who waited to see which side was likely to win, though at first invited to help Gessi, went over to Sulieman. The latter had 6000 men, while Gessi had only three hundred soldiers, two guns, and seven hundred irregulars, very badly armed. Gordon had been asked to send reinforcements, but the "sudd" at that time prevented any letters from going up the Nile. Gessi had to wait, and while he did so he made many discoveries respecting the way in which the province was governed. He found that far too much money was spent upon it, and that the men who were paid had so little to do that they passed much of their time in play. While they were still waiting the troops became mutinous, and some of them deserted. Gessi soon put a stop to this, for he shot the ringleader and flogged others.

On the 17th of November he began his march, which was one of the most difficult, for he had to go through depths of forests, and wade through rivers, encumbered though he was with a lot of women, and children, and slaves. For some days he saw no one: Sulieman's men had fled. Boats were destroyed, and he had great difficulty in getting his men across. He made a stockade at Wari, behind which he could leave the women and children. The natives hailed his approach, and told him that ten thousand persons had been taken away from the Bahr Gazelle into slavery by Sulieman. The latter promised that he would take the men, and let them get their wives and children back. He found plenty ready to help him, for the cruelties of Sebehr's son made them eager for revenge.

At Dem, Idris, a friendly Arab, gave Gessi seven hundred armed men to help him; and with these he took possession of the stronghold, which he strengthened, and in which he waited for the approach of Sulieman. In this stronghold he had to remain a considerable time. Sulieman attacked him four times. Gessi was often in great straits; and once he had to collect and re-cast the bullets which Sulieman fired into the camp.

On the 12th of January 1879 there was very severe fighting, and Gessi won a decided victory. Of Sulieman's force more than a thousand were slain; but Gessi dared not follow the enemy, for Sulieman had many more men than he. After that there was a fortnight of quiet; but on the 28th of January Sulieman again made an attack. Gessi had a little more ammunition by this time. A terrible onslaught was made, and Gessi was compelled to meet the enemy in the open, for his huts had been set on fire by the shells. Again, however, he was victorious.

Some time passed, and then Gessi had some powder sent him, which made him feel that he might attack the enemy. His men were as brave as the Ever-Victorious Army had been; they won one victory after another, and rescued hosts of slaves. He proved himself a man after Gordon's own heart, doing the same kind of work, and very much in the same way as the Governor-General.

Early in May he went to find Sulieman. When he had

nearly reached the robber's den, an attack was made upon him, but he (Gessi) pressed on and got into Sulieman's camp. The men plundered the camp, and Sulieman managed to escape. Gessi tried to follow him, but the troops did not do so well as they might have done. Sulieman had passed through a village, and only one woman was left behind to tell the tale. Gessi told his men to search for stragglers in the grass; they found one, and compelled him to act as guide.

They went on, trying to overtake Sulieman, and their march revealed many atrocities. They came upon the murdered bodies of little children, who had not been able to keep up with the others, and had been slaughtered. They found a great slave-chief (Abu Shnep), and entered into conflict with him. A strange thing happened to Gessi. Seven men mistook his camp for that of Rabi, who was Sulieman's companion. They told him that Sultan Idris was coming with a force to assist Sulieman. This information helped Gessi very much. He managed to get Rabi's men and the Sultan's into conflict; and then had a fight, and won, which victory provided his men with food. Rabi escaped, and so did the Sultan. The league of the slave-drivers was broken up, and Gessi marched back to Dem.

Early in July Gessi again heard of Sulieman, whom he at once pursued. Sulieman, knowing this, fled before him. Gessi followed with three companies; and on the night of 15th July he overtook the enemy at Gara. He had no compunction, for these men had devastated villages, and murdered families and tribes in cold-blooded cruelty for so long, that the very babes seemed crying for revenge. Gessi had two hundred and ninety men, and the rebels were seven hundred; but Gessi's men had excellent rifles. He sent to Sulieman, calling upon him at once to lay down his arms, and giving him ten minutes in which to decide. The slave dealers were quite taken by sur prise; for Gessi had come upon them while they were asleep. They could not tell but that the latter had an immense force to back him, so they sent word that they would surrender. They were told to come and lay down their arms. Dr. Hill* relates the conversation which took place between Gessi and Sulieman :—

" What! have you no other troops ? "

" No, they were enough."

" And I had seven hundred men." He began to weep at the thought of the small force to which he had submitted. Turning to one of his chiefs, he said—

" They had not more than three hundred men! and *you* told me there were three thousand of them. If only my father had been here to take the command, we should never have been beaten."

The prisoners were taken care of; Gessi would not have had them bound but for the news that they intended to escape.

" Then," said Gessi, " I found that the time had come to settle with these people once for all;" and he proceeded to do it. To the common soldiers he offered pardon, on condition that they went back to their own country and settled down to a peaceful life. They accepted, and went off under an escort. The small slave dealers were made prisoners and sent away. The eleven chiefs were shot. They had been told two years before that if they went on with their slave-hunting, they should answer for it with their lives. They did so now. Sulieman sank on the ground in terror, and another wept; but they were all executed, as they deserved to be.

And so ended the great revolt of Sebehr, for in the person of his son he paid for the crimes that he had committed, although Sebehr himself was allowed to live on by the authorities in Cairo.

* *Colonel Gordon in Central Africa.*

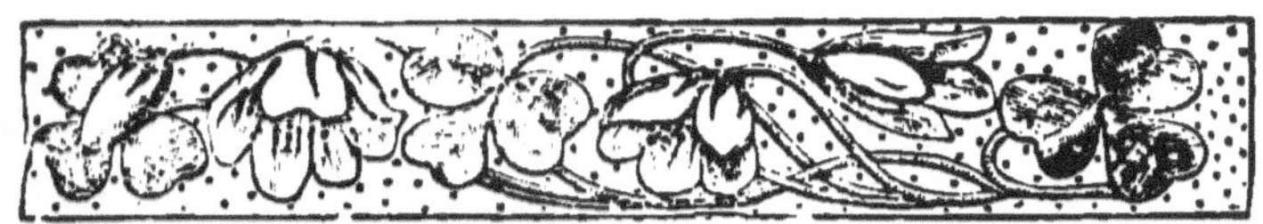

CHAPTER XXII.

KING JOHANNIS OF ABYSSINIA.

"His life was gentle ; and the elements
So mix'd in him, that Nature might stand up
And say to all the world, This was a man ! "
—Julius Cæsar.

O return to Colonel Gordon. We find that he had been occupied in many ways while Gessi was accomplishing the great work of punishing the slave dealers in the Bahr Gazelle. Two things troubled him more than all beside—the slave trade and the finances of the Soudan. But there were plenty of other troubles too. He had several times been so anxious about Gessi, that he had scarcely strength to endure the strain. Nubar had to look after the finances, and was half inclined to get money by becoming friends with Sebehr. He heard news which pleased him when he was told that Walad el Michael had sent in his submission to Johannis. He was not inclined to be severe upon the King of Abyssinia. He was summoned to Cairo three times, but he did not go. He was worried almost out of his life about the slaves. The Khedive told him he was to punish slave-dealing with death. But then the Khedive had also issued an order that the punishment of slave-dealing was to be an imprisonment from five months to five years. And, on the other hand, Nubar Pasha sent him a telegram to say that slave-purchasing in Egypt was legal. All this tried him exceedingly. He tells of passing caravans—one with two slave dealers and seventeen slaves, some of the women being quite naked; and another with seven slave dealers and seventeen slaves. "Nothing could exceed the misery of these poor wretches; some were children of three years old. They had come across the torrid zone from Shaker, a journey from which I and my camels shrunk. I got the slave dealers charged at once, and then decided about the slaves."

He had to go to Shaka soon after that. He ordered the slave dealers to get away from the village which they had thought their own; and they departed at the command of the Governor-General, who hoped they never would come back again. He found that there was a great panic among the slave dealers everywhere, for they had heard of Sulieman's defeat and death.

At Shaka, Gordon had a telegram ordering him to send up £12,000 to Cairo. He replied that his troops were several months in arrear, and had no clothes; so he sent to Cairo to ask them to send *him* £12,000.

At Shaka, Gordon's 25,000 troops were all black, and all recruited from slaves.

From Shaka, Gordon went to Kalaka, where he found at least a thousand slaves wandering about. From Kalaka he went to Dara, and then to Fascher and Kobeyt, in the north of Darfour. He heard that Kalkal was beset by brigands; so he went to see about it, travelling over a road which no one had travelled for two years. The lands were miserable, but he thought it was no use writing to the Khedive, who had enough on his hands. He sent out to

Khartoum four hundred Arabs, who needed food and clothes: "a great deliverance of useless mouths." In June he went to Toaschia; and his march was made horrible by the number of skulls which he found on the road. He had them put in heaps by the wells, as monuments of the cruelty of the slavers. As he was going from Oomchanga to Toaschia, he caught five or six hundred.

On the 25th of June the two heroes, Gordon and Gessi, met. Both looked much older. Gordon had Gessi made a Pasha of the Bahr Gazelle, and £2000 was presented to him for his useful services. The two men soon parted—Gessi to complete his work and Gordon to go on to new surprises—for at Fogria the news reached him that Ismail, the Khedive of Egypt, was deposed; and Gordon was ordered to proclaim throughout the Soudan the fact that Tewfik was his successor.

From that time he began to long for home. He was sorry for Ismail, although Tewfik was evidently inclined to be kind to him. Gordon cannot help getting attached to the people whom he serves. "It grieves me what sufferings my poor Khedive Ismail has had to go through."

On July 21st he wrote home :—"I shall (*D. V.*) leave for Cairo in ten days, and shall hope to see you soon : but I may have to go to Johannis before I go to Cairo."

This is exactly what he had to do. He reached Cairo on the 23rd of August, and left for Massawa, on a mission to King Johannis, on August 30th. The Khedive Tewfik sent a messenger, on Gordon's arrival at Cairo, to tell him that the palace was at his disposal; but he felt cross, and at first inclined to stop at the hotel. His secretary, Berzati Bey, however, advised him not to do so, and he therefore accepted the courtesy of the Khedive. The latter was glad to consult Colonel Gordon on many points ; and first, they had a talk about the threatened attack of the generals of Johannis, Aloula, and Walad el Michael, on the Bogos territory. Gordon was asked if he would go to Johannis on a special mission, and he replied that he would go, and then he would retire from the service of the Khedive. The Egyptian men thought that the Governor-General had been a little too friendly with Johannis, and Gordon found that there had been many absurd speculations and reports afloat concerning him. He said that if there were any more evil-speaking, he would ask the Khedive to punish the "evil-speaker," by making him Governor-General of the Soudan!

He started on his mission to Johannis on the 11th of September, taking with him one person only, his secretary and interpreter, Berzati Bey. He was first to visit Aloula. He had not proceeded far on his journey before he was told that Walad el Michael was imprisoned by Aloula, in accordance with Johannis's orders. Colonel Gordon was starting on a mission as difficult and dangerous as any in which he had previously been engaged. The Abyssinians were in possession of the Bogos district, and he was to ask the king to give it up; at the same time he was to understand that the Khedive wished neither to fight nor to pay.

The road was very bad, and Gordon suffered a good deal from palpitation of the heart, for he had to walk many miles, and had only a mule on which to ride. He had plenty of time to consider, and he thought through the details of his mission as he went. He was going with empty hands. He saw one thing clearly—that with or without the help of Johannis he must get rid of Walad el Michael and his men; and he was especially hopeful that the king would offer an asylum to Michael's men when they left Bogos.

He reached Gura on the afternoon of September 16th, and had his interview with Aloula, which he described in a most amusing manner. The chief was swathed in a white garment, so that only his nose was visible, and to the mouth both he and the rest applied their veils, as if something poisonous had entered. "Solemn silence prevailed, and I got quite distressed, for the figure at the end never moved, and I felt as if I must feel his pulse, for I thought he must be ill." After a time the solemnity was a little relaxed. Gordon presented the Khedive's letter, but it was slightingly put down on the table unread. Aloula said that the king had forbidden smoking, but Gordon might smoke if he chose. But he declined. After a great deal of fuss, the interview was over, and it was arranged that Gordon should go on to the king; and in the meantime Aloula promised that he would remain quiet, and not attack Egypt.

The envoy accordingly started for Debra Tabor, near Gondar, a journey which would occupy him twelve days. One night he camped near the place where Walad el Michael was in prison. On his journey he very narrowly escaped being taken by a chief and his men who were in revolt against the king. Some of Aloula's men were with him, or he might have been seized. The journey was altogether very difficult and dangerous; but on 27th October he reached the man who chose to be called "The King of Kings." The guns fired a salute, which Johannis informed him was in his honour. The king received him sitting on a raised dais, and had present with him his father on one hand and the high priest on the other. The king gave him audience for a few seconds, and then told him he could retire, which he did.

At dawn next morning the king sent for him, and immediately began to recount his grievances, declaring that he had been grossly wronged by Egypt. As Gordon agreed with him, he asked why he had come. He reminded him of the letter which he had already delivered, but which he found had not been read. The letter was found and read; and then the king stated his claim, which was an altogether preposterous one, and which the envoy said was not for him to reply to, but for the Khedive.

The king went away to the baths—"a hot spring coming up through a bamboo in an old hut," said Gordon, who had to wait some time before he could know the king's pleasure.

Gordon wanted him to state his wishes in writing; but this Johannis did not wish to do. Gordon heard that the Greek consul and others were urging Johannis to make great demands. He told the king that although he had positive orders not to cede Bogus to him, he would try to use his private influence with Egypt to get this secured to him. Johannis continued very cross and sulky, and at last told him to go back, and he would send his own envoy with his answer to the Khedive. Then Gordon asked that the Egyptian soldiers might be given to him, which made Johannis more angry still, and he told him to start at once.

After he had left, he was overtaken by the king's messenger, who brought him a letter and a thousand dollars. He would not take the money; and later he read the letter, as he had a right to do in his official capacity of Governor of the Soudan. When it was translated it was found to be very insulting. It said that Johannis had received the letters sent by *that man*, and he would not make a secret peace; if the Khedive wanted peace he must ask the Sultans of Europe. Colonel Gordon wrote to the Greek consul to ask what it meant; and having had an answer that the king would do as he pleased, he went on his way.

He had not gone far before he was taken prisoner by the king's orders. Gordon destroyed his journal and went on. He found that Ras Arya, the officer who had arrested him, was a worthless fellow, not in the least loyal to the king. Gordon gave him some money to send his telegrams safely, and after a time got free, although he was again arrested later on. He had to buy his way out of Abyssinia with gold. But at last he reached Massawa; and to his great delight and thankfulness found an English gun-boat, the *Seagull*, waiting for him.

The following amusing story was afterwards told:— " When Gordon Pasha was lately taken prisoner by the Abyssinians he completely checkmated King John. The king received his prisoner sitting on his throne, or whatever piece of furniture did duty for that exalted seat, a chair being placed for the prisoner considerably lower than the seat on which the king sat. The first thing the Pasha did was to seize this chair, place it alongside that of his Majesty, and sit down on it; the next, to inform him that he met him as an equal, and would only treat him as such. This somewhat disconcerted his sable Majesty; but on recovering himself he said, ' Do you know, Gordon Pasha, that I could kill you on the spot if I liked?' 'I am perfectly well aware of it, your Majesty,' said the Pasha. ' Do so at once, if it is your royal pleasure; I am ready.' This disconcerted the king still more, and he exclaimed, ' What! ready to be killed!' 'Certainly,' replied the Pasha; 'I am always ready to die; and so far from fearing your putting me to death, you would confer a favour on me by so doing, for you would be doing for me that which I am precluded by my religious scruples from doing for myself—you would relieve me from all the troubles and misfortunes which the future may have in store for me.' This completely staggered King John, who gasped out in despair, ' Then my power has no terrors for you?' ' None whatever,' was the Pasha's laconic reply. His Majesty, it is needless to add, instantly collapsed."

CHAPTER XXIII.

REST OR WORK?

"God shall be my hope, my stay, my guide,
And lantern to my feet."

—*Henry VI.*

THE next tidings that the world had of General Gordon were to the effect that he had resigned his post in Egypt. This caused more surprise to people then than it will to those who have been following his career as it is now written. Before he went to Abyssinia he had made up his mind to do so, partly because of events in Egypt, and partly because he needed and longed for rest. On the 15th December Colonel Gordon telegraphed to the Khedive:—"I asked your Highness, when I was taken by King John, on 14th November, by telegraph, to send a regiment and a steamer with two guns to Massowa. Your Highness has not done so; and had not the English gun-boat been here, the place might have been sacked."

It was a happy thing that the gunboat *Seagull* was ready; and England had her son, of whom she will for ever be proud, brought safely home.

Many things had occurred to give pain and annoyance to him. Some of the Khedive's ministers had wished to interfere much more than was pleasant to Gordon. The following characteristic letter, written to M. Ninet, and afterwards published in *The Echo*, throws a little light upon these matters :—

"My dear M. Ninet—I do not measure myself as a soldier with a Napoleon I., nor as an administrator with a Colbert. I claim only to have done my best for the land the government of which was entrusted to me. I dare to assert that, spite of all my faults, the population of the Soudan loves me. The Egyptian and European public are not capable of criticising me. A man must be in the Soudan, and see it with his own eyes, to know how things go there. If the councillors of the Khedive, and his courtiers, pretend that I have betrayed their land, in the matter of taking from them a foot on the Red Sea (for Abyssinia or Italy), then—they lie. I will tell you what I telegraphed in cipher to the Khedive :—' If France and England, after they put all Egypt's sugar into their own pocket, should leave Egypt in the lurch by refusing her the little salt she needs, then turn yourself straight to Italy, and give her a haven on the Red Sea.' It was my duty in this affair to give my straightforward opinion to the Khedive. One of his own ministers had said to a Consul-General that Egypt ought to give a port on the Red Sea to Abyssinia, and that such a concession would be no injury whatever to the Nile-land. Now, my dear M. Ninet, I said to the Khedive in cipher what one of his own ministers had already said in open language. After I have held the post of a Governor-General of the Soudan (a dignity second only, on account of its importance, to that of the Khedive), you will understand why I decline to hold any more subordinate place. I am going, and shall return no more to Egypt, where I could not even be Khedive. The Khedive is a noble man, and I am quite ready to die for him. As for the rest, whether they say bad or good of me, I am quite indifferent.—Your friend, "GORDON."

It was well for him to have the thought of the love of the Soudanese to comfort him, for he needed a little cheering. His health had given way. He had really been quite ill when he started for Abyssinia, and by no means in a fit state of body to undertake so important a mission. He had been doing work enough for several men. In the three years during which he had been Governor-General of the Soudan, he had ridden on camels and mules eight thousand four hundred and ninety miles. He was worn out, and needed rest. He had looked forward to it for some time. In his letters he had playfully written of the good things which he had promised himself when the work and the worry of his Soudan administration had come to an end. He would lie in bed till noon, and have oysters for lunch, and take no journeys, and receive no visits. We can imagine that if he had been allowed to carry out this programme, his life would soon have been again full of work; and, perhaps, if he could have chosen his own occupation, it would have been something like that which he had done at Gravesend.

In one of his letters, written when he was under great pressure, the following beautiful passage occurs :—

" I will tell you a story of 1848 years ago. There was a workman of Bethlehem who did not agree with the great teachers of an old religion, who answered them roughly, and who did not conform to their views, or pay them the attention to which they were accustomed. He was always in the slums with very dubious characters. This annoyed the church class. Why do you frequent those slums ?' He said, ' These slums need me to go to them; for they are sick at heart, and I bear them good news. I tell them they are worth something, in spite of their ill deeds. I tell them their God is a merciful God, and that He has worked out their salvation not for their merits.' Now, these slum people liked their visitor. He had kind words for them. He did not look on them as pariahs. He rather encouraged these people, and He never said words of despair against their evil ways; but he pointed out that happiness resulted from a holy life. His strong rebukes were against the white-robed, clean, respectable people, who thought they were everything that was good, because they had prayer meetings and sacrifices, and washed their hands before eating. Well, you know this story. The good people could not bear the home-thrusts they received, and so they murdered Him. They were too good to do it directly, but they worked up others to do it. The slum people liked this man; He was never hard on them. Some very dubious characters were well received by Him; but he was not polite to those who thought themselves good. He found fault with the invitations they gave to dinner, though He was their guest. He would have called on the ~ divorced.' He would have tried to cheer their life, and have aided them to see that, though the clerical party would not notice them, they were still God's children. Fancy that none of these slum people ever went to church, or ever gave a sacrifice! They were like our own slum people. They would not have liked any of the clerical people to come among them, for the clerical people would have exclaimed, 'I am better than you;' and human nature does not like that, and will never crush and crowd to hear it."

He knew so well what human nature needed and liked, and would crowd to hear, that it seems almost a pity he was not allowed to remain in quiet and talk to them. What a splendid missionary he would make! How well

he could have taken his place among those who are engaged on the Royal Commission to inquire into the
housing of the poor! He would be as well received in
London as he was at Gravesend; and the poor people
would soon learn to bless the kindly, care-worn face, and
the generous hand of Chinese Gordon.

But he was not left to enjoy the rest and quiet that he
needed. Early in May there was a good deal of discussion
on the appointment of Lord Ripon to the Governor-
Generalship of India.

Many considered that he ought not to have been appointed, and that it was a mistake on the part of the
Government; but before the surprise evoked by the
appointment had died away, it was increased by another
astonishing report to the effect that Lord Ripon had
invited Colonel Gordon to become his private secretary, and
that Gordon had accepted the post.

Most persons were not only surprised, but displeased;
though a few thought it would prove a good thing.

The Afghan war had led people to think of establishing
a border-line between the English and Russian empires;
and Mr. Charles Marvin, in *Merv, the Queen of the World,*
pointed out the man to do it :—

" We should choose a good man for the solution of the
Anglo-Russian frontier question; we should allow him to
choose his own advisers ; we should give him abundance of
time to form his own opinions on the subject. He should
have unlimited funds to conduct explorations, and to
appoint assistant explorers. He should visit in succession
Russia and Persia, to realise correctly the genius of those
countries. He should have absolute freedom in the preparation of his plans, and the plan, when complete, should be
made the basis of a definite and final settlement of the
Central Asian question.

" I may be asked to point out the Atlas who can bear

this enormous responsibility upon his shoulders. We have
not to go far to seek him. His name is well known. He
is not the offspring of a clique; he is not the creature of a
faction. He has fought well; he has ruled well. His
Christian piety is a proverb among those who know him;
his scorn of pelf and preferment is so remarkable, that he
almost stands alone—he hardly belongs to a place-hunting,
money-grubbing generation. He possesses the entire confidence of all parties; he enjoys the admiration and love of
the nation. Russia knows nothing to his detriment, and he
has recently earned her respect by his disinterested exer-
tions on her behalf in the distant East. I have no need to
utter his name. It springs spontaneously to the reader's
lips—Chinese Gordon!"

Colonel Gordon accordingly proceeded to India with
Lord Ripon, and some of the newspapers there were very
hopeful that his coming would do great good. "There is
not in the world," said one, "a man of gentler, kindlier
nature than Colonel Gordon."

But he had not been in India many hours when he saw
that he had made a mistake, and felt that he must at once
turn round and come back again. He declared that nothing
could exceed the kindness and consideration which had been
shown to him by Lord Ripon; nor had he ever met a man
with whom, in the arduous task he had chosen, he could .
have felt greater sympathy. Nevertheless, he decided to
leave, and thus wrote his reasons :—

"In a moment of weakness I took the appointment of
private secretary to Lord Ripon, the new Governor-General
of India. No sooner had I landed in Bombay than I saw
that, in my irresponsible position, I could not hope to do
anything really to the purpose, in the face of the vested
interests out there. Seeing this, and seeing, moreover, that
my views were so diametrically opposed to those of the
official classes, I resigned. Lord Ripon's position was

certainly a great consideration to me. It was assumed by some that my views of the state of affairs were the Viceroy's, and thus I felt that I should do him harm by staying with him. We parted perfect friends. The brusqueness of my leaving was unavoidable, inasmuch as my stay would have put me into the possession of secrets of state that—considering my decision eventually to leave—I ought not to know. Certainly I might have stayed a month or two, had a pain in the hand, and gone quietly; but the whole duties were so distasteful, that I felt, being pretty callous as to what the world says, it was better to go at once."

Immediately before he had left India a telegram was sent him urging him to go at once to China. He wrote home for permission to go; but leave was refused, as it was not known in what capacity he wished to serve. So he sent in his resignation to the War Office, which, however, was not accepted; and permission was then given him to go to China on condition that he did not accept any military appointment.

He knew that war was probable between China and Russia, and he was most anxious to do anything he could to prevent it. "To me it appears that the question in dispute cannot be of such vital importance that an arrangement could not be come to by concessions on both sides. Whether I succeed in being heard or not, is not in my hands."

He accordingly paid a hurried visit to China, reaching Hong-kong on the 2nd July, and going to see his old friend Li Hung-Chang at Tien-tsin, who, when he saw him, was so overcome with joy that he fell on his neck and kissed him.

We have already briefly referred to this visit; and given the memorandum which on this occasion Gordon gave to Li. He assisted his former companion in assuring peace instead of war; and he left the land of his former exploits with the thanks of almost every one.

The *Times*, in an article on Russia and China, which appeared in April 1881, bore the following testimony to the good effected by Colonel Gordon :—

"The outbreak of hostilities seemed imminent, when one more attempt was made to bring about a peaceful solution. The Marquis Tsêng, Chinese Ambassador at the Court of St. James, was ordered to St. Petersburg, to endeavour to amend the action of his predecessor ; and Colonel Gordon, in response, it is understood, to an indirect invitation of the Imperial Government, went personally to Pekin, and threw the weight of his great personal influence into the scale of peace. The efforts of both were so far successful that the danger of immediate collision was staved off. . . . .

" This, then, in the spring of 1880, seems to have been the political position at Pekin. Prince Chun and the Empress-Regent were eager for war, and Tso Tsung-tang, with the tattered legions which had never dared to meet the army of Yakoob Khan, vainly believed himself able to cope with the Russian forces; while Li Hung-Chang and other great satraps, who, with a juster appreciation of the relative strength of China and Prussia, desired peace, were dominated by the power of the Imperial name. There is no need to dwell on the circumstances of Colonel Gordon's visit, or on the intrigues which attended his advent. It is enough to say that he paid a visit of several days to the great Viceroy, with whom he had acted in the days of the great Tai-ping rebellion; and both to him, and subsequently to the high authorities at the capital, urged every argument in favour of peace. Exposing the weakness of their forts and ships, and the unweildiness and imperfection of their whole military organisation, he is said to have warned them that the outbreak of hostilities at Kulja would be followed by the invasion of Manchuria, from the Amoor, and that they might expect a hostile army within two months before the gates of Pekin."

After returning from China, Colonel Gordon went to Ireland for a short time; and afterwards visited the King of the Belgians, who was at that time greatly occupied in preparing to send an expedition to the Congo. He had a real holiday, if a short one, on the shores of the Lake of Lausanne; and then turned his thoughts to the Mauritius, whither he was ordered to proceed as Commanding Royal Engineer. On his way to Mauritius he went to Suez to visit the grave of his former helper and lieutenant in the Soudan, Romulus Gessi, who had died in the hospital there from the effects of the terrible privations he endured when shut in by an impassable barrier of weeds in the Bahr Gazelle river. Gordon was exceedingly pained to hear of the death of his friend.

He went to Mauritius, and appeared greatly to enjoy the ten months he spent there. It was while he was there that news came to the effect that he had been made a Major-General.

In the meantime, fresh work was offered to the able worker.

On the 23rd of February 1882 Sir Hercules Robinson sent the following telegram to the Earl of Kimberley :—

"Ministers request me to inquire whether Her Majesty's Government would permit them to obtain the services of Colonel Gordon, R.E., C.B. Ministers desire to invite Colonel Gordon to come to this country for the purpose of consultation as to the best measures to be adopted with reference to Basutoland, in the event of Parliament sanctioning their proposals as to that territory, and to engage his services, should we be prepared to renew the offer made to his predecessor in April 1881—to assist in terminating the war and administering Basutoland."

A telegram was also sent to Gordon telling him that

matters had become very grave, and asking if he would place his services at the disposal of the Cape Government. The telegram added that application had been made to Lord Kimberley, and the War Office had given consent. Accordingly he started for the Cape, and arrived there to find that he had been a little misled. He was told that he would eventually have the affairs of Basutoland placed in his hands; but at present he was asked to take command of the forces. The few months that followed were somewhat disappointing ones, and, in the result, very much so indeed.

On the 1st of July 1882 General Gordon took command of the Colonial forces in South Africa; and he at once issued a report on the state of the troops. His paper was, like himself, exceedingly direct and outspoken; and he told the truth about them, although the truth was, on many points, very unpalatable. He advised the formation of a native militia, with block-houses garrisoned by Europeans. He declared that the field artillery was of no use whatever. In regard to the Basuto question, he said that the limits of the native locations should be then and there fixed by legal deeds, and that all who encroached upon the borders of the tribes should be legally proceeded against, as this would sstisfy the natives, and cause them to become quiet and contented.

In September General Gordon, in company with the Secretary for Native Affairs, visited Basutoland, in the hope of settling the disputes that had arisen between the natives and the white squatters. A thousand armed Basutos met and escorted them, and they had an interview with several chiefs, who professed an ardent desire for peace, and disgust at the conduct of Masupha, the rebel chief who had been the principal factor in the rebellion. Gordon next had an interview with Masupha himself, but he could not bring the chief to reason: he would make no offer of submission, and declared he would not be satisfied with any settlement which did not give him independence. Whilst negotiations were going on, and General Gordon was urging Masupha to pay the hut tax and submit to the authority of the Government, news arrived that an expedition under Lerothodi was on its way to attack Masupha. The latter was so enraged at the tidings that he immediately broke off negotiations; and General Gordon was so displeased at such a step being taken at a moment when he thought his efforts might prove successful, that he tendered his resignation to the Cape Government. This was accepted with unseemly haste, and he started forthwith for England. The loss to the colony of a man like Gordon, at such a critical time, was most serious, and indicated a want of justice and wisdom on the part of the authorities that was exceedingly surprising.

At the end of the episode he returned to London, and soon after set off for the Holy Land, which he had long wished to visit. He took up his abode near Jerusalem, and spent the time in pleasurable quietness, until a cry of many voices reached him, " Wanted—Chinese Gordon ! "

CHAPTER XXIV.

TROUBLES IN THE SOUDAN.

"List his discourse of war, and you shall hear
A fearful battle."

—*Henry V.*

IN many Mussulman countries there existed a belief that on the completion of twelve centuries from the Hegira, the Mahdi, or new deliverer, would appear. The twelve centuries were reckoned to come to an end on 12th November 1882. But one who would not wait for that eventful day had already arisen, and declared himself the Mahdi. This was a man about thirty years of age, who is described as being tall and slim, and having a light brown complexion. His name was Mahomet Achmet, and he was the son of a carpenter. He was apprenticed to his uncle, who one day gave him a beating, which so enraged him that he ran away, and went to a free school kept by one of the dervishes at Hoghali, a village near Khartoum. This school is attached to the shrine of the patron saint of Khartoum, and is greatly venerated by the natives. From this school he went to another at Berber, where also there is a shrine; and he there seemed to be a religious boy.

In 16.. he became the disciple of Sheikh Nur-el-Dami, a name which means "Continuous Light," and he ordained him a faki or sheikh. After this he went to live in the island of Abba, on the White Nile, where he dug a cave for himself, which he called a retreat, and into which he went constantly to worship. He began to be known as a very pious man, greatly given to fasting, and incense-burning, and prayers. After a time he was joined by followers, who gave him presents, so that he became very wealthy. He married as many wives as he was allowed to have, and always took them from wealthy families, by which means, of course, his own wealth and influence were increased. In May 1881 he began to write letters declaring himself the Mahdi whom Mahomet had foretold. He said that he had been sent to reform Islam, that he would bring a new state of things into the Mahommedan world, that he would establish the equality of man, and make the rich share with the poor. A great many people at once believed in him, and followed him. Then he went further, and said that those who did not receive him should be destroyed, whoever and whatever they were.

Among the people to whom he wrote was Mahomet Saleh of Dongola, whom he ordered to collect his followers and join him at Abba. But this chief, instead of doing so, wrote to the Government an account of the doings and pretensions of the False Prophet. His Excellency Raouf Pasha thought it time to interfere; and in August 1881 he sent an expedition to meet him.

The world had been so occupied with Arabi Pasha in Egypt, that very little notice was taken of the Mahdi for some time; but on the 19th December 1881, news came that there were troubles in the Soudan. The False Prophet, at the head of one thousand five hundred men, totally annihilated an Egyptian force of three hundred and fifty men, who were led against him by the Governor of Fashada.

The governor himself was among the killed. The Governor-General of the Soudan at once sent for reinforcements, and the Black Regiment, under the command of Abdallah Bey, was ordered to advance. But the Egyptian forces were very half-hearted in the matter, and were beaten again and again.

In July 1882 the Mahdi brought his followers, and made them surround the Egyptian soldiers under Yusef Pasha. The Egyptians were without food, and were easily overcome, the entire army being massacred by the Mahdi. After that he marched northward, to occupy Shata Domen; and his army attacked Schatz, and slaughtered the people.

He had set his heart upon the capture of El Obeid, which town was garrisoned by 6000 men. Obeid was kept supplied with food and for some time the rebel could not succeed in his purpose. At Bara and at Duern the Mahdi was defeated. He lost 2300 men at Zidora, Kordofan, and Shcitfan.

On the 8th of September he attacked Obeid, and was repulsed. He made a second and a third attack with the same result; and on the last occasion 10,000 of his men were slain. On 15th September the following report was made :—" Abd-el-Kader, the commander in charge of the Egyptian forces in the Soudan, and now at Obeid, is in despair at not receiving reinforcements from the Khedive. Khartoum is fortified, but the soldiers are said to be demoralised, and the population secretly giving their adherence to the False Prophet." Obeid had then been under siege for forty days.

On 24th October some reinforcements sent to Kordofan were entirely destroyed. Other reinforcements sent from Khartoum to attack the rebels at Bara were defeated, but afterwards got into Bara, and won a victory.

On the 8th of December a man arrived on the scene who was likely to make things better, if it were possible, and that was Colonel Stuart; but in the beginning of January 1883 both Bara and Obeid surrendered to the Mahdi, who at once entered the latter town, and took up his residence there. There had been some terrible fighting over El Obeid. It is described as a long straggling town at the foot of an open slope, down which, in the rainy season, the water pours. There are many mosques in Obeid, which are built of mud bricks, of which also the houses are made. The houses, except that of the Governor, have no upper storey. In the front of the Governor's house was the gallows. The market-place consists of booths of matting, and presents a lively scene, especially in the morning. Arab women are busy selling milk; their hair decorated with coral and gold. Mixing with them, or in another part of the bazaar, were Soudanese, Nubian, and Egyptian women, selling merissa, hair-grease, sour milk, khasheesh—a very intoxicating drug—liquorice water, thenna—a paste prepared with dry leaves of the mignonettee tree, used by the Arabs for, the purpose of dying their nails red—and kohhl, which is a powder made of frankincense, used also by the Arab ladies for dyeing the lids and brows of the eyes. Tobacco is also sold in the Obeid market, and so are iron and brass vessels. In the market may be seen Greeks, Arabs, and Egyptians, who buy the wares offered for sale, and frequent the coffee shops. They are dressed in all sorts of gorgeous colours and costumes. Plenty of fruits and flowers, especially wild flowers, grow in and around El Obeid.

The *Daily News* published a very curious letter which had been forwarded by its special correspondent, Mr. O'Donovan, and which shows how some of the Mahdi's followers regarded him :—

"The following is a copy of a letter received from Yusef Effendi Mansoor and Mahommed Iskender Bey, officers of the regular army in Kordofan, who are at present prisoners at Obeid :—

"In the name of God, the Merciful and Compassionate. Thanks be unto God. the Bountiful Ruler; prayers and salutations unto our Lord Mohammed, and to his people resignation. From the servants of God, Sheikh Mohammed Iskender and Sheikh Yusef Mansoor, formerly officers in the Kordofan army, now auxiliaries of the Mahdi (peace be unto him !), to all Muslim officers of the regular troops in Khartoum, and to the Bashi-Bazouks, and to civil employées from the rank of general down to that of second lieutenant. We warn you, oh friends, and counsel you conscientiously, by the traditions of the Prophet (peace and salutation unto him ?). He has said, 'The faith of man will not be perfect until he loves his brother as he loves himself.' We have not been constrained to write you this our warning; but, fearing your worldly destruction and a bad end, we freely offer you advice. Friends, we are with the Mahdi, and as we have seen him regularly for the past six months, we watch his proceedings attentively ; we hear all that he says, and we have not found in him a grain of anything that is bad or unbecoming his holy mission. (Peace be unto him !) By the great God and the excellent Koran we swear that he is the true Mahdi—the Expected One. There is no other but he, and the man who doubts his holy mission is an infidel, and God has already decreed it. As a proof of this, the large amount of gold and silver, with immense stores of goods which came into his possession, has no interest whatever for him ; and it lies in the Muslim treasury, with a faithful and trustworthy man in charge of it all, and who distributes it to widows and orphans and emigrants. The Mahdi seeks nothing but God. He is kind, and speaks civilly to all. He abhors falsehoods, and his pride is to spread the glory of our religion. He fights in the path of God, and only with those who refuse to obey him. His daily life (peace be unto him !) is quite opposed to worldly matters, nor does he care for its enjoyments. He is simple in his diet and plain in dress. Kisaret dourra (millet) steeped in water is all that he eats. A plain shirt, and trousers made from the native cloth is all that he wears. · He is always smiling, and his face is as resplendent as the new moon. His body and form is of the sons of Israel, and on his right cheek is a mole (khal), and also other marks which are written in the books of the holy law are stamped upon him. He neither honours the rich for their riches nor does he neglect the poor on account of their poverty. All Muslims to him are equal. Like a kind father to his children, so much is his kindness towards us. Had he punished us for what we have done none of us would be saved, but he forgave us on our repentance. We all receive a sufficient sum from the treasury for the support of our family, but do not get any fixed pay. If I were to describe to you all the good qualities of the Mahdi, it would take a long letter to do so. He is following the footsteps of his grandfather [ancestor?]—peace be to his bones!—and if you are Muslims and the sons of Muslims, banish worldly affairs, and follow not the inclination of sinful souls, which leads its possessor to destruction, but look to the end and to Paradise. The way to it is to surrender to Sayed el Mahdi, son of Sayed Abdallah. By doing this you will be victorious, and be auxiliaries of the Faith. Beware of fighting against Muslims. We and you, God willing, shall fight infidels, the enemy of the Faith. If you are believers in God and His Prophet, strengthen yourselves by rebellion, and avoid assisting infidels. And remember that victory comes from God, and He gives it to whom He pleases.

"With the numerous army of the Mahdi, which is about two hundred thousand fighting men, whose souls are offered to the Lord, we have also Remingtons, cannon, and rockets, which have been taken from the Turks, besides an ample supply of ammunition. The Mahdi, however (unto whom be peace !), trusts to God only, and will prevent fighting by fire-arms, spears, and swords. He fights otherwise, and his connection with the angels is well known, as we well know from the history of Mohammed. If you still prefer worldly enjoyments, and insist upon fighting with us, you should remember what happened in the battles of Abba, Fashoda, Ghedeer, and Kordofan ; and at the time his army was small, especially at Ghedeer, where he had no fire-arms nor weapons, when most of his followers had sticks only. By the great God, the God of all times, he has not bidden us to write this : but we ourselves do so of our own free will, fearing for your safety. We have begged Khalifa Ledeek and the Prince of the Mahdi's army, Abdallah, son of Sayed Mohammed, to write this letter for us. Our lord the Mahdi was opposed to its being written. For our sake he consented. The matter stands as we have explained, and we think it well of you to accept our advice. If you go against it you will repent; but your repentance will not avail you when destruction comes. Peace !

" Seals of { SHEIKH YUSEF MANSOOR.
 SHEIKH MOHAMMED ISKENDER.

"EL OBEID, 13*th Shaban*, 1300 (16*th June* 1883)."

Before this time all indifference on the part of the English towards the affairs of the Soudan had passed away. On the 6th of February Lord Dufferin, when writing on the re-organisation of Egypt, wrote the following in reference to the Soudan :—

" Some persons are inclined to advise Egypt to withdraw altogether from the Soudan and her other acquisitions in that region ; but she can hardly be expected to acquiesce in such a policy. Possessing the lower ranges of the Nile, she is naturally inclined to claim dominion along its entire course ; and when it is remembered that the territories in question, if properly developed, are capable of producing inexhaustible supplies of sugar and cotton, we cannot be surprised at her unwillingness to abandon them. Unhappily, Egyptian administration in the Soudan has been almost uniformly unfortunate. The success of the present Mahdi, in raising the tribes and in extending his influence over great tracts of country, is a sufficient proof of the Government's inability either to reconcile the inhabitants to its rule or to maintain order. The consequences have been most disastrous. Within the last year and a-half the Egyptians have lost something like 9000 men, while it is estimated that 40,000 of their opponents have perished. Nor does this chronic slaughter seem to be nearer its conclusion than when it first commenced. Reinforcements to the extent of another 10,000 men have been despatched to Khartoum; but they seem to be raw, undisciplined, and disheartened levies. In the meantime, Egyptian garrisons at Obeid and Bara, and various scattered posts in Darfour and Kordofan, are cut off from communication with their base, many of them are surrounded, and some are pressed by famine. Obeid still holds out, but Bara seems to be on the point of surrendering.

"Colonel Hicks, a distinguished retired Indian officer, has been engaged by the Egyptian Government to join the commander-in-chief of the Soudan army as chief of the staff. A few retired European officers accompany him, who, perhaps, will be able to inspire the troops with confidence. Both Colonel Hicks and his companions have entered the Egyptian service on their own responsibility, nor have either Sir Edward Malet or myself been concerned in the arrangement.

"In the expectation that the fresh efforts about to be made will result in the restoration of tranquillity, a plan should be carefully considered for the future administration of the country. Hitherto, it has caused a continual drain on the resources of the Egyptian exchequer. The first step necessary is the construction of a railway from Suakim to Berber, or what, perhaps, would be still more advisable, to Shendy, on the Nile. Another scheme of railway communication has been proposed down the Nile valley, but it has many disadvantages. The promoters of the Suakim route maintain that the construction of their line would bring Cairo within six and a-half days of Khartoum—the time required to run from Suakim to Berber, on the Nile, being only sixteen hours—and that the cost would be under a million and a-half. The completion of this enterprise would at once change all the elements of the problem. Instead of being a burden on the Egyptian exchequer, these Equatorial Provinces ought to become, with anything like good management, a source of wealth to the Government. What has hitherto prevented their development has been the difficulty of getting machinery into the country, and of conveying its cotton, sugar, and other natural products to the sea. The finances of the Soudan once rehabilitated, the provincial adminstration would no longer be forced to visit its subjects with those heavy exactions which have been, in all probability, at the bottom of the present disturbances, and the natural expansion of commerce would eventually extend the benefits of civilisation for some distance through the surrounding regions. I apprehend, however, that it would be wise upon the part of Egypt to abandon Darfour, and perhaps part of Kordofan, and to be content with maintaining her jurisdiction in the provinces of Khartoum and Senaar."

On the 6th of June news reached England of Hicks Pasha's first victory. Five thousand of the enemy were engaged, and five hundred killed; and a subsequent telegram stated that the Senaar campaign was over. The Khedive sent a congratulatory letter thanking the forces. With Abd-el-Kader on the Blue Nile, and General Hicks on the White, the rebels had been crushed. They boasted that they would wait at Gebelain; but they fled at the approach of Hicks Pasha to Kordofan.

After this several chiefs sent in their submission, and it was hoped that the Mahdi would do so too, but he did not. They gave to Hicks the name of the "Great Magician." Several of the men fighting were clad in coats of armour like the old crusaders. The correspondent also mentions that Sir Samuel Baker's steamers, *Ismailia* and *Khedive*, were doing good service.

In August General Hicks was making his preparations to take Obeid from the Mahdi. Reports came to the effect that the Mahdi's followers were deserting him. In consequence of this the Egyptian army was full of hope; and so was England.

The Mahdi's movement being professedly a religious one, it was deemed inadvisable to place at the head of the Egyptian army in the Soudan a foreigner and non-Mussulman, lest this might be taken hold of by the insurgent leader to arouse still further the fanaticism of his followers. Accordingly, Suleiman Pasha, whose early military career dates back to the time of Mehemet Ali and the Crimean war, was elected to the chief command, but with the distinct agreement that he was to pay strict attention to, and carefully carry out, General Hicks's wishes and plans.

The march was a very tedious one, and the little army of Hicks made up their minds to live on biscuits and grain. They dreaded the famine and the climate much more than the enemy, but their greatest anxiety was on account of the water supply. They were encouraged by the submission of the principal sheikh of Obeid, with three hundred horsemen. But the enemy was resolute, and the way was very weary.

Accompanying Hicks Pasha were Ala Eddeen Pasha (the Governor-General), Abbas Bey, Colonel Farquhar, Majors

Seckendorff, Massy, Warner, and Evans; Captains Heath and Walker; Surgeons George Bey and Rosenberg; Mr. O'Donovan of the *Daily News*, Major Brody of the Royal Horse Artillery, with other pashas and beys, and a considerable number of Egyptian officers.

In England, although people hoped for the best, there were many forebodings, and it seemed as if the air was full of coming trouble. Other countries felt likewise, for the news that came told of the dangers of the little army under Hicks. An Austrian officer—Major von Seckendorff—described the march from Khartoum to Duem as most trying on account of the baggage, but as there was water, they were able to effect it. He feared, however, there would be a dreadful dearth of water during the advance on Obeid, since the wells along that route were very scarce, and the camels only carried sufficient water for one day. The Mahdi, he said, was in possession of 15,000 good breech-loaders, fourteen guns, and a numerous and excellent cavalry. His people, too, were roused by fanaticism, and would fearlessly ride to their death.

Hicks Pasha had 10,000 men, 6000 camels, and many pack-horses and mules. The latter necessarily impeded the advance into a desert without water, The writer concluded with the following words:—"If our cavalry suffices for out-post duty, success is possible, otherwise the issue will be very disastrous. In case of defeat not a soul of ours will return, and Khartoum and the entire Soudan will then be irretrievably lost, since all believe that the Mahdi is the Messiah." A letter from the Austrian Consul at Khartoum described the departure of Hicks Pasha with his army from that place on the 9th of September, and estimated that his forces consisted of 6000 infantry, 4000 Bashi-Bazouks, five hundred horses, 5500 camels, four Krupp and ten mountain guns, and six Nordenfeldts. The expedition took no apparatus for sinking artesian wells such as was used in Abyssinia. It was intended by the General to establish between Duem and El Obeid six depôt forts.

The Consul declared in his letter that in case of the Mahdi being victorious, the whole of the Soudan would be lost to Egypt.

For some time there was no news of Hicks and his army. On 22nd November the daily papers declared that Hicks Pasha's silence was beginning to cause anxiety in Government circles. The prevalent opinion was that in the event of his defeat a complete abandonment of the Soudan provinces would be preferable to a continual drain of blood and treasure.

The next news was terrible. The English people were not prepared for the awful catastrophe which the press made known on the morning of the 23rd of November.

The news was, that there had been three days' fighting, and that Hicks Pasha and his army had been utterly annihilated.

It seems that Hicks went to Kamua, near Obeid, a place with hills on either side. He sent half his men to Obeid to demand its surrender. The Mahdi was advancing from the south-east, and he fell in with that portion of Hicks's army which was on its way to Obeid, and attacked it. Hicks heard the firing, and brought the rest of his army to join the force attacked by the Mahdi. The battles were on the 3rd, 4th, and 5th of November. The Mahdi was backed by immense numbers, and he supplied the vacancies with fresh men. Hicks's army had formed into square, and his whole force was destroyed. The English officers fought gallantly, but they could not stand against the overwhelming might and fury of the enemy. Hicks had 10,000 men, and the Arabs numbered 200,000.

At first it was hoped that the news was really too bad to be true. It was thought that further details would not confirm the first horrible tidings; but subsequent telegrams only verified them, and increased the anxiety that was everywhere felt. For a day or two it was hoped that Mr. O'Donovan would not be among the slain; and great interest was felt in the last letter that had been received from him, in which he said that the troops scarcely deserved the name of soldiers, they were so ignorant of the art of fighting. They had not sufficient clothing, and had received no money for several months. They had no heart for the work, for many would not have gone at all if they had not been com pelled. O'Donovan also said that Hicks was greatly inconvenienced by the conduct of Suleiman Pasha, whc just then opposed him in many points.

We have already mentioned that Suleiman had been ap pointed to assist Hicks; but he had shown such apathy and apparent jealousy of the Englishman, that Ala Eddeen Pasha, the present Governor-General of the Soudan, removed him, and General Hicks received the whole of the responsibility, and was made Commander-in-chief of the army. Altogether, the suppression of the insurrection was felt to be one of enormous difficulty; and the able correspondent himself was very sad at heart as he contemplated the possible defeat of the army to which he was attached.

Very little can ever be known of the particulars of the disaster, for those who would have written them were killed.

The following is a *Times* telegram, published later, and sent from Khartoum :—

"The first and only survivor of Hicks Pasha's army, a man who marched with Hicks Pasha from Duem, and who has now come back in safety, arrived here last night. He is a native of Khartoum, and is well known here. He states that he was in the battle of Kashgate, and has a lance wound in the back.

"During the fight, owing to the rocky nature of the

ground and the number of trees, no proper formation could be preserved among the soldiers. They fought in detached groups, each body of men surrounded by Arabs, who picked them off in turn. Hicks Pasha fought like a lion, discharging the contents of his revolver three times, and then using his sword. He was the last of the staff to die. The members of the staff all fell in one group.

"After the battle about one hundred and fifty soldiers were found lying wounded, and the Mahdi ordered that no wounded man should be injured. My informant says nothing about any wounded officers. The heads of the staff officers and of the Egyptian officers were struck off and exhibited to the prisoners, and then fixed over the gate of El Obeid. The Arabs resolved to build a tomb over Hicks Pasha's body, in recognition of his great bravery.

"The Mahdi had sent an expedition against Slaten Bey, an Austrian commanding the garrison of Darfour. He also threatens to punish the Fargalla tribe for not assisting in the rebellion. The Sheikh of the Fargallas sent him a defiance, saying that he had 15,000 warriors and provisions for seven years, and that he was ready to meet the Mahdi. The Mahdi is also embroiled with the great Kabbabish tribe, some of whom were allies of the Government. He says that he will punish them for their loyalty.

"The survivor who states all these facts escaped from El Obeid owing to his being a black man and not in uniform."

The battle of Kashgill, in which Hicks was killed, was fought on the 5th of November, and on the very next day, the sixth, another battle was fought in the Eastern Soudan, at Tokar, also with lamentable results. Some months before the disaffected tribes in the east had broken into open insurrection, and surrounded the garrisons at Sinkat and Tokar. They stopped communication between

Berber and Suakim, and threatened to march on the latter garrison. Captain Moncrieff was sent with a force to the relief of Tokar. They were surrounded by the rebels and overcome, and Captain Moncrieff himself was slain.

There was great difficulty in getting a supply of men to go; and even while they were waiting, another defeat occurred. People began to get intensely anxious, while telegrams like the following that came to hand were by no means reassuring :—

" Owing to the small size of the steamers plying between Suez and Suakim, the transport of the whole body of two thousand five hundred men will require some time. Baker Pasha himself will leave in about ten days.

" The Egyptian contingent was reviewed by the Khedive this afternoon. The review was followed by an unpleasant incident. The Turkish officers came in a body to Baker Pasha and plainly refused to go to the Soudan, on the plea that their contract of service was for Egypt alone. This most serious step on their part was quite unexpected ; but it is hoped that some arrangement may be made for arriving at a quiet settlement.

" None of the Egyptian officers refused to go; but many of them wept when they heard what was to be their destination. There can be no doubt that the men of the Gendarmerie have been very hardly treated. While bearing the whole brunt of the suffering and hard work entailed by the cholera they were comforted by the assurance that thenceforth they would be employed as a purely civil force; but now, on the first emergency, they find themselves being used as the only available military force for the defence of Egypt against the Mahdi, while the army takes over their civil duties.

" In estimating their grievances we must remember that among the natives the feeling has always prevailed that being sent to the Soudan is equivalent to a sentence of death. Recent events have certainly not tended to diminish that impression.

"It has now become a melancholy military necessity to abandon the garrison of Sinkat, under Ibrahim Bey, to their fate, as it is impossible with a small force to attempt to push through the dangerous passes on the road, which are held by some fifteen thousand of the enemy, who appear to be well armed.

"I have also heard, on most trustworthy authority, that for some time past the rebels have been supplied with arms and provisions by Government employés at Suakim."

And now people began to ask in decided tones, "Where is Gordon ? Why not send him ?" The *Pall Mall Gazette* especially advised his going.

"But if we have not an Egyptian army to employ in the service, and if we must not send an English force, what are we to do ? There is only one thing that we can do. We cannot send a regiment to Khartoum, but we can send a man who, on more than one occasion, has proved himself more valuable in similar circumstances than an entire army. Why not send Chinese Gordon with full powers to Khartoum, to assume absolute control of the territory, to treat with the Mahdi, to relieve the garrisons, and do what can be done, to save what can be saved from the wreck in the Soudan ? There is no necessity to speak of the pre-eminent qualifications which he possesses for the work. They are notorious, and are as undisputed as they are indisputable. His engagement on the Congo could surely be postponed. No man can deny the urgent need in the midst of that hideous welter of confusion for the presence of such a man, with a born genius for command, an un-exampled capacity in organising ' Ever-Victorious Armies,' and a perfect knowledge of the Soudan and its people. Why not send him out with *carte-blanche* to do the best that can be done ? He may not be able, single-handed, to reduce that raging chaos to order, but the attempt is worth making, and if it is to be made it will have to be made at once. For before many days General Gordon will have left for the Congo, and the supreme opportunity may have passed by."

These words were echoed by many voices immediately; and it was felt in many circles, and almost without reference to politics, that Charles Gordon was the man for the hour.

CHAPTER XXV.

GORDON'S RESPONSE.

" Life every man holds dear, but the brave man
Holds honour far more precious dear than life."
—*Troilus and Cressida.*

THE newspaper correspondents in the Soudan had been for some time giving hints in regard to General Gordon. "Would that Gordon Pasha were here !" was a wish often expressed by the Europeans. Nor were they alone. Some of the natives, who remembered him lovingly and gratefully, often remarked that the former Governor-General would be the man to help them in their present troubles. That "Gordon Pasha was the most popular and beloved Governor-General that ever ruled the Soudan" was the testimony borne by Dr. Schweinfurth and many others. Those who knew him wondered why he was not sent. Mr. Allan, the secretary of the British and Foreign Anti-Slavery Society, and a personal friend of Gordon's, tells us in his interesting little pamphlet, *The Life of Chinese Gordon*—which it is to be hoped everybody has read—that "an eminent person, well known in the philanthropic world," sent to him the follow-

ing respecting the wonderful man who was then quietly living at Jaffa :—"Would that an angel would stand at Earl Granville's side, and say unto him, 'And now send men to Joppa, and call for one—Gordon. He shall tell thee what thou oughtest to do.'"

There appeared no time to lose, for so far as Egypt was concerned the New Year appeared gloomy enough.

The telegrams were not re-assuring.

On the 1st January news came that two European officers had resigned. They were Major Holroyd and Colonel Giles. These men had been badly treated by the Egyptians ; and the feeling between the officers of the Egyptians and the Europeans was becoming almost hostile. News had reached them that the widow of Consul Moncrieff was not to receive the ordinary widow's pension ; for it was said that Moncrieff went on his own accord, and was not sent. But Moncrieff had said beforehand that he felt it his duty, as the consul of the whole of Eastern Soudan, to go with the Egyptian force to Tokar, that he might be able to report to the Government on the real object of the rebellion, and the state of affairs in the interior. The news from Suakim was that Baker Pasha had reviewed the troops on Christmas Day.

On the 10th January the following telegram was published :—"Communication with Khartoum is interrupted, a fact which causes some anxiety. The wires are believed to have been cut by the Kababash tribe. Hostile forces in the rear of Khartoum would make the abandonment of the place by its garrison and non-combatant residents a difficult matter."

This difficulty occupied the public mind in England for a day or two ; for it was decided that the Soudan must be abandoned, and Khartoum evacuated, although no one knew how it was to be managed. Apart from the immense mass of stores which had to be left, there were a thousand families of protected subjects and Egyptian officials, who had to quit the town. At least six thousand camels were needed for their transport from Berber to Assouan, and the season was against the refugees, for the simoom winds were coming on.

But on the 18th of January the news was flashed throughout the country that General Gordon was going to the Soudan, and hope and joy filled thousands of hearts at once.

Every one felt that he was the man for the hour.

The *Times* said, "It is impossible to exaggerate the feelings of relief and satisfaction universally inspired by the knowledge that General Gordon has undertaken the pacification of the Soudan."

The *Pall Mall Gazette*, which had all along been urging this, was delighted and satisfied.

The name of Chinese Gordon was at once upon a million lips; and while those who had not read of him were asking, "Who is he?" and those who had were rejoicing in thankfulness, and only anxious to hear the latest news, all parties seemed to have trust in the magic power of the man, and Conservatives and Liberals alike hailed the news with profound satisfaction.

The Central News gave the particulars that all were longing to hear :—

"We are enabled to state authoritatively that General Gordon ("Chinese Gordon") has been instructed by the British Government with an important commission in the Soudan. Whilst General Gordon was in Brussels on Thursday, on business connected with his Congo appointment, he received a telegram from the English Government asking him if he would be able to go to Egypt, and if so, when. He promptly replied that he would most certainly go, and that he was prepared to start at the shortest notice. On receipt of this reply, instructions were at once telegraphed to the General to return to London without delay. He obeyed this order to the letter, and arrived in London yesterday morning. About noon General Gordon had an interview with such members of the Cabinet as are at present in town, and subsequently received the fullest instructions as to the character of his appointment. The Central News is informed that the chief duty entrusted to General Gordon is the difficult and delicate one of conciliating the various tribes scattered throughout the Soudan, with the ultimate object of bringing about some arrangement between the several conflicting elements in that country. General Gordon, however, was distinctly given to understand that the Government strictly adhere to their intention to evacuate the Soudan. The General was further informed that he will be the accredited agent of the British Government. He will take his future instructions solely from Sir Evelyn Baring, as the mouthpiece of the British Government, and will be in no way accountable to the Khedive or any Egyptian authority. General Gordon was so sufficiently satisfied with the terms of his engagement that he completed his personal arrangements within a few hours, and left Charing Cross station by the Indian mail last evening, accompanied by Colonel Stewart, who will act as the General's Chief of the Staff and confidential assistant generally. So quietly were General Gordon's arrangements made that the only persons who assembled at the station to wish the gallant officer God-speed were the Duke of Cambridge, Lord Wolseley, Colonel Brocklehurst, and Lord Hartington's private secretary. General Gordon will not go near Cairo, as his instructions are to get to Suakim with the least possible delay. He will join the Peninsular and Oriental steamer with the Indian mails at Brindisi, and on arriving at Suez will go on board a British gun-boat, which he will find waiting for him there. From Suez he will proceed direct to Suakim. The King of the

Belgians is naturally much distressed at this arrangement, as it was at his request that General Gordon recently returned from Syria. General Gordon has informed His Majesty that he much regrets that he cannot, under the peculiar circumstances, proceed to the Congo, as arranged, but he hoped to be able to carry out his engagement to His Majesty on his return from the Soudan."

It was afterwards said that Colonel Brocklehurst opened the carriage door for the man who was just then the hope of all. Lord Wolseley insisted on carrying the portmanteau of the hero, and the Duke of Cambridge got his ticket.

General Gordon was unaccompanied, except by Lieutenant-Colonel Stewart, of the 11th Hussars, who had been at Khartoum on duty the year before, and who went with Gordon in the capacity of military secretary.

As he went forth on his solitary mission of peace, many English hearts prayed that God would bless and prosper him. There was something so romantic in it all that the imagination could but follow him with thought and sympathy. But his instructions were very matter of fact. The following was the communication made by Earl Granville to him :—

"FOREIGN OFFICE, 18*th January* 1884.

"Sir—Her Majesty's Government are desirous that you should proceed at once to Egypt, to report to them on the military situation in the Soudan, and on the measures which it may be advisable to take for the security of the Egyptian garrisons still holding positions in that country, and for the safety of the European population in Khartoum. You are also desired to consider and report upon the best mode of effecting the evacuation of the interior of the Soudan, and upon the manner in which the safety and the good administration by the Egyptian Government of the ports on the sea coast can best be secured. In connection with this subject, you should pay especial consideration to the question of the

steps that may usefully be taken to counteract the stimulus
which it is feared may possibly be given to the slave trade
by the present insurrectionary movement, and by the withdrawal of the Egyptian authority from the interior. You
will be under the instructions of Her Majesty's Agent and
Consul-General at Cairo, through whom your reports to
Her Majesty's Government should be sent under flying seal.
You will consider yourself authorised and instructed to
perform such other duties as the Egyptian Government
may desire to entrust to you, and as may be communicated
to you by Sir E. Baring. You will be accompanied by
Colonel Stewart, who will assist you in the duties thus
confided to you. On your arrival in Egypt you will at
once communicate with Sir E. Baring, who will arrange to
meet you, and will settle with you whether you should
proceed direct to Suakim, or should go yourself or despatch
Colonel Stewart to Khartoum, *viâ* the Nile.—I am, etc.,

" (Signed)　GRANVILLE."

He went from Dover by the mail packet *Samphire.* He
reached Port Said on the twenty-fourth, and he and
Lieutenant-Colonel Stewart went at once to Cairo, which
place they reached at nine o'clock at night. They were not
generally expected, and there was no crowd to greet them.
General Evelyn Wood and Major Watson were with them,
having joined them at Port Said. They drove at once to
the house of General Wood, and there met Sir Evelyn
Baring. Gordon was dressed in plain clothes, and seemed
cheery and well.

He received, as he was told to expect, his final instructions from Sir Evelyn Baring. He also had given to him
£40,000 with which to pay the troops ; and on the night of
26th January he left Cairo for Assiout.

The following was written by Sir Evelyn Baring to
Gordon on the twenty-fifth :—

"It is believed that the number of Europeans at Khartoum is very small; but it has been estimated by the local authorities that some 10,000 to 15,000 people will wish to move northwards from Khartoum only when the Egyptian garrison is withdrawn. These people are native Christians, Egyptian employés, their wives and children, etc. The Government of his Highness the Khedive is earnestly solicitous that no effort should be spared to ensure the retreat both of these people and of the Egyptian garrison without loss of life.

"As regards the most opportune time and the best method for effecting the retreat, whether of the garrisons or of the civil populations, it is neither necessary nor desirable that you should receive detailed instructions. A short time ago the local authorities pressed strongly on the Egyptian Government the necessity for giving orders for an immediate retreat. . . . You will bear in mind that the main end to be pursued is the evacuation of the Soudan. This policy was adopted, after very full discussion, by the Egyptian Government, on the advice of Her Majesty's Government. It meets with the full approval of His Highness the Khedive and of the present Egyptian Ministry. I understand also that you entirely concur in the desirability of adopting this policy, and that you think it should on no account be changed. You consider that it may take a few months to carry it out with safety. You are further of opinion that 'the restoration of the country should be made to the different petty Sultans who existed at the time of Mehemet Ali's conquest, and whose families still exist;' and that an endeavour should be made to form a confederation of those Sultans. In this view the Egyptian Government entirely concurs.

"It will, of course, be fully understood that the Egyptian troops are not to be kept in the Soudan merely with a view to consolidating the power of the new rulers of the country.

But the Egyptian Government has the fullest confidence in your judgment, your knowledge of the country, and of your comprehension of the general line of policy to be pursued. You are, therefore, given full discretionary power to retain the troops for such reasonable period as you may think necessary, in order that the abandonment of the country may be accomplished with the least possible risk to life and property. A credit of £100,000 has been opened for you at the Finance Department, and further funds will be supplied to you on your requisition when this sum is exhausted. In undertaking the difficult task which now lies before you, you may feel assured that no effort will be wanting on the part of the Cairo authorities, whether English or Egyptian, to afford you all the co-operation and support in their power."

Sir Evelyn Baring states that when he read over to him the draft of this despatch the General expressed his entire concurrence in the instructions. "The only suggestion he made was in connection with the passage in which, speaking of the policy of abandoning the Soudan, I had said, ' I understand also that you entirely concur in the desirability of adopting this policy.' General Gordon wished that I should add the words, ' and that you think it should on no account be changed.' These words were accordingly added."

The news of his arrival in the Soudan was received with the wildest joy, as the following telegrams, taken from the *Standard,* prove :—

CAIRO, Friday Night.

"After rising very early this morning, General Gordon called on the Khedive, by whom he was most cordially received, as also by Nubar Pasha. Afterwards, accompanied by Sir Evelyn Wood, Lieutenant-Colonel Stewart, and Major Watson, he paid a visit to Sir Evelyn Baring, with whom he discussed the whole situation in the Soudan for several hours; the conversation, which was only interrupted for luncheon, lasting until six o'clock in the evening. Sir Evelyn Wood, however, left about three to attend to his duties elsewhere.

"These deliberations were, of course, strictly private, and absolutely nothing is known of the result, but there is reason to believe that General Gordon is to be entrusted with a mission, half military half diplomatic, and without any very definite instructions such as might hamper his initiative while on the spot. His primary object will be to secure, in whatever way possible, by negotiation or otherwise, the safety of those inhabitants of the Soudan who remain loyal to the Cairo Government.

"Should it appear to General Gordon on his arrival at Khartoum that the strength of the Mahdi is exaggerated, and that there is a reasonable prospect of holding the town by the opening up either of Suakim-Berber or the Massowah-Kasala route, there is little doubt that an effort will be made to carry out what are known to be his personal feelings on the subject.

"General Gordon leaves Cairo to-morrow evening. He goes by train to Assiout, whence a steamer will be chartered which will take him as far as Wady Halfa, at the Second Cataract. Thence he intends to strike directly across the desert for Abu Hamad, following the course of the river from this point to Khartoum. This plan, however, may be modified by circumstances.

"The extent to which confidence has been restored amongst all classes, European and native, by General Gordon's arrival is almost miraculous. An old Pasha, named Tohami, who served under him in his previous undertaking in the Soudan, predicts that, immediately on the ex-Governor's arrival, the Mahdi's hordes will 'melt away like dew,' and the Pretender will be left 'like a small man standing alone, until forced to flee back to his

Island of Abbas.'　Making all allowance for Oriental exaggerations, one can only hope that these anticipations will be verified.

"It is not only the enthusiastic and possibly interested natives who are so impressed by the advent of General Gordon. Sir Evelyn Wood, speaking of him after their meeting to-day, expressed himself in the warmest terms, ending by saying that the General had only one fault—that he was too good for his time, and should have lived centuries ago ; and compared him to the Chevalier Bayard.

"'Although Generals Wood and Gordon have not met since they served together in the Crimea, the mutual recognition, when Gordon appeared on the poop of the *Tanjore* at Port Said, was instantaneous, and a warm friendship has already sprung up between the two, as, indeed, is the case with all whom General Gordon comes in contact.'"

The question has been asked since, What is General Gordon's mission ?　In the following, which was his answer to the instructions he had received, the General himself answers the question :—

"Memorandum by General Gordon.

"I understand that Her Majesty's Government have come to the irrevocable decision not to incur the very onerous duty of securing to the peoples of the Soudan a just future Government.　That, as a consequence, Her Majesty's Government have determined to restore to these peoples their independence, and will no longer suffer the Egyptian Government to interfere with their affairs.

"2. For this purpose Her Majesty's Government have decided to send me to the Soudan to arrange for the evacuation of these countries, and the safe removal of the Egyptian employés and troops.

"3. Keeping Paragraph No. 1 in view—viz., that the

evacuation of the Soudan is irrevocably decided on, it will depend upon circumstances in what way this is to be accomplished.

" My idea is that the restoration of the country should be made to the different petty Sultans who existed at the time of Mehemet Ali's conquest, and whose families still exist ; that the Mahdi should be left altogether out of the calculation as regards the handing over the country; and that it should be optional with the Sultans to accept his supremacy or not. As these Sultans would probably not be likely to gain by accepting the Mahdi as their Sovereign, it is probable that they will hold to their independent positions. Thus we should have two factors to deal with—namely, the petty Sultans asserting their several independence, and the Mahdi's party aiming at supremacy over them. To hand, therefore, over to the Mahdi the arsenals, etc., would, I consider, be a mistake. They should be handed over to the Sultans of the States in which they are placed.

" The most difficult question is how and to whom to hand over the arsenals at Khartoum, Dongola, and Kassala, which towns have, so to say, no old standing families— Khartoum and Kassala having sprung up since Mehemet Ali's conquest. Probably it would be advisable to postpone any decision as to these towns till such time as the inhabitants have made known their opinion.

" 4. I have, in Paragraph 3, proposed the transfer of the lands to the local Sultans, and stated my opinion that these will not accept the supremacy of the Mahdi. If this is agreed to, and my supposition correct as to their action, there can be but little doubt that, as far as he is able, the Mahdi will endeavour to assert his rule over them, and will be opposed to any evacuation of the Government employés and troops. My opinion of the Mahdi's forces is, that the bulk of those who were with him at Obeid will refuse to cross the Nile, and that those who do so will not exceed

3000 or 4000 men, and also that these will be composed principally of black troops who have deserted, and who, if offered fair terms, would come over to the Government side. In such a case—viz., ' Sultans accepting transfer of territory and refusing the supremacy of the Mahdi, and Mahdi's black troops coming over to the Government, resulting in weakness of the Mahdi, what should be done should the Mahdi's adherents attack the evacuating columns?' It cannot be supposed that these are to offer no resistance; and if in resisting they should obtain a success, it would be but reasonable to allow them to follow up the Mahdi to such a position as would ensure their future safe march. This is one of those difficult questions which our Government can hardly be expected to answer, but which may arise, and to which I would call attention. Paragraph 1 fixes irrevocably the decision of the Government—viz., to evacuate the territory, and, of course, as far as possible, involves the avoidance of fighting. I can, therefore, only say that, having in view Paragraph 1,. and seeing the difficulty of asking Her Majesty's Government to give a decision or direction as to what should be done in certain cases, that I will carry out the evacuation as far as possible according to their wish to the best of my ability, and with avoidance, as far as possible, of all fighting. I would, however, hope that Her Majesty's Government will give me their support and consideration should I be unable to fulfil all their expectations.

" 5. Though it is out of my province to give any opinion as to the action of Her Majesty's Government in leaving the Soudan, still I must say it would be an iniquity to reconquer these peoples and then hand them back to the Egyptians without guarantees of future good government. It is evident that this we cannot secure them without an inordinate expenditure of men and money. The Soudan is a useless possession, ever was so, and ever will be so. Larger than

Germany, France, and Spain together, and mostly barren, it cannot be governed except by a Dictator, who may be good or bad. If bad, he will cause constant revolts. No one who has ever lived in the Soudan can escape the reflection—' What a useless possession is this land.' Few men also can stand its fearful monotony and deadly climate.

" 6. Said Pasha, the Viceroy before Ismail, went up to the Soudan with Count F. de Lesseps. He was so discouraged and horrified at the misery of the people, that at Berber Count de Lesseps saw him throw his guns into the river, declaring that he would be no party to such oppression. It was only after the urgent solicitations of European Consuls and others that he reconsidered his decision. Therefore, I think Her Majesty's Government are fully justified in recommending the evacuation, inasmuch as the sacrifices necessary towards securing a good government would be far too onerous to admit of such an attempt being made. Indeed, one may say it is impracticable at any cost. Her Majesty's Government will now leave them as God has placed them ; they are not forced to fight among themselves, and they will no longer be oppressed by men coming from lands so remote as Circassia, Kurdistán, and Anatolia.

" 7. I have requested Lieutenant-Colonel Stewart to write his views independent of mine on this subject. 1 append them to this report."

" Observations by Colonel Stewart.

" I have carefully read over General Gordon's observations, and cordially agree with what he states.

" 2. I would, however, suggest that, as far as possible, all munitions of war be destroyed on evacuation.

" 3. I quite agree with General Gordon that the Soudan is an expensive and useless possession. No one who has visited it can escape the reflection—' What a useless possession is this land, and what a huge encumbrance on Egypt.'

"4. Handing back the territories to the families of the dispossessed Sultans is an act of justice both towards them and their people. The latter, at any rate, will no longer be at the mercy of foreign mercenaries, and if they are tyrannised over it will be more or less their own fault. Handing back the districts to the old reigning families is also a politic act, as raising up a rival power to that of the Mahdi.

"5. As it is impossible for Her Majesty's Government to foresee all the eventualities that may arise during the evacuation, it seems to me the more judicious course to rely on the discretion of General Gordon and his knowledge of the country.

"6. I, of course, understand that General Gordon is going to the Soudan with full powers to make all arrangements as to its evacuation, and that he is in no way to be interfered with by the Cairo Ministers. Also that any suggestions or remarks that the Cairo Government would wish to make are to be made directly to him and Her Majesty's Minister-Plenipotentiary, and that no intrigues are to be permitted against his authority. Any other course would, I am persuaded, make his mission a failure.

"(Signed)   "D. H. STEWART, Lieutenant-Colonel,
"11th Hussars.

"Steamship *Tanjore*, at sea, Jan. 22, 1884."

On the meeting of Parliament many eulogistic words were spoken.

On the 22nd of January Sir Charles Dilke, addressing his constituents at Chelsea, referred to the mission of General Gordon as follows :—

"General Gordon is not against but in favour of the policy of the evacuation of Darfour, Kordofan, and the interior of the Soudan. The greater part of what is called the Soudan is not, and never has been, an integral part of Egypt. The Egyptian is a foreigner there. The Soudan has always been a strain and a drain upon Egypt; and instead of being a help, these countries always have been, in our opinion, a weakness to it, and if they be a weakness to Egypt it would be simple madness to this country to insist upon their retention. We have no interest that the Egyptians, rather than the Sultans of Darfour, should rule in Darfour; our interest is that there should be peace in the country. We have, I think, an interest that the Egyptian rule should be maintained on the coasts of the Red Sea, but we have no interest whatever in upholding Egyptian rule in the interior of the continent of Africa. The Conservatives have told us that we have shown upon this subject a singularly vacillating policy, and they seem to think we were suddenly driven to the employment of General Gordon at a day's notice by the news we got in the Conservative press. We first suggested the sending out of General Gordon to the late Egyptian Government very many months ago, but at that time the suggestion was not received with favour, either by the Egyptian Government or by our own representatives in Cairo. They thought that, under the circumstances then existing, it would not be desirable that General Gordon should go out. This reluctance lasted until quite recently, and it was a mutual reluctance, for General Gordon did not wish to go. It was only about ten days ago we were informed that General Gordon, although he had no wish to go to Egypt, would willingly obey the orders of Her Majesty's Government if he were directed to go, and that he would gladly act under the instructions of Sir Evelyn Baring. As soon as we had obtained by telegraph the concurrence of Sir Evelyn Baring in our view, the matter was arranged. A reply was received, I think, on Wednesday last. General Gordon's instructions were given to him on the Friday, and with the remarkable public spirit which characterises him, he started with Colonel Stewart, as you know, on Friday night."

In the House of Commons, Sir Stafford Northcote, while censuring the Government, said :—

"There is one point upon which all our minds are fixed —I mean the mission of General Gordon. On that point I am anxious to say little or nothing. General Gordon is now engaged in an attempt of the most gallant and dangerous kind. No one can speak with too much admiration of his courage and self-devotion. No one can fail, in this country, to sympathise with him, and earnestly to desire his safety and success. It would be the greatest possible misfortune if, by any word carelessly allowed to drop here, anything were done that would in the slightest degree imperil or disturb the success of his mission. I trust the Government are not proceeding in the case of General Gordon as they have done in too many instances— that they are not throwing all the responsibility upon him, and keeping none for themselves—that they are not confusing his position, and making it uncertain whose servant he is, or to whom he is responsible."

Mr. Gladstone, in his reply, thus spoke of the circumstances connected with his mission, and in praise of the hero :—

"General Gordon, in our estimation, is a very great feature in the case. What is General Gordon! He is no common man. I thank the right hon. gentleman for the manner in which he referred to him. I may almost say that General Gordon is not alone. · Other very able men are with him—one in particular, Colonel Stewart, his second and coadjutor. And, in fact, we have acted all along on the principle of obtaining for this difficult Egypt problem the very best services we could possibly get. It is no exaggeration, in speaking of General Gordon, to say that he is a hero. It is no exaggeration to say that he is a Christian. It is no exaggeration to say that in his dealings with Oriental people he is also a genius;

that he has a faculty, an influence, a command brought about by moral means—for no man in this House hates the unnecessary resort to blood more than General Gordon —he has that faculty which produces effects among those wild Eastern races almost unintelligible to us Western people. Perhaps it may be said, 'If General Gordon has all these gifts, why did you not employ him sooner ?' Again you have fallen into an error, for you have not taken the least pains to ascertain whether it was possible or not. The suggestion to employ General Gordon in the Soudan was made at a time so early that it really is not within the limits of the direct responsibility of the present Government.

"As early as in the month of November 1882 Sir Charles Wilson suggested the employment of General Gordon. But there were difficulties on both sides. It is very difficult to marry two people when one of them is averse, but it is still more difficult to marry them when, unfortunately, there is an aversion on both sides ; and that, I believe was found to be the case at that period between the Khedive and General Gordon. However, when it came to the grave period, and the increased responsibility upon us for the affairs in the Soudan that followed Hicks's defeat, then it was again our duty to have regard to the possibility of what might be got through General Gordon. The right hon. gentleman will recollect that we have contended all along—he might have done it, but we could not have done it—that down to the time of General Hicks's defeat, we should not have been justified in interfering. It was already known to us that the Egyptian Government objected to General Gordon. On the 1st of December Lord Granville had reason to believe that he was in a condition to offer the services of General Gordon to the Egyptian Government. Unfortunately, they were refused, but they were refused not entirely without reason. The reason was one with which we were not satisfied, but it went far to silence us, and I think the right hon. gentleman will find it to be the case too. The objection made was this :—' The Soudan is a country of strong Mahometan fanaticism, and to send a Christian as our agent would be a dangerous course, and might cause a more dangerous outbreak.' We were not satisfied, but at the same time it was very difficult to brush that objection rudely aside, and that led to some further delay. That was on the 1st of December. But we became acquainted with the sentiments of General Gordon, and, as time went on, the objection of the Egyptian Government became mitigated and entirely changed. However, it was not until the 10th of January—that is to say, eight days after Nubar Pasha came into office, that we had forwarded to us a request to send officers to conduct the evacuation of the Soudan, and on the 16th of January General Gordon was on his way.

" At Cairo General Gordon formed his plan, and the paper laid on the table we received first in the shape of a valuable memorandum. We have had some doubts whether it was our duty to produce his plan. If it could have been produced to this House or this country alone, it would have been a different matter, but the promulgation of the plan in Egypt might cause its failure. All I can say on this occasion—but I would rather not enter into particulars at all—is that it was evidently a well-reasoned and considered plan, that it was entirely pacific in its basis, that it proceeds on the plea—which would have been fanatical or presumptuous in my case, or in the case of most of those in this House, but which, in the case of General Gordon, with his experience and his gifts, was neither the one nor the other —not that he must, but that he might, hope to exercise a strong pacific influence by going to the right persons in the Soudan, and it was his desire as much as ours that this should be done without any resort whatever to violent means.   Now, General Gordon went, not for the purpose of reconquering the Soudan, or of persuading the chiefs of the Soudan, the Sultans who were at the head of the tribes of the Soudan, to submit themselves again to the Egyptian Government.   He went for no such purpose as that.   He went for the double purpose of evacuating the country by the extrication of the Egyptian garrisons, and of reconstituting it by giving back to the Sultans their ancestral powers, as I may so call them, which had been withdrawn or suspended during the period of Egyptian occupation.   I have told the House already that General Gordon had in view the withdrawal from the country of no less than twenty-nine thousand persons paying military service in Egypt.   The House will see how vast was the trust which was placed in the hands of this remarkable person.   We cannot exaggerate the importance we attach to it.   We are unwilling to do anything which should interfere with this great pacific scheme—the only scheme, absolutely the only scheme, which promised a satisfactory solution of the Soudanese difficulty, by at once extricating the garrisons and reconstituting the country on its own basis of local privileges."

The following telegraphic correspondence respecting the affairs of the Soudan was presented to Parliament :—

" Earl Granville to Sir E. Baring.

Foreign Office, Feb. 7, 1884, 6.25 p.m.

If possible, ask Gordon whether change of circumstances affects his judgment as to going to Khartoum, and whether he has any suggestions to make.

Earl Granville to Sir E. Baring.

Foreign Office, Feb. 8, 1884, 5.40 p.m.

Make it clear to Gordon that request for his suggestions

is not confined to the single point of Khartoum, but extends
to any alteration for assisting the object with which he is
charged.

Earl Granville to Sir E. Baring.

Foreign Office, Feb. 10, 1884, 11 p.m.

Ask Gordon whether he can suggest anything respecting
Sinkat and Tokar.

Earl Granville to Sir E. Baring

Foreign Office, Feb. 11, 1884, 1.45 p.m.

Send on following to Gordon :—
'It has been suggested by a military authority that, to
assist the policy of withdrawal, a British force should be
sent to Suakim sufficient to operate, if necessary, in its
vicinity.   Would such a step injure or assist your
mission ?'

Sir E. Baring to Earl Granville.

Cairo, Feb. 12, 1884, Noon.

Gordon telegraphs as follows :—
'I have formed a Committee of Defence with Hassan
Kalifa Pasha.
'They meet to-day They have announced my assump-
tion of the supreme power in the Soudan. I hope to
conciliate whole Province of Berber under my presidency.
Question of getting out garrison and families is so inter-
laced with preservation of well-to-do people of this country
as to be for the present inseparable. Any precipitate
action separating these interests would throw all well-
disposed people into the ranks of the enemy, and would
fail utterly in its effects. Therefore I trust patience will
be shown, and that you will not be at all anxious as to issue.

Sir E. Baring to Earl Granville.

Cairo, Feb. 12, 1884, 2.20 p.m.

Gordon replies :—

'As to sending forces to Suakim to assist withdrawal, I would care more for rumour of such intention than for forces. What would have greatest effect would be rumour of English intervention.'

Sir E. Baring to Earl Granville.

Cairo, Feb. 12, 1884, 4 p.m.

Gordon replies :—

'About Tokar and Sinkat, you can do nothing except by proclaiming that the chiefs of tribes should come to Khartoum to Assembly of Notables, when the independence of the Soudan will be decided. As for money, it would be well to try, but difficult to arrange.'

Sir E. Baring to Earl Granville.

Cairo, Feb. 12, 1884, 7 p.m.

Gordon telegraphs :—

'Not least probability of any massacre of women and children. Efforts of rebels confined to raising revolts among their neighbours. It seems no instance has occurred where rebels of one district invaded neighbour's soil. Have not least apprehension for safety of Khartoum or Berber being in jeopardy by events at Suakim. Kassala is, of course, in danger from rising of its own lower classes ; but even if they rise, action will be confined to robbery, and perhaps murder of few Beys, their oppressors.'

Sir E. Baring to Earl Granville.

Cairo, Feb. 13, 1884, 8.30 a.m.

Gordon leaves Berber to-day for Khartoum with several influential chiefs. He will not hurry, as he wishes to see people on banks.

Consul Baker to Earl Granville.

Suakim, February 18, 1884.

All quiet in town and camp. Enemy has abandoned position near here in consequence of latest news of British troops *en route.* The general opinion is that Tokar will be able to hold out till relieved."

CHAPTER XXVI.

SUBSEQUENT EVENTS IN THE SOUDAN.

" He can report,
As seemeth by his plight, of this revolt
The newest state."
                                        —*Macbeth.*

IN the meantime the troubles in the Soudan were as great as ever.

Tewfik Bey, the gallant commander of the little force in Sinkat, was hoping against hope that relief would come to him. Some spies succeeded in reaching him, who, on their return, said that Tewfik was delighted to see them, as no news had been received for a long time from Suakim, and the soldiers were getting faint-hearted. Parties of the enemy gathered every day on knolls outside, and shouted curses to the little garrison. A few men made attacks, but the garrison chased them. Tewfik had no cavalry, and he was not sure of the strength of the enemy. He said that "a large party among the Arabs really believe that the Mahdi is a real prophet sent from God, and that Osman Digna is his Calif." On the 10th of January Tewfik said he had not enough provision for a dozen days more. He begged the Government to send troops and provisions, as every day their state was becoming more desperate.

A few days later Tewfik wrote to say that he was at his last extremity; the dogs and all other animals had been devoured, and the men were receiving but half-a-pound of grain a-day on which to live. He had only one sack of grain left. It was hoped that the friendly tribes known to be near would relieve him; if not, he was resolved, on the 2nd of February, to try and fight his way to Suakim, as he preferred death in battle to starvation. He had continually to fight, and on one occasion he lost nineteen men.

It was impossible that Baker's army could reach Sinkat, owing to the waterless state of the roads. But Tokar was in as bad a plight as Sinkat. The commander of the forces there thus described his state :—

"It is impossible for us to be in a worse condition than we now are. The enemy have filled up all the wells outside the town, and the water in the inside wells is brackish and bad. The troops are suffering greatly from diarrhœa, and I fear that in two or three days we shall be obliged to surrender. We have dried grain enough for three months, but no meat or ghee, and only from ten to twenty rounds of ammunition per man. The rebels fire upon us night and day."

When Baker Pasha received this news he at once decided to march on Tokar. It was hoped that Osman Digna, the leader of the rebel tribes, would go to engage with him, and so lessen the pressure around Sinkat. If this were so, Tewfik's army would have a better chance of getting away. Baker offered £100 to the first sheikh who would enter Sinkat with supplies, and large rewards to all tribes who would convey food to the place.

On Monday, the 4th of February, occurred another terrible defeat. The Egyptian army seemed to have no courage, otherwise the battle of Teb must have had another conclusion. It was a dull morning, which turned to rain, under cover of which the rebels advanced. They charged suddenly, uttering wild cries; and at the sound the Egyptian horsemen became panic-stricken, and, turning rein, hurried away. Some of the soldiers refused even to defend themselves, but threw away their rifles, and fell on the ground screaming for mercy. The generals tried to get the men to form into square; but there was wild confusion everywhere, and the Egyptians could not be induced to fight. It became a total rout, and the shattered columns streamed across the plain towards Trinkitat, the cavalry flying before them. The enemy pursued, killing them as they went. When last seen, Dr. Leslie, Morris Bey, and Captain Walker, with drawn swords and pistols, were standing in a group close to the guns, facing the enemy, and quite surrounded by them. The pursuit was kept up for five miles, and then the fugitives made their way to Trinkitat. On reaching the shore they were so eager to get into the boats that the English soldiers had, in order to prevent them from swamping, to keep them back with revolvers. Lieutenant Cameron, in his graphic description of the battle, remarks :—

"After yesterday's experience no one here will ever trust themselves in action again with Egyptian troops, except, indeed, with bodies of well-drilled Blacks, who, under such circumstances, only can be relied upon. The enemy had not three thousand men in the field, but it must be owned that these came on with all the pluck and gallantry of the Moslems of old. Those of us who saw their long line charge down through the scrub at a steady pace, after uttering a wild whoop, will not soon forget the sight."

Indeed, this battle may be said in one sense to have settled the fate of the Soudan ; its result making it evident that the Egyptians have not ability to rule the Arabs.

While this reverse was occurring at Teb, the little garrison at Sinkat was in despair. Letters arrived from Tewfik imploring assistance. He would have known the impossibility of sending it had he been informed that Baker had been routed; but he did not know, and his men were starving. His last despatch said they were chewing leaves in order to assuage the pangs of hunger. At last news came that the gallant little band at Sinkat had been massacred.

Tewfik is reported to have pointed out to his men that by fighting they might save themselves; by remaining, all must in a few days die of hunger, while flight was impossible. Having animated his men with his own spirit, he burned all the stores, spiked the guns, and blew up the magazines. Then each man having filled his pouches with as much ammunition as he could carry, the six hundred issued out. Osman's hordes at once rushed down to the attack. Tewfik and his men fought nobly, and for a long time repulsed every effort to break their ranks; but at last numbers prevailed. With a tremendous rush the Arabs burst into one of the sides of the square, and a general massacre then took place. Reports received by the *Standard's* correspondent at Suakim speak of five men and thirty women having been spared; and the first statement that the women and children had not been massacred was thus contradicted. The streets of Suakim, when the news arrived, were filled with crowds of weeping women; and although the English there are less demonstrative in their grief, Lieutenant Cameron represents them as feeling it well-nigh as deeply and bitterly.

When the news reached London it was decided to take energetic measures for the relief, if possible, of Tokar, and for assuring the safety of Suakim. A force of four thousand men were at once collected and despatched to the western shore of the Red Sea. Lord Wolseley, the Adjutant-General of the forces, entered into communication with the general officer commanding the British troops in Egypt. General Graham was to command, and Oolonel Redvers Buller to be the second in command. General Stephenson was to select the three best battalions of infantry from among his troops. Some Irish Fusiliers and Marines were also ordered to the Soudan. The 10th Hussars, on their way home from India, were to be stopped at Suakim, and provided with horses. Provisions were to be taken; and the expedition was to go forth promptly, and with every hope that its work would be speedily accomplished.

This news was warmly welcomed at Suakim. Admiral Hewett sent to Tokar to say that if they could hold out a little longer an English force would march to their relief. The commandant replied in a hopeful strain that he thought he could manage to hold out until relieved by English troops.

Better news then reached England. The Marines arrived at Suakim first, and then the Hussars and Irish Fusiliers. It was feared that the *Jumna*, in which the relief party were hastening, might come into contact with Osman Digna's forces; but all went well.

In consequence of the rapidity with which news reaches England by telegraph, it became known that probably on a certain day in February a battle would be fought; and so strongly was the imagination wrought on, that we could almost see the blaze and the dust, and hear the noise of battle. We knew that the stores had all been landed, and the whole force had moved to Fort Baker, and that it was intended to bivouac there, and early in the morning march to Teb, for the battle was to take place on the ground which had proved so fatal to Baker and Moncrieff.

War is always horrible. We cannot but mourn that it has ever to take place, and wish for the time when it shall cease for ever from the earth; but while it lasts, every one feels an interest in the success of his own soldiers, and rejoices when the victory is on his own side.

Great courage on both sides was exhibited at the second battle of Teb. Everything was ready. The surgeons were there, prepared to do their best for the wounded. The newspaper correspondents were there, ready to write the whole particulars for their readers; and so were the artists who sketched the terrible scenes, that in a week or two the whole reading world might realise the event almost as fully as those who were eye-witnesses of it. And the soldiers were there, ready to die doing their duty.

They cheered as they advanced, and the pipers of the Black Watch played the bagpipes. Some one said that as they were not stationed in front, they would try to do their best to frighten the enemy away with their strains of unearthly music. The battle lasted between three and four hours; and then a loud cheer from the Gordon Highlanders, and a blast from the bagpipes, told of victory.

Sir E. Baring at once telegraphed the news of the victory in Arabic to General Gordon, so that it was known all up the line.

The next thing was for the troops to occupy Tokar. They imagined that the enemy might probably come up again and try to prevent this; but no opposition was offered, and the troops marched in, to the great joy of those who were left in Tokar. They found that the Egyptian garrison only numbered about seventy, and they were in a starving condition. Many had gone over to the enemy, and some had died. Those who remained, as well as the population of the town, welcomed their deliverers with tears of joy.

There were great rejoicings everywhere; but the list of the killed and the wounded could not be read without a shudder. On the British side four officers, thirty-two privates, and two marines were killed; and seventeen officers and one hundred and forty-two soldiers and marines were wounded. On the side of the enemy it was estimated that over a thousand had been slain.

It was hoped that this loss on the enemy's side would ensure his submission; but it did not. Many, no doubt, who had believed the Mahdi's troops invincible lost faith, and were inclined to waver; but it is to be feared that his power over the Arabs will yet prove a source of trouble.

The following order was issued by General Graham at the close of the battle to the troops who had fought under him :—

"The objects of the expedition are now achieved. Tokar has been relieved, and the rebels so thoroughly humbled, that the force before Tokar may safely retire. But before the force is broken up, the General desires to record his sense of the gallantry and good discipline displayed by all arms. The cavalry have shown that dash which has always characterised that arm of our military force, and have also rendered invaluable service in reconnaissance and scouting duties. The action of the infantry generally has been characterised by steadiness and firmness in the presence of the enemy. The first operation carried out, that of moving to a flank under a heavy fire, was very trying to the steadiness of young soldiers, as was the great daring shown by the foe in charging down to close quarters in the face of an overwhelming force. The result of the action shows the British soldier that as long as he keeps steady in formation and cool in firing, desperate rushes like those made by these brave Blacks only ensure their destruction. The Arabs have now felt the terrible effects of the fire of the British infantry. The lesson will not easily be, forgotten. The General thanks the Naval Brigade under Commander Rolfe, for their cheerful endurance during the severe work of dragging the guns across the difficult country, when suffering from the heat and scarcity of water;

for their ready gallantry and steadiness under fire when serving their guns, they have contributed materially to the success of the action. I cannot too highly express my thanks for their services.

"The guns of the Royal Artillery were also admirably served, and these, in conjunction with those of the Naval Brigade, succeeded in silencing the enemy's fire, and prepared the way for the advance of the infantry. The staff officers of all departments also worked without sparing themselves. The supplies were never stopped, in spite of the difficult country. The General especially commends the absence of all crime on the part of the troops. He is proud to command them; they deserve well of their country."

A few days afterwards Admiral Hewett and General Graham issued a joint proclamation to the tribes. They asked all the sheiks to come in and meet them at Suakim. "You have already," says the proclamation, "been warned that the English forces have come here, not only to relieve the garrison of Tokar, but to redress the wrongs under which you have so long suffered; nevertheless, you have gone on trusting that notorious scoundrel, Osman Digna, well known to you all as a bad man, his former life in Suakim having proved that to be the case. He has led you away with the foolish idea that the Mahdi has come on earth. The great God who rules the universe does not send such scoundrels as Osman Digna for His messengers. Your people are brave, and England always respects such men. Awake, then, chase Osman Digna from your country. We promise you that protection and pardon shall be granted to all who come in at once; otherwise the fate of those who fell at El Teb shall surely overtake you."

This proclamation was followed a few days la'er by another, sent especially to the sheiks of thirty-three hostile tribes :—

" We, the Admiral of the English fleet and the General of the English army assembled at Suakim, do hereby summon you to disperse peaceably, and to return to your homes. The English army is about to march to your camp in the Valley of Tamanieh, and will treat all found there in arms as rebels in the same way they treated those at El Teb. Be warned in time. Listen no more to the evil counsels of Osman Digna. If you have any grievances, send delegates to Khartoum to meet General Gordon, whom you all know to be a good and just man. If you desire to send delegates to us, we, promise them protection, and will transmit their statements by telegraph to General Gordon, and obtain a reply in one day. We desire you to send a reply by the bearer of this letter, or the consequences will be upon your own head."

The following reply was sent to the British Generals from the camp of Osman Digna :—

" In the name of the most merciful God, the Lord be praised, etc.—From the whole of the tribes and their sheikhs who have received your writings, and those who did not receive writings, to the Commandant of the English soldiers, whom God help to Islam. Amen. Then your letters have arrived with us, and what you have informed us in them—to come in—then know that the gracious God has sent his Mahdi suddenly who was expected, the looked-for messenger for the religious and against the infidels, so as to show the religion of God through him, and by him to kill those who hate him, which has happened. You have seen who have gone to him from the people and soldiers, who are countless. God killed them, so look at the multitudes." Here follow verses from the Koran. "You who never know religion till after death hate God from the beginning. Then we are sure that God, and only God, sent the Mahdi, so as to take away your property, and you know this since the time of our Lord

Mahomet's coming. Pray to God, and be converted. There is nothing between us but the sword, especially as the Mahdi has come to kill you and destroy you unless God wishes you to Islam. The Mahdi's sword be on your necks wherever you may escape, and God's iron be round your necks wherever you may go. Do not think you are enough for us, and the Turks are only a little better than you. We will not leave your heads unless you become Mussulmans and listen to the Prophet and laws of God, and God said in His dear book those who believe Him fight for Him, and those who do not believe in Him shall be killed." Here follow many verses from the Koran referring to permission to kill infidels. " Therefore God has waited for you for a long time, and you have thought that He would always go on waiting for you; but God said He would wait for you as you were bad. People but know that during the time of the Mahdi he will not accept bribes from you, and also will not leave you in your infidelity, so there is nothing for you · but the sword, so that there will not remain one of you on the face of the earth, therefore Islam. Sealed by sheikhs of twenty-one tribes."

The troopship *Jumna* took the wounded to Suez, and a special train, with invalid carriages, conveyed the wounded from the wharf to the Victoria Hospital. The Eastern Telegraph Oompany kindly offered to send messages from wounded officers to their friends free of charge. And the Queen telegraphed her thanks for the services of her soldiers, her sympathy with the wounded, and her sorrow for those who mourned the dead.

On the 11th of March the news reached England that General Graham had had another victory. He engaged with Osman Digna's army at a place called Tamanieb, and completely routed it. Osman himself fled to the hills, and the day after the battle they marched on Osman Digna's village, and destroyed it, burning all the guns, and arms, and ammunition they found there. They met with no opposition; and it was felt that the cause of the Mahdi had, in that decisive battle, received a blow from which it could not recover. He had little difficulty in persuading his followers to believe in him when an unbroken series of victories seemed to them to confirm his own statements. But when reverses and defeats told another story, it was far less likely that they would be faithful to him. Unhappily the British losses in this engagement were very heavy. One hundred and ten were killed, including five officers, and about one hundred and fifty wounded.

General Graham offered a reward for the capture of Osman Digna himself, but the reward was afterwards withdrawn. It was resolved to make a final effort to disperse the force still remaining under Osman Digna; and the English troops, after much suffering, owing to the intense heat and total absence of water on the line of route, reached the Arab position at Tamanud on the 27th of March. After some desultory firing, in which the English sustained no loss, the enemy abandoned their position and fled, completely routed and demoralised. The troops then returned to Suakim, and the campaign was announced as at an end, its object—the relief of Tokar and the dispersion of the Arabs—being accomplished.

Rather an interesting trophy of the war was presented to Her Majesty the Queen. It consisted of the Mahdi's standard, which was captured by the British troops at the relief of Tokar. Lieutenant Wilford Lloyd, Royal Horse Artillery, on his return home, was commissioned by General Graham to convey the trophy to Her Majesty. The gallant officer, who has already seen considerable active service, left Trinkitat on the 5th of March, travelling *viâ* Cairo and Alexandria to Venice, and thence to London, where he arrived on the ninth. He soon after proceeded to Windsor. The standard, which is about two-and-a-half yards long and two yards wide, is composed of red and yellow silk. On one side is an Arab inscription, stating that it was presented by the Mahdi to the Governor of Tokar, and on the other a text from the Koran: "There is no God but God, and Mahomet is His Prophet. Every one professes the knowledge of God." The Queen, accompanied by Princess Beatrice, received Lieutenant Wilford Lloyd in the corridor after luncheon. Having been introduced by General Sir H. F. Ponsonby, he presented the flag on behalf of General Graham to Her Majesty, who was greatly interested in the trophy.

CHAPTER XXVII.

SLAVERY AND GORDON'S PROCLAMATION.

"The good I stand on is my honesty.
                          I fear nothing
That can be said against me."

—Henry VIII.

GENERAL GORDON went on his way as swiftly as possible, and the people everywhere rejoiced to see him. It was known that one of the most dangerous parts of his journey was that from Korosko to Berber, which was over the desert of Abou Hamid. He was a day later in arriving than he expected to be, and wild rumours began to be circulated respecting him. But he was safely helped on his journey, and no one molested him. Soon after he left Korosko some friendly Bedouins had gathered together and offered their assistance in crossing the Desert. They were quite ready to accompany him if he cared to have them ; but he thanked them, and declined, giving as his reason for refusing the escort his anxiety to travel with the utmost possible rapidity.

He reached Berber in safety, and telegraphed the good

news immediately. He said that he was safe and well, and thought there was no danger. He considered that the country was quieting down, and said he had every hope that, in the end, his mission would prove successful. He thanked most heartily the Egyptian Government for the arrangements which they had made for him on the way. Everyone was rejoiced to hear of his safety.

From Berber to Khartoum he went by water, and was received by his old friends there with every demonstration of joy and enthusiasm of welcome, which showed how much he was loved.

When he left Cairo, his last words to Nubar Pasha were, " I will save the honour of Egypt." Before entering the desert, he sent a brief message to the garrison he was hastening to relieve, exhorting them to be brave: " Ye are men, not women," he said. From Berber, where he emerged from the desert, and was about to take steamer down the Nile to Khartoum, he telegraphed back to the Egyptian Premier at Cairo: " I am sending down many women and children to Korosko. I wish you would send a kind-hearted man to meet them. A European is best." At the same time he said, " Give yourself no further anxiety about this part of the Soudan. The people, great and small, are heartily glad to be free of a union which has only caused them sorrow."

The *Times* correspondent, telegraphing the same day, stated :—" His speech to the people was received with enthusiasm. He said:—'I come without soldiers, but with God on my side, to redress the evils of the Soudan. I will not fight with any weapons but justice. There shall be no more Bashi-Bazouks.' It is now believed that he will relieve the Bahr Gazelle garrisons without firing a shot. Since they heard that he was coming, the aspect of the people has so changed that there are no longer any fears of disturbances in the town. They say that he is giving them more than even the Mahdi could give. He is sending out proclamations in all directions. Such is the influence of one man, that there are no longer any fears for the garrison or people of Khartoum."

Mr. Power, the correspondent of the *Times*, further telegraphed :—Yesterday was one series of acceptable surprises for the people of Khartoum. General Gordon's proclamation preceded him ; and immediately on his arrival he summoned the officials, thus preparing the people for some salutary changes. He next held a *levée* at the Mudirieh, the entire population, even the poorest Arab, being admitted. On his way between the Mudirieh and the Palace, about one thousand persons pressed forward, kissing his hands and feet, and calling him " Sultan," " Father," and " Saviour of Kordofan."

He at once set to work with all vigour to give the people some much needed reforms. First, he had the telegraph repaired, so that messages might be sent. Then he had offices opened in the Palace, and invited the people to come to him and Colonel Stewart, and state their grievances. He found that many were suffering from the burden of taxation that lay upon them, and dreading that their outstanding debts to the Government would be demanded. But Gordon had a great fire made in front of the Palace, and the Government books recording these debts were burnt. " Now," said the kindly General, " we will have no more of the whip. No one else is going to be bastinadoed; so bring all the kurbashes and implements of punishment to me, and we will make a grand fire of them also."

This was accordingly done, amid the glad shouts of the delighted people, who seemed to feel that their deliverer had indeed come. He telegraphed also that he had appointed Colonel Coetlogan to the supreme command at Khartoum ; and with him and Colonel Stewart he visited the prison, the hospital, and the arsenal. He found the

prison a den of misery ; two hundred wretches were loaded
with chains. He had before created a council of Arab
notables residing in Khartoum, in order to help him.
He gave to Colonel Stewart the duty of examining into
the cases of the prisoners, and reporting thereon. There
were boys and old men, and even women, there, some
of whom were not yet condemned, but who had been
wearily waiting in that terrible place during many months,
and actually in some cases for several years, for their trials
to take place, when it should be decided whether they were
guilty, and must continue to be incarcerated, or innocent,
and allowed to be free. The sight of the kind English
faces, full of pity for their sufferings and of indignation at
their wrongs, must have brought hope into many a hopeless
breast. One woman lifted her beseeching eyes to the new
judges who had come, and began to plead her cause—

. "All the best of my life has been spent in this place. I
was only a child when I committed the crime. May I not
now go free ?"

"How long have you been here ? "

"Fifteen years."

And after fifteen years of darkness and captivity the
woman was sent out into the bright sunshine and the fresh
air, to bless her deliverers with tears of gratitude.

The prisoners were not liberated indiscriminately. That
would not have been holding the balance level. Their cases
were all examined, and those who ought to be retained
were kept. But all had their chains struck off, and many
of them were set at liberty ; to be, let us hope, faithful
friends and helpers of the man who had rescued them from
injustice and wrong.

That was a wonderful day ; and at night the people gave
themselves up to rejoicing. All parties united to make the
fête a grand one ; and the town was in a blaze of illumina-
tion. Flowers and lanterns, bright banners and variegated

lamps, coloured cloths and bangles, were freely used every-where. The bazaar was especially gay, and every house was decorated, while the entire negro population exhibited a fine display of fireworks. Indeed, the scene must have been quite wonderful, and exceedingly picturesque, with a brilliancy of adornment such as we can scarcely imagine in England.

The motto of General Gordon, in which he heartily believed himself, and which he caused to be understood by the people, was a very simple and a very just one—

"THE SOUDAN FOR THE SOUDANESE."

In order at once to begin to make this theory a fact, he gave orders that all the white troops should go to the other side of the Nile—themselves and their families being sent down the river in detachments. The Europeans who chose to leave might also do so. He had two new gates opened in the fortifications, and introduced generally a feeling of security and freedom. Unfortunately (for he hates war), the town of Khartoum appears since to have been attacked by the Arabs, and General Gordon, who devoutly hoped there would be no need for a single shot to be fired, has had, in self-defence, to send some of his men out to fight.

But, so far as the internal management of Khartoum was concerned, he had nothing to fear. In a letter of thanks which he addressed to Colonel Coetlogan, in which he gave him very high praise for his services, and assured him that the good work already accomplished had been greatly through his aid, he said :—" My belief is that there is not the least chance of any danger being incurred by Khartoum, which I consider as safe as Cairo. Therefore, your services here in a military capacity would be wasted. I consider this place was in imminent danger, not from an external enemy, but from the people of the town, who, bullied by the effete government of Hussein Pasha Cheri, became favourable to the El Obeid people.　Rest assured you leave this place as safe as Kensington Park."

Every one hopes that events will prove the Governor-General to have been correct in the sanguine opinion which he thus expressed.

One thing made him exceedingly angry with the ex-Governor of Khartoum, Hussein Pasha Oheri.

Among the other cases which demanded enquiry and attention was that of Sheikh Belud of Khartoum.　The old man had to be carried into his presence, for he was quite unable to walk; indeed, it is to be feared that he may never walk again.

"What is the matter ?" asked the Governor; and then the story of the old man's wrongs was unfolded to him.

Six weeks before, Hussein Pasha Oheri had bastinadoed the feet of this man so severely that the skin was all torn off and the sinews exposed.　When Gordon saw them he declared that Husseim should be punished for his cruelty, and he at once telegraphed to the authorities of Oairo to stop £50 of his pay, which money was to be handed to the bastinadoed sheikh for compensation.　If the ex-Governor objected, then he was to be sent back to Khartoum for trial.

We have said that two new gates into the palace grounds had been opened.　At each of these gates General Gordon had boxes placed, into which the people might drop their petitions and complaints.　This he has ever found a good plan, for previously the people could only get access to the Governor by the payment of large sums of money.　He also made the market free from tolls and taxes.

The next thing that the General did aroused in England a great clamour of astonishment and displeasure.

He had pasted on all the posts and public places, so that everyone might read it, the following proclamation to all the inhabitants :—

"As I have been appointed Governor of all the Soudan, with the approval and by the decree of the Exalted Khedive, and Britannia, the All-Powerful, the Soudan and its Government have become independent, and will look after their own affairs, without interference by the Egyptian Government in anything whatever.

"I also proclaim an amnesty, and grant you the privileges given during the reign of Said Pasha ; and inform you that His Majesty the Sultan, the Exalted, had made up his mind to send Turkish soldiers, the well-known valiant and courageous conquerors. But when His Majesty heard of your wretched condition, and of my compassion for you, he sent me, at great risk, putting my faith in the God of all mankind, to prevent the declaration by His Majesty the Sultan of war between Moslems. . . .

"Your tranquillity is the object of our hope. And as I know that you are sorrowful on account of the slavery which existed among you, and the stringent orders on the part of the Government for the abolition of it, and the punishment of those who deal in them (the slaves), and the assurances given by the Government for its abolition, seizing upon and punishing those concerned in the trade ; the punishment of those who trade in slaves, according to Imperial decrees, and the firmans forwarded to you—all this is known to you.

"But henceforward nobody will interfere with you in the matter, but everyone for himself may take a man into his service henceforth. No one will interfere with him, and he can do as he pleases in the matter, without interference on the part of anybody ; and we have accordingly given this order.

"My compassion for you.

" (Signed)   "GORDON PASHA."

Whatever effect this proclamation might have had in

Khartoum, it made a great stir in this country. Every one was surprised; and perhaps it is not too much to say that every one was sorry. The hatred of slavery and the slave trade by English hearts is consistent, uncompromising, and most intense; and that General Gordon should declare that he permitted it filled every one with disappointment and dissatisfaction. In the House of Commons the Opposition demanded, in indignant tones, the meaning of it. Was England going to be untrue to all her traditions, and, in the person of one who was beloved and honoured as one of her greatest heroes, undo what she had previously done !

In the midst of the commotion a few people continued calm. The Ministers declared that they would stand by the man who had gone at their bidding to the Soudan, with the understanding that he was to use his own judgment as to the best methods of bringing about the peace that was so desirable.

The Earl of Derby, in the House of Lords, said :—" My Lords, my noble friend asks me whether we approve or disapprove of the Proclamation which has been recently issued by General Gordon. The only answer I can give at the present time will be an extremely short and simple one. As the House knows, the instructions which have been given to General Gordon leave him in possession of practically unlimited powers. This Proclamation was not issued in consequence of any instructions sent from here, and, in point of fact, our first knowledge of it arose from seeing the summary in the papers. We have no doubt got the text of the document, and what may be regarded as a brief telegraphic statement referring to it; but we have not yet got that full explanation of the circumstances which led to it, the conditions of the people to whom it was addressed, and generally the state of the case with which General Gordon has to deal, which it is absolutely necessary

for us to know before we can form a judgment on the
action which General Gordon has taken.

"I do not wish to throw any doubt on the action of
General Gordon. I have the highest opinion, not only of his
devotion to the cause which he is engaged in, but of the
detestation which all his life he has expressed of the slave-
trade. We know what he has done in China and elsewhere,
and this has all shown us the marvellous influence which
he seems to have exercised over the minds of the natives.
Knowing, then, his capacity for dealing with persons of
that class, it is only reasonable that we should wait for
that full explanation of the circumstances under which it
was issued before we proceed to discuss it. Meanwhile, I
think General Gordon is entitled to be treated with that
fairness which his antecedents and the whole history of his
life would indicate. But while we do not know precisely
what happened, I should rather be disposed to think that
what occurred was something of this kind. General
Gordon found a very strong opposition to the present
Government in Egypt, as being under European influence,
and as it was well-known that the English Government is
advising the Egyptian Government, it is quite possible that
one of the leading topics of those who are endeavouring to
advocate the cause of the Mahdi would be the well-known
hostility of the English Government to slavery and the
slave-trade, and I think it is extremely possible that the
emissaries of the Mahdi were persuading the people that
the pledges hitherto given would be of no value, and since
the English had taken possession of Egypt the property in
slaves would be instantly taken away from them. It is
obvious that any report of that kind must operate dis-
astrously on the cause which General Gordon was sent out
to promote, and he, I think, justifiably took means to
prevent its spreading. It has been assumed that this
Proclamation legalises slave-hunting. That, my Lords, is

simply i, ,possible, and circumstances would not require him to re, ort to an explanation of that kind. There is a wide disti netion between domestic slavery and the slave-trade carried on by foreigners in the adjoining countries. What, I ,uppose, this Proclamation refers to, is the right of holdi ,; slaves, which is a right, be it remembered, recognised by Egyptian law ; and if any one was endeavouring to put it into the minds of the people of Khartoum that their rights would be confiscated without notice and without compensation, this Proclamation would be necessary to ensure them that they would not be disturbed in their rights, and that what had been legal before would be legal still."

Mr Gladstone said :—" Any explanation I can give on the subject must necessarily be of a conjectural character. I have not the least doubt in my own mind that the key to the difficulty lies in the distinction between slavery in the Soudan and slavery generally. And hon. gentlemen will find very full, curious, and interesting material on the subject in a book called *General Gordon in the Soudan*, and principally between pages 334 and 354, I think, they will find ample illustration of what I now state. I think it is set out among other things by General Gordon, that seven-eighths of the population of the Soudan are in a state of slavery, moreover that this state of slavery has been made the subject of legislative consideration, and I believe hon. gentlemen will find details of that consideration explained in a despatch of Lord Dufferin which is on the table. That state of slavery has a term of existence fixed by the Egyptian law, and until the expiration of that term in 1889 it is under the distinct guarantee of that law. I think that is as much as I can say now. It will be seen from the book I have already referred to that General Gordon, with the noble enthusiasm of his character, exclaims in one passage : "Would to God by laying down my life I could put an end to the slave trade;" and he afterwards shows how his whole mind and work were devoted to that object. But the whole of the work I have spoken of shows that slavery was so inter-woven with the texture of life in the Soudan that it would be impossible to put an end to it by any summary proclamation."

It was felt by all reasonable people, that to judge, and especially to condemn, General Gordon without knowing more, was altogether unjust, and by no means an illustration of holding the balance level. People turned to his own words with great interest, and read in the book referred to by Mr. Gladstone that which gave some light upon the subject. The following extract is from letters to his own people, published in Dr. Hills' book:—

"You will think I might do more. I cannot. Slaves are, to all intents and purposes, property until their owners are compensated, or till a certain number of years has elapsed. We cannot compensate, but we can decree their liberation after a term of years. Slave-hunting must be put down; but when men see that they have no hold over slaves acquired after the 1st of January 1878, they will not buy them. At any rate, slaves acquired after that date can run away, and the Government will not force them to go back. I consider this will succeed (*D. V.*). I feel that I have been most unjust to the Khedive, knowing, as I now do, the great difficulties in abolishing slavery. That the question of domestic slavery is no easy one, the debates on the abolition of slavery in our colonies would show. There it was a question of colonies only; here it is a question of home interests. You are, no doubt, better versed than I am in the history of our abolition of slavery. Men possessed slaves; to liberate them without compensation was ruin to the owners; and our people, feeling that to do so would be robbery, did compensate them. Now, in our case, England dealt only with a colony. The question did not affect us directly, but still she gave compensation. How different is this case! Here slavery abolition touches every one. How can you deal with it so as to avoid a civil war or a rising of the people? You must either pay compensation, or you must allow a term of years in order that slavery may die out. Egypt is ahead of us if we consider the state of affairs as before the Abolition Act. . . . I have an enormous province to look after; but it is a great blessing to me to know that God has undertaken the administration of it; and it is His work and not mine. If I fail, it is His will; if I succeed, it is His work. Certainly He has given me the joy of not regarding the honours of this world, and to value my union with Him above all things. May I be humbled to the dust and fail, so that He may glorify Himself. The greatness of my position only depresses me, and I cannot help wishing that the time had come when He will lay me aside and use some other worm to do His work. You have reached your happy eventide. I would that the heat of my life-day was over; but He will aid me, and not suffer me again to put down anchors to this world. . . .

"People think you have only to say the word and slavery will cease. Now, here the Gallabat merchants, I have told you of, have taken thirty of this tribe. I am trying to search them out, but I dare not do anything against these Gallabats on account of my present position with respect to Shaka. I fear to raise these men against me; they are well disposed at present. Of course, I must let time soften down the ill effects of what is written against me in the papers, on account of my purchasing the slaves now in possession of individuals in order to obtain the troops necessary to put down slavery. I need troops—how am I to get them but thus? If I do not buy these slaves, unless I liberate them at once, they still remain slaves; while, when they are soldiers, they are free from that reproach. I cannot liberate them from their owners without compensation, for fear of a general revolt. I cannot compensate the owners, and then let the men go free, for they would only be a danger. Though the slaves may not like to be soldiers, still it is the fate of many in lands where there is the conscription, and, indeed, it is the only way in which I can break up the bands of armed men, which are owned by private people—slave dealers—and get these bands under discipline.

" When I have those bands of which Sebehr's son and others are the chiefs, then the slave dealers will have no power to make raids ; while at the same time I get troops able to prevent any such like attempt. I want you to understand this, for I doubt not people will write and say :— 1. Colonel Gordon buys slaves for the Government. 2. Colonel Gordon lets the Gallabats take slaves. To No. 1 I say : 'True, for I need the purchased slaves to put down the slave dealer, and to break up their semi-independent bands.' To No. 2 I say : 'True, for I dare not stop it to any extent, for fear of adding to my enemies, before I have broken up the nest of slave dealers at Shaka.' I should be mad if I did. We should not, if at war with Russia, choose that moment to bring about any change affecting the social life of the Hindoos. The slaves I buy are already torn from their homes ; and whether I buy them or not, they will, till twelve years have elapsed, remain slaves. After twelve years they will be free, according to the treaty. It is not as if I encouraged raids for the purpose of getting slaves as soldiers. But people will, of course, say : ' By buying slaves you increase the demand, and indirectly encourage raids.' I say : ' Yes, I should do so, if, after buying them, I still allowed the raids to continue, which, of course, I shall not do.' . . This slave question is most troublesome and difficult to manage. A number of the slaves who were taken in the

last raid, made near here on the sly by the Gallabats,
refuse to go back, for they find they are better fed with
their new masters than they were with their old. . . . It
is a queer country.

"The slaves came from Dara, and had been captured and
sold to the pedlars by my own officers and men. . .   One
of the Shaka men who is riding with me tells me hundreds
and hundreds die on the road, and that when they are too
weak to go the pedlars shoot them.   I believe this man to
be quite truthful. . . . In all previous emancipations either
there has been a strong government to enforce obedience, or
a majority of the nation wished it.   Here, in this country,
there is not one who wishes it, or who would aid it even by
advice.   I know there are many who would willingly see
the sufferings of the slave-gangs cease, and also the raids on
the negro tribes ; but there they would stop.   Besides this,
the tenure of slaves is the A B C of life here to rich and
poor ; no one is uninterested in the matter. . . .

"These captures make the total number of captured
caravans since June, 1878 sixty-three.   I am not good at
a description, but you can scarcely conceive the misery and
suffering of these poor slaves.   I heard at Khartoum from
one who came from Cairo that some of the Consuls-General
did not take the least interest in the suppression of the
slave-trade; they only moved in it because their Government, fearful of public opinion, obliged them to do so.   I
do not believe it ; no one who has had a mother, or sisters,
or children could be callous to the intense human suffering
which these poor wretches undergo.   All the place is agog
to-night, and I expect parties will go out to intercept those
en route ; and, I daresay, will quietly take for themselves
the slaves they may fancy.   Yet I cannot help it.   Now I
have been here only two days, and yet these two captures !
I feel sure that several caravans passed me *en route* from
Obeid to this place ; but they were warned off the road

before I came along it. What I shall try to do is to get up
a subscription for £2000 a-year, and get English Consuls at
Obeid and Khartoum, with £1000 a-year each. What are
the £1, 1s. which are now given by rich people to the
Anti-Slavery Society ? Let them give £20 a-year; they
will not feel it.

"If the liberation of slaves takes place in 1884 (in Egypt
proper), and the present system of Government goes on,
there cannot fail to be a revolt of the whole country; but
our Government will go on sleeping till it comes, and then
have to act *à l'improviste*. If you had read the account
of the tremendous debates which took place in 1833 on the
liberation of the West Indian slaves, even on payment of
£20,000,000, you would have some idea how owners of
slaves (even Christians) hold to their property. . . . It is
rather amusing to think that the people of Cairo are quite
oblivious that in 1884 their revenue will fall to one-half,
and that the country will need many more troops to keep it
quiet. Seven-eighths of the population of the Soudan are
slaves, and the loss of revenue in 1889 (the date fixed for
the liberation of slaves in Egypt's outlying territories)
will be more than two-thirds, if it is ever carried out.
Truly, in a small way, the Egyptian problem is a very
thorny one, if you look beyond your nose. The 25,000
black troops I have here are either captured slaves or
bought slaves. How are we to recruit if the slave trade
ceases ? . . .

"Just as I wrote this I heard a very great tumult going
on among the Arabs, and I feared a fight. However, it
turned out to be caused by the division of the slaves among
the tribes ; and now the country is covered by strings of
slaves going off in all directions with their new owners.
The ostriches are running all about, and do not know what
to make of their liberty. What a terrible time of it these
poor, patient slaves have had for the last three days—

hurried on all sides, and forced first one day's march in one direction, then back again, and then off again in another. It appears that the slaves were not divided, but were scrambled for. It is a horrid idea, for, of course, families get separated; but I cannot help it, and the slaves seem to be perfectly indifferent to anything whatsoever. Imagine what it must be to be dragged from your home to places so far off—even farther than Marseilles or Rome. In their own lands some of these slaves have delightful abodes, close to running water, with pleasant glades of trees, and seem so happy; and then to be dragged off into these torrid, water-forsaken countries, where to *exist* only is a struggle against nature. . . .

"The plan suggested in June last to Earl Granville for the appointment of Consuls in the Soudan and the Red Sea has not yet been tried; and whilst still advocating such appointments, the Anti-Slavery Society would now further propose a complete registration of existing slaves, by which they believe a great check would be placed upon the increase of domestic slavery in Egypt. Such a check could not fail to render slave-hunting less remunerative in the future.

"The following mode of registration is respectfully submitted:—

"1. Registration of all existing slaves in the Mudiriehs of the Soudan and of Cairo (Lower Egypt) by the Governors.

"2. Registers to be kept in each government office of the names of slaves and their owners, with description of each.

"3. Every slave to be free, if not registered, after expiration of six months (the period given for registration). All slaves born after signature of this decree to be free.

"4. Register books to be closed for ever after the expiration of six months.

" 5. Owners of slaves thus registered to be bound to produce government certificates, corresponding with the register books, when required to do so by the Government of Egypt.

" 6. The Governors of Egypt and of the Soudan to proclaim this throughout the land.

" 7. All purchases or sales of slaves from family to family are to be endorsed on the registration papers, and inscribed in the Government books of registry.

" Assuming that the Khedive will issue a decree adopting these provisions, it may be justly asked, Where is the guarantee that they will be effectually enforced ? "

That General Gordon hates slavery with a hatred as intense and earnest as that of any Englishman is abundantly proved by these extracts and other letters in his book ; but at the same time he knows, what other Englishmen do not, the exceeding difficulty of the whole question. No one need fear to trust him ; and those who are acquainted with the man, as his whole life has revealed him, will be quite ready to do this utterly and with every confidence.

From the time of his departure, many could not help feeling anxious as to his own personal safety. Nothing was heard of him for many weeks ; and the news was often so far from being reassuring, that fresh tidings were looked for with great concern. And for all who are interested in him there was real comfort in the thought, not only of his greatness and cleverness, but also of his goodness. He was not afraid to die. He had been so often in circumstances of extreme danger, that he had become inured to the thought of death ; and his faith in the future life was so strong, that he had no doubt that when death came to him it would be to change from weariness and care to perfect peace. He was safe, living or dying, for he was a Christian.

GENERAL GORDON.

IS GORDON SAFE ?

" A message from one who had gone in haste
    Came flashing across the sea ;
It told not of weakness but trust in God,
    When it asked us, ' Pray for me ; '
And since, from churches and English homes,
    In the day or the twilight dim,
A chorus of prayers has risen to God—
    ' Bless and take care of him.'

A lonely man to these strange far lands
    He has gone with his word of peace,
And a million hearts are questioning,
    With a pain that does not cease,
' Is Gordon safe ?   Is there news of him ?
    What will the tidings be ? '
There is little to do but trust and wait,
    Yet, *utterly safe is he !*

Was he not safe when the Tai-ping shots
    Were flying about his head ?
When troubles thickened with every day,
    And he was hard bestead ?
Was he not safe in his weary rides
    Over the desert sands ?
Safe with the Abyssinian king ?
    Safe with the robber bands ?

We know not the dangers around him now
    But this we truly know :
He has with him still in his time of need
    His Protector of long ago ;
An unseen Shield is above his head,
    And a strong arm comes between
The strong brave heart that rests in God,
    And the death that might have been.

He is not alone, since a Friend is by,
    Who answers to every need :
God is his refuge and strength at hand,
    Gordon is safe indeed !

He trusts in the mercy of God for all,
    And finds it a rock to last ;
And back to us now come the ringing words
    He spoke in years gone past :

' I am a chisel that does the work
    The master directs above,
Ever the Gospel must be good news,
    Kind is the God I love.
His salvation is full and free,
    He will never cast us out ;
I may say I have died a hundred times,
    But I never yet had a doubt.'

It is true he may pass from the far Soudan
    To rest, and reward, and Heaven ;
But he is not less safe because from thence
    His freedom may be given.
Safe in living, in dying safe,
    Where is the need of pain !
God give the hero long life—but death
    Will be infinite joy and gain."

These verses, written by Marianne Farningham, and taken from the *Christian World*, which has always exhibited a generous appreciation of General Gordon's career, express the feelings of many people concerning the hero of the Soudan. Even in danger he is safe. If he could send a message home, it would no doubt be such as that which he once sent before :—

" Now you must not be surprised at anything happening to me. Supposing we subdue Sebehr's son, and he happens to be killed, some of his people may avenge themselves on me. This is not improbable. You must screw yourself up to bear it, and will remember that a quick departure is better than a long and lingering one, and, also, that I did not seek the position here. If it is so decided, depend upon it, it is because my work is finished upon this earth."

But the fact of his stay among them is sure to make it so much the better for the Soudan. His previous sojourn among the tribes had made him capable of judging what was best for the Soudanese ; and his determination to be JUST ALL ROUND rendered him an able administrator of their affairs. His wish was, as we know, to establish matters upon a firm basis, and then to leave the Soudanese to manage the country for themselves, as certainly, if they show themselves capable, they have the right to do. We can only hope that, as the result of his labours, great blessings may follow, especially that of the abolition of slavery in the land of the Blacks.

CHAPTER XXVIII.

THE YEAR IN KHARTOUM.

"Right is he, who, loving duty,
    Bravely does his best ;
Safe is he, who in God's keeping
    Finds his work or rest."

NGLAND is a very busy nation; so busy that she only gives a little time and a passing thought to her greatest heroes. The excitement caused by the departure of General Gordon, and the subsequent reception of his proclamation, soon died away, and the interest which had been at fever heat calmed down into quiet waiting. But whenever the newspapers announced "News from Gordon," it sprung up again; and throughout the year, so full of intense anxiety to the solitary hero of the Soudan, every word despatched from him was eagerly read by the British hearts that followed his movements with so much admiration and sympathy.

It was on 18th February 1884 that General Gordon arrived at Khartoum. As if he had foreseen the weary waiting that was to follow, both for him and for us, he sent home the significant message. "No Panic." We have already described the welcome accorded to him in Khartoum, and the General's wise efforts to inspire confidence by liberating all prisoners, burning all records of debts, and remitting taxation. One of his first telegrams recommended the Government to give Zebehr a commission, and stated his belief that "to withdraw without being able to place a successor in his seat would be the signal for general anarchy throughout the country, which, though all Egyptian elements were withdrawn, would be a misfortune and inhumanity."

In another telegram he said—"If Egypt is to be quiet, Mahdi must be smashed up. I repeat that evacuation is possible, but you will feel effect in Egypt, and will be forced to enter into a far more serious affair in order to guard Egypt. At present it would be comparatively easy to destroy Mahdi."

General Gordon's first duty was to create a stable government in the Soudan, and in order to do this he strongly urged the British to allow him to secure Zebehr as a coadjutor; but this request being peremptorily refused, he could only attempt that which was possible. Very cleverly did he send out of the fortress, and despatch safely to Egypt, the women and children—more than two thousand in all— whom he found there. Sir Evelyn Baring stated that there were 15,000 persons in Khartoum who ought to be brought back to Egypt—Europeans, civil servants, widows and orphans, and a garrison of a thousand men, one-third of whom were disaffected. To get these people out was General Gordon's first duty.

The resident population is generally estimated at from 50,000 to 55,000 souls, of which two-thirds are slaves. There is also a floating population estimated at from 1500 to 2000 souls, and consisting of Europeans, Syrians, Copts, Turks, Albanians, and a few Jews. The free resident population are mostly Makhass or Aborigines, Dongolawees from Dongola, Shaghives from a district along the Nile north of Khartoum, and Rubatat, a district north of Berber. The slaves belong mostly to the Nuba, Dinka, Shulook, Berta, and other negro tribes. Both the free population and the slaves are all Mahommedans of the Maliki school of divinity, and are also followers of either the Rufai, Kadri, Hamdi, or Saadi sect of dervishes. They are very superstitious. Their political creed is to side with which ever side is the strongest.

The following description of the town, given in the official "Report on the Egyptian Provinces," and published by authority, will enable the reader to form an idea of the place in which Gordon was to spend the year :—

"Khartoum is situated near the confluence of the Blue and White Niles, at a height of 1450 feet above the sea. It lies chiefly along the left bank of the Blue river, from which, however, it is partially separated by gardens, and is also so near the White Nile that the inundations of tho latter frequently reach the earthern wall by which the place is surrounded. The town, as approached from the White river, presents a mass of dirty grey houses, over-topped by a single minaret, and in front lies a sterile sandy plain without trees or bushes. It is entered by a long narrow street, stretching from west to east, and terminating in the market. This street is dirty in the extreme, and bordered by mud houses, whose doors are their only openings to the street. In other parts of the town there is no semblance of regularity ; the houses are of all sizes and shapes, and the streets mere labyrinths. Here and there are open spaces large enough for gardens, and even for corn-fields.

"There are also numerous hollow flats, in which, during the rainy season, water collects and stagnates, rendering the place very unhealthy. The street above mentioned is the best in Khartoum ; it contains the Governor's residence and offices, and many spacious mansions belonging to Turks, Copts, and Arabs. All the other houses are of a miserable description, consisting of sun-dried clay, cemented with cow-dung and slime. In the market-place is the mosque, built of brick, and here also are the bazaar, coffee-houses, brandy shops, etc. In addition to the buildings already mentioned, there is a Coptic and a Roman Catholic chapel, a Roman Catholic school, an infirmary, a gaol, and barracks.

"The gardens along the Blue Nile produce vegetables and fruits in great variety. The date palm here reaches its most southern limit, and ceases to fully ripen its fruit, though as a tree it still grows vigorously.

"There is much land for cultivation along the borders of the Blue Nile, but the tax on the water-wheels and the contributions levied on the produce cause the Arabs to limit their agriculture to their bare necessities."

It was on the 24th of March that the British expeditionary force landed at Trinkitat. That affairs were serious in Khartoum was seen by the following proclamation issued by General Gordon to the Soudanese on 26th February :—

"From the date of my arrival until now I have given you sound advice, and everything has been done to ensure tranquillity and put a stop to bloodshed. My advice has not been listened to, and I am therefore forced against my will to send for British troops, who are now on the road, and will arrive in a few days. I shall severely punish all who will not change their conduct. You know well that I am not ignorant of anything that is going on, and I write this that you may know my resolution."

News also came that General Gordon had sent Colonel Stewart up the White Nile to punish the marauding tribes, who had become exceedingly troublesome ; but nothing was known as to the force with which Colonel Stewart was to carry out his mission.

After this scrap of information came the news of General Graham's victory, and the rout of Osman Digna's army at Tamanieb ; and then the troops were recalled to Suakim.

On the 12th of March Gordon, feeling that he had only two alternatives, as he might not have his wish granted in regard to Zebehr, and that he must either surrender absolutely to the Mahdi or strengthen his position at Khartoum, was doing his best in the latter direction, when 4000 rebels marched to the Nile and cut off 800 of his men who were at a village called Halfaya, to the north of Khartoum. In consequence of this, General Gordon sent down a steamer to reconnoitre. The moment the vessel came within range of the enemy a volley was fired into her, and an officer and a soldier were wounded ; but Gordon resolved to extricate the little garrison if possible. It proved possible, though very difficult. Three companies of Gordon's troops had gone out to cut wood, when the enemy came upon them, cut them off from the main body, captured eight of their boats, and killed or wounded nearly 150. The Halfaya garrison could not retreat, for the rebels covered the river and kept up a heavy fire. But Gordon was determined on rescuing them. Two grain barges, with 1200 men on board, were towed by three steamers, defended with boiler plates, and carrying mountain guns protected by wooden mantlets, and by means of these, with the loss of only two men killed, Gordon's force contrived to extricate the remaining 500 men and bring them into Khartoum. They brought also from Halfaya seventy camels and eighteen horses.

But although this was so far a success, yet as the rebels held Halfaya, General Gordon on the 16th of March resolved upon making an effort to drive them away. He marched out of Khartoum at the head of 2000 irregular troops—very irregular indeed, probably a mixed multitude of Soudanese and Nubians, out of whom the courageous General hoped to make good soldiers. They advanced across the open in square, supported by the fire of the guns of two steamers. The Mahdi's forces came out on the other side to give him battle. At first it seemed that Gordon was to be victorious, but the treachery from which his greatest sufferings have resulted was at work to prevent this. The rebels were actually retreating when Gordon's two native generals, Hassan and Seyid Pashas, rode into the wood and called the enemy back. The Egyptians, finding themselves thus betrayed by their own officers, broke and retreated in great confusion, leaving their ammunition and two mountain guns in the hands of the enemy. They managed to carry off some of their wounded, but left two hundred on the field.

When they had got safely back to Khartoum one of the first things the Governor did was to have a court-martial held in order to try Hassan Pasha and Seyid Pasha for treachery in the face of the enemy. Seyid had only been a Bey until Gordon promoted him. Both men were found guilty upon the clearest evidence, and Gordon sentenced them to be shot. Later on he sent a telegram announcing what he had done, and conveying a reminder—that was, a warning— to the effect that the forces, whom he seems even then to have expected to come to his aid, should keep in mind the fact that his guns in the hands of the enemy made them additionally dangerous.

In a despatch received at Cairo on the 31st of March, the General intimated that notwithstanding the defeat he had suffered things were not altogether dark and hopeless at Khartoum. Supplies were coming in from the White Nile, while the rebels at Halfaya were in want of food and apprehending a famine.

The enemy, however, was exceedingly troublesome, and made it difficult for the supplies to arrive in safety. A steamer coming up from Berber was attacked with great determination ; but Gordon's men behaved resolutely, no less than 15,000 rounds of ammunition being fired amongst the enemy, who suffered considerable loss, and had to retire.

In the meantime efforts were made on both sides to effect a negotiation. General Gordon sent to the Mahdi a message to the following effect—"I will make you Sultan of Kordofan." "I am the Mahdi," was the only answer vouchsafed in return.

The Mahdi then sent Gordon a letter, in which he advised him to embrace the Mohammedan faith. He added that the European prisoners in Obeid were kindly treated and well-cared for. The letter was rather friendly than otherwise; but the emissaries were insolent. In the Governor's presence they kept their drawn swords in their hands, and spread a filthy patched dervish's coat before him.

" Will you become a Mussulman ! " they asked.

"No !" shouted Gordon, flinging the coat across the room.

He then cancelled the offer he had made to the Mahdi, and from henceforth there was no hope of negotiation.

No day passed afterwards without some shots being fired into Khartoum from the Mahdi's forces outside.

The town being invested, General Gordon set to work to defend it. There were 10,000 men who sympathised with the Mahdi within the walls, and these were allowed to go outside and join the enemy. Gordon's steamers kept up a brisk skirmish on both the Niles. All the houses on the north side were loop-holed, and those on the northern bend of the Blue Nile were fortified and garrisoned by Bashi-Bazouks. A 16-pounder Krupp gun was mounted on a barge, and blockading wires were stretched across the river. Omdurman, a village on the west, was held and fortified, and the same was done with Buri on the east.

During the last week of March various items of news were forwarded from Gordon to Cairo. A steamer had been sent down to shell the enemy at Halfaya, but the shells fell short. Another steamer was sent up the Nile with a Krupp gun, which rendered better service. On the 25th of March two hundred and fifty irregulars were ordered by Gordon to attack some villages on the opposite bank of the river. They refused to obey, and Gordon at once commanded them to lay down their arms. On the following day several of his steamers shelled the rebel camp on the Blue Nile, and did some damage to the enemy. On the twenty-seventh the rebels came up close to Khartoum and maintained an attack for several hours, the Krupp gun replying. On the thirtieth the outlying enemy was attacked by some of Gordon's irregulars, who, however, had to flee back into Khartoum. All the night of the thirty-first the rebels kept up an incessant fire on the town. Gordon gave it as his opinion that the rebels had only one gun left, the other gun having been spiked, and two rounds of ammunition. He spoke hopefully of his power to hold out; and it was felt at Cairo that if only the garrison remained faithful to him, he would be able to do so. But no one could know but himself the difficulty there was in keeping those around him contented and true to the tasks imposed upon them.

A post-card was received at Berlin from General Gordon, dated "Khartoum, March the 7th," from which the *Nord Deutsche* published the following extract:—"I doubt not that the King of Abyssinia will receive Sula, Bogos, and some other districts, but it is no longer in our power to give him Galabat, which is already in the hands of the rebels. The king should be satisfied with this indemnification, which, however, I doubt." In the same missive, moreover, the General speaks of the difficulties of the slave question, but some of the words are so illegible that it is impossible to make out the meaning of the passage.

During April a false report was circulated to the effect that Khartoum had fallen, and that General Gordon was captured. But a few days later a letter was received from himself, stating that the Fagallâh tribes had twice defeated the Mahdi. That he was greatly disheartened, and knew himself to be in the midst of danger, no one doubted, but that he had also some things to encourage him was made clear by a telegram from Mr. Power to the *Times*, which, to the intense relief of the English nation, was published early in April. Among other things, it stated that a number of prisoners taken by the Arabs were being sent with a gun and ammunition as trophies to the Mahdi at El Obeid, when they attacked their escort, broke the elevating screw of the gun, and made their way back to Khartoum. Again, a young man of rank, who had been landed from a steamer by one of the traitorous Pashas—who was sent with him to effect the rescue of the lad's family, threatened at that time by the foe—and was then basely deserted, had rejoined the General's forces, and brought the fullest confirmation of the treachery for which the Pashas were executed. The number of Arabs fighting against General Gordon was then estimated at about 4000 foot and 100 cavalry.

But on the 5th of May a Blue Book was issued, from which it was seen that General Gordon had on the 16th of April telegraphed the following significant words to Sir E. Baring :—"As far as I can understand, the situation is this : You state your intention of not sending any relief up here or to Berber, and you refuse me Zebehr. I consider myself free to act according to circumstances. I shall hold on here as long as I can, and if I can suppress the rebellion, I shall do so. If I cannot, I shall retire to the Equator, and leave you the indelible disgrace of abandoning the garrisons of Senaar, Kassala, Berber, and Dongola, with the certainty that you will eventually be forced to smash up the Mahdi under great difficulties, if you would retain peace in Egypt."

Colonel Stewart and Mr. Power telegraphed that they

would remain and follow the fortunes of General Gordon to the end. Evidently the General felt that he had been forsaken by the English Government. He sent a telegram to Sir Samuel Baker, asking that, as he was abandoned by the Government, an appeal might be made to the millionaires of England and America to equip a Turkish battalion to march to Berber. Many of the English people, and almost the entire press, were greatly indignant at the attitude of the British authorities, who persisted in declaring that Gordon was in no danger. Nearly every one except those authorities believed his danger to be most imminent. In both Houses of Parliament questions in reference to the General's safety were repeatedly asked ; but they were, as a rule, treated very lightly. Lord Granville declared that if General Gordon felt himself abandoned, it was because he had not received the Government telegrams. Mr. Gladstone said that the General was at liberty to leave Khartoum if he pleased : an assertion which the foreign press ridiculed most derisively. In the *Standard* the following telegram from Cairo appeared on the 22nd of April :— "General Gordon has telegraphed to Sir Evelyn Baring expressing the utmost indignation at the manner in which he has been abandoned by the English Government, and stating his resolution henceforth to cut himself entirely adrift from those who have deserted him, on whom will rest the bloodguiltiness for all lives hereafter lost in the Soudan."

At this time private enterprise was busy. A lady wrote to the *Times* offering £5000 as the nucleus of a sum to be contributed voluntarily by the nation ; and it was sought to enrol a band of two hundred volunteers to go out and rescue the brave man and his two companions who had evidently been left to shift for themselves. The entire news from Egypt was gloomy in the extreme. It included a massacre of some three hundred refugees from Shendy, a military post midway between Berber and Khartoum, while endeavouring to escape in a steamer down the Nile to Berber. The governor of that place, when telegraphing the news to Cairo, asked if reinforcements were coming, as otherwise there was no course open to him but to make the best terms possible with the Mahdi, whose troops were investing the place. Later telegrams from the same quarter stated that the Arabs were occupying the desert route from Abu Hamed to Korosko, which separates the two points on the Nile where navigation to the north and to the south commences, so that it was most probable the telegraph line connecting Berber with Cairo would be cut.

The popular feeling found some vent in a meeting which on the 8th of May was held by the Patriotic Association in St. James's Hall, London. The Earl of Cadogan presided; and the following resolution was moved by Mr. Chaplin, M.P., and seconded by the Earl of Dunraven : "That this meeting condemns the abandonment of General Gordon by Her Majesty's Ministers as dishonourable to them, and discreditable to the country." It was declared both at that meeting and at others that the officials who had sent Gordon out had told him to use his own judgment, and had given him to understand that he would be supported and his wishes carried out. But he had asked for money, and it had not been sent; had asked for Zebehr, and had been refused; had prayed for troops, and been informed that they were not forthcoming.

Still the Government persisted in declaring that Gordon was in no danger; adding that they had taken the responsibility of his safety upon themselves, and that as they were better informed than other people, they would move in the matter when it became necessary. There was an attempt to pass a vote of censure, which was only lost by twenty-eight. But the next news was, that an order had been sent to the British military authorities at Cairo to prepare for the despatch in October of an expeditionary force for the relief of the General. Immediately after the following telegrams appeared in the papers :—

" Further news has been received from Khartoum. It is stated that the authorities there have a stock of maize sufficient to last for eighteen months, but that other provisions are short.

" Four men have been shot by General Gordon for treachery.

" Advices from the same source state that the country appears quiet between Wady Halfa and Berber.

" General Gordon has stated to Greek merchants that he expected English troops, and that, therefore, they need not leave the town, as they were quite safe. He has appointed a Greek Sub-Governor of Khartoum.

" The Governor of Dongola telegraphs that the whole country south of Debbah—a place which is close to Dongola —is in open revolt.

" There are no further hopes of communicating with either Berber or Khartoum. Nevertheless, only a few days since a Greek trader arrived at Cairo, having left Khartoum on the day after date of General Gordon's last message.

" The belief here is that General Gordon could even now effect an escape, if he could be prevailed upon to attempt it alone. But it is evidently impossible to bring out even a small force with him."

General Gordon would certainly not escape alone, but would be faithful to those who had stood by him. There followed an interval of little or no news until a telegram from Mr. Power, sent to the *Times*, relieved the anxiety of the nation. In the meanwhile, the following diary had been kept by Mr. Power, and it is probably the best and most reliable account we shall ever have of the life in the besieged town from 23rd March to 31st July. Since that date there has been no record of events from within the city :—

" *March* 23.—Hassan and Seyid Pashas were put to

death for treachery in the battle of the sixteenth, in which we lost 350 killed and wounded.

"*April* 16, 17, 18, 19, and 20.—Attacks by rebels on the Palace from the villages opposite. Fearful loss of life to the Arabs from mines put down by General Gordon.

"*April* 21.—We heard of the surrender of Saleh Bey at Mesalimieh to the rebels with fifty shiploads of food, seventy boxes of cartridges, 2020 rifles, and a steamer.

"*May* 1.—The officer commanding engineers having put down a mine of 78 lbs. of powder, trod on it, and with six soldiers was blown to pieces.

"*May* 3.—A man reported an English army at Berber.

"*May* 6.—Heavy attack from the Arabs at the Blue Nile end of the works; great loss of lives from mines we had placed at Buri.

"*May* 7.—Great attack from a village opposite; nine mines were exploded there, and we afterwards heard that they killed 115 rebels. The Arabs kept up a fire all day. Colonel Stewart, with two splendidly-directed shots from a Krupp 20-pounder at the Palace, drove them out of their principal position. During the night the Arabs loop-holed the walls, but on the ninth we drove them out. They had held the place for three days.

"*May* 25.—Colonel Stewart, while working a mitrailleuse at the Palace, was wounded by the rebel fire, but he is now quite well.

"*May* 26.—During an expedition up the White Nile, Saati Bey put a shell into an Arab magazine. There was a great explosion, sixty shells going off.

"During May and June, steamer expeditions were made daily under Saati Bey. Our loss was slight, and much cattle were captured.

"*June* 25.—Mr. Ouzzi, English Consul at Berber, who is with the rebels, came to our lines and told us of the fall of Berber. Mr. Ouzzi has been sent to Kordofan.

"*June* 30.—Saati Bey captured forty ardebs of corn from the rebels, and killed 200 of them.

"*July* 10.—Saati Bey having burnt Kalaka and three villages, attacked Gatarneb, but three of his officers were killed. Colonel Stewart had a narrow escape. Saati's loss is serious.

"*July* 29.—We beat the rebels out of Buri, on the Blue Nile, killing numbers of them and capturing ammunition and eighty rifles. The steamers advanced to El Efan, clearing thirteen rebel forts and breaking two cannon. Since the siege began our loss has been under 700 killed."

General Gordon was blamed by many parties for engaging in so many fights, but they were all purely defensive. He did but try to clear the road of the attacking force, which would have been easily done if he had possessed a single reliable regiment; but he did not, and since the middle of April the rebels had attacked the city in ever-increasing force. He was utterly cut off from the outside world, and compelled to rely wholly upon his own resources. Negroes were sent out to entice the slaves of the rebels to come over, promising them freedom and rations. This he thought would frighten the rebels more than bullets; it would be the beginning of the end of slavery there, and the Arabs would desert a locality so dangerous to their hold on human chattels. On 26th April he made his first issue of paper money to the extent of £2500, redeemable in six months. By 30th July it had risen to £26,000, besides the £50,000, borrowed from merchants. On the same day he struck decorations for the defence of Khartoum—for officers in silver, silver-gilt and pewter for the private soldiers. These medals bear a crescent and a star, with a quotation from the Koran, the date, with an inscription—"Siege of Khartoum"—and a hand grenade in the centre. "School children and women," he wrote, "also received medals; consequently I am very popular with the black ladies of Khartoum."

Facsimile of a Letter written by
GENERAL GORDON.

22nd June 1884.   *Received 23rd August.*

Translation.

First Side.

Mudir of Dongola,

Khartoum and Sennaar in perfect security
and Mahomed Ahmed carries this to give you
news and on his reaching you give him all
the news as to the direction and position of the
relieving force and their number and as for
Khartoum there are in it

Second Side.

8000 men and the Nile is rapidly rising on
the arrival of the bearer give him 100 reals
Megidich from the State.

C. G. Gordon.

1301 Shaban 28th.

---

*The official stamp in indigo is too indistinct to
decipher the characters on it.*

*The letter was folded and placed in a quill and
hidden in the hair of the messenger.*

He wrote subsequently, in little notes to friends—" Be assured that these hostilities are far from being sought for, but we have no option. Retreat is impossible, unless we abandon the *employés* and their families, which the general feeling of the troops is against." These words show that he was in great straits ; and although he was obliged to fight, he mourned the necessity. " *You may rely on this,*" he wrote further, " *that if there was any possible way of avoiding these wretched fights, I should adopt it, for the whole war is hateful to me.*"

Still, honour was dearer to him than peace.

" I will not leave these people after all they have gone through. I shall not leave Khartoum until I can put some one in."

" I stay at Khartoum because Arabs have shut us out. I also add that even if the road was open the people would not let me go unless I gave then some government, or took them with me, which I could not do."

On the 22nd of June Gordon wrote to the Mudir of Dongola to say that he had 8,000 men with him in Khartoum, and to ask if reinforcements were coming ; and later news was received to the effect that himself, Colonel Stewart, and Mr. Power were all well, and that he had provisions for four months.

On Midsummer-day Gordon met at the wells Mr. Ouzzi, formerly his own agent at Berber, but now a prisoner of the Mahdi's, who had been sent by the latter to announce to the General the sad news that Berber had been taken, that the garrison were massacred, and that 3500 persons had been killed.

The hearts of the three Englishmen had need to be brave ; and they were. The officer, Saati Bey, who had command of the steamers, was also brave, and for two months he had had uninterrupted success. In July Mr. Power went up to Gareff, on the Blue Nile. taking with him five armoured steamers and four armoured barges, which had been made more effective by General Gordon, who had erected castles twenty feet high on each, so that a double line of fire could be poured from them upon the enemy. The Arabs had constructed fourteen small forts between Gareff and Khartoum, but Gordon's forces cleared them all away. There were two strong earthworks at Gareff, bound together by trunks of palm trees and defended by cannon. The Krupp gun disabled the cannon.

In the four months Gordon's troops had fired about half-a-million cartridges, and two of his steamers had received on their hulls nine hundred and eight hundred hits respectively; yet only thirty of his men were killed and sixty wounded.

But the strain upon the besieged must have been simply terrible. They lived in constant expectation of the arrival of relief from England; but no relief came. Gordon endeavoured to keep up the spirits of his people, and they behaved admirably. The ammunition was stored in the large mission premises on the river; and as time passed on it became necessary to use it with the utmost caution. Great economy had to be exercised in regard to food. All were rationed, but at the beginning of August food had become thirty times dearer than its usual price. Still none came to his aid. "We appeared even as liars to the people of Khartoum." These were General Gordon's words, and there is much heart-break in them. He knew the people trusted him, yet he could not keep his word. Zebehr and relief had been promised them, but neither came. He had borrowed money to feed the starving, and now it seemed as if his paper money would never be redeemed. Still he did not altogether lose heart, for the Nile was rising; and if Colonel Stewart could only get through to Dongola much might be done. He was able to seize five thousand quarters of grain and replenish his almost exhausted granary. Moreover, he performed a very plucky action in the beginning of August. He reached the garrison of Senaar, and caused the Blue Nile to separate the rebels into two forces. At last the following strange and ominous despatch, dated Khartoum, 26th August, was received from General Gordon by the Khedive, Sir Evelyn Baring, and Nubar Pasha respectively :—

"I am awaiting the arrival of British troops in order to evacuate the Egyptian garrisons. Send me Zebehr Pasha, and pay him a yearly salary of £8000. I shall surrender the Soudan to the Sultan as soon as 200,000 Turkish troops have arrived. If the rebels kill the Egyptians, you will be answerable for their blood. I require £300,000 for soldiers' pay, my daily expenses being £1500.

"Within a few days I shall take Berber, where I have sent Colonel Stewart, Mr. Power, and the French Consul, with a good number of troops and Bashi-Bazouks, who, after a fortnight's stay there, will burn the town and then return to Khartoum. Colonel Stewart will first go to Dongola and then to the Equator to bring back the garrisons from thence. I disbelieve the report of the Mahdi's coming, and hope the Soudanese will kill him.

"If the Turkish troops arrive, they should come by Dongola and Kassala, and you should give them £300,000."

Two days later, England at least approved of one step which was taken, and Gordon would have been encouraged had he known of it—Lord Wolseley was appointed to conduct an expedition for his relief to the Soudan.

CHAPTER XXIX.

THE RELIEF EXPEDITION.

"I know the gentleman
To be worth and worthy estimation,
And not without desert so well deported."
—*Two Gentlemen of Verona.*

N the 5th of August the House of Commons having gone into committee, Mr. Gladstone moved a vote of credit for £300,000, "to enable Her Majesty to undertake operations for the relief of General Gordon, should it become necessary, and to make certain preparations in respect thereof." The vote was opposed by Mr. Labouchere and Mr. Bourke; the latter, however, declaring that he and his friends were anxious to see General Gordon in a place of safety. The vote was carried by one hundred and seventy-four to fourteen. Preparations were commenced with great activity. From Cairo news was telegraphed that the Mudir of Dongola would provide 2000 men to accompany Major Kitchener to Khartoum, in which direction Major Chernside was also making progress. It was considered both advisable and practicable to construct a railway from Suakim to Berber; and a portion of the necessary railway

plant had already been landed at the latter place; but the project was ultimately abandoned, and the Nile route adopted. Four hundred boats, of light draught, were immediately ordered for the expedition. Shipbuilding firms at Liverpool, Dundee, Hartlepool, London, Hull, and on the Clyde and Tyne, were engaged to build them at a cost of £75 a-piece, and men were kept employed at them day and night, in order to expedite their delivery. An additional order was given for other four hundred, to be delivered in London by the 1st of October.

The hearts of the British people beat more freely when it became known that Lord Wolseley was appointed to conduct the expedition. It proved that the Government fully realised the gravity and importance of the undertaking; and Lord Wolseley's past successes encouraged the hope that he would speedily bring the difficulty to a satisfactory termination. The War and Admiralty officials were busy late and early; and a Mobilisation Committee was formed, including the Duke of Cambridge, Lord Hartington, Lord Wolseley, Sir Ralph Thomson, Lieutenant-General Sir H. Herbert, Quartermaster-General, and the heads of the principal departments, to arrange as to the disposition of the forces comprising the expedition, and to consider Lord Wolseley's plans, so far as they were formed, for conducting the campaign. The Marquis of Lansdowne, Governor-General of Canada, issued a proclamation for the enlistment of a contingent of six hundred Canadian river boatmen to conduct the boats up the rapids of the Nile, of which Major Denison, of the Governor-General's bodyguard, was to take command.

On the thirtieth an official telegram from Assouan announced the fact that the Nile was rising, and that seven steamers had been got over the first cataract.

It was decided that Lord Northbrook should accompany Lord Wolseley, and on the last day of August they both proceeded to Osborne to take leave of Her Majesty ; and the following evening started on their journey. On the 9th of September they arrived at Alexandria, and were received with enthusiasm by a large assemblage, and by Nubar Pàsha and the Khedive. A special train conveyed them to Cairo, which they reached in four hours. General Earle, as senior officer, introduced to Lord Northbrook the various officers and native officials. Fifty men of the Black Watch, accompanied by their band, formed a guard of honour, and escorted Lord Northbrook and Sir Evelyn Baring to their residence. The following is the appointments approved by the Queen :—

General the Lord Wolseley, G.C.B., to be General Officer Commanding in Chief the Forces in Egypt.

To be Military Secretary—Brevet Lieutenant-Colonel Swaine, C.B., R.A.

To be A.D.C.—Major Wardrop, 3rd Dragoon Guards ; Brevet Major Creagh, R.A. ; Lieutenant Childers, R.A. ; Lieutenant Adye, R.A.

To be Major-General on the Staff—Major-General Sir R. Buller, V.C., etc., as Chief of the Staff.

To be A.D.C.—Lieutenant Lord W. Fitzgerald, King's Royal Rifles.

To be Assistant-Adjutant and Quartermasters-General— Colonel W. F. Butler, C.B., and Lieutenant-Colonel G. A. Furse.

To be Deputy Assistant-Adjutant and Quartermaster-General—Brevet Lieutenant-Colonel J. Alleyne, R.A.

For Special Service.—Colonel Sir C. W. Wilson, K.C.M.G., R.E., as head of the Intelligence Department ; Colonel R. Harrison, C.B., R.E. ; Colonel H. Brackenbury, C.B., R.A. ; Colonel Sir H. Stewart, K.C.B., 3rd Dragoons ; Colonel Webber, C.B., R.E. ; Colonel Henderson, King's Royal Rifles ; Brevet Lieutenant-Colonel J. F. Maurice, R.A. ; Captain Lord Airlie, 10th Hussars.

Lord Northbrook presented to the Khedive his credentials as High Commissioner, and an autograph letter from Queen Victoria, in which Her Majesty assured the Khedive of her personal esteem, and expressed the hope that he would lend every help in his power to her High Commissioner while in Egypt.

The Mudir of Dongola telegraphed from Debbah that there had been a defeat of the rebels on the Nile, and on the 17th of September news came of renewed fighting in the Soudan, in which it was said that Osman Digna's nephew had been killed.

A parliamentary paper was issued on the same day, containing a despatch from Earl Granville to Mr. Egerton, requesting him to send a message to General Gordon, to the effect that Her Majesty's Government continued to be anxious to learn from himself his views and position, so that if danger had arisen, or was likely to arise, they might take measures accordingly.

It was on the 17th of September that the three identical cipher telegrams from General Gordon reached Cairo for the Khedive, Sir Evelyn Baring, and Nubar Pasha, in which he said he was awaiting the arrival of British troops in ordei to evacuate the Egyptian garrisons, asking again for Zebehr Pasha, and stating that he required £300,000 for soldiers' pay. These telegrams are given in the previous chapter. A day or two later five other telegrams were received in Cairo from the General.

On the 23rd of September a report was published to the effect that Gordon had won several victories over the rebels. Lord Wolseley hastened his departure from Cairo, General Earle took command of the forces at Wady Halfa, and Colonel Stewart started for Dongola. The Mahdi had sent messengers to Suakim to say that having heard of General Gordon's recent successes he intended to despatch troops to Khartoum. In the meantime all hands were at work

making preparations for the advance. Great things were
hoped from the armed steamer *Nasefra*, for it was thought
that the presence of a vessel flying the British flag in the
upper waters of the Nile would produce a great effect upon
the natives, who would then be convinced for the first time
that a force was on its way to Khartoum.

During the time the Expedition was advancing, the
Nile boats were gradually making their way, and the
infantry had reached Dongola.

Early in October the news from General Gordon was
exceedingly grave and important. It was reported that he
had conducted a force in two steamers and bombarded
Berber. But immediately afterwards came the news that
Colonel Stewart and Mr. Power had been murdered.

After he had driven the rebels out of Berber, General
Gordon returned to Khartoum, and then Colonel Stewart,
with about forty men on board a steamer, went down the
Nile in order to proceed to Dongola to open up communications with the Mudir. The steamer was making its way
down the river when it struck upon a rock and was disabled.
Stewart and his men did their very utmost to get the
steamer off, but were unable to accomplish it. Several
natives then came on board, and appeared to be friendly.
They invited the crew to their dwellings and gave them
presents; and they informed Colonel Stewart that he was
only a short distance from Meranee. They said that in
that village they would be able to procure men to remove
the steamer; and an Arab chief engaged to provide the
party with camels and guides. Colonel Stewart, after a
little natural hesitation, decided to trust the natives. The
chief requested them to lay down their arms, as otherwise
the natives would not trust them, and they consented to do
so, Colonel Stewart retaining only a small pistol in his
pocket. Suleiman Wad Gamr, who conducted the negotiations, and who undertook to guide them, received a present

of a sword and dress, after which Colonel Stewart and his party prepared to go ashore and start on the journey. At that moment he and his two English companions were treacherously murdered.

At first, when the news came, it was hoped that Mr. Power had escaped, or that he had not been one of the party ; but as time passed on that hope proved fallacious. It was several months before the English public had the whole story told them. At length Husseim Ismail, who had been stoker on board the *Abdai*, one of Stewart's steamers, escaped from the Arabs, and having joined General Earle's column, made the following statement, which we extract from the *Standard :—*

"We left Khartoum about six months ago. There were with us two other steamers. On board the *Abdai* were Colonel Stewart, two Pashas, two European Consuls, Hassan Bey, twelve Greeks, and some Egyptian soldiers, besides the crew.

"When we reached Berber we shelled the forts there. After this the other steamers went back. We came on down the Nile. Nothing happened till we passed Abu Hamed ; but on the 18th of September the steamer struck on a rock. We were then passing through Wad Gamr's country. As we had passed down we had seen the people running away into the hills on both sides of the river.

"When it was found that the steamer could not be got off the rock, the small boat, filled with useful things, was sent to a little island near us. Four trips were made. Then Colonel Stewart himself spiked the guns, and threw them overboard, and also two boxes of ammunition.

"The people now came down to the right bank in great numbers, shouting, 'Give us peace and grain.' We answered 'Peace.' Suleiman Wad Gamr himself was in a small house near the bank, and he came out and called to Colonel Stewart to land without fear, but said that the soldiers must be unarmed, or the people would be afraid of them.

"Colonel Stewart, after talking it over with the others, then crossed in the boats, with the two English Consuls and Hassen Bey, and entered the house of the blind man, Fakri Etman, to arrange with Suleiman for the purchase of camels to take us all down to Dongola. None of the four had any arms, with the exception of Colonel Stewart, who carried a small revolver in his pocket. While they were in the house we began to land in the boat.

"After a little time we saw Suleiman come out of the house, with a copper water pot in his hand. He made signs to the people who were all gathered near the house. They immediately divided into two parties, one entering the house, the other rushing down towards us who were gathered on the bank, shouting and waving their spears. I was with the party who had landed when they charged down. We all threw ourselves into the river. The natives fired, killing some in the river, many others were drowned, and the rest speared as they came near the bank. I swam to the island, and hid there till dark, when I was made prisoner with some others, and sent to Berti.

"I heard that Colonel Stewart and the two Englishmen were killed at once. Hassen Bey held the blind man before him, so that they could not spear him. They spared his life, and he afterwards escaped to Berber. Two artillerymen, two sailors, and three natives are, I believe, still alive at Berber, where they were sent by Suleiman. All the money found on board and in the pockets of those they killed was divided among the men who did the murder. Everything else of value was placed in two boxes and sent under a guard to Berber. The bodies of Colonel Stewart and the others were thrown at once into the river."

Before the full particulars of this massacre reached England, another telegram had been received from General Gordon, complaining of the slowness of the expedition, and declaring that the rebels were increasing.

There was at first a considerable amount of sickness among the troops at Dongola, but as the month of October wore on the health of the men improved, and the officers arranged some slight diversion for them. The programme comprised races for horses and camels, and foot races for the men, and the relaxation was much enjoyed by all ranks. To witness a camel-race was a new experience for Englishmen, and occasioned considerable amusement.

Lord Wolseley made Wady Halfa his headquarters. This place is situated at the foot of the Second Cataract, and is 793 miles from Cairo. His presence there gave considerable impetus to the expedition. He had a force of 6000 men at his disposal.

Lord Northbrook started on his return journey towards the end of October. About the same time it was announced from Cairo that the Mahdi, having heard that General Gordon was running short of provisions, determined to render the investment of Khartoum so complete as to starve out the garrison. For this purpose he was preparing to despatch a force of 15,000 men.

Additional particulars in regard to Gordon's cipher telegrams were published before October was ended. He informed Sir Evelyn Baring that the best route for an expedition would be from Wady Halfa, along the right bank of the Nile, to Berber; that if Berber had not fallen, the campaign would simply have been a picnic.

On the 3rd of November several newspapers in England published intelligence of a startling character, but which afterwards proved to be false. It purported to come from the Cairo correspondent of the Central News, and stated that a noted sheik had brought news to the effect that General Gordon was a prisoner in the hands of the Mahdi. A very circumstantial story was told, to the effect that Gordon had been compelled to yield to the remonstrances of the people in Khartoum, who were dying of starvation; that he had left

Khartoum in September, accompanied by the 2000 troops who had remained faithful; that his steamers had sustained, in sight of Berber, a murderous cannonade, which destroyed nearly all the flotilla; and that Gordon was a prisoner, heavily ironed, and at the mercy of the Mahdi.

The news scarcely created a panic, for most people received it with caution, and the next intelligence disproved the report. On the 4th of November a telegram from Dongola stated that the troops of the Mahdi had closely surrounded Khartoum, and that the Mahdi himself had called upon Gordon to surrender.

"Not for ten years," was the reply of the intrepid General.

He afterwards said, " When you, Mahdi, order the Nile to dry up, and walk across with your troops, and come into Khartoum to me, and take me, then I will surrender the town to you, and not before."

Some remarkable stories were told of the tyranny and rapacity of the Mahdi, and of his endeavours to work miracles by jugglery. It was asserted that he took in earnest the taunt of General Gordon with regard to the drying up of the Nile, and that he ordered three thousand of his men to cross the river, assuring them that it would become dry ground as they advanced. They were forced to obey the order, and the result of the experiment was that almost the whole number were drowned.

On the 8th of November a letter was received from General Gordon stating that he was safe, and that so far from starving, he had enough provisions to enable him to hold out until the expedition arrived.

A few days later came the news of the daring ride of Major Stuart Wortley across the desert. His ride from Selimah round to Dongola completed a survey of the entire flanking route from Kordofan to Assiout by the Western Desert, with a view to ascertain the possibility of a rapid hostile advance by that line cutting the British force from their base. With four attendants Major Stuart Wortley struck south from Selimah, and penetrated to Laghen, one hundred and fifty miles distant, and then went over a desert of one hundred and eighty miles to the nearest point of the Nile, and then eastward to Dongola, steering himself by the aid of the compass alone. Bedouins followed the little party for some distance, but they were evidently afraid to attack. Fifty miles from the Nile, Major Wortley struck the great Wady-el-Kab, and found it a fine grazing country for camels, well supplied with water. The Major considered that this route should be watched; and his journey, described as "one of the most plucky events of the expedition," doubtless effected good and prevented evil.

The progress made by the expedition appeared, to those who in England waited for news, to be exceedingly slow; but the difficulties of getting the boats up the Nile were almost insurmountable. The advance began; our men worked with a will, and all that genius and courage could achieve was doubtless accomplished; but, all the same, it was weary waiting in England, and what it must have been in Khartoum no pen can describe. In November Khartoum and Dongola were within ten or fifteen days' communication from each other; and in answer to a letter which he had received from Lord Wolseley, General Gordon sent one containing eight hundred words. It expressed the General's regret at the wreck of the steamer which he had despatched from Khartoum with Colonel Stewart, Mr. Power, Mr. Herbin, and thirty others on board, and confirmed the news of the massacre. It declared his delight to hear of the advance of the British troops, and his belief that he could hold out until they arrived. It affirmed that the Mahdi was at that time only a day's march from Khartoum, and that he (Gordon) continued with his steamers to harass the enemy, who were attempting to reach Khartoum. It stated also that he had received letters from his sister Sir Samuel Baker, and Mr. Stanley, through Major Kitchener. The letter gave many directions as to the best means of reaching him, and repudiated the idea that the expedition was coming to rescue him.

"You are coming" he wrote, "not to relieve me, but to rescue the garrisons which I was unable to withdraw."

This letter was dated 4th November, and reached Lord Wolseley on the thirteenth of the same month.

A later message was received which gave an account of Gordon's proceedings in Khartoum. He was engaged in making powder, repairing disabled steamers, and building new ones. His Admiral, Kasham Amors, had, with five steamers and 500 men, driven the rebels from the banks of the Nile as far as Shendy. Large supplies of grain had been brought in ; and, notwithstanding that the Mahdi had 15,000 troops on the west bank of the Nile, all was well in Khartoum, if only the brave commander could have no fear of treachery.

On the 1st December Lord Wolseley published the following order, which was to be read at the head of every regiment, battalion, battery, and detached body of troops, and to appear in all orders for three days :—

"The relief of General Gordon, and of the garrison which has been so long besieged in Khartoum, is the glorious mission which the Queen has entrusted to us, an enterprise which stirs the heart of every soldier and sailor fortunate enough to be selected to share in it, and the very magnitude of the difficulties only stimulates us to increased exertion.

"We are all proud of General Gordon's gallant and self-sacrificing defence of Khartoum, which has added, if possible, to his already high reputation. He cannot hold out for many months longer, and now calls us to save the garrison. His heroism and patriotism are household words wherever the English tongue is spoken, and not only has his safety become a matter of national importance, but the knowledge that a comrade is in danger urges us to push forward with redoubled energy.

"Neither he nor the garrison can be allowed to meet the sad fate of the gallant Colonel Stewart, who, carrying out an enterprise of unusual danger, was cruelly murdered by his captors. We can, and, with God's help, we will, save General Gordon from such a death.

"The labour of working up this river is immense, and to bear it uncomplainingly demands the highest soldierly qualities, and that contempt for danger and determination to overcome difficulties which in previous campaigns has always distinguished all ranks throughout the Army and Navy.

"The physical objects which impede rapid progress are considerable ; but who cares for them when we rememember General Gordon and his garrison are in danger ? Under God, their safety is now in your hands. Come what may, we must save them.

"British soldiers and sailors, it is needless to say more.

"The General Commanding will give a hundred pounds to the battalion of the Nile force which makes the quickest time, with the fewest accidents, between Sarras and Debbeh, and will do all he can to give the place of honour to the battalion which wins the prize. The hundred pounds will be distributed, on their return to Egypt, amongst the non-commissioned officers and privates of the winning battalion."

The *Times* in a leading article thus speaks of Mr. Power :—"We are proud to pay a tribute to the memory of our brave and ill-fated correspondent, Mr. Power, who, thrown on a sudden into the midst of great events and formidable dangers, showed himself fully equal to the occasion. It must not be forgotten that it was almost exclusively through Mr. Power's despatches published in these columns that England and Europe first of all learnt the details of the disaster which befell Hicks Pasha's army, and the triumph of the Mahdi, and the gradual closing of the enemy around Khartoum. Afterwards it was from him we had the graphic and stirring accounts of General Gordon's arrival, and of his energetic efforts to establish order, and to keep the hostile tribes around him at bay, of his victories and his misfortunes, of the valour of his Bedouin foes, and the treachery and cowardice of his Turkish and Egyptian troops. Then for a long time the curtain fell. It was lifted for a moment when Mr. Power was enabled to send us his journal of events, as romantic as any recorded in history, which had been happening while Khartoum was cut off for months from the outer world."

In the meantime a glimpse of the life of the defender of the garrison was given by a native of Khartoum, who had reached the Mudir of Dongola. He had accomplished the journey between Khartoum and Dongola in a fortnight, but in accordance with General Gordon's orders he had stayed four days at Omdurman, in order, if possible, to learn something of the movements of the Mahdi, and report upon them to the Mudir. The messenger said that the Mahdi and his followers were suffering severely from famine, and that the dead bodies of several of their number were to be seen lying unburied in the surrounding country. He stated that the Mahdi's followers were discouraged by the repeated attacks made upon them, and that many, hearing of the approach of the British, had dispersed.

He also reported that five hundred of the Mahdi's regulars had deserted him, entered Khartoum, and surrendered to the General.

As to the daily life of the hero within the walls, we have since learned that at this time he spent his nights in constant expectation of attacks. Throughout the entire night he kept careful watch, visited the outposts, and by personal scrutiny assured himself that every sentry was on the alert. He had two palaces, and on the roof of each he had mounted a gun. At daybreak he carefully primed this gun and reconnoitred the enemy's position, after which he usually partook of breakfast, and retired to his bed for rest. He was said to be looking well, and keeping strong and courageous.

Nevertheless, it was known that the Mahdi had drawn a complete cordon round the city of Khartoum, and had declared that he would reduce the place by famine. He had himself received abundant supplies from Kordofan. It was said that Gordon had inflicted some losses upon them by means of his mines; but it was known that his position had become exceedingly critical.

The close of the year witnessed a rapid advance of the troops. No sooner were the Christmas festivities over than Lord Wolseley issued an order for all the troops to be ready to proceed at once. That a crisis had come was evident from the desperate character of the work given to the troops to do. General Stewart was to leave with the Mounted Infantry and the Camel Corps, and make a dash across the desert to Metemmeh. General Earle was to force his way up the Nile.

Perhaps Lord Wolseley knew that at length the heart of the solitary hero of the Soudan had begun to fail him; for one of his friends at Cairo had received the following letter:—

"Farewell. You will never hear from me again. I fear that there will be treachery in the garrison, and all will be over by Christmas."

CHAPTER XXX.

THE END OF THE STORY.

"England, thou hast not saved one drop of blood in this hot trial."
—*King John.*

"KHARTOUM all right, 14th December.—
C. G. GORDON."
This brief message, which arrived on
New Year's Day, put everyone into better
spirits. It was on a tiny scrap of paper no bigger than a
postage stamp, and could have been swallowed if the
messenger had found it necessary. It was put in a quill,
and hidden in the messenger's hair.

The column under General Stewart was making a quick
march across the Desert. The Arabs were astonished at
the rapidity shown by the troops. The camels were so
placed as to make a compact column, which would be able
to resist any attack by the enemy. No attack, however,
was made. The troops met a small convoy of camels, on
their way to the Mahdi with dates; and General Stewart
took seven prisoners. The journey continued; and after
the march across the desert, of a hundred miles over rough
ground, Gakdul Wells was reached on the 2nd of January.
The long and perilous march had only occupied sixty-five

hours, and had been accomplished without casualties of any kind. The journey had been made more toilsome by the absence of water; but when they reached Gakdul Wells they found an unlimited supply. Sir Herbert Stewart left the men encamped in a position which Lord Wolseley had described as impregnable; and then rode back to Korti—the present headquarters of Lord Wolseley—taking the camels to fetch more troops. About halfway on the journey some men were left at Hombok Wells, and General Stewart arrived at Korti on the fifth. Lord Wolseley rode out five or six miles to meet him, and congratulated him on his splendid achievement. The prisoners whom he brought with him tore from their dress the braid, which was the sign of their allegiance to the Mahdi, and spat upon their uniform, and freely cursed their former master. The camels needed rest before restarting across their desert journey; but on the seventh Lord Wolseley sent the following telegram to the Secretary for War:—

"KORTI, *7th January*, 1885, 4.10 p.m.

"Strong convoy now leaving camp for Gakdul.

"General Stewart starts with another to-morrow for Metemmeh. Expect him to occupy it on the 15th instant. If steamer there, will communicate with Gordon without delay."

A day or two after the able correspondent of *The Standard* sent the following amusing paragraph describing the scene of preparations at Korti :—

"The Naval Brigade paraded this evening on camels, and were inspected by Lord Wolseley. The sailors are hugely delighted at finding themselves on camels, and cause great amusement to all here by their joviality and fun. Their ideas as to the pleasure of this kind of locomotion will probably be considerably modified by the time they arrive at Gakdul. Everything is conducted in nautical fashion, and the camels are steered to the words of command, 'Port' or 'Starboard.' The animals themselves appear puzzled with their new riders, whose vivacity and energy contrast strongly with that of the natives who are accus-tomed to pilot them. 'Steer small, Bill;' 'Mind your helm, Jack, or you will run me aboard,' were the sentences one caught as the camels got in motion."

The correspondent also announced that he was going on with General Stewart's column, probably little thinking that he was going to his death! The forces under General Stewart's command were only to make a halt for one day at Gakdul Wells, and then march on to Metemmeh. The arrangement was that as soon as Stewart and his men reached Metemmeh, Colonel Wilson, Lord Charles Beresford, who had part of the Naval Brigade under his command, and others, should go up to Khartoum.

At this time General Gordon was sending several of his steamers up and down between Khartoum and Metemmeh, with the object, not only of keeping the water-way open, but of assisting those who were making their progress towards him. It seemed, therefore, that the end of the expedition was in view. If once Colonel Wilson and General Gordon could communicate with each other by these steamers it appeared that little more would be left to accomplish.

On the 10th of January a messenger reached Korti, who had previously been sent by Lord Wolseley to General Gordon. He had accomplished the journey both ways with great speed, and spent one day in Khartoum; but on his return was stopped by tribesmen, and beaten and robbed, Gordon's despatches being taken from him, excepting a *fac simile* of the little note already referred to. He said that Gordon was in good health, and that his steamers were taking cattle and grain safely into Khartoum.

The second party travelled much more slowly to Gakdul than the first. ' Every ounce of food and water had to be carried. The heat was intense, but the men's allowance of water was only two pints a day. They so suffered from thirst that they sometimes could not take their food, and the camels were nearly three days without water. At Howeiyat Wells, though the water was like pea-soup, the soldiers offered a dollar for a glassful of it.

Still they kept on, and plans were laid for the future with care and caution. General Earle was making his way up the Nile, and the forces would unite as speedily as possible.

The march across the Desert met with nothing particularly noteworthy until the afternoon of the sixteenth, when the Hussar scouts brought in a report to the effect that the enemy were in force at Abu Klea.

These wells were then in sight. General Stewart having marched his force in square column formation, rode forward to reconnoitre. He discovered the enemy at the neck of a valley leading from the desert to the Nile. The General decided that it would not be wise at once to make the attack, as the night was coming on, and the troops were weary with their march. A zereba was formed, and strong pickets were posted on the hills in front. A harmless fire was kept up during the night, and twice the troops were summoned to arms.

In the morning the enemy was discovered strongly posted on the right front, and scouts were seen creeping round to the left. It was ten o'clock when General Stewart gave the order to advance. The camels and heavy impedi-ments were left in the zereba. The force moved on in the direction of the Abu Klea wells, which wells are situated about twenty-five miles north of Metemmeh. The enemy occupied favourable ground, and, as the *Daily News* cor-respondent said, "Our square moved forward under a hail

of bullets, men dropping from the ranks right and left."
In an hour the body of the enemy was in full sight, and
General Stewart tried to pass round their left flank; but
the enemy wheeled suddenly to the left, and charged full
upon the left rear of the square.   There was a temporary
confusion at the point where the Heavy Cavalry Camel
regiment stood; but the men quickly rallied, and remained
steadily at their post, maintaining a hand-to-hand combat.
The enemy was beset on all sides, and eventually gave way;
and the Abu Klea wells were in the hands of the British
about five o'clock in the afternoon.

General Stewart, in sending his report to Lord Wolseley,
bore this testimony to the valour of the men—"It has been
my duty to command a force from which exceptional work,
exceptional hardships, and, it may even be added, exceptional fighting has been called for.   It would be impossible
for me adequately to describe the admirable support that
has been given to me by every officer and man of the
force."

Unhappily, the Abu Klea victory was only secured at
great cost and by heavy British losses.   Nine officers and
sixty-five non-commissioned officers and men were killed,
and eighty-five wounded.   The names of the officers were—
Lieutenant-Colonel F. G. Burnaby, Royal Horse Guards;
Major Carmichael, 15th Lancers; Major Atherton, 5th
Dragoon Guards; Major Gough, Royal Dragoons; Captain
Darley, 4th Dragoon Guards; Lieutenant Law, 4th Dragoon
Guards; Lieutenant Wolfe, Scots Greys; and Lieutenants
Pigott and De Lisle, Naval Brigade.   Lord St. Vincent,
Major Dickson, Lieutenants Lisle and Guthrie, and Surgeon
Magill, were severely wounded.

Colonel Frederick Gustavus Burnaby had been a most
adventurous soldier.   He entered the Royal Horse Guards
Blue in 1859, was made captain in 1866, and lieutenant-
colonel in 1881.   It was in 1875 that he started on his

famous " Ride to Khiva." Later he rode on horseback through Asia Minor and Persia. At the very beginning of the Soudan expedition from Suakim against the Mahdi's forces, Colonel Burnaby served under General Graham, and in the battle of El Teb he was severely wounded by a fragment of a cannon shot which struck his face. He returned to England in order to recover, but before his wounds were healed, hearing of Lord Wolseley's expedition, he decided to join the forces which, however, he was only able to do a week before his death.

Major Carmichael of the 5th Royal Irish Lancers, though he joined his regiment in 1861, had not before been in active service. His death awakened considerable public sympathy for his orphan child, only a few months old, whose mother died at the time of his birth. Major Carmichael had spent nearly £400 in purchasing promotion, but the system had since been abolished, and the child would only receive an annuity of £21.

On this circumstance becoming known, the Queen made inquiries, and the child will no doubt be cared for. Her Majesty, on receiving news of the victory gained by Sir Herbert Stewart, instantly telegraphed to Lord Wolseley the pride she felt at the conduct of her brave troops, and her deep concern at the loss of so many gallant officers and men, and asked that she might be kept informed of the state of the wounded, after whom she anxiously inquired.

For several days following the Abu Klea victory no news was received from General Stewart and his forces, excepting a report that was calculated to inspire the gravest anxiety, which was to the effect that Omdurman, which lies on the left bank of the river opposite Khartoum, had been taken, and was occupied by the Madhi. It was felt that this would greatly increase the peril of General Gordon's position, and England waited in suspense for the next tidings.

It was something, however, to know that the boat column, under General Earle, was making satisfactory progress up the Nile, although that was the only satisfaction possible till further news arrived. A report was issued that General Earle's column had passed beyond the fourth cataract, and was still moving onward.

The silence was broken on the evening of Wednesday, the 28th January, when telegrams were published announcing the fact that an engagement had taken place at Metemmeh, that Stewart was dangerously wounded, that the fighting had been very severe, and five of the Mahdi's Emirs were killed; but that communication had been established with General Gordon, and that Sir Charles Wilson had gone to Khartoum.

The whole of this news was subsequently confirmed. General Stewart's force, after the battle of Abu Klea, pushed on to a point about five miles south of Metemmeh. The enemy appeared to be waiting for them, and as they were seen approaching in great numbers, an endeavour was at once made to form an entrenchment where the hospital and baggage might be placed in safety. The camels were unloaded and a fortification was thrown up, principally composed of the saddles and baggage. Sir Herbert Stewart sent out a detachment of the Hussars in the direction of Metemmeh. While the zereba was being formed, the enemy fired upon the men at their work, which was thereby made exceedingly dangerous. Their sharpshooters were concealed behind bushes and by tall grass on all sides, and, therefore, could fire with effect. Our men were, however, not prevented from working at the fortification, and it was soon thrown up, the hospital being placed in the centre, protected by guns. Sir Herbert Stewart gave orders to form square and attack the enemy in that formation; but before the square could be completed, the general was struck by a shot from the enemy and severely wounded. Almost at the same time, Lieutenant C. Crutchley, of the Scots Guards, was also wounded, and Mr. St. Leger Herbert, the war correspondent of the *Morning Post* was killed. Nor was he alone; Mr. Cameron of the *Standard*, from whose reports we have just quoted, and whose graphic accounts were always read with interest, was also shot through the back and killed instantly.

This expedition has cost many lives; and few men were more deeply regretted than the three correspondents who had gone with others to the seat of battle in the interest of the public. The respective papers bore testimony to the esteem in which the correspondents were held, and every reader added his regrets.

The force garrisoning the zereba was commanded by Lord Charles Beresford, and for two hours the enemy continued to attack it. Twelve of our men were killed, and more than forty wounded.

As General Stewart could no longer continue in charge of the column, Sir Charles Wilson assumed the command. The men marched in square amid a storm of bullets towards the Nile. The enemy came upon them in great force, directing their fire especially against the Foot Guards and the Naval Brigade, who returned the fire, while the Royal Artillery played upon the enemy with terrible effect. This arrested the enemy, but several times their leaders rallied them, and led them forward, until at last they were finally repulsed and drew off towards Metemmeh, leaving several hundred dead behind them. Before the British started they buried their dead. The correspondents of the different papers bore sadly to the grave the bodies of Mr. Cameron and Mr. Herbert, Lord Charles Beresford reading the burial service. At sunset the enemy ceased firing, but a most anxious night was spent, the call to stand to arms coming once in the darkness. The next morning the main body established itself upon the river. The wounded were carried up on stretchers. Eventually the forces occupied a strongly fortified post at Gubat, close to Metemmeh. Opposite Gubat was a large island with plenty of green forage for horses and camels. Lord Wolseley considered that Gubat could be held against any force that the Mahdi could send to attack it. A hospital was established for the care of the wounded near Metemmeh, Metemmeh itself being occupied by about two thousand of the rebels.

On the following day, to the great joy of all, four of General Gordon's steamers came from Khartoum, having on board five hundred soldiers and five guns. Thus reinforced, the troops made an attack upon Metemmeh, but without success. They however, with a number of black troops, two companies of mounted infantry, and six guns, bombarded Shendy on the opposite side of the river, and destroyed it.

The Mahdi was said to have 6000 men near Khartoum, and it was felt that General Earle's force was certain to encounter opposition at Berti, and again near Berber, but it was still the general belief that the worst was over, and Khartoum would shortly be reached.

General Stewart was taken on board one of the steamers, and Lieutenant Oruchley was with him. The hospital tent was pitched on the bank, and the wounded placed in comfortable beds. They appeared to be doing well. Lord Hartington telegraphed to Lord Wolseley :—

"I have received the Queen's gracious commands to express her satisfaction and warm thanks to her brave troops, and her deep concern for their losses and sufferings, and especially for General Stewart's severe wound. Her Majesty has, in consideration of that officer's gallant services, been pleased to promote him to the rank of Major-General."

The next news that reached England was the occupation of Berti by General Earle's column. Generals Earle and

Butler had reconnoitred the position, and a deserter had told them that the enemy had evacuated the village. This story they found to be true, and the British took possession of Berti without opposition.

"A few hours more and Gordon will be relieved." These were the words on the lips of the people on Thursday morning, 6th February. Lord Wolseley had telegraphed that he had received one line from him to say that Khartoum was all right, and he could hold out for years. There seemed no need for anxiety, for the end was all but gained: when suddenly, without any preparation, a terrible blow fell upon us. The morning papers of 5th February had nothing new to publish, the most interesting items of news being that Lord Wolseley had declared that the prize of £100 which he had offered to the regiment that should make the quickest passage from Surras to Debbeh had been gained by the first battalion of the Royal Irish.

But early in the day, first London, and then England, was startled and shocked by the dreadful tidings that Khartoum had been captured by the Mahdi, and that the fate of General Gordon was unknown.

The excitement in the Metropolis cannot be described. People thronged to the newspaper offices, and an anxious crowd gathered round the War Office in Pall Mall. Further details were demanded with intense eagerness. These were forthcoming, and the whole story was too soon confirmed.

Khartoum was only thirty-six hours from Metemmeh, and on the 24th of January Sir Charles Wilson, Captain Trafford, and twenty men of the Sussex Regiment, with three hundred and twenty of Gordon's faithful Soudanese, left Metemmeh in three of Gordon's steamers, in order to accomplish the journey. As they neared Khartoum they found themselves passing through hostile forces relentlessly pouring fire upon them. As they approached Omdurman they discovered that the report of its being in the hands of the enemy was true. Four Krupp guns had been placed on the banks at Halfiyeh, and their fire was directed against the little party pluckily making their way up to the capital. Alas! not only Halfiyeh and Omdurman, but also the Island of Tufti, which lies just outside of Khartoum, had been appropriated by the Mahdi. Notwithstanding all these facts, Sir Charles Wilson and his party steamed on, and managed to get within eight hundred yards of Khartoum, but then, to their great dismay, instead of the welcome which they hoped for from brave Gordon and his followers, they saw thousands of Arabs wildly waving flags, and a storm of shot was poured upon them from twelve guns and about a thousand rifles. Friends nowhere, enemies on all hands—this was the state of things found by the relieving party who had reached the capital.

The truth flashed upon them that the Mahdi must have gained admission to the city, and everything confirmed this impression. No flags were flying from the public buildings, and the Palace, in which Gordon had lived, was gutted.

Sir Charles Wilson and his men, knowing it to be impossible to land in the face of such an overwhelming enemy, were compelled to retreat out of the range of the guns. But as they were making their way back the steamers were wrecked some miles below the Shabukla cataract; the whole party, however, were saved, and landed in safety on an island. The wrecking of the boats was due to the treachery of the pilots. A man, second in command of the Soudanese, Abdul Hamid Bey, managed to escape, and ran away. Treachery was the foe before which the expedition had failed.

Sir Charles Wilson and his party were three days on the island on which they had been wrecked. A messenger who went ashore took the news to Gubat, which he reached on foot, and the disastrous tidings were at once forwarded

to Lord Wolseley. Lieutenant Stewart Wortley, who had
been with Sir Charles Wilson, also reached Gubat in a
small boat, and confirmed the terrible news. The only
thing that seemed for the moment possible was at once
attempted—namely, the rescue of Wilson and his men.
On the 1st of February Lord Charles Beresford left Aboo
Krou, flying the British ensign on board General Gordon's
steamer *Sofia*, and taking two Gardner guns, detachments of
Blue Jackets and Mounted Infantry under Lieutenant
Bowe, and some natives. The steamer went on successfully
until she was within three miles of the island where Sir
Charles Wilson and his party were; and then two guns,
which had been mounted in embrasures on a level with the
water, opened fire, and riflemen lining the banks seconded
the attack. The steamer returned the fire, and had almost
got out of the danger, when a round shot went through the
boiler. Enough steam remained to enable the vessel to go
five hundred yards further up the river, and more out of
reach of the enemy's fire. Then the vessel was at once
anchored, and Lord Charles Beresford ordered the men to
proceed to repair the boiler; the sailors in the meantime
shifting the guns to the stern, and continuing to fire upon the
enemy. Sir Charles Wilson, who was anxiously watching
from the island, seeing a dense cloud of steam rise, concluded that the boiler had burst; he therefore landed his
party, guns, etc., on the opposite bank from that on which
the enemy was placed, and marched down to the point
nearly opposite the battery, and assisted Lord Beresford in
silencing the enemy's guns. A nuggar on which Captain
Gascoigne started from the island, bearing several guns and
a considerable quantity of ammunition, was grounded upon
a rock, in a position which placed it in imminent peril
from the enemy. Every effort to get it off proved
ineffectual, and it had to remain all night on the rock.
Fighting went on until sunset. At night Lord Charles

Beresford's steamer was rapidly repaired, and Sir Charles Wilson marched his men three miles lower down from the river, and encamped for the night. In the morning Lieutenant Keppel, R.N., started off from Lord Charles Beresford's steamer with a boat-load of sailors to the assistance of the nuggar. The men threw all their energy into the work, and by their skill and perseverance got the vessel clear of the rock. This piece of gallant work was done under heavy fire from the enemy, who gave much attention to the operations of the sailors; but Lord Charles, under a continuous fire, towed the craft triumphantly away. Lord Charles Beresford then steamed down the river to the spot where Sir Charles Wilson and his men were encamped, and there stopped and took the whole party on board, after which they went on to Gubat, which place they all reached in safety.

The next fighting news referred to General Earle's column, and stated that tho gallant officer was killed. The Black Watch, the South Staffordshire regiment, and others, reached Dulka Island, and at once prepared for the enemy, who was known to be near in strong force. While they were preparing a zareba the rebels opened fire; but the pickets drove them back. The night was coming on, and an outpost was stationed ready for an attack; but the night passed quietly. In the morning the troops went out to meet the Arabs, and the fight commenced. The ground was very difficult, but the troops drove back the enemy, until they were surrounded. The enemy occupied a high hill of rocks, and loopholed walls strengthened their position. Seeing that it was impossible to dislodge them otherwise, General Earle gave orders to the Black Watch to carry the position with the bayonet. The pipers struck up, and the Highlanders responded so gallantly that the General, who was himself leading, could not repress an exclamation of admiration. It was almost his last speech,

for, as the Black Watch rushed on and drove the enemy
from their shelter, General Earle fell as he reached the
summit, and never knew how completely was the victory
gained that day.

But what of the hero of the Soudan? Was Gordon
really a prisoner in the hands of the Mahdi? or was he
killed when the garrison he had defended so nobly fell?

These questions were agitating not only all England, but
the whole world. The anguish of suspense was scarcely to
be borne : such days were like a lifetime of anxiety, and
every fresh edition of the papers, every scrap of news, was
read with an eagerness which proved that General Gordon
was not only a hero to be admired, but a man to be loved.

The reports were very conflicting. At first it was said
that he was a prisoner in the power of the Mahdi, and
hopes were entertained that this might be so, as in that
case he could be ransomed. His friends believed that the
Mahdi himself would not treat him cruelly, for it was
known that he felt much personal esteem for him. It was
even reported that he had, with great glee, declared that
General Gordon had adopted his uniform, and become a
Mohammedan. It was also said that he had taken refuge
in a Catholic church with some Greeks, and was still holding out. All felt that if he lived he must be rescued at any
cost. A spirit of most intense and enthusiastic admiration
of the man took possession of all people, and the papers
were filled with laudatory notices, which praise might have
been considered exaggerated but for the fact that the
matchless man deserved the highest that could be said of
him.

The five or six days of suspense passed at last, and on
the 11th of February the newspapers, some of which were
put into mourning, announced the heavy tidings that the
dreaded calamity had really fallen upon us—General
Gordon was dead, and the whole garrison massacred.

The papers declared that the catastrophe had been entirely brought about by treachery. The little band of faithful adherents had remained loyal to their commander, and shared with him the hope that a few days would see the end of their troubles, and bring safety and reward. But General Gordon's fears of treachery, as expressed in the last sentence of the previous chapter, were verified. It seems almost certain that the five hundred deserters from the Mahdi's troops were really loyal still to their old leader, and traitors to their new master. If this be so, Khartoum had to all intents for some time been in the power of the Mahdi; and whenever the British troops approached, the doom of the city and its heroic defender was sealed. We could almost hope that it was so, for that Gordon should be lost because the troops were two days too late, is too dreadful to contemplate.

However that may be, the stories that have since been told confirm the opinion entertained from the first in regard to the treachery of some of Gordon's troops. His most trusted officer, Kashim Elmoos, remained true to the last, but Almud Ahmed deserted. And there was another man, a traitor, whose name will for ever be covered with infamy.

Faragh Pasha, who commanded the Soudani troops, had been a betrayer throughout. General Gordon had reason to mistrust him. On a previous occasion treason was proved against him, and he was condemned to death. He begged so passionately for pardon, he uttered such strong protestations of attachment to General Gordon, that the latter, who always hoped the best and judged generously, forgave and reinstated him. But it is said to have been this man, who owed his life to General Gordon, who opened the gates to the Mahdi and his forces. Another treacherous pasha marched the Khartoum garrison to the Omdurman side of the city, telling them that they must be ready

for an attack which the Mahdi's troops were expected
to make there; and as soon as they were well out of the
way, Faragh Pasha opened the gates of Khartoum, and the
Mahdi's forces swarmed in. As far as can be ascertained,
General Gordon was in the Government House at the time,
and hearing the unusual commotion in the street, he—
perhaps hoping that the British had really arrived at last
to rescue him—advanced to the door, and was killed on
the threshold. The correspondent of the *Daily Chronicle*
said :—

"The Mahdi's troops—the wild hunters of Kordofan and
those Cossacks of the Soudan, the Baggara horsemen—
rushed in swelling hordes into the devoted city, and the
word was given to slay. A massacre of indescribable
ferocity followed. Those who had remained faithful to the
gallant Englishman who had stood between them and the
knife so long, regardless of age or sex, were ruthlessly
butchered. The women, for the most part, were murdered
in cold blood, and little children were spitted on the Arab
spears in pure wantonness. All those relatives of the faithful five hundred under Nusri Pasha, who met and assisted
us at Gubat, shared the general fate. From the accounts
of an eye-witness who boarded Sir Charles Wilson's steamer
on the return voyage from Khartoum it would appear that
"for an entire day the streets of the city ran with blood;"
but allowing for Oriental exaggeration, there can be no
doubt that the scene of carnage which followed the entry of
the Mahdi's fierce warriors into the city which had defied
them so long, was one of unparelleled horror since the days
of Tamerlane."

And so, if these reports are true, the brave hero had at
last died a martyr's death. He must have expected it
again and again. It is known that from the first, when in
obedience to the request of the Government he started on
his perilous mission, he had a foreboding that he might

never return. But the foreboding did not in the least deter him from going. Nor did it make him the less resolute in his determination to hold out in Khartoum, and fulfil his duty toward those who trusted him.

Writing to his sister on 11th March 1884, General Gordon said—" Remember our Lord did not promise success or peace in this life. He promised tribulation, so if things do not go well after the flesh, He still is faithful. He will do all in love and mercy to me. My part is to submit to His will, however dark it may be." That was the philosophy of his life, and "however dark it may be," that strong faith shines ever like a pillar of fire in a dark and desolate wilderness.

Gordon was true to God and duty ; and he was also true to the Soudanese. Forced sometimes by the cruel exigencies of war to do things which his humane soul must have abhorred, he was yet a loyal Christian, who, in the spirit of his Master, loved the people among whom he lived. and was willing to die for them. He said repeatedly, before leaving London for the last time—"*I would give my life for these poor people of the Soudan. How can I help feeling for them? All the time I was there, every night I used to pray that God would lay upon me the burden of their sins, and crush me with it instead of these poor sheep. I really wished it and longed for it.*"

We may not dare to say that God did not hear and answer this passionate, oft-repeated prayer. General Gordon, unless, happily, the reports prove false, *has* laid down his life for the Soudanese—nay, he has yielded it to them ; for it was the very people for whom he was willing to die that treacherously slew him. He has crowned his life of self-sacrifice by a hero's death. Again and again it was urged that he might have come away from Khartoum if he had chosen ; but he chose death rather than desert the little band of his followers, who could not all have got away, and who remained faithful to him. So he stayed, weary himself, but striving to cheer them; weighed down by anxiety and worn out in the endeavour to save, at any cost, the ives of the people of Khartoum; hoping day by day for rescue, and increasing his own risk by sending assistance to those who were coming to his aid; until at last relief was so near that he only waited to hear the hearty greeting of any Englishman who should be the first to grasp his hand and receive his thanks. And then, instead of the friendly faces of the English, he saw—but only for a moment—the hostile numbers and the flashing steel. So much at least we imagine; but of this we are certain, that if he is dead, he heard above the clash and the roar the voice of *his Commander* ending the struggle of His true soldier, and bestowing upon him his reward, "Well done, good and faithful servant; thou hast been faithful over a few things: I will make thee ruler over many things: enter into the joy of thy Lord."

We cannot forbear quoting two out of a hundred tributes of the press :—

The *Daily Telegraph* said—"We fear we shall see the face of Gordon no more. In such a case, the noble story of his life has been terminated by a death as dutiful, as unselfish, as heroic as a gentleman and a soldier could die. Faithful unto the last to his Queen, to his country, and to his desperate task, he will have fallen amid the garrison and the population whom he struggled to save—matching his mighty heart, in solitude and abandonment, against all the daily dangers which beset them. He will have attained a rest unspeakably sanctified by sacrifice and devotion, and will have left a name, brightest, like the setting sun, at its moment of departure, and glorified more perfectly by failure than that of other heroes has been by success. The civilized world will mourn for him along with England; for political jealousy has grown dumb and rivalries were forgotten wherever men spoke of Charles Gordon. All Christendom turned its eyes to that lonely Englishman ready to ransom the lives of his black people by his own blood; and comprehended that the divine story of its Founder had found a new illustration. If, indeed, he be dead, the world is poorer, and humanity at large has cause to bewail; for never beat a heart more gallant, and never was a soldier truer to his flag, or Christian to his faith."

The *Daily News* said:—"So closes a career which, more than any other in modern times, has aroused the hearty sympathy and affection of his countrymen and the admiration of the world. The age of chivalry is not gone: it revives again in Gordon's history. It is a life which seems like a story of old romance. Arthur and the Table Round had no more blameless knight. He was Lancelot and Galahad both in one. He has died in the service of his country, and his admiring countrymen will cherish his memory among their brightest and tenderest recollections. He has brought something of the glamour and brightness of the heroic ages into the dull realities of these prosaic times. He has added a new chapter to the glorious story of British heroism, and has left a name to which our young men will look back, and which all that is best and truest among us will reverence, so long as truth, and faith, and self-devotion, and a lofty sense of duty stir the admiration of men who are worthy to call themselves his countrymen. This nineteenth century will hand down to posterity no higher and worthier and no more lasting fame."

CHAPTER XXXI.

A CHRISTIAN HERO.

" Heaven doth with us as we with torches do;
Not light them for themselves : for if our virtues
Did not go forth of us, 'twere all alike
As if we had them not.   Spirits are not finely touched,
But to fine issues : nor nature never lends
The finest scruple of her excellence ;
But, like a thrifty goddess, she determines
Herself the glory of a creditor,
Both thanks and use."

—Measure for Measure.

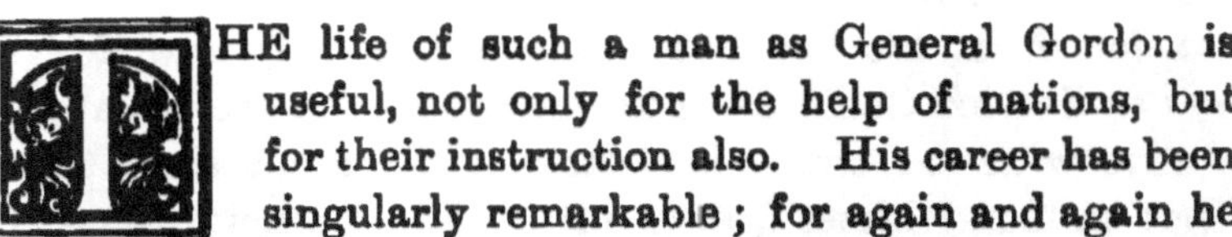HE life of such a man as General Gordon is useful, not only for the help of nations, but for their instruction also.   His career has been singularly remarkable ; for again and again he has been singled out of the multitude, and called away from his life of quietness, as the only man sufficient for a crisis which affected multitudes of people, and more or less touched all the nations of the world.   The very fact of his being so frequently in request in emergencies that had arisen proves that he had the power to meet them, and not only the power, but the willingness also.   And yet his life can scarcely have been what he would himself have chosen ; but, indeed, the whole tenor of it is an exemplification of

his own firm belief that every individual is under the control of a directing Providence, who orders the event and chooses the lot. And his conduct throughout is an illustration of the way in which the Christian should fall in with the designs of Him who is the ruler of the universe, and the guide of the individual.

And therefore his biography is a lesson. We may get from him, as from all good men and women, lights to guide us in the formation of our characters, and the direction of our actions. To the young especially, who desire to make the best of their lives, an account of Gordon and his work cannot be other than useful; and if they will stop to ask what has made him great, they will be able to discover in him the qualities out of which all heroes are made. That which is most pronounced, and was the foundation of his usefulness in China, Gravesend, and the Soudan, is undoubtedly the

SINGLENESS OF PURPOSE

which always governs him. It has never entered into his mind to suppose that a man should live to himself; but he has felt from his boyhood that his one duty and delight was to live for God. He has gone where he has been sent always with the single intention of doing his duty there. That he found himself, as he often did, in circumstances of great discomfort and danger affected him very little, and only made him the more resolute to rise to the demands of the case. Often a weaker man would have run away from the intricacies and perplexities that beset him; but Gordon never thought of withdrawing from any position because of its embarrassments. On the contrary, he always elected to remain until the entanglement was at an end, and the way smooth for his successor.

"Others sow, and one will reap all the success of their labours." "A man here must be prepared to find a week's negotiation fall to the ground in a minute, and all his work to be gone over again. It is this continual failure of one's efforts which tempts one to despair, until one realises that one must never count on anything till it is performed." But he did not despair. He took things as they came, fulfilling the day's duties, and leaving the rest to God. "I know that I have done my very best, as far as my intellect has allowed me, for the Khedive, and have tried to be just to all." "Difficulties make my spirits rise, and I feel quite lively over my innumerable troubles." "If you are mis-judged, why trouble yourself to put yourself right? You have no idea what a deal of trouble it saves you." God is the sole ruler, and I try to walk sincerely before Him." This singleness of purpose has no doubt kept the man steady and true to his principles amid all the changes of his most eventful life. It is this that has made him so willingly, and without delay, put down one kind of work and take up another—remove from one place, and settle complacently in a distant land—be sometimes a king, and sometimes a servant, as circumstances, or rather as God, directed.

Great as these changes have been they have made no change in him; they have not really touched his inner life at all. Charles Gordon has been precisely the same man, leading his armies to victory in China, teaching boys in the Ragged School at Gravesend, or riding over the deserts on the swift-footed camel. It was very much the same to him whatever he did, for he was just a child obeying his father, a servant gladly and reverently obeying his master. And, added to his singleness of purpose, were the invaluable qualifications of

DILIGENCE AND SELF-HELP.

General Gordon cannot be idle. He has had very few opportunities, but when they have come he has been only eager to break away from them. He feels that the day is given for work, wherever the day may find us. He hesitated at nothing, and took the work as it came, whether it was waving the rebel Wangs into submission with his magic cane or pulling a boat through the water. Whatever was worth doing at all he considered was worth doing well. "I would sooner, I think, have the Saubat Government than the whole Government. To do anything, there is nothing like beginning on a small scale, and directing your energy, like a squirt, on one particular thing. I have made *such* a pair of trousers for one of the Blacks, and the housewifes are so useful."

We find him sometimes weary of overwork. He knew as well in the Soudan as any one can know in England the meaning of over-pressure ; and now and then he got quite bewildered with the amount of duties that were upon him. On one occasion at least he could not sleep, for when he lay down the strain upon him during the day had been so severe, that at night, instead of sleeping, he was in imagination reading petitions, finding measures of relief for the oppressed, and punishing the guilty. But he would rather have been overworked than idle.

The days when he had little to do were the most irksome of his life, and we find him resorting to all kinds of occupation rather than do nothing. Not only did he set himself to do a little tailoring, as we have seen, but on one occasion he made two good rocket-cases, and on another he repaired some clocks, pulling them to pieces and putting them together again in good workman's style, though he confessed himself beaten by a watch and a cuckoo clock. No work came amiss to him, though he was certainly at his best when the work was great. He got into good spirits when accomplishing a tremendous march, or quelling a mutiny, or settling a few scores of people who came to him with requests.

He has always proved himself a very painstaking and persistent worker. They say at Gravesend that he never took a poor boy in hand to forget him afterwards, as so many well-meaning people do. He rescued the boys, then he taught them, then he found situations for them, going to London often on their account, seeing captains, looking into all matters that concerned them, and giving them a cheery good-bye as they went away. Surely then he had finished with them! Oh no. He wrote letters to them, to reach them at the different ports at which the ships would call, and he followed them with his thoughts and his prayers all round the world until they were home again, and he could see for himself the state in which they were. And the same unwearying energy and thoroughness characterised all his work. He has known the importance of giving personal attention to the details of the business in hand, as well as to its broader features; and he has taken pains with the task whether in itself the occupation was pleasant or unpleasant, agreeable or the reverse. He has brought the high aims of his life to bear upon all duties, the little as well as the great; and none can read his life without seeing that it has been based on Paul's advice to Timothy—"*Study to show thyself approved unto God a workman that needeth not to be ashamed.*"

He sometimes get a little impatient of others, for it happened very frequently that he had none but most incapable people about him. They were so slow that he was always before them ; and often so stupid that he took the work from their hands and did it himself. On one occasion his servant left him; and he said, "So much the better! The best servant I ever had is myself: he always does what I like." He had a great objection to being treated like a Czar, and having everything done for him. He had no patience with the number of servants or hangers-on that were supposed to be necessary to a Ti-tu or a Pasha. If

he wanted a thing done he delighted in doing it himself; if
the action shocked the prejudices of people who were particular in regard to etiquette he liked it all the better.
Indeed, few things are more marked in General Gordon
than this

STRONG COMMON SENSE,

which is always coming to the front, and which helps him
over many difficulties. He says in one of his letters that
the Soudan soldiers like nothing better than watching him.
They stared so that he had to suffer a little as royalty does;
but, he added, "Yet I am not like royalty a bit, for I
cleaned a duck gun in public to-day. I will be natural,
coûte que coûte, and I am quite sure I cleaned the gun
better than any Arab would." His common sense is
brought to bear upon everything, even upon his religion.
He is said to be a mystic; but he sees things more clearly
than most people, both as regards life and revelation. His
belief in God does not in the least interfere with his own
self-reliance. He quite believes that he has power given
him to do the work that has been placed in his reach, and
although he knows that he is only a tool in the hands of
another, the tool is a very intelligent one, that does his
work well.

His great intelligence and common-sense have made him
able to deal successfully with so many kinds of people. He
has had the penetration which enables persons to read
others, and know exactly how to manage them. He is
trusting to this now, in his mission to the Soudan. He can
be firm and immovable as a rock, even when a host is
against him, if a question of right be involved. But he
will not set the host against him if he can help it. "With
all due deference to what the son of Michael said about the
stockade having been made six months ago, I cannot help
seeing that the wood of which it is composed is *green*, and

recently cut." But he did not say so to Michael. He exclaimed once, "Oh, dear! what a people to slave for! They never have a knife, nor a hammer, nor a bit of yarn, nor anything of the sort. They have not the least idea of preventing a rope running out too rapidly—in fact, you have, as it were, in *war* to teach your men to *drill*." Sometimes he got angry, and tried to shout them into better ways. But when he found that this was not the wise way to manage them, he controlled himself, and endeavoured to be patient. And this was the more possible to him, notwithstanding a certain warmth of temper which he undoubtedly possesses, because his heart is full of

KINDNESS AND LOVE TO OTHERS.

He is following in the very footsteps of his Lord, for he is willing to lay down his life for the sake of any poor creature who may be benefited by his self-sacrifice. His consecration to the work of delivering the oppressed is very marked. He has "compassion on the multitude," and he cares a great deal more for the poor, and the outcast, and the afflicted, than for any other portion of society. He has been thanked and praised by kings, and persons in very high places; but we can believe that the chalked wish on the paling, "God bless the Kernel," is more to his mind than the carefully worded phrases of a Prime Minister.

During almost the whole of his life, the poor he has always had with him, and whenever he could he has done them good. He has, indeed, been going about doing good for many years. He has been always the same in this respect as in others, in all the places and spheres in which he has been called to live: in China sharing among his men the salary that was paid to him; at Gravesend giving part of his simple meal of bread and tea to any poor lad who was hungry; in the Soudan sparing some of his small stock of dhoora for the slaves, taking care of the little orphan and neglected babies that he found, or sheltering the slaves that fled to his tent for refuge. "This morning, when I got up, my servant told me that, on coming early, before I was awake, he found a female slave sleeping very quietly in the corner of my hut. She had crept in during the night, and one must hope she had a good night's rest. She was chained, and had escaped from her master."

General Gordon was often imposed upon. Every one who knew much of him at Gravesend says that people took advantage of his kindness, as unprincipled people will often do if there be a chance. And no doubt the same thing occurred both in China and in the Soudan. Now and then, indeed, it seemed that this conduct was by no means confined to the poor, and those who had not received the benefit of education and refining influences; for it has seemed that kings used him for their own purposes only, and rulers took advantage of his generous good nature and able service. But these things, if they grieved him, did not cause any change in his spirit and conduct. His motives lay so deeply within his soul, that neither man's praise nor man's ingratitude affected him very deeply "The more one lives," he wrote, "the more one learns to act towards people as if they were inanimate objects—namely, to do what you can for them, and to utterly disregard whether they are grateful or not. This is what God does to us. He lets His rain fall on the just and the unjust. He never gets gratitude, and is furthermore totally ignored in the ordinary circumstances of life."

But more than anything else that has made General Gordon what he is, is the

GODLINESS

which is his chief characteristic. He is another illustration of the fact that the Christian is the highest style of man. Let those who wish to imitate him try rather, as he has always done, to imitate Christ, and be willing to take up the cross and follow Him. It is only so that the greatest work can be accomplished—the noblest life lived. It is so that the spirit can be kept tranquil and steadfast amid all the changes of life. It is so that the young can learn the beautiful lessons of obedience and humility, of loyalty to God, and devotion to others for His sake, that the life of General Gordon so well illustrates. "Take my yoke upon you, and learn of me." This is the invitation of Jesus; and the sincere and earnest response to it has been the starting point of every Christian Hero.

Printed by WALTER SCOTT, "*The Kenilworth Press*," *Felling, Newcastle-on-Tyne.*